Praise for *Until All Curses Are Lifted*

"An inherently riveting read by an author with a genuine flair
for originality and a distinctively engaging and entertaining
narrative storytelling style, *Until All Curses Are Lifted* by
Tim Frankovich will prove to be an immediate and enduringly
popular addition to community library Science Fiction & Fantasy
collections."
— Midwest Book Review

"Frankovich leads readers down twisting paths, traveling with
unforgettable characters, in a story with evocative depth.
Highly recommended!"
- Eric Wilson, NY Times bestselling author

"I was part of this world. I cared for its people. Even the leper
assassin Kishin tugged at a corner of my heart. I genuinely cried
over a pivotal scene at the temple of Theon, the one that proved just
how powerful a mother's love can be. I felt shivers when the two
seemingly separate tales of Marshal and Seri finally intertwined.
The good people are set on their sworn duties and even the
most villainous of creatures had something significant to fight for...
I can't wait to read more."
- Elle Espiritu, Reedsy Discovery

"I enjoyed this book almost more than I can say."
- Lelia Rose Foreman, author of the Shatterworld Trilogy

Until All Bonds Are Broken

Tim Frankovich

WARPSTEEL
PRESS

Cover Design by Rofiatul Adawiyah
Map Design by Alexandra Lindgren

For Joel. Some Bonds should never be broken.

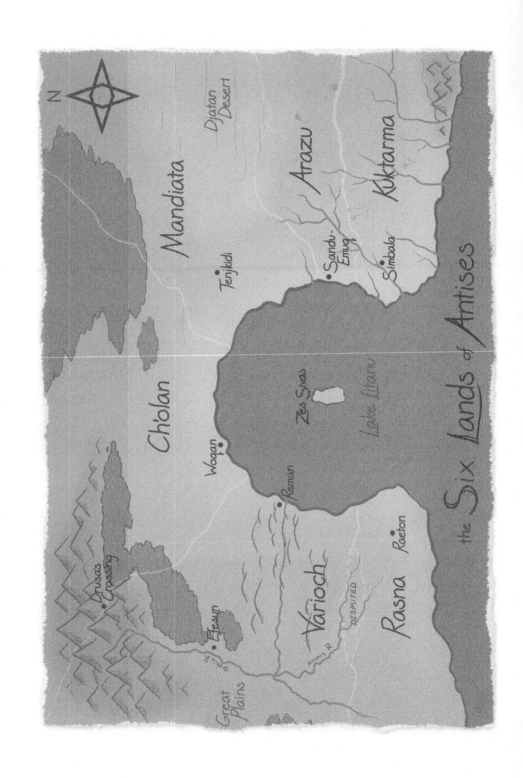

the **Six Lands of Antises**

N

Mandiata

Djatan Desert

Arazu

Kıktarma

Tenjikidi

Sandu-Emvg

Simbala

Ch'olan

Zes Sivas

Lake Itiaru

Woqan

Reman

Rasna

Raeton

Great Plains

Drusas Crossing

Etesun

Varioch

Annis R.

DISPUTED

(((1)))

"Watch out for the Curse Boy," Titus warned.

Victor scowled as little Marshal trotted up beside him. Though all three boys were eight years old, Marshal hadn't kept up with the other two's growth spurts. He seemed much younger. Plus, the curse and all.

"You're going to follow us if we don't let you come, aren't you?" Victor asked.

Marshal's face twisted as he seemed to be thinking hard. Then he nodded.

Victor sighed. "All right. Come on."

"Do we have to?" Titus asked. "He's just going to be in the way."

"If we don't, he'll follow us and we'll probably get in trouble. If we let him come, we can keep an eye on him."

Titus rolled his eyes and pushed past Marshal onto the trail. The three boys set off, following the well-worn path through the mountainous terrain. All of them were accustomed to this part of their quest, having spent their entire lives on the edge of the mountain pass known as Drusa's Crossing.

"It's the left turn," Titus said.

"I know, I know," Victor grumbled. Of course it was the left turn. The right turn led to the river where they did all their fishing. That was the path they always took, the path they were supposed to take. The leftward path led somewhere else, somewhere higher.

Victor took the lead and turned left, pausing only long enough to glance toward the right and make sure no one could see them. It would be just his luck if his father—or worse, his mother—chose this exact moment to wander down the path.

He felt a strange thrill as they moved out of sight of the trail's fork.

1

They were truly in the unknown now. No parents. No adults at all.

"My older brother took me up here a few weeks ago," Titus said. "It's not that far now." He had to remind them this wasn't his first time up the path.

The trail led up a rough incline that proved challenging for the boys, especially the shorter Marshal. In places, they had to scramble up onto rocks using all four limbs. One day, Victor vowed, he would be able to stride up these rocks with single steps. Why did growing up have to take so long? He had so many things he wanted to do, especially once he got out of this tiny village.

Marshal slipped on an angled rock, but recovered before his knee hit the ground. Victor glanced at him. The smaller boy smiled. Without the ability to speak, Marshal struggled to communicate in even simple ways. Victor felt sorry for him, but if he showed any sympathy, it would open him up to the mockery of Titus and the other village children.

"Right up there!" Titus said.

Victor pulled himself up the last step. He wobbled and managed to stand up straight. He almost lost his balance as Titus pushed his way up beside him. Both boys held on to each other as they moved to make room for Marshal on the narrow ledge. The smaller boy pushed between them.

The view was spectacular. From this slim vantage point with their backs to a rock wall, the boys could see for miles. Behind them, Mount Cassius soared another two hundred feet or more before it reached its final peak. The climb from here would be almost impossible, even for a well-trained adult.

"We're almost as high as you can get!" Victor said. His mouth remained open as he looked from side to side. Aside from the path they had scrambled up, the ground dropped off rapidly all around them. The rocky slopes cascaded down toward the valley far below.

For the first time, Victor felt uneasy. He could understand why their parents did not want them climbing this high. The ledge was very small, and a fall from this height… he doubted anyone could survive. Maybe this hadn't been the best idea.

Marshal pointed insistently at something to their left. Victor peered in the indicated direction. "It's… it's home!" he exclaimed. Amidst all the trees, a single thatched rooftop peeked out from an area that leveled off and curved mostly out of sight behind them. It had to be one of the houses in Drusa's Crossing.

"Whose roof do you think that is?" Titus asked.

Victor squinted. "Might be Marshal's," he said. "His cabin is the furthest out."

"That's on the opposite side," Titus disagreed. "This is the other end of town."

"Wouldn't that be too close to the actual pass?" Victor furrowed his brow. The climb had twisted back and forth several times, making him unsure of their actual facing.

"No, because if we were facing the other way, we would be looking into Ch'olan. People are strange there."

"You only say that because your brother does."

"It's true! Some of them wear feathers!"

Marshal yanked on a spiraling root as thick as his arm. Loose dirt and pebbles rained down on all three.

"Watch it!" Victor griped.

"Dumb Curse Boy." Titus feinted a lunge at Marshal, who wavered, a look of panic crossing his face. He grabbed at the root again.

"Stop that!" Victor said. "We should go down. It's too dangerous up here."

"Coward."

Victor's face felt hot. "What did you say?"

Titus waved his arms. "We came all the way up here for this, and you want to go down because you're scared! I expected that from Curse Boy here, but not you!"

"You can't call me a coward!"

"I already did!"

Victor balled up his fist and stepped around Marshal toward Titus. "If we weren't up here, I'd teach you a lesson!"

Marshal grabbed at Victor's arm, but he shoved the hand away.

"I'd like to see you try it." Titus snorted. He turned and deliberately dropped down on his behind before sliding off down onto the trail. "Whenever you're ready."

Victor took another step. As his right foot touched the ground, he knew he had done something wrong. His stomach plummeted and he felt a strange feeling wash over his entire body. The gravel and dirt gave way under his foot and he lost his balance.

"Victor!" Titus screamed.

Victor pivoted as he began to fall. His eyes swept past Titus' shocked expression, past the wall of the ledge, and past Marshal, who looked... determined? Before Victor even realized what was happening, a thick root, the one Marshal had been yanking, looped over him.

In desperation, Victor grabbed at the root. He slid three feet and came to an abrupt halt. His knees banged against the rock. The root wrapped beneath one of his armpits. He seized it and looked up.

Marshal held on to both ends of the root, his teeth gritted and legs braced. Victor couldn't grasp how he hadn't been yanked down along with him.

"Ahhh!" A cry finally escaped Victor's lips. He scrambled against the sheer rock wall, trying to gain a foothold of some kind. Marshal continued to hold on, but couldn't pull Victor any higher. Titus shouted something incoherent.

Leaning on the root that encircled him, Victor released it with one hand, reached up and grabbed it a few inches higher. He pulled, legs still searching for anything at all to brace against.

Marshal looked back over his shoulder at the root's source. Victor followed his look. One end of the root extended from the ledge's wall about three feet above Marshal's head. The other curved around out of sight. Marshal nodded. He released the side whose end wasn't visible, and bent down, still holding onto the other side of the root. His outstretched hand didn't come anywhere near Victor, but he did take hold of a lower spot on the root and pulled.

Victor also pulled and managed to scramble up a few more inches, grabbing a higher spot.

Titus attempted to get onto the ledge to help, but between Marshal and the spot Victor had collapsed, he couldn't find room. He slid back down onto the trail.

Inch by inch, Victor repeated his earlier movements, slowly working up the root. His arms felt like they might give way at any moment from the strain.

"You can do it!" Titus called.

Victor's fingers brushed against Marshal's. The silent boy dropped onto his stomach and reached as far as he could, still holding the root with his other hand. Victor swung himself upward and reached. Marshal grasped his hand, but couldn't hold it. Victor slipped loose and screamed as all his weight hung from one hand. It slid another inch and splinters cut into his palm.

He swung himself up again, not sure if he could make it. This time, Marshal caught his hand and held on. They hung there for a moment. Then Marshal began to pull. Victor pulled back, then lunged upward to catch a higher spot on the root with his other hand. A few moments later, Marshal pulled his hand up over the lip of the ledge. In a few more moments, Victor struggled onto the ledge himself and lay still. Safe.

"Theon's pillars!" Titus said. Standing down below, his face was almost even with Victor's, lying on the ledge. "I can't believe… Theon's pillars!"

Victor turned his head and leaned on his elbow. It shook with fatigue. He looked back at Marshal. "Thank you."

"Who would have thought? The Curse Boy saved your life!" Titus looked from one to the other, then his eyes widened. "He saved your life," he repeated. "That means…"

Victor let his head drop down onto the rock again. "Devouring fire!" he whispered.

• • • • •

Victor looked across their meager camp at Marshal, sound asleep. Though he had been immensely grateful to the other boy for saving his life, for ten years he had resented the Bond it created between them. That resentment included Marshal himself.

Who would have ever guessed Marshal would drag him off on this grand adventure they were having now? Sure, it had hurt to leave behind his home, friends, family. But that faded over time. He could barely remember Careen's face now. He frowned. That wasn't right. But he had gotten to fight monsters, meet magical beings, and learn how to wield a sword. He wouldn't trade all this for the world itself.

When Marshal disappeared into the Otherworld, the Bond between them had become a painful thing. When Marshal encountered any kind of danger, Victor always knew, always felt a pull, sometimes physical in nature. But this had been different. The pull couldn't pinpoint a direction most of the time Marshal was gone. At times, Victor felt pulled in every direction. It felt like his insides were going to explode out of his chest. He couldn't rest, barely slept.

But now Marshal was back, escaping the danger. The Bond had faded away. Victor felt immense relief to have his friend back. Because that's what Marshal was now: his friend. A better friend than he'd ever had. And now his curse had been lifted! The possibilities for both of them were infinite. Marshal might very well become the Lord of Varioch! And Victor…

He lowered his head. During Marshal's Otherworld venture, the other thing had faded. But now, now it was back. Victor hadn't mentioned it to anyone yet. He had no idea what to think. But being around Marshal for so long seemed to be changing him. That had to be the reason.

Victor lifted his hand before his face and watched.

His fingers vibrated.

(((2)))

Seri's head exploded in violent pain. Despite the control she worked so hard to maintain, she screamed and grabbed at her hair.

Beside her, someone else screamed. Dravid. He dropped his crutch and fell, clutching at his own head.

Seri had never experienced pain like this. It felt like someone had jammed a hot iron into her brain and stirred it around. At the same time, something happened inside her chest. Her heart felt pulled, pulled back toward the island of Zes Sivas. The pull became almost as unbearable as the pain in her head, and then…

It snapped.

Seri staggered and collapsed. The pain in her head seemed almost inconsequential now, compared to her chest. It felt like an iron ball slammed into her chest, then ricocheted around inside it. Surely all of her ribs had shattered. She heard a voice yelling at her, but couldn't figure out the words. The pain overrode her hearing. She rolled back and forth.

Hands grabbed her shoulders. Strong hands that kept her in place. The voice yelling at her gradually became more distinct, though her pain did not lessen.

"…broken! You can get through this! My Lady! Can you hear me?"

Ixchel. Dimly, Seri recognized only Ixchel would have strong enough hands to hold her this way, and be willing to do so.

"Hold him! Hold him steady!" Ixchel said to someone else, her voice blurring. Then she was speaking at Seri again. "You must focus, my Lady! You are strong! You can do this!"

Do what? Seri didn't even know what was happening. But it hurt. So. Much.

"You must listen to me. Listen! Master Hain is dead."

Dead? Her mentor? He...

"You and Dravid were both Bonded to him. His death has broken the Bond. You are both..." Ixchel's voice faded.

Seri's head filled with memories of Master Hain, the powerful mage who had been training her for the last few months. Yet each memory appeared twisted, distorted in pain, with different, horrible outcomes. In her arrival at Zes Sivas, a tower collapsed on the Master. An assassin stabbed him in the back. An earthquake swallowed him. One of his fellow Masters blasted him apart with magic.

"No! No!" Her voice screamed her denials, but she had no conscious thought of doing so.

"Hailstones!" she heard Ixchel curse. "I can't help them both. Not at the same time..."

The memories shattered apart in the all-consuming pain. And then Seri sensed the real threat. Something came toward her. Something deadly. From the East, in the direction of Zes Sivas, an avenging being strode across the waves toward her. She had no idea how she knew this, only that it came.

"What is that?" Dravid cried, and she knew he sensed it too.

In her mind's eye, Seri saw the creature, a figure of flame and magic incarnate, coming for her. Inexorable. Unstoppable. It walked across the water, every step creating explosions of steam. Then, within her mind, Seri's star-sight activated and she saw the being as it looked in the Otherworld.

If her first vision of the creature had been a flame, its appearance now made that look like a simple candle. It shattered the Otherworld's darkness with a light so intense, it seemed as if... as if...

Seri's brain could not pursue that train of thought any further. Her eyes snapped open to see Ixchel holding her head, her face almost touching her own. "Deny it!" Ixchel said, her face fiercer than Seri had ever seen, even when she fought Volraag's assassin. "You are not to blame! You are innocent of the Master's blood!"

Of course she was. She had done nothing wrong. Why should she suffer like this? What would that creature do to her if it reached her? What—?

"Say it!" Ixchel screamed, spittle hitting Seri's own lips. "Declare your innocence!"

"I..."

"Say it!"

"I'm innocent!" Seri cried, the words a plea of desperation. "He was my Master! I... I loved him!"

In her mind's eye, the being stopped and faded from view. It no longer came for her. The pain began to fade, as well, though her head and chest still ached with an unbelievable soreness that vibrated like her magic. Ixchel released her and she slumped back down to her hands and knees.

She looked down at rough wood. The ship's deck. They were on the ship. She and Ixchel and Dravid...

"Dravid!" she exclaimed, her voice weak and hoarse.

He thrashed a few feet away. Two sailors held on to his arms, though both looked completely baffled. His face alternated between horror and pain. His eyes stared east, locked onto something only he could see. Seri blinked, trying to focus her vision and thoughts. Were Dravid's eyes glowing?

Ixchel scrambled over to him and grabbed Dravid's head as she had Seri's. "Deny it!" she said, repeating her instructions. When Dravid did not respond, Ixchel looked back at Seri. "It may be too late for him!"

Seri staggered to her feet. No. She would not let Dravid fall to this, not after all he had been through already. She didn't know what would happen if the shining creature reached Dravid, but she had sensed vengeance in her own contact with it. It did not intend anything good.

Seri closed her eyes. She had transported herself to the Otherworld fully in a moment of self-preservation, and had not been able to repeat that feat since. But she had also slipped over to it another time, or at least partially, when she saw a monster roaming the ruins of Zes Sivas. Perhaps that kind of transport was all she needed here. She opened her eyes, her star-sight fully activated. Multi-colored beams of pure magic shot around her. Nowhere near as many as she constantly saw on Zes Sivas, but this would have to be enough.

She grabbed as many beams as she could, heedless of their colors, and absorbed them into herself. She knew the danger. Too much magic might tear her apart. But Dravid's life might depend on it. Desperately, she grabbed more and more. Her entire body began to vibrate.

"My Lady?" Ixchel's voice seemed to come from far away.

Seri could not take the time to respond. She focused as much of the magic as she could into her left eye, her star-eye. The power pushed against her eyelid. She felt like the skin itself would explode.

Her eyes flew open. Whether she stood fully within the Otherworld or not, she did not know. The avenging creature filled her vision, consumed her senses. She stood between it and Dravid, and its presence dwarfed them all. They were gnats before a giant, chaff to be consumed by one touch of its outstretched hand.

In that moment, Seri's mind made the connection she had sought earlier. The light appeared as intense as if... a star had come down to walk the earth.

"You can't have him!" Seri screamed. "He is innocent too!"

Her words had no effect, as far as she could tell. It reached forward, drawing nearer and nearer.

Seri shrieked. She swept her arms in a wide circle outward, trying to gather even more magic. Then she swept her arms forward, channeling every iota of power she had forward at the creature. With her star-sight, she saw beam after beam after beam of colored light burst from her hands and strike the creature. She emptied herself, throwing everything into one desperate effort.

The creature paused. Seri knew that it perceived her now, turning from Dravid back to her. Its hand, if hand it could be called, came towards her. A single appendage of light, like a finger, came toward her face.

"No!" Seri screamed once more. The finger touched her left eye.

Seri fell backward, felt arms catching her, Ixchel's strong arms, felt her head spinning in vertigo, felt the pain renewed in her head and chest. Yet none of that mattered, for she knew—she knew!—what the creature had done to her, the price it had exacted for her interference in its duty. Her consciousness faded away.

When she finally woke many hours later in her hammock, she blinked and blinked until tears coursed down her cheeks. Her fears were confirmed.

Her star-sight was gone.

(((3)))

Volraag idly pushed a pile of dust out of his way with a magical vibration. With every use of his power, he became more proficient. He stopped and turned in a circle, examining the ruins of the temple of Reman.

"The witnesses all say the same?" he asked.

Otioch, the head of Volraag's personal guard, eyed the rubble. "They all agree that the temple fell apart before the earthquake," he answered after a pause.

Volraag ran a hand over what remained of the temple's outer wall. The stone had been pulverized. Whatever force had done so had come from within. The angles of the destruction showed that much clearly.

"Furthermore, they all agree that the scar-faced young man came out of the temple, and that he... flew." Otioch said the last word with distaste, as if he couldn't believe someone would even suggest such a thing.

It had to be Marshal. Didn't it? But one detail did not match what he knew. "Tell me about the scars."

"No one seems to have been close enough to see them clearly," Otioch answered. "Accounts vary. Some claim multiple scars criss-crossing his face. A couple insist that it's a single, large X-shaped scar. Others aren't sure of the shape at all, but all of them insist he was scarred."

Marshal had not been scarred when Volraag spoke with him. But that had been months ago. Something could have happened to his face since then. In fact, with Kishin in pursuit of him, such injuries could be expected.

Volraag frowned. Kishin's failure and disappearance troubled him, perhaps more than anything else in this strange saga. The assassin had never failed before. A message dispatched to his home received no response. Death seemed the most likely answer, though how Marshal could have accomplished that boggled the mind.

He stepped out of the ruins into bright sunlight. Volraag winced and shaded his eyes. For some reason, he had been sensitive to light since his return. A side effect of his new power? He hoped the adjustment period wouldn't take much longer.

"What other news have you gathered this morning?" he asked.

"Messages are still sporadic," Otioch said, "No doubt due to the damage on Zes Sivas. But the Consuls received an outraged missive from the new Lord of Mandiata, demanding you restore his father's power to him."

"Tell them to ignore it, of course."

"Of course. But I do think we should send a spy or two to keep an eye on them, in case they decide to sail here and start a war."

"That will take time, but it is a distinct possibility. And that is why we must accelerate our plans for dealing with Rasna." Volraag strode toward the temple courtyard's gates.

"Accelerate? Are you sure that particular fight is worth it?"

Volraag stopped and turned on him. "There are two things that are of the utmost priority in my plans now. Only two. First is finding my half-brother and regaining my father's power from him. The second is winning a quick and decisive victory over Rasna. For what is buried on that border land is... worth whatever it takes.

"In fact..." Volraag turned back toward the gates. "Send out the recruiters and pick up another century's worth of conscripts."

"As you command, sire."

Volraag walked through the gates and stifled a scowl at the carriage awaiting him. He would much prefer his own horse, but his newly elevated position meant certain practices were expected. He climbed into the carriage and smiled at the dark-haired woman inside. Cyra did not smile in return.

"Are you through climbing through ruins?" she asked.

Volraag chuckled. "It was a little more involved than that, my dear. Do you recall our visit to a little village up in the mountains a few months ago?"

"I remember you dragging me to a bunch of little villages. I hated every minute of it."

"But we got to sample all those quaint inns along the way." Volraag nodded out the window to Otioch and the carriage began rolling. "So many different beds together…"

The concubine smiled. "I didn't hate those minutes," she admitted.

Volraag leaned in closer and playfully tapped Cyra on her small, upturned nose. "I didn't think so." He kissed her and then relaxed back against the cushions.

Cyra adjusted her skirts absently. "Have you decided on your speech at the ceremony tomorrow?"

Volraag took a deep breath. His father's funeral. Much of the city would be there, regardless of how they felt about Varion. They would be curious to see their new Lord and hear from him for the first time.

"I know exactly what I will be saying."

"Any hint at… a marriage?" Cyra asked pointedly.

"We've been over this." Volraag closed his eyes and tried not to react in anger. "I will not marry you. Not yet. I will not give the populus reason to expect a child."

"It doesn't have to mean a child…"

"But they would expect it!" Volraag's eyes flew open. "I will not father a child until and unless all my plans succeed! I will force no curse upon an innocent. My father sired at least a dozen cursed children, my brothers and sisters. And I lived, each and every day, in fear that I would be the one to suffer from his actions next. I will not continue that. I will not!"

Cyra whimpered. "You frighten me when you talk like that."

Volraag sighed. Beautiful Cyra, all he could want in a concubine, simply could not understand all that he had been through, or all that he wanted to do. The Lordship of Varioch was an important step, but only the first of many. When he finished, all Antises would be transformed.

• • • • •

The palace of Reman was a cold, sterile home. Since the death of Volraag's mother, it had lacked a female influence on its decor. Even the day-to-day operations were run by men. As he descended the steps leading to the lowest levels, Volraag made a mental note to encourage Cyra to be more involved in palace operations. It would make her feel more important.

He passed several red-cloaked Remavian Guards and spoke a word to each in turn. He made a point of knowing at least one personal detail about each of his elite warriors. Familiarity bred loyalty.

Volraag paused at the top of the final staircase. Everyone had strict orders to stay away from this part of the palace. Even so, he glanced around to be sure no one saw and followed him. Satisfied, he made his way down to a solid oak door. A quick vibratory wave pushed it open.

Inside, the leper assassin, Rathri, sat polishing a dagger. Volraag restrained a shudder. No matter how many times he saw Rathri's uncovered face—or Kishin's, for that matter—he could not stifle the disgust. The peeling, diseased skin revolted him. At least Kishin kept his hidden most of the time. Rathri simply didn't care what others thought.

"I assume he is still well?" Volraag asked, gesturing at another door beyond Rathri's seat.

"No thanks to you!" called a voice from inside.

Volraag approached the door. A familiar face stared out from a narrow window cut into the door at eye level.

"Tezan."

"Why am I here, tyrant?" the false king demanded. "Why even keep me alive?"

"Because I am not done with you," Volraag said. "You and I still have much to do together."

"I will not help you again!"

"Yes. You will. When you fully understand… you will."

"You are a murderer. There is no threat you can give me any longer. I'd rather die than help you."

"Threats worked with you the first time," Volraag pointed out. "But I prefer reason. When I have more time, we will talk. I will show you what I am doing. And you will help me. Willingly."

"You are delusional."

"Possible. But I doubt it." Volraag turned to Rathri. "Are you in need of anything?"

"You do not need me here," Rathri said. His voice, so raspy, made Volraag wonder what the man's curse had done to the interior of his throat. Was it as damaged as his exterior skin? The thought made him wince.

"No, I don't. I can assign any guard here now. They all know I have a Rasnian prisoner. You wish to leave, then?"

"No." Rathri stood and slipped the dagger into a hidden sheath somewhere in his sleeve. "I want to stay near you."

Volraag's brow wrinkled. "I… don't see how that would work. I can't have you walking about in public."

"Of course you can. Make me the head of your Remavian Guard."

"Otioch serves that role quite ably. He has been with me for many years."

"Then make me second. Either way, I must be near you. Especially when you demonstrate your power to the people at your father's funeral."

"I don't understand." Volraag knew he owed multiple debts to Rathri, but had been hoping to pay the assassin with his usual gold.

"No, you don't. But you will in time." Rathri gestured at the prison door. "You told him that he would understand you in time. I am telling you the same thing. In time, you will understand… and agree."

Volraag found himself intrigued. "Very well. You will be part of the Guard. But you must conceal your… condition."

Rathri nodded. He took a step closer. An unpleasant odor of decay brushed Volraag's nostrils.

"I must be near you as you learn your power. And the more you use it, the more powerful you will become." Rathri smiled, and Volraag could not repress the shudder this time. The assassin was missing a portion of his upper lip. "And as your power grows, so too will mine."

The assassin swept down in an exaggerated bow. "And then, you will find me truly irreplaceable."

(((4)))

Victor looked up to see Marshal returning from the creek. His friend flexed his bandaged arm as he approached their camp.

"I think… it's getting better," Marshal said. Victor tried not to wince. Every time Marshal spoke, it sounded wrong somehow. The words were all correct, but they didn't sound right together. But what could you expect from someone who hadn't used his voice for the first eighteen years of his life? His brain knew what to do, but his lips were still learning.

"I don't get it," Victor said. "Last time you went there, the stars healed you, right? So why didn't they heal you this time?"

Marshal furrowed his brow. "I don't know. Maybe the Eldanim did something else to me besides the starlight." He stared off into the distance.

Victor had grown accustomed to that look. It happened any time Marshal thought about that other place, the Otherworld or whatever they called it. For some reason, he wanted to go back. Victor had only caught a glimpse through the portal. It hadn't looked so fantastic then.

"Hello!" a voice called from nearby. Marshal tensed, but Victor waved it off. "It's Nian," he said.

A few moments later, the dark-skinned priest emerged through the trees. He put his hands on his knees and caught his breath. "Did you have to camp on the top of a hill?" he asked between deep breaths.

"Yes," Victor said. "It's the most defensible location, and—"

"Yes, yes," Nian interrupted. "You needn't go into detail. I was merely complaining."

Victor attempted a laugh. The priest was a strange one. He had helped them with everything at the temple, and had stories galore of his travels in the six lands, but still seemed off. He tried too hard to be friendly, sometimes.

Nian straightened and approached. "I found something of yours, Marshal," he said. He reached into his robes and pulled out Marshal's sword and sheath. The sheath looked battered and torn, but when Marshal drew the sword, it appeared untouched.

"Buried in the ruins," Nian said. "Found it while helping clean things up. I'm still trying to work my way into the other priests' good graces."

Marshal hung the sheath on his belt and replaced the sword. But he kept one hand on the hilt. Victor noticed he did that quite frequently during their travels. Perhaps he found comfort or stability in it.

"What's new in the city?" Victor asked.

Nian took a seat on the ground. "Lord Volraag is wasting no time in consolidating his power," he said. "He's been seen all over, making friends with the leading citizens, visiting the merchants' guild. He even showed up at the temple today, to look over the damage." Nian looked pointedly at Marshal. "His men have been questioning the priests over and over, trying to find out more about the scar-faced man who destroyed the temple."

"I didn't... mean to do that," Marshal said.

"That's not in question. He just wants to find you. For obvious reasons. And just as obviously, we can't let that happen."

"Once Marshal's power is back, he could take him down!" Victor said.

"Why?" Marshal asked.

"Because he's not the rightful Lord," Victor said. "We should stop him."

"I think what Marshal is suggesting is that overthrowing Volraag may not do much to advance your primary goal," Nian said.

Victor didn't remember anyone mentioning a primary goal. He picked up a stick and broke off a twig, waiting for someone to say something.

"Hope," Marshal said.

"For all those who are cursed," Nian added. "I told you that the lifting of Marshal's curse was a sign that all curses would soon be lifted."

"But how do we do that?"

Nian sat in silence. Marshal joined the other two on the ground. Victor looked from one to the other.

"Nothing? No idea?"

"It seems an impossible task," Nian admitted. "How does one undo the very nature of reality?"

"Not reality," Marshal said. "Not everywhere. Just Antises."

"That's a fair point. Even so…"

"How were the Laws put in place at the beginning?" Victor interrupted.

Nian also picked up a stick and toyed with it absently. "That's the question to ask. The histories as I've read them tell of the great Conclave of Mages uniting all the magic of the land and placing it in the hands of the Lords and King, while also implementing the Laws of Cursings and Bindings. Exactly how they did this is never spelled out. Perhaps someone from the current Conclave could explain it."

"The… Durunim told me that the mages stripped the magic from the Otherworld to do it," Marshal said.

"Was he telling the truth?"

Marshal shrugged. It looked awkward; his body still wasn't used to the movement and its meaning.

"Regardless, it is understood that it took all of the mages together to do this," Nian said. "And that the Conclave has never again reached that height of power."

"So… to undo it would require at least as much power," Victor suggested.

"So it would seem."

Victor held up two fingers and ticked them off with his stick. "We need power and knowledge. We have neither. So what do we do?"

"Talinir," Marshal said abruptly.

"He's still in the Otherworld, right?"

"Yes. I think." Marshal struggled with the right words. "He vowed to help me. But I left him there. We should get him back. He can help."

"Can you open a portal to the Otherworld?" Nian asked.

Marshal shook his head.

"Then we go back to the Eldanim city! They'll have to help us now!" Victor insisted.

Marshal frowned. "I'd… like to. But I don't know how. And it's so far."

Victor pointed his stick at his belongings. "I have that stone from your mother. We can try to call them. Maybe there's another warden around."

"There are other alternatives," Nian said.

Both young men looked at him.

Nian gestured broadly. "There are three places where the barrier between the worlds is said to weaken. Where wild magic erupts from time to time. One is in Kuktarma. One is in Ch'olan. And the last one…" He paused.

"Where?" Victor demanded.

"The disputed land between Varioch and Rasna," Nian said. "Where they're threatening war."

"That's much closer than the Eldanim city. But we'd probably have to get through all the soldiers." Victor frowned and tossed his stick. It bounced off a tree trunk and spun into the grass.

"If that is where you need to be, Theon will provide a way," Nian said.

Marshal did not look convinced.

(((5)))

Dravid never found climbing out of a rowboat an easy task. Wearing robes made it even more awkward. Attempting it with only one leg? Ridiculous.

Dravid nearly plunged onto his face, but Ixchel caught him. It wasn't too embarrassing. He glanced at Seri to see her reaction, but she hadn't noticed. Instead, she gazed off into the distance, looking at nothing in particular.

Ixchel stepped up beside Seri and looked around. "This is Varioch," she said. "I am not impressed."

Dravid didn't agree. He couldn't see much from the beach, of course, but what he could looked pleasant enough. From the narrow strip of sand, the ground sloped gently upward into a low hill dotted with evergreen trees. Beyond it, he could see larger and taller hills, also covered in green.

Dravid turned back toward the two women. Not for the first time, he wondered why he had come. And as always, he knew the simple answer: Seri. Back on Zes Sivas, his future had been tied first to Master Simmar, then to Master Hain. Without them, Dravid had no future as a mage. No one else would train him. But Seri. She had a mission. One he might be able to help. And more significantly: she was incredible.

From the moment Dravid had laid eyes on her sitting alone at the table in the dining hall, he had admired her. Seri was beautiful, confident, and powerful, especially as she had developed her unique "star-sight." She could see magic in a way none of them could.

But she lost it. Seri had effectively sacrificed her special power, and for what? To save him? He wasn't worth that. A failure as a mage. A failure as a friend.

The sailor who helped them to shore tossed Dravid's pack to him and bid them farewell. Dravid gave him a half-hearted wave and watched him pull back out into the water. In a sense, he waved farewell to their last connection to other places. The three of them now stood alone in a strange land. None of them had ever visited Varioch before.

"I still can't see it," Seri said. She moved her gaze in either direction. "It hasn't changed."

Dravid moved up near the girls. "But do you have to?" he asked. Time to make himself useful. Or at least pretend.

Seri looked at him with confusion in her eyes. "I don't have to, of course, but... it was a part of me," she said. "And how are we to find the boy, or... or the lost King, if I can't see the magic?"

"You'll have to stumble through like the rest of us," Dravid said. "You can still sense the magic, can't you? Like a regular mage?"

Seri hesitated. She closed her eyes for a moment. "Yes, I... I guess I can. It's very weak here."

"We're already a long distance from Zes Sivas. That only makes sense."

Seri nodded and took a deep breath. "All right. Then what we need to do is see if we can sense any magic sources other than the island."

"Exactly. Let's do it together." Dravid held out his hand.

Seri paused only briefly before taking his hand with her own. It felt cool and soft. He put the feeling out of his mind, noticing Ixchel eyeing him with a strange look. He closed his eyes and tried to reach out with his magical senses. The magic of Antises, based on vibration, created a somewhat tactile sensation. Where did he feel vibrations and how strong were they?

Dravid put everything else aside and focused. When doing this before, cutting out all other input gave him the most success. Eyes shut. Ignore any sounds. Focus.

"South," Seri said, just as Dravid felt it himself. The vibrations felt distant, but definitely there, and definitely powerful.

"The city of Reman is to our south," Ixchel said.

"Then it's Volraag we're sensing," Seri said.

"I don't think we should go anywhere near him, if we can help it," Dravid said, opening his eyes.

"Agreed." Seri opened her eyes and frowned. "It must be him. I can feel the Bond toward him in that direction too."

Dravid tried not to sigh with relief and closed his eyes again. He didn't want to see Volraag again, in any way whatsoever. He tried to focus on the southern impression a little longer, to see if he could guess at the distance.

"West," Seri said abruptly. "Maybe a little northwest?"

Dravid changed his focus, but just as he did, he thought the southern impression split into two. Odd. But then he noticed the western impression.

"What is that?" It felt different, strange. The vibrations were there, yet they seemed… discordant, somehow. Normally, the vibrations felt completely natural, an integral part of the world around him. Not like this.

He opened his eyes to find Seri looking at him. "You felt it, right?" she asked.

"I don't understand. It's different."

"What is happening?" Ixchel asked. "Are we going west?"

"No," Dravid said, as Seri said, "Yes." They looked at each other with raised eyebrows.

"That felt wrong," Dravid said. "Something was… it was just wrong."

"But powerful," Seri said.

"Yes…"

"We have to investigate. It could be the young man that I saw. I never did get a good look at his power. Maybe this is it." She paused. "Maybe it's the King himself and he's returned to our world!"

"But you felt his power, right? Did it feel like this?"

Seri frowned. "No, I… I don't think so. But I'm not really sure. Everything happened so fast that day."

"Then are we going west or not?" Ixchel asked again.

Dravid frowned, but Seri gave a slow nod. "Yes. We're going west."

(((6)))

Volraag looked out over Reman's coliseum. The granite structure seemed ready to explode with the enormity of the crowd packed within it. Many, the nobles especially, had come out of obligation. Others had come to see their new Lord. Still others had come to satisfy themselves that Varion was truly dead. But they all shared one thing in common: none of them knew what to expect.

Varion's casket lay on a pedestal in front of the stage. Volraag had already heard some gripes about it being closed. Again, some wanted proof of Varion's death. Idiots. Volraag's power displays should be enough proof for anyone. But he would satisfy them all, if the morning went as planned.

The high priest droned on, delivering a eulogy that skirted the edge of praising Varion, without ever quite getting there. Volraag tried not to smile. The priest considered it inappropriate to condemn the dead Lord, but everyone knew he wanted to.

He glanced at the others on stage. Otioch and two other Remavian Guards stood behind him. Cyra sat to his right. To his left, the three Consuls who held most of Varioch's economic power sat stone-faced and impassive. Behind them all sat another half-dozen officials whose names even Volraag struggled to remember, yet somehow they were important enough to be here.

The high priest finished and returned to his seat. Volraag stood, but did not move forward. He waited until murmurs began to sweep through the coliseum. When the volume reached a sufficient level, he bent and pretended to whisper something to Cyra. This only served to increase the murmuring.

With their attention now fully engaged, Volraag stepped up to the front of the stage. The crowd quieted. His moment waited. All of the politicking over the last week had won most of the nobility to his side. Today, he would win the hearts of the common people. Then Varioch would truly be his, and follow wherever he led.

"My father is dead!" he announced, gesturing toward the casket. His voice echoed across the coliseum. The crowd remained quiet. Most of them probably didn't know how to react, or rather, if they would be allowed to react the way they desired.

Volraag stepped to the edge of the stage and looked down at the casket. "I do not come to praise him." He paused and let the impact of those words sink in. "He was not worthy of my praise. Nor yours, either!" A quiet murmur swept through the crowd. They had not been expecting something like this.

"Varion was a monster! Most of you know this. Many of you feared him." The murmur grew a little louder.

"What you do not know is how much I knew this. How much I feared him." Volraag moved around the stage as he spoke, peppering his speech with broad gestures.

"Do you know how many brothers and sisters I have? I don't know, exactly. But because of Varion's appetites, there are many... and because of his sins, most of them are cursed!" Volraag held both hands pointing toward his chest. "I lived in daily fear—daily!—that a curse would fall on me because of my father. Do you know what that is like? To strive to live your life under the Law, but knowing that your life depends not on your own actions, but on the actions of a tyrant?

"You do know it!" Volraag pointed at the crowd. "You felt the same way! Perhaps not with the daily fear that I lived under, but with fear nonetheless. When Varion passed through your neighborhoods, did you hide your daughters? Did you conceal your wealth? Your food? I don't blame you!"

The crowd was with him now. He could tell. They knew he spoke the truth.

"This is not right! This is not how a people should be led! This is not how a Lord should behave! A Lord should serve his people, not prey on them! I tell you, here and now, that I am not my father!" Volraag shouted the next sentence one word at a time. "I. Will. Never. Be. My. Father!"

The crowd roared. Volraag held out both arms and let their adulation wash over him. The magic seemed to respond and vibrations swept over his skin. After a few moments, he raised his arms and waited for them to quiet.

"Varion was unworthy of the title of Lord in life, and he is unworthy of it in death!" He pointed at the casket and unleashed a burst of magic. The wood of the casket shattered and splintered, spilling his father's corpse onto the ground. "Do not bury him in the tombs of the Lords! Take his body to an unmarked grave outside the city walls!" Loud gasps were followed by a brief moment of absolute silence, and then the crowd roared again.

This time, Volraag let them cheer on and on. They believed what he said, regardless of truth. Of course he wasn't going to throw his father's body in an unmarked grave. But only close family members and a few loyal guards would ever know that.

This was the crucial moment. He had the crowd. But now he needed to turn them, to focus them where he desired.

He fell to his knees and looked down at his father's body. The cheers faded away. The crowd didn't understand his actions, as he intended.

"My father is dead!" he cried out again, but this time his voice swelled with grief. He got up on one knee, but didn't stand. "Yes, he was a monster. But… he was still… my father."

On cue, Otioch stepped forward to offer help to the new Lord. Volraag waved him away and stood on his own. He made a show of taking a deep breath.

"He was a monster. And he deserved to die. But… you do not know how he died!" The sound of the crowd grew. Many rumors circulated through the city over the past week, some started by Volraag himself, but no one really knew.

"Varion was right about one thing." Volraag held up a single finger. "One thing! And being right about that one thing is what led to his death. No! It is what led to his murder!"

The crowd erupted. Again, Volraag raised his hands for silence. Then he gestured back at his Remavian Guard. "Bring him."

Rathri and another Guard dragged Tezan out from behind the stage and threw him down next to Volraag. He had been beaten, and his hands were tied. Volraag stared down at him and waited for the crowd to quiet.

"This man. This man killed my father on Zes Sivas. How, you must wonder? How could he infiltrate the gathering of Mages and Lords and succeed in such a deed? How?" Volraag pointed at him. "He played on all our hopes! He pretended to be the lost King of Antises!"

Shouts of outrage filled the coliseum. Volraag gestured down at his father's body. "He deceived us and then killed my father. And why? Because my father was right! About one thing!"

Volraag grabbed Tezan by the back of his collar and yanked him upright. "Tell these people, false king! Tell them! Who persuaded you to pretend? Who made you act like you were our king?"

Tezan glared at Volraag, but his lips began to move, seemingly against his will. "Lord... Tyrr."

The crowd exploded. Cries of "Death to Lord Tyrr!" and "Death to Rasna!" poured out from hundreds of voices.

Volraag swept his sword out of its scabbard and held it high. The crowd grew silent. Volraag shoved Tezan down and pointed the sword at his neck. He lifted it high again. "Kill him! Death to the Rasnian! Death to the murderer!" screamed the crowd.

Volraag aimed and lifted the sword again. The cries escalated. But then he turned away from Tezan and sheathed the sword. Shouts of outrage followed him as he strode several feet away before turning back. He lifted his hands and waited for the quiet again.

"The murderer will pay!" he promised. "But first we will learn all we can from him. Because what we need now is information. Information that will help us in what is to come. I said my father was right about one thing. That one thing? Rasna! He knew Rasna was preparing for war against us! They want our land!"

"No!" cried the crowd.

"Lord Tyrr sent this man to pretend to be king, so that he could kill my father and pave the way for his invasion!"

The crowd roared louder. Volraag raised his voice to be heard above them.

"I say he does not know our land! He does not know our people!"

Volraag pointed to his father's corpse. "We will not trade one tyrant for another!" he screamed.

This time, he waited a full minute while the crowd vented their rage. He lifted his hands and they grew quiet. One last time. Once he spoke the next words, everything would change.

"I, Volraag, Lord of Varioch..." he began.

The crowd, realizing what he was doing, screamed their approval. Volraag began again.

"I, Volraag, Lord of Varioch, do hereby declare..."

Louder and louder the crowd grew. In a brief moment where the roars faded slightly, Volraag shouted into it.

"I, Volraag, Lord of Varioch, do hereby declare WAR on the land of

Rasna and their Lord!"

The coliseum shook with the screams of the crowd.

The words had been spoken, words that superseded even the Laws of Cursings and Bindings. For the first time in generations, Antises was at war.

(((7)))

Talinir blinked and looked around. How long had he stood there, staring at the stars? His legs felt weak and his stomach empty. He faced a huge problem being in the Starlit Realm in this form. A glance at the sky could turn into hours of star-gazing.

Fortunately, no tunaldi wandered by during his reverie. That would have been the end of Talinir, warden of the Eldanim. And all because of a pledged vow to a human, who dragged him here at the end of their association.

That wasn't fair. Marshal hadn't known what he was doing. And for all Talinir knew, Marshal might be dead now. Or taken by the Durunim.

Time to focus. He needed to find a way back to the primary world. He could probably get to Intal Eldanir, his home, but one of the high places might be closer. It would be southwest from here. He looked up to get his bearings.

"You won't get out that way."

The voice snapped Talinir out of his star-gazing again. His legs collapsed and he fell like a marionette whose strings had been cut.

Dust erupted in all directions as the speaker hastened down a crater's wall to reach him. Talinir shook his head and tried to take control of his own thoughts. His consciousness swam.

"Here. Eat something." A hand offered him a cold strip of cooked meat. He took it with a shaking hand and ate quickly. How had he gotten so ravenous? The stars. He had been trapped by them again. Who knew how long it had been this time?

He managed to sit up and found himself looking into the eyes of his rescuer. A human. Here. And not Marshal.

His height, though tall by human standards, barely put him at Talinir's eye level while seated. He did not look well fed. His clothes hung in tatters, and his gray hair and beard long and disheveled. Pale, sun-starved skin was broken up by blotches of pure darkness, some around the size of a coin, others much larger. Talinir recognized the symptoms, but not on a human. He must have been here for many years.

"Who—" Talinir began.

"Who I am is not important," the man interrupted. He stuck a spear into the ground and removed a battered water pouch from his belt. "Your identity matters more just now. Am I right in thinking you are Talinir?"

The warden nodded. His benefactor offered him the water pouch and he drank. The water, though warm, felt exquisite on his parched throat.

"Good to know. I was looking for you. But I didn't expect to find one of your kind caught by the stars. Why is that happening?" The man stared at Talinir with such intensity, the warden felt uncomfortable.

"I am... all here," he said.

"I can see that you're here. What— oh. You mean you're here, as in, all of you is here? What does that mean?"

Talinir started to rub his eyes and found them dry. He blinked multiple times. "An Eldani is normally a part of both worlds," he said. "As a warden, I spend most of my life in the primary world. That is, most of my physical essence is there. A part of me remains here, which allows me to see with this eye." He pointed at his right eye. "And even interact with things here, to some degree. Many of my race, however, do the opposite, keeping most of their essence here and only a portion in the primary world."

He made a sweeping gesture to reference his entire body. "But now... I was dragged into the Starlit Realm all at once. I am here, all of me. I cannot see the primary world at all."

The man's expression did not change. "And this is a problem for you, is it?"

"Yes!" Talinir pulled his knees up. "It is wrong! Unnatural. And if I stay here like this for very long, I risk..." He stopped.

"You risk becoming one of the dark ones," the man finished for him.

Talinir nodded. "The Durunim."

The man removed his eyes from Talinir for the first time and looked around. He made his way to the remains of a fallen tree and sat down. He leaned his long spear against the tree trunk, keeping it near him, and sighed.

Talinir eyed him. "I don't know who you are, but I cannot do this on my own," he said. "You have already assisted me greatly. Can you help me further?"

The man looked up. "Help you? Oh, yes. I'll do that. It's why I was looking for you. I promised my... that young man that I would do that."

"Young man? Marshal?"

"Marshal? Is that his name? Marshal." The man seemed pleased to hear that.

"Was his face covered in scars?"

The man nodded.

"That was Marshal. Is he still here?"

"No, he's returned to his proper place. But I strongly suspect that you'll meet again. In the meantime, what are we to do with you?"

Talinir looked away. "I had thought to go southwest, to the high place. It's on the border of Varioch and Rasna."

"You won't get through there," the man said. "That one's been buried on the other side. But I hear they may be fighting over it now."

"Of course. The war." Talinir closed his eyes. "Then I suppose I should head toward Intal Eldanir. It's the most likely place."

"Let me offer another suggestion," the man said. "I could take you that way, but it's far away from where I eventually want to go. What about the northern high place instead?"

Talinir opened his eyes again. "The one in Ch'olan? Why there?"

"It's on my way. And it's not much further than the trip to Intal Eldanir, if I'm calculating correctly."

Talinir nodded. "I suppose that will work. If you don't mind, I will rest, and then we can start."

"You do that. I don't think you could get more than a few yards right now, anyway."

Talinir made himself as comfortable as he could. "I will repay your kindness," he told his rescuer. "What do I call you?"

The man snorted. "I've picked up a few names in my time. For now... call me Janaab."

Janaab. The name sounded like it came from Ch'olan. Perhaps it explained the man's desire to travel in that direction. But it didn't explain how he got here, his true identity, or what... Talinir could think no more about it. He fell asleep.

(((8)))

Victor finished filleting the two fish and handed the dagger back to Marshal with a chuckle. "Your brother may have meant that dagger for a twisted purpose, but it's come in pretty handy."

"Half-brother," Marshal said. He wiped off Volraag's dagger and put it away.

Victor pushed a skewer through one of the fish and set it carefully on the smoldering fire pit. He repeated it with the second. "Should be just a few minutes," he murmured. "Who needs Talinir, anyway?"

"You can make tea?" Marshal said. "With sugar?"

Victor rolled his eyes. "This is gratitude. Keep that up and—" He broke off as Marshal shot a look over his shoulder. A moment later, he heard it too: voices.

"Up here!" one called. "Coming!" came the answer from a different direction.

Victor got to his feet and took a quick glance around their makeshift camp. His flail lay on the ground near the fire, but it wouldn't be much use with so many trees around. He put his hand on his sword hilt, noting that Marshal had done the same.

Two soldiers approached over the edge of the hill. They wore regular Varioch army uniforms and carried short swords and triangular shields. A rustle behind Victor signaled the arrival of more. He looked back and saw three more soldiers, one of whom wore a helmet. The leader, maybe?

"Watch yourselves," one of the first soldiers said. "They've got swords."

"And we know how to use them," Victor said, moving back-to-back with Marshal. "What do you want with us?"

The helmeted soldier circled around in front of them. Victor kept facing him, while Marshal maintained their defensive posture.

"Two young men, both with swords, both who know how to use them," the leader said. "Sounds like you're practically perfect for the army."

"We're not interested," said Victor, but a slight thrill went down his back. Being part of the army had been his dream for years, before any of this, before Marshal.

"That doesn't matter," one of the other soldiers said. His companion elbowed him.

The leader stopped circling. "Indeed, it really doesn't. You see, we're the Lord's conscriptors. It's our job to find new soldiers for his Lordship's army."

One of the soldiers, a large man who stood a head taller than his comrades, gestured at Marshal with his sword. "What about that one, venator? Those scars. He might be cursed."

The venator waved it off. "Well, put him in the curse squad. I don't care."

"No," Marshal said.

"No?" The venator chuckled. "Did you hear that, boys? The freak said no. He thinks he has a choice."

"Will you try to force us?" Victor asked. "Are you willing to risk getting cursed?"

"You haven't heard," the venator said. "Lord Volraag has declared war. While carrying out his orders, we don't risk a thing!"

At that moment, Nian burst onto the scene in a flurry of robes. "What is going on here? I insist you leave these two alone!"

The venator raised his hands and took a step back. "Your pardon, priest. But we are here under his Lordship's orders."

"And I am telling you, in the name of Theon, to let these men go. They are engaged on a vitally important mission."

"And what would that be?"

"I am not... authorized to tell you."

"He's making it up," one of the other soldiers said.

Nian spun on him. "You accuse a priest of Theon of telling lies?"

"How do we even know he's a priest?" the larger soldier asked. "I mean, he's obviously not from around here, is he?"

"Albus raises a good point," the venator said. "Tell me your name, priest. And if I go to the temple—what's left of it—will they know you there?"

Nian glared at him.

"Nian," Victor said softly. "Let it go. We'll deal with them."

The priest looked at him. "I will not allow it. There has been enough fighting and killing already."

"Take them," the venator said.

The four soldiers lowered their swords and moved in. Marshal and Victor swept out their swords and took defensive stances.

"I will not countenance this!" Nian insisted.

"You can't stop us," Albus said. He took another step toward Marshal.

Nian shoved his way between Marshal and the soldier. Victor tried to keep an eye on both of them while watching the soldiers in front of him. Two against five were not good odds, but he and Marshal might be better trained. And if Marshal's magical blade ward still worked, and if he could summon some of his power...

"Get out of the way, priest!"

"I will not."

Albus tried to push him out of the way with his shield, but Nian dodged around it. The priest grabbed Albus's sword hand and tried to push it away.

"All right, that's enough," the venator said, moving forward to intervene.

"Let go!"

"Leave them be!"

It happened faster than anyone else could react. Albus yanked back and forth, trying to get Nian to release his sword hand. When the priest's grip finally weakened, Albus didn't realize it and shoved forward again. His sword cut cleanly through Nian's chest.

"Nian!" Marshal screamed. Victor spun around and lunged forward. He caught the priest as he fell.

Marshal dropped his sword and fell to his knees beside Nian as Victor lowered him to the ground. Albus stepped back, his mouth and eyes open in horror, his sword dripping Nian's blood. The other soldiers looked equally horrified.

"You killed a priest!"

"No! No, I... I didn't mean to..."

Victor ignored them. He pulled Nian's robe aside to look at the wound. His breath caught at seeing the size of it. Marshal pushed him aside and shoved parts of the robe into the wound, trying to stop the blood flow.

"Marshal..." Nian wheezed.

"It's all right," Victor said. "Don't try to talk. We'll... we'll get help. We..." He looked up. "Are any of you trained in healing?"

The soldiers looked helplessly at each other. The venator snorted.

"No curses, Marshal," Nian said, his voice growing weaker. "Blessings."

"Nian..."

"Blessings..."

The priest gasped once more, and then the air left him in one final breath. He grew still, his eyes staring up at the sky that somehow seemed much darker than a few moments ago.

For another moment, no one moved or spoke.

"My eyes!" Albus screamed. He dropped both sword and shield and grabbed at his head. "I can't see!"

The other soldiers backed away and murmured as Albus staggered from side to side. Two of them dropped their shields so they could touch their palms with index fingers.

"It's the curse!"

"I thought we were immune to curses!"

"But it's a priest!"

Albus screamed and dropped to his knees. Victor stood, sword in hand, at first intent on avenging his friend. But as he took a step, he hesitated. Albus began to weep, making pathetic sounds for a man his size.

"Idiots!" the venator bellowed. He stepped up and slapped Albus across the face, silencing him.

"Curses don't apply to us if we're doing our jobs!" He glared around at the other three soldiers. "Killing a priest is not part of the job! Now pull yourselves together!"

He turned to Victor. "This has gone far enough, don't you agree?"

Victor's eyes narrowed. "It went too far the moment you arrived."

The venator met his stare. "We have a job to do, by the orders of Lord Volraag. Now. You can come along with us, or we fight, and more people die."

"You and your men will be the ones who die."

"No." Marshal stepped up and put a hand on Victor's arm. He shook his head.

"Marshal?"

"We'll come," Marshal said to the venator.

"I'm glad one of you has sense. Fine. Let's—"

"Wait." Marshal pointed at Nian's body. "You must... take him to the other priests."

The venator raised an eyebrow, either at the request or at Marshal's stumbling voice. He looked at them for a moment, then nodded. "I will see it done."

He gestured to one of the soldiers. "You. Take the priest's body to the temple. The rest of us will escort these two to the camp."

"Venator, Sir? What about Albus?"

"Bring him too."

Victor took one last look at Nian. The priest had annoyed him from time to time and perplexed him often, but he had done everything he could to help them during Aelia's plan for Marshal and ever since. He would be missed.

"The pillars of Raeton," Marshal said.

"What?"

"He never... got to see... pillars of Raeton."

Raindrops began to fall, sizzling on the abandoned fire pit and the crisp, burnt fish.

(((9)))

"What is that horrible sound?" Seri asked.

Ixchel paused from laying out her bedroll. "That would be frogs, my Lady," she said. "We're not far from a creek. They will probably sing all night."

Seri frowned. She didn't remember sleeping outside much. Actually, she didn't remember doing it at all. Sleeping on the ship that brought them here had been a new experience. But this… she didn't know what to think about this.

She also wasn't used to this much walking. Ixchel led the way, but allowed frequent stops for the other two to rest. Dravid, despite his impairment, seemed less tired than Seri. That just wasn't fair.

Still, she would make the best of it. She reached for her pack, then hesitated. How was she supposed to change into sleep clothes with Dravid around? These were things she had never considered before agreeing to go on this quest.

"You may change over there," Ixchel said, as if reading her thoughts. She pointed to several trees close together. "Behind those trees. I will watch out for you."

Dravid glanced up from his bedroll. His eyes darted back and forth between them, then returned to the tiny fire he had started. He even knew how to start fires!

Seri went behind the trees and struggled with changing into her sleep clothes. Where was she supposed to put one set of clothes while she took off the others? With no other choices, she set them carefully on the ground, but examined each one thoroughly for bugs before putting it on. Shoes were the hardest. How did Ixchel walk around without them all the time, anyway? She decided to wait until back at

37

her bedroll before removing them.

She hesitated only briefly before returning to the fire. Even this, walking in front of a man in her night clothes, would be unthinkable back home in Arazu. For Theon's sake, she exposed her bare feet! She wasted no time in gathering her blanket around herself as she sat. Arazu's customs dated back before the founding of Antises. Seri had been raised to respect those customs, to be proud of them. Yet tonight she felt silly.

Dravid looked up and smiled. Why did his smile have to be so... so cute? He had the barest hint of dimples in his cheeks during each smile.

Stop it. Those kind of thoughts did not belong, at least not right now. The unusual circumstances threw off her self-control. She took a deep breath.

"Tell me how you made the fire," she said.

Dravid showed little surprise at her request. "When we gathered the wood," he began, "I filled the lowest level of this pile with debris: twigs, small broken pieces, everything as small as possible..."

Seri listened intently. When Dravid explained things, he often used broad gestures. Tonight was no exception. His mannerisms had always fascinated her, along with his looks, and that smile. Her eyes drifted and settled briefly on the point where his left leg ended so abruptly. She felt a pang in her heart at the wrongness of it. So completely wrong.

Dravid stopped talking and followed her gaze. He looked away.

Seri gasped. "Oh, I'm so sorry, Dravid! My mind was drifting. I wasn't... I didn't..."

"It's all right." Dravid took a deep breath and looked back at the fire. "Everyone will look at that part of me. For the rest of my life."

"I said my mind was drifting!" Seri insisted. "You know that doesn't bother me."

"It should. It bothers me. Every moment. Sometimes it hurts, even though it's not there."

Seri sighed. She pulled her knees up to her chin and looked into the fire herself. Stupid, stupid, stupid. Every time she even thought about a man in... that way... she said or did something stupid. It felt worse this time, because Dravid was her friend. She really did care for him, even if she wasn't sure how much. She took a quick look up at his face to see what he might be thinking.

He wasn't looking at her. He seemed greatly distracted by

something off to his right. Seri looked.

Ixchel knelt on her bedroll. She had washed off her face paint and unbound her braid. Her dark brown hair, surprisingly long when released, reached almost to her mid-back. She brushed it with care, not noticing the other two watching her.

Seri's hand unconsciously felt for her own hair. It had been growing since she arrived at Zes Sivas and fell well past her shoulders now. Even so, Ixchel's was longer and darker. Is that why Dravid watched? Is that what he liked? Or was it simply Ixchel's overall allure? Seri had grown accustomed to Ixchel's odd clothing, no longer scandalized by the amount of skin she showed. Of course she knew men did not think the same way. But... Ixchel acted so cold, so fierce. She did not seem like a woman at all.

"Let's try to sleep," Ixchel said, her voice breaking Seri's inner thoughts into shards that tumbled away. "You especially, my Lady. It may take you some time to adjust. You're not used to this environment."

As if she needed reminding of that! Nevertheless, Seri nodded her assent and let her body relax onto the bedroll. She faced away from the fire and the others. The air felt cool against her cheeks.

She blinked. Had she seen a flash of color? She lifted her head and stared. Nothing. Her imagination, her hopeful imagination. She lowered her head and blinked again. And again. She blinked until her eyes watered, and she wasn't even sure whether the tears came from the blinking or from her heart.

Master Korda had sent her on this mission because of her special power, because she could see the magic. And now she couldn't. Why even continue? Dravid tried to encourage her, telling her she could still use magic as all other mages did. But he didn't understand. The starsight had become a part of her. Losing it felt like losing her hearing or vision.

Her eyelids drooped. They had walked a lot today. The sounds of the frogs weren't really that horrible, after all. In fact, they almost formed a peaceful rhythm. Perhaps sleeping outside would not be as much trouble as she had worried...

(((10)))

Kishin wandered without comprehending where his feet took him. He had no concept of time, no idea how many days, or even weeks, had gone by since... since the world stopped making sense.

He came to himself as he stood in a narrow stream, rubbing desperately at his skin with a rough stone. What did he hope to accomplish? Restore his leprosy?

Kishin's rational brain began to assert itself. His entire life had been altered. That was true. But it had been altered in a good way... hadn't it? Thousands of people across Antises would give anything to remove their curses. He gave nothing.

But it changed the very nature of reality. He believed all men were cursed; everyone suffered, whether caused by magic or Theon. Everyone bore a curse, and those curses were eternal. How could he accept he had been wrong all these years?

When his curse first fell on him, his mentor gave him four words of advice: "Surrender or fight back." Kishin had chosen to fight back, killing and killing again. Because he endured the worst curse possible, he never suffered any consequences for any of his subsequent sins. He fought back in every way he could, even killing his mentor when he could gain from it.

And yet... he also surrendered. Surrendered so fully to his curse that he let it define him. That could not be right. Surely a man was more than his sin and its consequences.

Kishin climbed out of the stream. He needed to rediscover himself, return to who he used to be. He would start by going home to Woqan, capital city of Ch'olan. How would people treat him now? And how...

Kishin stopped. A thought struck him with such force that he

40

trembled. He almost dared not think it. The magnitude overwhelmed him.

His daughter.

He had not spoken to her in almost two decades. He had barely even seen her from a distance in several years. Did he dare to approach her now? What would she think of him?

Kishin began walking. Woqan lay many miles to the north. Maybe by the time he got that far, he would think of something to say to the daughter who believed him dead.

(((11)))

Victor pushed his hair out of his face, squeezing water from it in the process. The rain had stopped, but not before thoroughly drenching them. As if things weren't miserable enough with Nian's death, and being conscripted.

He glanced at Marshal. His friend had remained silent throughout their long march heading to the temporary camp for new conscripts. His scarred face looked even grimmer than usual.

"Listen," Victor said, "I've been thinking. This might work out well for us."

Marshal looked at him, chin down and eyebrows arched.

"No, I mean it. Nian said that the place where all these soldiers were going to fight is the place where you might be able to cross into the Otherworld, right? Well, we're going that way now, whether we wanted to or not."

"Not worth it," Marshal said.

"No, that's not what I meant. I just mean... we're going there, anyway."

Marshal didn't answer.

Victor slipped on the slick ground, but recovered. The heavy pouch hanging on the right side of his belt smacked his thigh. The Ranir Stone from Aelia. Not for the first time, he wondered why she had given it to him instead of Marshal. But she had entrusted him with even more. As far as he knew, Victor was now the only person alive who knew the truth about Marshal's ancestry—his grandfather's side, anyway. Marshal himself didn't even know. Yet Aelia had cautioned him not to tell his friend until... "the right time."

"What is the right time?" he grumbled out loud.

"We're here!" the venator escorting them announced.

Victor and Marshal looked down from a hilltop. The temporary camp appeared despondent under the cloudy skies. Grayish tents in haphazard lines dotted the landscape. The rain had doused any cooking fires, but a thin trickle of smoke still rose from some ashes somewhere toward the middle of the camp.

The camp of conscripts they had seen a few weeks ago hadn't been very impressive. But compared to this one, it had been the height of military readiness. The few soldiers Victor could see moved with all the speed of a depressed cow.

"Edin Na Zu," Victor muttered.

"Where's the curse squad?" the venator asked his men.

"Down on the left," one answered.

As they descended the hill, a scribe of some sort approached to inquire about their success. The venator gestured at Victor and Marshal, then explained about Albus. The scribe wrote something down and shuffled away.

The venator walked up beside Victor. "Congratulations. You're now a decanus, in charge of the curse squad."

"What?"

"Did I stutter?"

Victor blinked. "I—I don't..." He pointed at Marshal. "He's the one who needs to lead."

"Needs to?"

Victor lowered his voice. "You don't know how important he is."

The venator shrugged. "You can surrender your leadership to him, for all I care. Just make sure one of you jumps when your centurion barks orders." He tossed Victor a small red badge showing a black spear at an angle. "One of you pin this insignia on your shoulder."

A soldier led the way toward some tents on the left end that looked even more disheveled than the rest. As they approached, an enormous man with light brown skin emerged from one of the tents. He noticed their approach and took a few steps forward to meet them.

"Look sharp, Ch'olan," the venator said. "Here's three more for the curse squad. Make 'em welcome. One of them's your decanus now."

"I am happy to surrender that duty," the big man said. "Which one?"

Victor pointed to Marshal.

The big man scratched his chin and looked from one to the other of them. "Whatever you say, boss." He gave a short nod to Marshal.

One of the escorts stepped in front of them, an anxious look on his face. "You'll keep a good eye on Albus, won't you?" he asked. "He didn't mean to... you know... what happened."

Victor glanced over at Albus, who stared off into the distance unseeing.

Marshal gave a slow nod. "We'll... watch him."

The soldier went to say farewell to his former comrade. Then he and the other escorts left with the venator, leaving them behind with the big man from Ch'olan. Marshal took a deep breath, then faced him.

"I'm Marshal," he said. "This is Victor. You are?"

"Ha! A Marshal for a decanus, eh? Good one. I'm Topleb, but everyone keeps calling me Ch'olan." He shrugged. "I guess because you Variochs think we're all alike?"

"I'll call you Topleb," Marshal said.

He chuckled. "We'll see." He gestured for them to follow and led the way back among the tents.

A skinny man with long gray-streaked hair sat huddled near the first tent, knees drawn up to his chest. Somehow, he appeared more thoroughly soaked than Victor. Had he been sitting there throughout the rain?

Topleb gestured at him. "That's Wolf. At least, that's what we call him because of his hair. Can't get a real name out of him."

Victor tried to catch the skinny man's eye, but he turned his head rapidly, avoiding eye contact. Strange.

"I don't belong here," Wolf whispered.

"None of us do," Topleb said. He pointed to the next tent. "You two can take that one. I'll move out and share with Merish. He's asleep in the next tent." He pointed to his head. "Good with a sword, but his pyramid isn't complete, if you know what I mean."

Two nearly identical young men approached, carrying buckets of coal. Topleb greeted them. "Ho, you two. Here's our new decanus, who's also a Marshal. He brought a couple more for our squad too." The young men nodded, set down their buckets, and hurried away. Topleb turned back to Victor and Marshal. "I call them Callus and Gallus. Don't know if those are their real names and don't care. Farmers. Don't know one end of a spear from the other."

"I thought this was the cursed squad?" Victor said. "You and those two don't seem to have any curses."

"Neither do you, flail-man," Topleb said, eyeing him. "Not everyone here is cursed. They just threw us together because we don't fit anywhere else. I'm here because I'm not one of you. Wolf's here because no one can figure out what's wrong with him. And the brothers? They just make people feel weird." He glanced around. "Merish is cursed. Your boy there who can't see is cursed. And Gnaeus is here somewhere. He's cursed. Stole something. His right hand is all twisted and useless. Kind of like most of these men."

Topleb shrugged. "Once we get to the front, see some actual fighting? All of them will die."

Victor looked around the camp. Everywhere he looked, he saw men who didn't know what they were doing or why they were here. More than the curse squad would die when they started fighting. From what little he knew, none of these men were ready to fight. They were all sheep to the slaughter for the Lords' amusement.

• • • • •

It didn't take long for Victor and Marshal to learn their place with the curse squad. As part of a century of conscripts, Victor had expected they would be thrown together with the other ninety-plus men in some kind of basic training. Such was not the case.

The decanus of the squad camped closest to theirs explained everything.

"No one cares," he told Marshal. "Look, we're all conscripts here, except for the centurion and his assistants. But your squad is… well, you're cursed." He glanced at Victor, clearly wondering what his curse might be. "You'll get the same basic supplies as everyone else, but that's it. No one else wants to be around you."

"What about marching? Formations?" Victor asked.

The decanus shrugged. He at least had the conscience to look a little guilty. "When we move the camp, just follow everyone else. They won't care if you're organized."

"And when… we get to battle, you'll put us in the front lines. To die," Marshal said.

"Two weeks ago, I was a farmer," the decanus said. "In another couple of weeks, we'll all be on the front lines, dying together." He looked off toward the city. "That's what our new Lord has decreed. And he has the power to enforce it."

Victor watched him leave, but Marshal had turned back to look at the tents of his squad. Wolf sat nearby, giving no indication that he had heard any of the conversation. He stared into the distance, his face a mask of desolation.

"What can we do?" Marshal said, his voice barely audible.

"I don't know. Maybe once we get near that magic place, you'll..."

Marshal looked at him.

"I don't know. Maybe you'll feel something? Are your powers coming back at all?"

"My powers," Marshal repeated. He stomped the ground and Victor felt an almost imperceptible tremor pass under his feet. "That's all I can do."

Victor nodded. Marshal had burned himself out fighting in the Otherworld. But it couldn't all be gone, could it? He had a Lord's own power! He blew apart the entire temple! That kind of power didn't just disappear. Not in any of the stories he knew, anyway. It would just take time. Marshal would get it back.

In the meantime... Victor jumped as his eyes settled on Wolf and saw the thin man's eyes staring back. He stared unblinking at Victor for a moment, then looked at Marshal. Those eyes. They weren't like any he had ever seen. The pupils were black, but a slate blue surrounded them, instead of white. His skin tone matched Victor's own, so he appeared to have come from Varioch or Rasna. In fact, everyone in the army, save Topleb, appeared to be a native of Varioch. So where did the conscriptors find Wolf?

"Nian didn't die for this," Marshal said, again so quiet Victor barely heard him. "Mama didn't die for this."

The decanus turned out to be right. When the conscript army moved out the next day, another officer ordered the curse squad to fall in at the rear, just in front of the supply wagons. The centurion and his aides rode by them only once, and barely glanced at Marshal and his men. The army marched southwest, passing by Reman on their left.

As they set up a new camp, Victor tried to calculate their travels. "If we do this every day, I'm guessing we'll reach the border of Rasna in... a couple of weeks?"

"What difference does it make?" Marshal dropped a rolled-up tent and stared at it, his frown pulling the rest of his face downward. "A day. Two weeks. Who cares?"

"It gives us time," Victor said. "Time to prepare."

"How?"

Victor pointed to an open area apart from the tents. "Tomorrow morning. We'll find a way."

Marshal's expression did not change. A light rain began to fall, eliciting groans from the conscripts. They forgot everything else as they hurried to get the tents up again.

(((12)))

Dravid tried to keep a smile from his face. Seri looked so pitiful. He had wondered how she would handle sleeping outside. After the first night, he knew the answer: not so well.

"Water?" He offered his waterskin. Seri, her eyes bleary and hair a complete mess, took it and drank. She groaned.

"Some people do this all the time?"

"Some people have no choice," Ixchel said. She stood nearby, finishing her braid. "And others do so when traveling. Like us."

Dravid watched as Ixchel carefully attached her two green feathers to her braid. Curious. "What is the significance of the feathers?" he asked.

Ixchel looked up. "They come from a... special bird in my homeland."

"Do they signify anything important?" Seri, seeming a little more conscious, asked. "Your rank, maybe?"

Ixchel held the feathers and her braid and did not respond for a moment. "They are... special."

Dravid looked to Seri. She met his eyes and shrugged. Her bodyguard remained a mystery in so many ways. Yet Dravid wanted to know more. She fascinated him. She possessed an undeniably attractive appearance, but her demeanor and skills could make any man a little fearful of even speaking to her.

Ixchel set to work educating Seri on proper morning procedures while on the road. Dravid pretended not to listen as Seri expressed indignation over being thought ignorant, at which point Ixchel pointed out that she was, in fact, ignorant in this regard, just as Ixchel herself was ignorant concerning magic. And on they went. Dravid found their conversation highly entertaining, especially once Seri woke up enough to fully express her opinions.

They provided such a contrast in so many ways, even their clothing. Seri in her mage's blue robe arguing with Ixchel in her short skirt and torso wrap. The thought made him consider his own clothing choices for the day. He picked up his orange acolyte robe, looked it over for a moment, then tossed it away. Time for a change.

Dravid pulled on a cotton tunic and a pair of breeches. They were not, in any sense, similar to the traditional garb worn back home, but they seemed appropriate for traveling. He added a leather vest, looked himself over, and nodded.

He ran a hand through his hair, still too short to require combing, but at least it was growing back out. Why had he shaved it on Zes Sivas in the first place? Had it been Jamana's idea? Probably. If only Jamana had been able to come on this trip. That would have made things much more entertaining.

"No robes?" Seri stared at him.

Dravid shrugged. "I'm not exactly an acolyte any more, am I?"

"My Lady," Ixchel interrupted. "We have not completed our tasks."

After more instructions and arguing, some breakfast and packing, they finally resumed their journey. Seri gave the general heading, based on her magic sense, which Dravid confirmed. Ixchel blazed the trail across mostly pleasant terrain: rolling hills, scattered trees, very little undergrowth. Dravid often traveled through Kuktarma with friends and family, but his homeland consisted mostly of low plains and wetlands. This much up and down travel was new to him, especially with a crutch. He despised being the slowest member of the group.

Late that day, they found a road which seemed to move in the same general direction they wanted. Parts of the road had been paved with stones, but although it showed signs of frequent use, it had not been maintained in quite some time. It took little discussion to agree to use the road, despite its poor condition.

They spent another two days traveling without incident. As the nights passed, Seri grew a little more used to outdoor life. Dravid struggled with sleeping. Though he felt extremely tired each evening from their travel, the phantom feelings of his missing leg made him toss and turn for hours.

Each day, he and Seri confirmed to each other that they traveled in the right direction, yet they could not be wholly certain they moved any nearer to their destination.

"Maybe we're following him as he's traveling," Seri suggested as they paused for a moment on the road.

"I think it's stronger," Dravid said, stifling a yawn. "I really do think we're getting closer."

"If I had my star-sight, I could probably tell." Seri looked so despondent that Dravid almost reached out to put an arm around her.

"Hail!" called a voice behind them.

All three of them turned, Ixchel with her hand on sword hilt, to see a young couple approaching. Dravid guessed they were near to his own age, if not younger.

"Well met, travelers!" said the young man. "There are few of us on this road to meet! Especially ones who have traveled so far!"

How did he know... oh. Right. Dravid had gotten so used to the constant diversity on Zes Sivas, he forgot other places didn't share so many skin tones as the three of them exhibited. This couple possessed the typical fair skin of Varioch's inhabitants. The woman had curly blonde hair and green eyes that looked ready to burst out of her head. The man, slightly taller, had short brown hair and a narrow beard.

"Are you on your way to see the Forerunner?" the young woman piped up, before they could respond to her companion.

"Who is the Forerunner?" Seri asked.

The couple exchanged a bemused look. "You've traveled this far, and you don't know? What other purpose could you have in this part of Varioch?" the man asked.

"We are on a... pilgrimage," Dravid said. He gestured at his companions. "This is Seri, mage of Arazu, and Ixchel of Ch'olan. My name is Dravid, of Kuktarma."

"What fascinating names," the woman said. "I'm Junia, this is Cato."

"Tell us about this Forerunner," Seri said.

"He came out of nowhere, only a week or two ago," Junia said. "He's amazing!"

"They say he works miracles," Cato said. He gestured toward Seri. "Seeing your robes is what made us wonder if you were also going to see him, since he's such a powerful magic user."

Dravid and Seri exchanged a quick glance. Magic user. The one they were looking for?

"What kind of miracles?" Dravid asked.

"All kinds!" Junia's eyes widened even more. "But mostly, he heals people!"

"Healing?" Seri exclaimed.

Dravid furrowed his brow. How could one heal with magic? He had never heard of such a thing. Nor could he imagine how it could be possible, based on all he had learned so far from Master Hain.

"Yes," Cato said. "We've heard several stories of people getting healed—diseases, sickness, even blindness and... lameness." He glanced briefly at Dravid.

"Is he... is he lifting curses?" Seri said.

Cato frowned. "I don't think so. I don't think these people were cursed."

"It's impossible to get rid of a curse," Junia said. She glanced at her Cato. "Isn't it?"

"Of course it is."

"But if anyone could do it, I'm sure it would be the Forerunner," she went on. "His power sounds amazing!"

"Who is he? Where did he come from?" Dravid said.

"No one knows. We'll ask him when we meet him." She cocked her head and looked him over. "Tell me about Kuktarma. Is everyone there as handsome as you?"

Her forwardness took him aback. "I..." He looked to Seri, who smirked. "I'd like to hear that answer too," she said.

Right. She asked for it. "Well, I haven't been home in around a year now," he said. "But when I left, many young female hearts were broken and left to wander without hope of finding another so"—he smiled and bowed—"handsome."

Seri rolled her eyes. Junia giggled. Cato laughed. "I like this man!"

Ixchel had moved on ahead a dozen or so paces. She returned and frowned. "Are we going to keep moving today?"

The conversation continued as they moved along the road. The two newcomers kept pace, much to Ixchel's displeasure. But their goal might be what—or who—Seri sought. It only made sense to stick together. Dravid and Seri both tried to draw more information out of them about this mysterious Forerunner, but neither seemed to know much.

He had come out of nowhere, started working these miracles, and now people traveled to see him. Junia and her companion explained that they lived near the capital city of Reman, but not within it. From their lifestyle descriptions, Dravid gathered that both of them were quite rich, by most standards. Children of the nobility, with nothing better to do than to chase after strange rumors. And yet…

The magic called to him from somewhere ahead. If not this Forerunner, who could it be?

•••••

Junia and Cato appeared at least as ill-trained for this journey as Seri. As Dravid had surmised, they came from well-to-do backgrounds. While both carried some suitable supplies in their packs, neither seemed to know what to do with themselves. That night, when Dravid lit their fire, Cato quietly admitted they had slept by the side of the road the last two nights without a fire. Junia expressed such delight in the fire that Dravid felt embarrassed. He glanced repeatedly at Seri and Ixchel, hoping one of them would say something soon.

But Ixchel disdained their new company, pointedly ignoring them. And Seri… Seri sat by herself, staring off toward the west. Dravid couldn't get a good look at her expression. Was she thinking about this Forerunner, or her lost star-sight? Maybe both.

Dravid sighed and smiled back at Junia. Why be melancholy? He was young and on the road with three attractive women (though he had yet to figure out the exact relationship between Junia and Cato). Why not enjoy it while he could?

Around the fire that evening, Dravid entertained the party with elaborate descriptions of the great walled cities of Kuktarma. He told exaggerated tales of the antics of Lord Meluhha's seven sons, embarrassing to the Lord, of course, but highly amusing to his people.

After a somewhat dramatized recount of the second son's failure to seduce the princess of Mandiata, Dravid could truly smile in satisfaction. Seri had been as enthralled with the account as their guests (though he did notice her blush multiple times over the subject matter). And even Ixchel appeared interested.

"Are all families in Kuktarma that large?" Cato asked.

"Not all, but many," Dravid said. "I have two brothers and two sisters, myself. You?"

"I have one younger sister."

"Ladies? What about you? Brothers or sisters?"

"I have none," Seri said. She seemed a little saddened to admit it.

"I have no siblings," Ixchel said.

Dravid turned to the girl beside him. "Junia?"

She looked down. "I have a brother."

"Older or younger?"

"He's older. I... I don't know where he is right now."

"Is he lost?" Seri asked.

Junia bit her lip and shook her head. "No. He..." She sniffed and looked away.

"He ran off and joined Lord Volraag's army," Cato said.

"Why?" Ixchel asked.

Cato jumped at being addressed by her. "Ah, lots of young men are doing so. We're going to war with Rasna any day now. That's what everyone says."

"Why would they go to war?" Seri asked. "I mean, I've heard the rumors, but I don't understand it."

Cato shrugged. "There's some land around the border that belongs to us, but the Rasnians claim it belongs to them."

"That's it?"

"It's stupid!" Junia burst out. "The whole thing is stupid! Why would they go to war over some land? Who cares? It can't be that important. Not important enough for people to— to die!"

Dravid didn't know what to say. What little he knew of war did not make him want to see one, either. Men killing other men, without fear of curses. It sounded horrible. It had only been a few weeks since he had seen Volraag and his assassin kill two other Lords. Between that and Lord Varion's attempt to assault Seri, he had seen enough of men harming others. How could they do that?

He glanced across the fire at Ixchel. She carried weapons, had been trained to fight. She fought on Zes Sivas, against the assassin. Did that explain her rough manner? If it came to war, would all of the people involved become like her? War between Varioch and Rasna had been rumored for some time, as Seri mentioned, but now... not only did it seem probable after Lord Tyrr's machinations with the false king, but Volraag had also murdered the Lord of Mandiata and stolen his power. Might war come from that too?

Dravid had no answers. He wondered if anyone did.

(((13)))

Victor drew his sword and took a deep breath. He flipped his left wrist a few times, feeling the chain of his flail clang against itself, the heavy iron ball on the end twisting in the air. Here in the real army, the flail seemed so old and rusty, not to mention a rarity among the soldiers. The last real flail he had seen on a soldier was on that day in Drusa's Crossing so long ago, when Volraag arrived and changed their lives.

But the flail felt like an extension of his own body. Had been for years now. He loved the feel of it as he whipped it through the air. And after weeks of training with the Eldanim warden, Talinir, he knew how to use it in combination with a sword.

Victor dropped into a defensive stance, bringing his sword up in a horizontal blocking move. At the same time, he began to spin the flail. He needed this. The last few days with Marshal had been in hiding as they considered their course of action. Their hidden camp hadn't allowed for much practice time, especially not the way he liked to practice.

The open ground here remained wet from yesterday's rain. His feet squelched through a thin layer of mud with every step. Topleb and Gnaeus wandered out from the tents and watched him.

Victor moved. He shifted from stance to stance, alternating between defensive parries and attacks, both with sword and flail. He performed his own combination of moves, something he had been working on for the last few weeks. Each day he practiced, he added another series of moves to it, and ran through it several times.

It felt good. His arms moved smoothly, but without hesitation, remembering the sequence flawlessly. No one watching would know if he made a mistake, of course, unless he managed to smack himself with the flail. Hadn't done that in around a year now.

He moved faster. He finished the sequence as far as he had devised it and immediately started over. Several moves into the new sequence, he realized he could feel the vibration in his hands again. But instead of loosening his grip, it seemed to help. The sword and flail felt more like extensions of his arms, molded directly into his hands.

He moved faster. The strange feeling spread into his legs, as well. His stances shifted and rotated without a hitch, far better than he had done the last time he tried this.

Halfway through the third time through his sequence, he experienced a thrill run through his entire body, rejuvenating but also frightening him. It felt as if his body had taken control of his mind and wanted to keep going, on and on.

He reasserted control, slamming the flail's head into the ground on one side of him, and slashing violently upward with his sword on the other. He came to an abrupt stop.

Marshal faced him from a few feet away, arms crossed, head tilted to the side in curiosity. Victor sheathed his sword and wiped sweat from his forehead as he approached his friend.

"When did you get so fast?" Marshal asked.

Victor shrugged. "I've always been fast."

Marshal shook his head. "Not like that. Those last few moves were… I almost couldn't see you. So fast."

"Thanks, but you're exaggerating."

"Tell that to them." Marshal gestured with his chin.

Victor looked back toward the tents. Topleb and Gnaeus had been joined by every other member of the curse squad, along with four or five other conscripts who had gathered to watch him. Even from here, he could see looks of awe on their faces.

What did it mean? That strange feeling, the vibrating? It did seem to have given him more speed and precision somehow. Was it magic, like Marshal?

Marshal looked toward the watchers and rubbed the scruff on his face that grew between the scars. "You… should train them," he said.

"That's what I was going to tell you. But you should do it. You're a better swordsman than I am."

"Maybe. But they don't all have swords. They need more… general training."

"You're the leader of this group now, Marshal. It should be you."

"I can't. My face and… voice."

"Your voice is getting better every day. And your face?" Victor shrugged. "Have you seen these men? They don't care."

"It should be you."

"Fine. How about we do it together?"

Marshal frowned, then nodded.

Victor laughed. "A few weeks ago, we were being trained. Now we're going to train others? What would Talinir say?"

"He'd be proud, I think."

"Yeah. Yeah, he would be."

Victor looked over at the curse squad. "No time like right now. Shall we get started?"

Marshal snorted. "Lead the way."

"You lead the way. I follow."

• • • • •

Marshal gathered the curse squad in the open space. The other conscripts who had watched Victor in awe now mocked the group from the sides.

"What are they doing?"

"I guess they want to learn to fight."

"Why? They're either going to scare the Rasnians off, or run for their lives at the first sign of enemy arrows!"

Victor looked to see what effect the mocking had on the squad. They stood in two disheveled rows, shoulders slumped, eyes following Marshal as he moved in front of them. Topleb, the exception, stood straight with a mocking grin of his own. He toyed with an odd wooden device, which Victor assumed had something to do with the collection of light spears that hung at his side.

Albus, having come straight from the regular army, still carried his own short sword and shield. Merish also held a similar sword, though his looked cleaner. The other four all held spears like most conscripts.

"Do you hear the mocking?" Marshal asked. He waited, as if he expected them to answer. "I have heard it all my life! It has not stopped me… and will not stop us now!"

Victor winced. Marshal tried to say the right things, but his voice created a problem. Even though he no longer bore a curse, those who heard him would assume he did. He said the correct words, and for the most part even pronounced them right. But they sounded awkward, as if they didn't belong together the way he used them. The odd pauses did not help. Even when he tried to project, he had no notion of his own volume. He was still learning, understandably, but maybe he had been right about his leadership ability for now.

Marshal drew his sword and pointed it at Victor. "Victor and I have… trained with a warden of the Eldanim. What we have learned, we will try to teach you. They"—he waved his sword toward the mockers—"expect you to die. I want to show them that… you can fight!"

"The Eldanim?" One of the twins snorted. "They don't exist!"

Victor walked over to him and held his own sword up. "See this? Eldanim forged. Seen any others like it in this army?"

"It's a sword." He shook his head. Clearly not an expert.

Beside him, Merish stirred. The big man had been watching Marshal and Victor with a child-like dreaminess. Topleb suggested his curse had something to do with his mind. But when he saw Victor's sword, Merish's eyes sharpened. His entire demeanor changed. He stepped out of the line and peered at the sword with an intense stare.

"You got his attention," Topleb said. "He likes swords."

Merish put out his hand and looked at Victor with a questioning expression. Victor turned his sword and handed Merish the hilt end. Merish stepped away from everyone else, dropped into a fighting stance, and began swinging the sword. His movements at first appeared random, but Victor slowly recognized a type of exercise, like he himself had done earlier.

Except Merish was better. One elegant and precise maneuver followed another for several minutes while everyone watched. Marshal approached. "He might be as good as Talinir," he whispered to Victor.

"Maybe."

"What's going on?" Albus asked in a loud voice.

Gnaeus explained it to him, but like everyone else, kept his eyes on the movements of the sword.

Merish came to an abrupt halt. He rested his free hand against the flat of the blade and closed his eyes for a moment. Then he offered the sword back to Victor.

As soon as Victor took the sword, the child-like disconnect returned to Merish's face. Victor gently guided him back into his position in the line. Each one of these men had strange abilities, secrets, oddities. A curse had robbed Merish of his intellect aside from this one thing. What had he been like before it? And a chill swept over Victor as he wondered what a master of swords had done to deserve such a curse.

"Well…" Marshal said. "One of you knows how to use a weapon. How about the rest of you?"

"Why am I here?" Albus said, again with the loud voice.

Marshal stepped in front of him. "Because you killed my friend."

"And I'm blind because of it. I can't fight." He hefted his shield. "What am I going to block with this? I can't see anything coming. I'll be dead in seconds."

"Maybe that's what you deserve."

Silence followed Marshal's words. Victor couldn't help agreeing with him, but he shouldn't have said it out loud. He joined them and took the shield from Albus's hand.

"You can't use this," he said. He turned to the next man in the line. "But Gnaeus here can."

Gnaeus, a wiry man with wrinkled skin and a handful of short scars on his face and arms, started. "Me, sir? I only have one good hand!" He held up his right hand, twisted and withered as if it were fifty years older.

Victor nodded. "Exactly. You only have one good hand. I want you to work with Albus here. You carry the shield and guard the both of you. In fact…" He glanced at the other soldiers. "I'll see if I can find a bigger shield you can carry. Maybe together, the two of you can equal one good soldier. He's the sword. You're the shield. And eyes."

Gnaeus hefted the shield and looked at Albus. "We can give it a try, I guess," he said.

Victor looked to Marshal, waiting for him to speak. He nodded to encourage him.

"Right. So we have… four… swordsmen, three spearmen, and…"

"And me," Topleb said. "I'm the one who starts it all."

"You… throw those spears?" Marshal asked.

"Throw." Topleb snorted. "Crazy Variochs. You throw a spear to hit something close. I don't want to be close. That's why I have this." He held up the piece of wood he had been toying with. Victor examined it. About two feet long, the smoothly-carved device had a pair of holes a few inches from one end. The other end, intricately carved, formed a kind of hook.

"You've been carrying that thing since you got here," one of the twins said. "Are you ever going to show us what it's for?"

"This, my ignorant young friend, is how we kill the enemy before he gets close."

"Like a bow and arrows?" the other twin asked.

"Bows! Bah! Bows are good for hunting squirrel or bird. You want to take down something larger—like a man—then you need something better," Topleb said. "Something stronger. The atlatl. Only in Ch'olan did we develop such a thing. Like most good things."

He held up one of his spears. It looked smaller than the ones the conscripts carried, but still larger than regular arrows. Topleb fitted the spear's base tip onto the hook on the end of his atlatl, lying it parallel against the device. He took hold of the other end, fitting his first two fingers through the holes.

Topleb pointed at a tree some forty feet away. He lifted the atlatl, took a step and propelled it rapidly over his head. The spear launched through the air at an unbelievable speed. Before the viewers could quite grasp it, the point of the spear embedded itself into the tree.

"If the tree is an enemy, then he dead," Topleb said.

"That's fantastic!" Gnaeus exclaimed.

"Impressive," Victor admitted. If Topleb could do that in battle, and quickly, and if they could get the others fighting even half as good as Merish, maybe… just maybe they wouldn't all die when the real war began.

(((14)))

The conscripted century marched south toward the Rasnian border every day. With Victor's assistance, Marshal tried to fit in some training time each day after the march ended. Some days, everyone claimed exhaustion. Other days, he could only persuade some of the squad to participate.

Albus was especially resistant. Gnaeus acted more willing, but without Albus, he couldn't do much. By contrast, Merish did whatever Marshal asked... but he didn't always understand. Topleb practiced his atlatl on his own each day, often watched by some of the others. Gallus, Callus and Wolf listened to Victor, though he wasn't very knowledgeable when it came to their spears.

Victor fought the air of depression that seemed to permeate the squad. The only ones who behaved at all pleasant were Merish, who never spoke, and Topleb, who complained about everything, but in such a jovial manner he didn't seem to mean it.

Marshal himself troubled Victor the most. As each day passed, he seemed to sink into melancholy more and more.

"I'm not a leader," he told Victor again one evening. They sat by the fire, alone save for Wolf who sat opposite them, staring into the blaze. He muttered to himself now and then, but never addressed anyone directly.

"You will be," Victor said. He snapped a stick in two and tossed it on the fire.

"Why? What makes you think that?"

"You have to be! I mean, you have this power. You're the son of a Lord, for Theon's sake!"

"Theon's sake," Wolf echoed. He chuckled.

"Did he just laugh?" Marshal asked.

"I'm not sure. Wolf, was that funny?"

"I shouldn't be here."

"Right." Victor sighed.

They sat in silence for several minutes.

"Why would my father's identity make me a leader?" Marshal asked.

"Because… that's what happens with every Lord? I guess. I mean, the magic passes down and they become the new Lord. It's the way things have always happened, isn't it?"

"Were they all good leaders, then?"

"I don't know."

"Not that it matters," Marshal said. "Volraag rules now. Even if I wanted to be a Lord, I can't."

"Aelia believed in you!" Victor insisted. "She wanted your curse lifted, not just because she loved you, but because of who she knew you could be!"

Marshal stared at him. "And she told you this?"

Victor hesitated. Once again, he considered telling Marshal what Aelia had told him on her last day. Yet her stern warnings held him back. Not yet.

"We all knew," he muttered. "You're supposed to lead."

"You should lead," Marshal said again. "You're the one who always wanted to be a soldier."

"I follow you." Victor had said it many times now, but he wasn't sure he believed it any more.

Marshal got to his feet. He gestured toward Wolf. "Then that makes you crazier than our friend here." He walked back to their tent and crawled inside.

Victor sat by the fire, watching it burn down. After a few moments, he heard footsteps. He looked up and blinked as his eyes tried to adjust to the darkness. The figure stepped closer to the fire and Victor recognized the decanus of the neighboring squad. He nodded in greeting.

"Where's your decanus?" the soldier asked.

Victor pointed. "He's gone to bed already."

"Don't blame him." The decanus eyed Wolf with a grimace. "We should all rest. Tomorrow, everything changes."

"Why?"

"Tomorrow, we join the main army. We'll be at the border. And the

Rasnian army waits for us. Good night."

•••••

The decanus had been right. After a brief march the next morning, the conscripted century arrived at the border of the disputed territory.

Victor couldn't make out anything definite about the locale. They never gained a high enough vantage point to look out over everything. As such, he saw confusion and chaos everywhere, perhaps controlled, perhaps not.

They crossed over a ditch around three feet deep. Victor took a quick look in either direction. The ditch appeared to encircle the entire camp, the entire army.

And beyond his current view, Lord Tyrr of Rasna waited with an army of his own. The Lords were at war over this spot. Volraag wanted it. Lord Tyrr wanted it. Victor had heard multiple theories from other soldiers during the days of their marching. The most popular theory held that a massive gold mine had been discovered on the border and both Lords wanted it. Of course, in true patriotic fashion, the Varioch soldiers insisted the mine was actually on their side of the border and the despicable Rasnians wanted to take it.

Somewhere out there, he knew, waited some kind of magic opening, or gateway to the Otherworld, or something. Nian hadn't been very clear on the exact nature of this spot. What had he said? The barrier between the worlds grew thin?

The supply wagons stopped just beyond the ditch. Victor barely caught a glimpse of that area of the camp. He noted a lot of activity: soldiers procuring weapons, armor, even more tents.

As they marched past the regular soldiers toward the front of the camp, the area closest to the enemy, Victor tried to get a better understanding of the layout. He saw towers evenly spaced around the camp's perimeter. The flag of Varioch with its soaring eagle hung limply near a large tent in the center of the camp, no doubt belonging to Lord Volraag. Workers even now scrambled to build an elevated platform outside it—not quite as high as the towers, but high enough to see over the entire area.

Victor caught his breath as three of the Remavian Guard, the elite of the elite, walked by, laughing with each other. Their gold-trimmed red cloaks fluttered in the breeze. Victor slowed to keep them in sight.

Gallus gave him a push. "Keep moving," he griped. "You can

admire their clothes later."

Victor stumbled and resumed his pace with the rest of the curse squad. None of them, Marshal included, appeared at all interested in their surroundings. They followed as they were told, looking downcast or resigned.

They didn't understand. How could they? Everything Victor ever wanted was right here. From the moment he found that flail so many years ago, he had dreamed of becoming one thing: a soldier. And now here he was.

The circumstances weren't quite as he had imagined them, of course. Not as a conscript, let alone part of a squad of cursed men. He was officially the lowest of the low in this army.

But he was a soldier.

(((15)))

Volraag looked over the command tent and nodded his approval. He turned to General Cassian and gestured to the nearby table. "Show me," he ordered.

Cassian stepped up to the table and spread out a map. "Our main army is here, of course, just south of the Amnis River." He pointed. "We have four legions of conscripts spread along the border to the west, ready to move on our command, to act primarily as distractions. Two more legions of conscripts will be joining us here shortly."

Volraag examined the map. Otioch and Rathri stood behind him. "And what about Rasna?"

Cassian shifted. "Our scouts report the primary Rasnian army is stationary just south of us, as they have been for weeks. The only difference is that they've been receiving reinforcements of their own. I believe we outnumber them, but only because of our conscripts."

"Any sign of Lord Tyrr himself?"

"Not as yet."

"I need to be informed the minute he shows himself. If he chooses to engage our soldiers, his power alone could devastate an entire legion."

Otioch eyed the map carefully. "And will you be doing the same to his troops?"

"Not unless it becomes necessary," Volraag said.

"But shouldn't we use every asset at hand to end this swiftly?" Cassian asked. "Your power could—"

"I will not. Our soldiers must have the opportunity to fight for their land. That which is born of blood is more highly valued." Volraag gestured and a light vibration shook the map. "Were I to hand them the victory, they would honor me, of course, but... they would not honor Varioch. And that is what matters here."

Cassian frowned. "Are you saying the end goal does not matter? Is the disputed land then so worthless?"

"Not at all. I am especially interested in seeing what is hidden here. But that is my personal goal. I am not altogether selfish. I have personal goals, and goals for our land. If I am a good Lord to our people, those goals will end up being the same thing."

Volraag glanced at Rathri. He had stepped forward a little too eagerly when Volraag vibrated the map. That man had an obsession with his power.

"Know this, all of you. Should the need occur, I will use my power to join our soldiers in battle. But that need will probably only occur if Lord Tyrr enters the fray himself. His power equals mine. We are playing a dangerous game here, both of us watching the other, waiting to see who uses their power first. Is it better to get in a first strike? Or to let the other weaken himself before striking back in full force?"

Cassian opened his mouth to answer, but Volraag waved his hand in dismissal. "I am not interested in a full strategic discussion of that question at this time, though I'm sure it will occupy your thoughts greatly, my general. You're dismissed for now."

"As you command, sir." The general left the tent, just as Consul Regulus entered. Volraag resisted a groan; he knew what to expect.

"Lord Volraag, I need to remind you about the finances of this campaign." The Consul, a thin man with a severe face, rested his hand on the map. Volraag assumed the sharp curve in his nose created the nasal quality to his speech.

"You have done so multiple times already, Consul." Volraag pulled up his camp chair and sat. He did not offer a chair to the Consul.

"And I will continue to do so." Regulus gestured broadly. "It is not inexpensive to maintain this many soldiers. The food cost alone is immense."

"I am aware."

"Are you? The nobility is paying for this, and they are only just now beginning to realize what that means. Varioch has not fielded an army this size since the last barbarian assault over a hundred years ago. We do not know what we are getting into here."

"I know." Volraag stood again. "I have studied this for some time. Do you think this is a large army?" He also pointed outside the tent. "I tell you that this is nothing. The Rasnian army. Our army. They are insignificant. In ancient times, our lands would gather armies that consisted of virtually every man of fighting age. That would include these nobles. It would even include you, dear Consul."

Regulus flinched, but only slightly. The man was difficult to shake. "Whatever happened in the past, this is happening now. And I need you to know that it can only last so long before your nobles refuse to pay its cost."

"You need not worry. I anticipate a swift victory."

"And what is 'swift'?"

"You will see. Be patient, Consul."

"Words will not keep the gold flowing, Lord. At least not for long." Regulus bowed and exited the tent.

Volraag waved to the two guards. "I need to be alone, if you don't mind. Just give me some time to myself."

Otioch and Rathri saluted and also left.

• • • • •

Volraag collapsed in his camp chair. This entire process was turning out to be much more complicated than he had originally bargained. Consul Regulus, unfortunately, wasn't wrong on many points. He buried his face in his hands. So many factors to consider. So many plans.

"You are wise to conserve your power."

"Rathri, I asked for some time alone."

"And Rathri honors your wishes, young Lord. I apologize for violating them myself, but I have little time to waste."

Volraag looked up. A stranger stood in the shadows near the tent wall. He found it hard to get a good perception of him. His height was evident, yet seemed taller somehow, too tall to fit inside the tent.

"Who are you? How did you get in here?"

"My methods of traveling are quite... extreme, young sir. As for who I am..."

The figure stepped out of the shadows into the lantern light. Volraag jumped to his feet, flipping the camp chair onto the floor. The strangeness of the figure's height became more confusing. He stood, smiling at Volraag, looking somewhere over six feet tall... and yet he wasn't. Volraag's stomach churned. The figure's tan facial features, framed by long white hair, were angular to the point of sharpness. His left eye shone with a crystalline green color. His right eye contained no white at all; only a pure orb of darkness with a sprinkling of tiny pinpricks of light, like a miniature star field.

"Eldanim," Volraag whispered.

"Yes. My name is Curasir." He strode next to the table and looked down at the map. "Your father cared little for my people, and we in turn avoided him. Perhaps you will be more amenable, more... friendly."

"What do you want of me?" Volraag reached instinctively for his power, but did not use it. For the first time in a very long time, he found himself completely surprised and unsure of his next move.

"I believe that we share similar interests, similar goals, perhaps," Curasir said. His voice, even casual, seemed filled with command. Volraag wanted to believe him, to listen to him, but his suspicious nature still came to the fore.

"What do you know of my goals?"

Curasir toyed with the edge of the map, almost like a cat batting at the curled edge of the paper. "I know many things. I know you killed your own father in an effort to gain his power."

"I did not kill my father."

"No, no, of course." Curasir gestured toward the command tent's doorway. "You had Rathri do it. What a fascinating creature he is. And to think there were two like him in this realm."

Two? "You know Kishin?"

"I know of him. But he's not at issue here. You are. When your father's power instead went to your brother, you found another way. That was quite creative, by the way. You learn quickly and adapt your plans to new input. I admire that."

Volraag clenched his fist to contain the vibrations that threatened to erupt outward. He moved to his left, putting the table between himself and the Eldani. As if he didn't notice, Curasir continued his movement around the table in the other direction.

"So the big question is: why? Were you so desperate for power? I think not, at least not in a way that most people would assume. You have larger plans, larger goals." He turned to face Volraag directly. "Tell me of them."

"Why should I?" Volraag lifted his fist. "Why should I even speak with you? You entered my private tent. I should defend myself."

"Were you able to actually strike me, you might succeed. I cannot stand against the power of a Lord." Curasir spread his arms. "But why would you? Have I threatened you? In point of fact, I believe we can help each other."

"So you have said. How?"

"Tell me of your plans. Surely you mean to do more than just hold on to the power you've stolen. After all, when you die, it will return to Lord Sundinka's heir. It is a temporary thing."

"Not if I claim all the power."

"Ah, now we're getting somewhere. You mean to claim all the Lords' powers?"

"What if I do? The Lords have abused their power. I have watched it my entire life."

Curasir picked up the fallen camp chair and sat on it. He pointed at Volraag. "And what makes you any better than them?"

"I will not use the power for myself!" Volraag felt heat rising in his face. "I will help everyone!"

"How? You've already started a fight in which people will die."

"It's a means to an end."

"What end? What is your goal?"

Volraag raised his fist to eye level, then released it. A burst of power shook the roof of the tent. "I will return the power to the land itself. No more Lords."

Curasir steepled his fingers together. "Fantastic. As I said in the beginning: we have similar goals."

"What do you care of the Lords? Or humans at all?"

"I care because the power, as you call it, should return to the land. In fact, we would like all things to return to the way they were before you Lords changed everything."

"You wish to help me?"

"I wish us to help each other." Curasir stood and strode across the room again. Volraag had to turn rapidly to keep him in sight. "You think the power of all six Lords will be enough for your purpose. I tell you it is not. You will need more. And I can tell you how to get it."

"How?"

Curasir pointed outside. "This spot you're... quarreling over."

"It's a war, not a quarrel."

Curasir snorted. "Please. This is not a war. It's a skirmish at best. You know nothing of real war. But the spot itself. Do you know what is there?"

"I know it is one of three spots of power. Legend tells of many things related to them. Strange creatures. Men who wander into another world. Wild magic of all kinds."

"It is more than that. It is a portal."

"To where?"

Curasir pointed toward his right eye. "Do you know what I see with this?"

Volraag shook his head.

"I see another world. We call it the Starlit Realm. The portal opens the way to it. Well, one of the ways."

"What good will that do me?"

"First, if you open it, as you can do with a Lord's power, then I will bring you another source of power."

"Another source?"

"You didn't really think your Lords and Mages held all the 'magic' of two worlds, did you?"

Volraag didn't answer. Until now, he hadn't been sure of the existence of a second world.

"After that," Curasir went on, "I ask only that you open the other two portals."

"Why?"

"When the gates between the worlds are fully open, then anyone and anything may travel through. Those who have been denied for so long may return."

Volraag blinked. The conversation had started out strange, then moved into making perfect sense. Now it veered in another new direction.

"Who are you talking about?"

"That is the part where you help me. I can promise you, however, that if you accomplish all this, you will have enough power to do as you desire, and more."

Volraag considered. "You seem to know a great deal about a great many things, Curasir," he said at last. "I want one more thing."

"And that is?"

"Where is my half-brother?"

"Far closer than you think. Less of a threat than you imagine. Yet more dangerous than you've guessed."

"I don't like being spoken to in riddles."

"Regardless. I actually don't know where your half-brother is, at the moment. He has eluded my sources, and seems to be hiding his power somehow. Yet he cannot be far. I suspect the portal will be drawing him, as well."

"Drawing him?"

"Just as it draws Lord Tyrr and you, and your father before you."

"That makes no sense. Then every Lord throughout history would have come here."

"But things are different now. Everything is changing."

"Why is that?"

"Didn't you hear? A curse was lifted. Two, in fact." Curasir took a step toward the door and began to fade. "I will see you at the portal." Another step and he turned grey and indistinct, a shadowy figure. And then he vanished completely.

"A curse? What do you mean?" Volraag stared at the spot where Curasir had been. An uneasy feeling grew in his stomach, as his mind connected several events. A lifted curse. The destroyed temple. Marshal.

(((16)))

Dravid stared at the trees on either side of the road. Someone had carved complicated patterns into the bark on two large oaks. He had never seen anything so elaborate on such a scale.

"We must be close!" Junia said, excitement in her voice.

Seri reached a hand out and caressed one of the patterns. "These were carved by magic," she said. "I'm not sure how, but I can feel it." She looked at Dravid. "Can you?"

He frowned and stepped up beside her. His fingers traced one of the lines engraved into the bark. This close, it looked almost like it had been burned. But he could feel a faint vibration within each one of the lines. "Barely," he admitted. "But..." He peered closer, then stepped back for a wider view. "I think I've seen this one before."

"On Zes Sivas?"

"No... back home. In Kuktarma." He struggled to remember. A book cover. That's it. He had seen it decorating a leather book cover in his parents' library.

Ixchel pointed to one of the patterns on the opposite tree. "This one is from Ch'olan," she said.

"There are six!" Seri said. She hurried to the other tree. "This one! Definitely from Arazu. I remember seeing it at the university, though I can't remember what it means. It's ancient."

Dravid looked from one tree to the other. Each held three patterns, now that he could tell them apart. Each one stretched at least a couple of feet square. One for each of the six lands of Antises?

"Do either of you recognize any of the other ones?" he asked Cato and Junia. They shook their heads.

"One of them has to be from Varioch," Seri said. She furrowed her

71

brow.

Dravid leaned in close. "I don't think our two friends here are likely to be well-versed in ancient lore," he whispered.

"Oh." She moved back to the other tree and ran her hands over the different patterns. "What do you suppose it all means?"

"We must be near the Forerunner!" Junia insisted.

"What makes you say that?" Dravid asked.

"Why else would these be here? You said they were magic! And it has symbols from all six lands!"

"Because all are welcome?" Cato guessed.

Ixchel looked down the road. "How far to the next settlement?" she asked.

"Settlement?"

"Town. Village. City."

Cato frowned. "If I remember right, there is not another town of any size for many miles along here. This isn't the most populated area."

"He wishes to attract a following, yes? Why make his home so far from the population?" Ixchel asked.

"Maybe he doesn't want a following," Dravid said.

"Or maybe he only wants those who are willing to make the journey," Cato suggested.

"That must be it!" Junia bounced on her heels. "Only those who are worthy can be in his presence! Our journey will show our worthiness!"

Dravid rolled his eyes. "By that logic, I'll be the most worthy, since I've come the furthest."

Junia scampered to his side and put a hand on his crutch. "And you've had the most difficult journey!" she said. "Oh, perhaps he will reward you greatly for your sacrifice!"

Dravid found it hard to maintain his cynicism. Junia's excitement, lack of inhibitions, and joy of life brought a smile to his face.

"Someone comes," Ixchel warned.

Dravid looked up and saw four figures approaching from the western road. From this distance, he could only make out white robes on three of them, an odd choice for traveling clothes.

As they drew near, he saw the three in white were all female, all with wheat-colored skin like other natives of Varioch, but three different hair colorings: blonde like Junia, brown like Seri, and a third whose hair shone like fire. But the fourth figure commanded their attention. Without any words spoken, Dravid knew this must be the mysterious Forerunner.

As he approached, he moved through shadows and light, the morning sun's rays piercing through the oak canopy in patches. The inconsistent light made it difficult to make out some of his appearance. His skin color at times appeared as light as the women around him, and other moments as dark as Dravid's own. As he drew near, Dravid grew more confused. The man's skin color appeared to change depending on how he looked at it, fluctuating with every blink or shift in lighting. His hair, at least, could be discerned: long and pale, almost like the whitest of rice. Yet his face lacked any hair growth, save pale eyebrows. He did not appear to be old, nor did he seem very young.

His clothing portrayed a mixture of practical elegance and bizarre touches. While his beige trousers appeared simple enough, his tunic flaunted multiple colors, mostly shades of blue. The sleeves grew ever wider from shoulders to wrist, hanging from his hands as he raised them in greeting. Four piercings held multi-colored earrings in his left ear, while the right remained bare. A lengthy purple cape, trimmed with crimson, hung from his broad shoulders.

His appearance did not proclaim his identity so much as the magic that radiated from him. Dravid could feel its vibrations growing stronger and stronger as he approached, yet it felt nothing like the power he knew from Zes Sivas, the Masters, or even the Lords. Whereas the Lords' power felt like it could burst forth at any time, this man's power seemed more contained, as if under greater control. Yet it did not vibrate the same, almost like an entirely different kind of power. But that made no sense.

"Like the Lady's power," Seri whispered beside him.

The Lady? Was she referring to Lady Lilitu, from her homeland? Seri did not know any other great ladies, that he recalled. And he didn't remember anything about Lady Lilitu having her own power. Dravid wanted to ask, but things happened too fast.

Ixchel moved beside Seri. Cato and Junia stepped forward, their eyes fixed on the amazing figure who stopped a few steps before them. He bowed. Cato and Junia returned his bow in elaborate but smooth motions.

"Welcome, children! Welcome to our sanctuary!" His voice resonated throughout Dravid's body. Instinctively, he knew: magic permeated that voice. But how? How did one project magic through the voice, and why? Theoretically, it made sense, but the purpose eluded him.

"I am Forerunner, and I am here to restore that which was lost." He placed a hand on Cato and Junia's shoulders. "You have each lost something, something dear to you. I tell you that it is not the end. What was lost can be found. What is gone can return." He looked from one face to the other. "And what has been taken can be restored."

Junia abruptly burst into tears and put her face in her hands. Cato started to reach for her, but Forerunner stepped between them. He placed a hand under Junia's chin and lifted her face to look into her eyes. "Do not weep, daughter. Your brother, even now, has left the Lord's army and is on his way back to your parents' estate. He will be there before another night falls."

Dravid felt a chill. The words could be false, but how would Forerunner even know of Junia's brother? This defied everything he knew of magic.

Forerunner turned to Cato. "Your loss is minor in the grand scheme, but no less important to you, I am sure. Rest assured that it will trouble you no more." Cato nodded, his eyes alight. He took Junia's hand and the women in white surrounded them. Forerunner turned to the others.

"I am Seri, mage of Arazu," Seri said with confidence. "Who are you, Forerunner? Are you a mage or Lord?"

Forerunner's smile could have been patronizing, yet it seemed sincere. "I am neither, child. I am Forerunner. I am. That is all that is needed for now." He leaned closer to look into her eyes. "Ah, your loss is recent. It pains you to be without it. Come. Stay in my sanctuary, and it will be restored to you. I can promise you that." He lifted a finger and tapped beside his own eye.

Seri trembled. Dravid reached a hand out to steady her. But just as he had done with Junia and Cato, Forerunner pivoted in between them. So smoothly had he done so, Dravid didn't even realize it until his hand touched Forerunner's shoulder. He felt the power beneath tight muscles, calling to him, like the constant pull from the power of Zes Sivas. Instinctively, he reached out to it, attempting to draw some of the power toward him.

Forerunner took Dravid's hand and removed it. He grasped his forearm in some form of greeting. Dravid's connection to the power vanished.

"Oh, my friend. You have lost so much," Forerunner said. Dravid looked up and saw Forerunner's eyes for the first time. He wavered in shock. Forerunner's eyes were green with gold flecks deep within... and two pinpricks of light on either side of each pupil. Like the star no longer in Seri's eye. No wonder she had been trembling.

"Anyone can see your obvious loss," Forerunner went on. As he spoke, Dravid could feel the slight vibrations from the magic in each word. "But you have lost something greater. You have lost your purpose. Your entire life revolved around one goal, one purpose, and now it is gone."

Dravid's mind whirled. He fought with wondering how Forerunner could know all this, the strangeness of his appearance, and more shockingly, whether Forerunner had the power to do all that he promised. Because if he did...

"I do. I can. I am here to restore that which was lost, and to prepare the way. Come. Spend some time in my sanctuary. You must decide what is most important to you. And that is what I will restore. You have my word."

Dravid wavered. If not for Forerunner's grip on his arm, he would have fallen. He took a deep breath and steadied himself.

"What is all this?" Ixchel's suspicious voice broke into the confusion.

Forerunner looked into Dravid's eyes once more and then released him. He turned to Ixchel, his expression never wavering.

"Greetings to you, daughter of Ch'olan, Holcan of the Lady."

"How do you know me?"

"I know... oh, so much. I know your struggles. I know the depth of your pain, your loss."

"You do not."

"Oh, but I do. Your loss happened so long ago, when you were so small. You believe that all hope is lost completely. But..." Forerunner reached toward her and put his thumb and forefinger together as if taking hold of something tiny. "A tiny strand of hope remains, buried deep within you. I will show you the truth of it."

Forerunner motioned as if he pulled a thread with his small grip. Ixchel gasped, and the stony demeanor melted from her face. In that moment, Dravid thought, she was truly beautiful, more so than he had ever realized.

Forerunner stepped toward Ixchel and gently pushed her shield aside. "That strand of hope would not exist if it were not anchored to something real," he said. "It will take time, but that which you have lost will also be restored. In time." He leaned in and gave her a hug.

Prior to this moment, Dravid could not imagine anyone hugging Ixchel. In fact, if anyone had made such an attempt, he would have expected them to be lying flat on their backs in seconds. Yet Ixchel did not resist Forerunner. Her eyes, over his shoulder, sought out Dravid and then Seri. "It cannot be," she whispered.

Forerunner stepped away from her and backed a few steps away. He spread his arms to encompass them all.

"Come! The sanctuary awaits! Let us be filled with life, celebrate hope rekindled, and look forward to your restorations! Come!"

And they did.

•••••

Dravid recalled little of the walk to Forerunner's sanctuary. They left the road soon after the marked trees, and followed a narrow path up a steep hill. Once they crested the top, they saw a plateau surrounded by three higher hills. From a central building, a narrow creek flowed out beside the main path and then down the hill behind them. Two larger, round buildings lay to either side.

"Rest from your journeys," Forerunner proclaimed. "We shall speak again soon."

The red-haired woman led Dravid and Cato to the right building. The girls were led to the left. None of them had anything to say as they were separated. Everything seemed to be as it should be.

Inside, the women gave Dravid his own spacious room. The red-haired woman took his crutch and assisted him in climbing into a bed more comfortable than those back home in his parents' estate. Sleep claimed him within a few moments, a deep sleep without difficulty from his leg.

When he woke, he felt disoriented. Where was he? How had he gotten here? His vision took a few moments to clear before he could look around the room.

His bed, tall and heavily cushioned, stood in the tip of a wedge-shaped room. Behind the bed, the room ended in a wooden wall. Dravid noted the Kuktarman symbol he had seen on the tree earlier decorated the wall as well. The two angled walls appeared to be only curtains, albeit very heavy curtains, both dyed a deep crimson.

The far end of the wedge drew his attention. A stone wall reached about two-thirds the height of the ceiling, letting sunlight pour in. Water also flowed over the top of the wall, down into an inviting pool, lined with paving stones. The sunlight struck the pool just right, casting dazzling reflections around the room. To his dismay, Dravid saw his crutch lying beside the pool, quite some distance from the bed.

He considered hopping all the way, but decided to crawl instead. It might not be dignified, but no one saw him. The pool of water beckoned him, reminding him how long since he last bathed. In fact, it seemed intentional, as his crutch rested on top of a couple of neatly-folded towels.

But something didn't seem right.

He couldn't see any doors in the room, but the side walls were only curtains, after all. He pushed his way through at the end closest to the pool and outside wall. He found himself in a narrow hallway formed by his own curtain wall and another one running parallel. Another room like his? It didn't matter, as he also found the one thing he most wanted: a door. It had no lock, and he easily pushed it open and stepped out into the sunlight.

He needed to see Seri. He moved past the building in which he lodged and crossed the main path toward the left-hand building where the women had gone. He took three steps onto the bridge over the creek before a blonde woman in white hastened to block his path.

"I'm sorry, sir, but men are not allowed in the women's lodgings," she informed him, holding a palm up to stop his progress.

"All right." Dravid looked past her to the building, seeing no sign of movement. "Could you take a message to my friend Seri? Tell her I need to see her?"

She cocked her head, considering him. "Oh, yes. You're the ones who arrived in the group yesterday."

"Yesterday?" Dravid looked at the sun's position. Late afternoon. They had arrived late morning. He could not have slept an entire day away. "No, no. We got here this morning."

The woman nodded, smiling. "You're a little disoriented, as would be expected. You were very tired after your long journey, and slept quite soundly."

"That's not possible."

"I hear those words many times here in Forerunner's Sanctuary."

Dravid did not know how to respond to that. "Well, um, could you take the message to Seri?"

"I will tell her, but I would also suggest that you simply wait until the evening meal. You just have time to bathe beforehand."

Dravid took that as a not-so-subtle hint. If he truly had slept over a day, then he probably didn't smell very nice. He nodded. "And where will the meal take place?"

The woman pointed to the central building. "Forerunner will

welcome all to his table in the pavilion."

Of course he will. Dravid turned and headed back to the men's building. Come dinner time, he would find Seri and figure out what was going on here.

(((17)))

"All right, that card is the wild mage," Victor explained to Callus. "We re-shuffle the deck now."

"But what if he ends up back at the top of the deck?"

"Uh, then we'd re-shuffle again."

"And if he's there again?"

Victor rolled his eyes. "It could happen, but it probably won't. Can we keep playing?"

The conscript nodded. Victor kept trying to teach the card game to members of the curse squad. So far, only Topleb had been able to grasp it, but he had little interest in playing.

"Now this is a soldier card. I can use it to take one of your Lords captive."

"Why?"

"That's how the game works."

"But a soldier can't capture a Lord."

Gallus, the other twin, leaned in. "This is what I told him. A single soldier doesn't stand a chance against a Lord!"

"He can if it's the right soldier," said a quiet voice above them. All three looked up. Marshal stood there, but he wasn't watching them. He stared off into the distance.

"Look, it's the way the game works," Victor said. "It's based on history or something."

"It still doesn't make sense," Callus said.

"It's a card. It takes another card. It's how you play the game."

"But a soldier can't stop a Lord."

"Fine. Pretend the soldier is actually protecting the Lord."

"Why would a Lord need protection?" Gallus asked. "They've got magic powers."

"They're cards! Just cards!"

"But it doesn't make sense."

"It doesn't have to make sense!"

"Then why would you want to play it?"

Victor started to pick up the cards. "I have no idea any more."

"Which one is this?" Callus picked up a card and handed it to Victor.

"That's the High Master Mage."

"Why is it a woman?"

"It's not—never mind." Victor took the last of the cards and stood up. The twins began to argue about whether a woman could become a mage.

Victor stepped over next to Marshal and looked him over. His friend continued to stare. Victor followed his gaze and saw the command tent.

"He's here, Victor. I can feel him."

"Your brother?"

"Half-brother."

"That doesn't mean... I mean, can he feel you?"

Marshal broke his stare and looked back at Victor. "I don't think so. My power's still not very strong. If I were at full strength again, maybe. I don't know how all this works."

"But you can feel his presence? How?"

Marshal gestured weakly. "I'm not sure. I can feel a disturbance in the air, sort of a faint vibration. And when I focus on it, I can follow it. And it leads over there." He pointed toward the command tent. "And there... it's kind of like I can tell there's a lot of vibrations. I know it's magic, and it pulls at me. I want to reach out and try to take it. My mouth even waters."

Victor now understood a little bit about the vibrations involved in magic, but everything else Marshal said sounded completely strange.

"Do we need to be worried? He has his own power now, so he doesn't need yours. And that freaky assassin hasn't come back."

"I don't know. I still don't understand why he even has power. Is that where mine went? Will it come back? Or does he have something else?" Marshal ran his hands through his hair. "And is he even the enemy we have to be worried about? He wasn't the one who killed my mama and almost killed me. That was those... Durunim. The eidolons. Or whatever they are."

"I haven't seen one of them since the temple, either."

"Neither have I. And that worries me. They followed us through our whole journey. And then told me that I was the key to restoring their world. I can't imagine they just gave up. Where are they?"

"Maybe they'll go after Volraag, since he has power now. That would solve a lot of our problems."

Marshal shook his head. "No. He... said it was me. And talked about his masters. They wanted me."

Victor felt a chill at the back of his neck. Marshal had told him some of what happened in the Otherworld, but he hadn't mentioned this part before. Masters? That didn't sound good.

"Look," he said, "let's not dwell on it. We have to deal with what's going on right now. Let's run the squad through some more practice."

Marshal nodded and took another look toward the command tent. "If you think it'll do any good."

• • • • •

Victor looked up as two regular soldiers approached, pushing another conscript before them.

"Where's your decanus?" one demanded.

Victor glanced at the tent. "I think he's asleep. We did a lot of practice earlier, and—"

"I don't care. Here's another one for your squad." The soldier shoved a red-headed gangly conscript to the ground.

As the soldiers departed, Victor called after them. "You will make sure our food allotment is increased, won't you?" One of them waved back. Victor grunted. "Bad enough they shorted us on the wine yesterday. Here, let me give you a hand."

He helped the newcomer back to his feet. Like most of the conscripts, he didn't have a uniform of any kind. He carried a standard spear and shield, and seemed to stumble a bit.

"Thanks."

"Don't mention it. I'm Victor. What brings you to our curse squad?"

The newcomer looked at Victor with questions in his eyes, no doubt wondering about his curse. "I'm Rufus. I don't know why my old decanus sent me here. I don't—I mean, I do have a curse, but it's just a twisted foot. I've been with him for months!"

"As curses go, that's not much," Victor agreed. "Well, I guess, um, you'll have to share a tent with Wolf. He's an odd one, but seems harmless."

Marshal crawled out of his tent. "What's going on?" He stood up and stretched.

Rufus stumbled back and nearly fell. "You!"

Marshal frowned. "Do I know you?"

Rufus gripped his spear and took a step forward. "It's all your fault they're dead! Your fault!"

"Wait..." Marshal's eyebrows went up. "I do remember you..."

Before Victor could react, Rufus lunged toward Marshal, thrusting his spear. Marshal spun into a defensive stance and struck at the spear with his palm. The tip caught his tunic sleeve and tore it. "What—" Marshal managed to say before Rufus struck at his face with his shield. The boss caught Marshal in the chin and knocked him back into the tent.

Victor grabbed Rufus's spear arm and yanked him off balance. "Stop it!" he yelled. "You're attacking your decanus!"

"He can't be a decanus!" Rufus shouted, his voice shaking. "He tricked us! Got my friends killed!"

Marshal scrambled out of the tent's ruins and drew his sword. "We have met, Victor," he said. "When Aelia needed medicine. For you."

"And you tricked us!"

Marshal lifted his palm, but kept his sword at his side. "We did. We needed medicine for my friend."

"It saved my life," Victor said. Without the starshine Aelia had obtained, he wouldn't be here now. The assassin's sword had ripped his back open. Even with Aelia's treatment, the wound never fully healed, leaving an ugly scar. He could feel it now.

"And killed three others." Rufus's voice was still raw, but he stopped struggling against Victor.

"When... we left you, no one had died," Marshal said.

"We came back. And that other man was there. The leper. He killed... he killed them all!" Rufus dropped his spear and sank to his knees. "He made me help him. I spent weeks worried that I got leprosy from him." He looked at his hands. "I washed my hands so many times..."

Victor let go of the conscript's arm. He looked to Marshal.

"I'm sorry for your friends," Marshal said. "But the killer was after me. He's the reason Victor was hurt."

Rufus looked up. "So if you had stayed away from us, he would have stayed away. It is your fault. Or the woman's. Where is she?"

Marshal did not answer.

"She's dead," Victor said.

"Oh."

All three stayed quiet for a few moments.

"Did you find him a tent?" Marshal asked Victor.

Victor nodded.

Marshal turned to Rufus. "You've been in this army longer than anyone here, I think. You can help us."

"Why should I?"

Victor leaned in close. "Because without all the help we can get, we're all going to end up dead in a few days."

(((18)))

Janaab put out a hand and Talinir stopped in his tracks. Wandering the Starlit Realm was always a dangerous endeavor, made more so by the company. While Janaab had been reticent about his own identity and background, Talinir learned one important thing: magic filled Janaab more than any human he knew. How he had survived this long was a mystery.

Talinir saw nothing, so he listened. Somewhere beyond the ridge in front of them, he heard the scuffling footsteps of a large creature. "Tunaldi?" he guessed in a whisper.

Janaab shook his head. "Curse-stalker," he answered softly. "A big one." He paused. "No. Two of them."

Impressive. As a warden, Talinir should be able to make those identifications himself. But his senses were still in disarray from the unnatural way in which he now lived. But Janaab's ability to be able to identify a creature by its sound indicated years of learning. Exactly how long had he been here?

They waited in silence until the creatures passed on. A few moments later, Janaab led the way up and over the ridge.

"I'm surprised they didn't come for you," Talinir said.

Janaab chuckled. "In my early days here, that's all they did." He glanced back at the Eldani. "Imagine my surprise to discover the misbegotten beasts are native here! They don't belong in my—in the primary world at all."

Talinir nodded. "Yet they have slipped through, over the ages, through the high places, drawn by the magic your people bound up." He waited a moment before adding, "Like the magic within you."

"Figured that out, did you? It's hard to disguise, especially from one such as you. Even so, I've gotten better at hiding it from the less intelligent denizens of this place."

"How?"

Janaab's glance displayed no obvious emotion. "Some things I'm not ready to discuss," he said.

Talinir accepted that. Change of subject, then. "You said Marshal had returned to the primary world. How did that happen?"

"You know, I'm not completely certain." Janaab stopped walking and straightened his back, stretching. "I think our power combined somehow and he just... slid back."

"I've never heard of anything like that."

"Neither have I. But it happened. Perhaps it had something to do with the Bond to his friend." Janaab looked off into the distance. "They should have been reunited pretty quick, I would assume. But how long will it take the girl, I wonder?"

"What girl?"

Janaab resumed walking. "She's the key, you know. The key to everything. If she left Zes Sivas within a few days, and made straight for Varioch, she'd have been there by now. But will she find him?"

"How do you know so much?" Talinir stared at his companion. He had made a habit of focusing on him as much as possible, to keep his eyes from wandering to the stars.

"It must be maddening, I suppose." Janaab tested the ground ahead with his spear point before moving on. "You're here, in a way you shouldn't be, you meet a human where he shouldn't be, and he hints at knowing things he shouldn't know. Insane, isn't it?"

"Outlining it does not make it any less strange," Talinir said dryly.

"No, I suppose it doesn't. How can I explain? You know that I have magic and that I have been here a long time. Is that not enough?"

"Many of my people have been here a long time, and we are all magical, in our way. Yet doing so does not grant us visions of the primary world."

Janaab raised a finger. "Most of you," he corrected. "Most of you are not granted visions. Some are. I met an old woman in Intal Eldanir once—"

"You have been there?"

"You were out on warden duties at the time, most likely," Janaab said. "But yes, I've been there. And an old woman looked into my future. She told me I had to go to Zes Sivas and meet the girl with the star in her eye." He paused. "And what I must tell her to gain her aid."

"What did you tell her?"

"It doesn't matter now. She helped Marshal against the Durunim. That's what matters. And if she finds him, she can help him again."

Talinir wondered what help Marshal needed now. His curse had been lifted. Where would he go now? Back to his home in that mountain village? Or would he attempt to claim the Lordship of Varioch? Somehow, Talinir couldn't see that happening. He returned his thoughts to his companion. Keeping his eyes on Janaab so often had revealed more than just magic. The wanderer tried to hide it, but his skin, pale from lack of sun, had dark blotches on it. Janaab himself was in danger of becoming Durunim, or a human equivalent, at least. How long did he have? And if he succumbed to it, what would Talinir be forced to do?

Absently, he glanced up.

Stars.

"Theon's pillars!" Janaab's epithet broke into his ears some time later. "You have got to stop doing that!"

(((19)))

After his bath, which he had to admit was luxurious, Dravid got dressed and exited. As he left his room, Cato emerged from the curtains concealing the next room.

"Ah, there you are!" Cato said. "Ready to see Forerunner again?"

"I'm ready for some answers," Dravid said. "Tell me: when did we get here?"

Cato wrinkled his brow. "Earlier today, of course. Are you all right?"

"One of the women told me we arrived yesterday."

"That can't be right."

"That's what I said. But she insisted."

"I've had some lengthy naps, but nothing like that." Cato frowned. "Maybe it's part of Forerunner's magic. He wanted to be sure we were well-rested."

Dravid grunted.

Together, they made their way to the central building. Unlike the quarters, which each held a round shape, Forerunner's "pavilion" resembled a long rectangle. Dravid and Cato entered through a central pair of doors that led to a small atrium. Multiple doors all stood open, leading them further into an immense dining room. The walls alternated between carved wood panels and red curtains similar to their quarters.

Eight wood tables stood in a u-shape. A couple dozen people were already sitting at them, while at least another dozen milled about, talking. About half of them wore white robes like the women who had welcomed them here.

Dravid spotted Forerunner with ease, thanks to his bright clothing. He stood near the central tables, engaging with a small crowd of admirers. Even from this distance, Dravid could feel the magic radiating from him. It called to him, inviting him to come nearer, to take it for himself, to gain the power, to—

"Dravid!"

He shook himself. What had he been thinking? He turned and looked at Ixchel. He felt a strange sense of relief in seeing her still clad in her warrior's garb. She frowned at him. "What is wrong with you? I called your name three times!"

"I'm sorry. I don't know what's happening to me." He looked past her. "Where is Seri?"

Ixchel pointed to Forerunner. Amongst the crowd, Dravid spotted dark hair and a blue robe. He started toward her, but Ixchel grabbed his arm.

"Listen!" she said. "Something is not right here!"

"I know," he said. "I've lost an entire day. And he has something to do with it. His magic is strange."

"Indeed. I slept too long as well. I missed my morning prayers. My Lady says her Lady of Arazu has a similar magic," Ixchel said. "I don't know what that means. She seems quite fascinated by it. I'm worried about her."

"I'm worried about all of us! The things he promises are… they're impossible." Dravid hesitated. "Either he is a great deceiver, or he really can do what he says. I'm not sure which frightens me more."

"He must be a deceiver," Ixchel said.

Dravid looked at her and raised an eyebrow. "When we met him, you seemed pretty shaken," he said. "You even let him hug you."

Ixchel's face did not change. "I do not know what happened there."

"Really? Because you seemed—"

"My friends!" Forerunner's voice projected across the room. All eyes turned to see their host now standing atop one of the tables. He clapped his hands and gestured broadly to include them all.

"Welcome to my home! It is a temporary dwelling, of course, as I have many travels to make. But for now, let us eat and drink! When we are satisfied, we shall speak further of the days to come. Enjoy!"

At his wave, a dozen or so women in white robes emerged from the curtains, bringing trays filled with food and drink. The crowd surged to find seats at the tables. Dravid tried to move toward Seri, but found himself urged to sit down, instead. Ixchel stepped in front of him and made a path. He followed her until they reached one of the central tables.

Seri sat beside Forerunner. Though no seats were available anywhere near her, Ixchel strode up directly behind her, followed by Dravid. "My Lady," Ixchel said.

Seri glanced up and gasped a little. "Oh, Ixchel. There you are. How did we get separated? Oh! You found Dravid!"

"Ah, there are your companions!" Forerunner interrupted. "Make room for these new arrivals, my friends! Make room!" At his urging, several of the other guests rose or slid down the benches. Ixchel sat beside Seri, and Dravid joined them.

"Seri, have you—"

A tray of food came down in front of Dravid, cutting him off. He looked it over. Fruits and vegetables of all shapes and colors were spread before him. Among the fruits, he recognized oranges and a wide range of berries. He spotted apples, a fruit he had first encountered on Zes Sivas. All of these must be native to Varioch, as he saw no grapes, bananas, litchi, or others he knew from home.

The vegetables also contained a mix of the familiar and unfamiliar. He saw carrots and a wide range of leafy greens. A plate of steaming potatoes completed the arrangement.

"No meat," Dravid observed.

"All life is sacred," Forerunner said. Dravid hadn't even noticed him get up and stand behind them. "Are there not many in your homeland who practice this?"

"Yes," Dravid admitted. "I grew up without meat. At least until I left my parents' home."

Forerunner tilted his head. "While you're here, I suppose you'll have to return to that diet."

"And I suppose I'll go hunt my own food," Ixchel said in a low voice. Dravid suppressed a chuckle.

Forerunner stood so close again, his power so close. Dravid turned and found their host looking straight at him. He smiled.

"Who are you?" Dravid asked. In the pause that followed, Dravid felt a longing he did not understand, pulling him toward Forerunner. The magic of Antises could not explain this. It felt different, like a genuine thirst for the answer to his question.

"I am the forerunner. I am the harbinger. I am the omen. I have come to pave the way, to restore that which was lost."

"Where have you come from?" Seri asked. Her voice startled Dravid, as if the sound pulled him back from somewhere else. He blinked and looked toward her.

Forerunner eyed her, still smiling. "I have been many places, and I may not truly be from any of them. Though most recently, I have come from another land."

"Far from here?"

"So very far. And yet, so very close."

Dravid groaned and rubbed his face. Forerunner spoke in riddles and veiled secrets. Why couldn't he give a direct answer to anything?

"You mean the Otherworld," Seri said.

Forerunner's smile faded ever so slightly. He sat back down next to Seri and said something to her Dravid couldn't hear.

Still the magic called to him.

With her star-sight, Seri could actually see magic and take hold of it. Dravid could not. Seri and Master Hain had both instructed him, though, teaching him the traditional method mages throughout history used to find and manipulate magical power. He closed his eyes and placed his hands flat on the table.

"Are you all right?" asked the woman on the other side of him.

"Yes, I just need to think."

Focus. That's what he needed. Focus. Feel the vibrations of the magic all around. As his senses sharpened, he could feel a tiny bit of power within himself, and some within Seri. That would be expected, as mages unconsciously absorbed minuscule amounts of magic from time to time.

But what about Forerunner? He possessed a different magic. Dravid could not feel it as vibrations, at least not like he usually felt. Instead, he felt occasional pulses of power radiating outward from what seemed a massive source. Once he knew the pattern, Dravid waited until just before another pulse expanded… and he opened himself up to it.

The pulse struck and Dravid took hold of the magic. He gasped. That one pulse filled him with power more than anything he had experienced at Zes Sivas. He would need to release it quickly. But instead, he realized he had grabbed hold of the power source and pulled it toward him. More power rushed into his body. He tried to stop the flow, cut himself off from it, but failed. It kept coming.

Earlier experiments with absorbing magic usually resulted in spasms in his chest and pools of saliva within his mouth. This power behaved differently. He felt his chest tighten. A burning sensation swept up his throat, leaving his mouth painfully dry. He could feel heat building behind his eyes. They flew open.

Everything glowed around him. Ixchel leaned closer to look at his face. Her lips moved, but he heard nothing but a dull roar building within.

He pushed against the table and fell off the bench. He rolled on the floor, feeling both exhilaration and terror. The power was everything. The power was too much. His body was not meant to handle this.

Seri knelt beside him, grabbing at him. Fear decorated her face, fear he could sense vibrating from her, as if it were a type of magic itself. Forerunner stood behind her. Dravid could not read his expression, but he glowed with the power, releasing another pulse that rushed into Dravid, filling him beyond his capacity.

In that moment, he knew. Somehow, he understood. Forerunner's power source did not come from Antises. He did not carry a portion of it within him like the Lords. His power, so strange and alluring, existed as a part of him, intrinsic to his nature. He could not possibly be human and contain such power. Only seconds remained to Dravid before the power tore him apart.

Forerunner gestured ever so slightly, and the power rushed back to him. Dravid felt it leave him like a tearing of cloth. He felt drained, more exhausted than he'd ever felt in his life, even after he lost his leg.

"Foolish acolyte." Forerunner's words reverberated within his head before he lost consciousness.

(((20)))

Seri relaxed in her own bathing pool, surrounded by lit candles. Such a stressful evening, but the warm water certainly helped her relax.

What had Dravid been thinking? The moment he connected to Forerunner's power, she felt it and understood. Forerunner called him foolish, and she couldn't deny it. Trying to tap into an unknown power source was like... like trying to grab one of these candles by the flame. Except the flame was a raging inferno. And Dravid tried to grab it with his whole body.

Seri frowned. She needed to work on her similes. That one didn't quite grasp the reality of what had happened. Fortunately for Dravid, Forerunner could reabsorb his own power.

Forerunner. What an intriguing mystery the man created. He certainly wasn't what she had set out to find on this journey, but he needed more investigation. Powerful. Oh, so powerful. At least as powerful as one of the Lords, if not more so. And yet he didn't fit within the structure of magic as she knew it. How was that possible?

He considered himself so clever with his implications tonight, but he let something slip. He tried to cover it up with smooth words, but he definitely implied he came from the Otherworld. The Eldanim lived in the Otherworld, at least sometimes, and they were beings of magic. Yet Forerunner looked nothing like them. Not human. Not Eldanim. So what was he?

Ixchel pushed aside the curtain and entered the room. Despite being given her own room, she had dragged a feather-stuffed mattress to the floor of Seri's room this morning, announcing her intent to sleep there.

"Is Dravid all right?" Seri asked.

"He is sleeping," Ixchel said. "The white robes raised quite a fuss.

They objected to my presence in the men's housing. But I did see that he was well treated. His sleeping chamber is much like yours."

"I hope he doesn't suffer any ill effects," Seri said. "Forerunner's magic is... unusual."

"Is that what happened to him?" Ixchel snorted. "Yet another reason to distrust that man."

"Distrust? I don't know." Seri rolled over and rested her elbows on the side of the pool.

"What is wrong with you?" Ixchel knelt and stared directly into Seri's eyes.

"What do you mean? Nothing's wrong with me."

"You are not yourself."

Seri's anger rose. "What do you know, anyway? I'm enjoying this place, and Forerunner is amazing."

Ixchel drew a dagger Seri didn't even known she had. She scratched a mark onto the paving stone in front of Seri. "You have said it yourself: we must be wary of all magic users," she said.

She scratched a second mark.

"Forerunner is using magic within his voice. It influences everyone around him. I fell prey to it at first, to my shame. I have to fight not to do so again."

"He is..." Seri wanted to object, but found she couldn't. She knew the truth of that statement.

Ixchel scratched a third mark. The screech of metal against stone made Seri wince.

"You have behaved in a leisurely fashion lately. Since coming into Forerunner's presence, in fact."

"I'm just happy to be in such a nice place!"

Ixchel scratched a fourth mark, and pointed the dagger at Seri.

"Finally, you are lying in the water totally naked. You have previously displayed a fear and aversion to this. You have avoided removing any clothing in another's presence, even mine."

The shock washed over Seri like ice water, and then her face flamed. She snatched a towel, scrambled from the water and wrapped herself. What had she been thinking? Her mother would be so ashamed of her!

Water dripped from her hair as she tried to calm her rapid breathing. How could she have done that? It did not make any sense! Except... she looked down at Ixchel's marks. Forerunner. His voice had been affecting her, altering her mood, her inhibitions.

"Are you yourself once more?" Ixchel asked.

"I think so." Seri took a deep breath and let it out in a shudder. "I was—I was becoming like—"

"Like one of the white robes," Ixchel finished. She pointed to the foot of Seri's bed. "They even have a robe laid out for you."

"How did you know? How did you resist it?"

Ixchel sighed and sat, crossing her legs. "I didn't, for a while. Then this morning, I was alone. I decided to check on you." She hung her head. "I couldn't find you."

"But isn't your room right next door?"

"It is. But I mean I could not... sense you." Ixchel looked up. "We are Bonded, you know. In more ways than you realize. My oath, my... promise as your guardian. It behaves in a similar way to a normal Binding."

"Like the Binding I have to you, and the one I had to Master Hain?"

Ixchel nodded. "That is more powerful. It is to my great honor that such a Binding exists. Except... It no longer does."

"What do you mean?" Seri felt a sick tightness in her stomach.

"The Bond is gone. Not broken. We would have felt that. But it's not there now."

"That can't be right."

"Close your eyes."

Seri did so.

"Now find me with our Binding."

Seri let herself relax. She tried to sense the magic, the vibrational hum that drew her toward Ixchel in their Bond. But she couldn't find it. In her mind, she turned back and forth, trying to sense.

"There!" She threw out her arm, pointing to her right.

"No." Ixchel's voice came from her left.

She opened her eyes and stared at her friend and bodyguard. "How can this be?"

"You are the mage." Ixchel's face softened. She looked... frightened. "I was hoping you could tell me."

"The Laws of Cursings and Bindings are inviolable," Seri said by rote. "I mean, they can't be broken. Curses and Bonds cannot be removed."

"And yet."

Seri paced, leaving wet footprints across the floor. "The Masters all insisted that a curse had been lifted here, in Varioch or Rasna. They saw it as more important than anything else that's been happening. Now we find someone who is removing—or blocking—Bindings. Is it connected? Did Forerunner lift someone's curse?"

"The travelers spoke of healing magic," Ixchel said.

"But we haven't seen anything like that since we've been here. But he promises all kinds of things, healings, restorations. For Theon's sake, he even implied he could restore Dravid's leg!"

Seri stopped pacing as a thought too impossible struck her. "It couldn't be. Could it?"

"What is that, my Lady?"

Seri turned back to Ixchel. "Could Forerunner be Theon?"

Ixchel's face twisted in skepticism. "Theon is not a man," she said. "He dwells in the light."

"But what if he came down here? Who else could change the Laws?"

"Your pardon, my Lady. If Forerunner is Theon, then... he is not a god I wish to follow. Would he treat you this way?"

"What way? I mean, don't take me wrong." Seri's words spilled out in a torrent. "I don't like what was happening to me. But was it all bad? I felt good. I've enjoyed our time here. I don't know. Maybe he's not Theon. Maybe he's one of Theon's servants or something? Even his name implies that something or someone else is coming, right? Forerunner?"

Ixchel opened her mouth to answer, but Seri hurried on.

"He says he can restore my star-sight. I can't—I can't tell you how desperate I am for that. I know you don't understand. No one can. Losing it was like... like losing one of my eyes. If he can bring it back, maybe he is someone we should listen to."

"I still do not trust him. He must be a deceiver."

Seri frowned. "How? What has he lied about?"

"He says he can restore what we lost, yes? He knew my loss came when I was a child. Yet he claims he can restore it."

"Maybe he can?"

"No. No one can raise the dead."

• • • • •

Dravid's eyes still burned when he finally forced them open. His entire body ached with a dull pain and a lethargy that pulled at every muscle. He looked up at the ceiling of his room in the men's quarters.

"I need to speak with him alone." The voice of Forerunner. Dravid could feel the tiny vibrations in each syllable. But this time, they generated sharp but tiny pains in his head.

He rolled his head and saw two of the white-robed women leaving his room. Forerunner stood alone a few feet from his bed, arms crossed. He waited until the women were gone and then spoke.

"You have behaved in a childish, foolish manner."

Dravid groaned and looked back up at the ceiling.

"What made you think you could draw from my power, anyway?"

"It called to me."

Forerunner snorted. "And when one tiger calls to another in your native land, do you try to take its teeth?"

Dravid frowned and then winced from the effort. "Who's the other tiger, then?"

"What?"

"If you're a tiger calling to another tiger, who is the other tiger?"

"That—it was an analogy. And apparently not a very good one. It's been some time since I've visited these lands."

These lands? Did he mean all of Antises?

"At any rate, you could have killed yourself. That would not be a polite action for a guest to take."

"I apologize."

"Well, that's something, at least. I suppose I forgive you."

"Can you stop… using magic with your voice? It hurts my head."

"Oh." Forerunner paused. When he spoke again, his voice no longer held the vibrations. "That comes natural to me. I have to make an effort not to do it."

Dravid lifted himself up on his elbow and looked at Forerunner. "I'm revising my earlier question. What are you?"

"Ah." Forerunner lifted a finger. "Now that's an interesting question. And yet the answer is the same as before. I am Forerunner."

"So… Forerunner is who you are, and also what you are?"

"I suppose it's also how I am and why I am."

Dravid sank back down. "Why can't you give a straight answer to anything?"

"I am answering as best as I can, as best as you can understand. It is quite frustrating for me, as well. Why do you not trust me?"

"Why?" Dravid waved his hand in the air. "You use magic through your voice to persuade people. You promise miracles, but we've yet to see anything. You made me sleep an extra day for some reason. Shall I go on?"

"Magic. What a limited word you all use to describe so many different forms of power."

"And you're fond of cryptic statements."

Forerunner chuckled. "That's fair. But to answer your charges: my voice, as I said, is natural. My promises will be fulfilled; I promise you that." He stepped up beside the bed. "I told you that you would have to choose what I would restore. You still have plenty of time to make that choice."

He touched Dravid's amputated leg. He felt a vibration and heat spread through his stump. For a moment, Dravid genuinely believed his leg was about to regrow. And then the feeling faded.

"And I'm actually not sure why you slept so long," Forerunner said, stepping back. "Or even why you're not sleeping right now."

"Now?" At the words, Dravid felt the lethargy in his body grow stronger. His eyelids seemed to pull themselves down.

"You absorbed a good deal of my... magic. It should exhaust your frail body."

"No, I..." Dravid couldn't keep his eyes open any longer. Sleep. It's what he needed, after all.

"Your questions will be answered. In time." Forerunner's voice had the vibrations in it again.

(((21)))

Kishin wavered many times on the road. Return to his old life? Preposterous. It could never be. But what else should he do? Start a new life somewhere? What kind of life? How would he do it? He had no answers.

His dire straits did not become clear to him until he met a merchant. The man appeared Mandiatan, which made him a long way from home. Traveling merchants were unusual. Most people regarded them with suspicion, since they seemed to defy the normal Bindings that everyone held to their homes. Yet they provided valuable services that no one wanted to avoid.

"Greetings!" the merchant called to him from some distance away. A somewhat portly man, he seemed at ease walking the road and leading a donkey who pulled a small cart of his wares.

Kishin nodded in response. He did not feel much like conversation.

"Are you in need of anything today, good sir? I carry a wide variety of—"

"No, thank you."

If the merchant wasn't used to rudeness, he didn't show it. He nodded and kept talking. "As well as you like, sir. I merely offer, as you seem to be all alone on the road with few supplies. It seemed a bit odd to me, it did. So I thought to myself that I would see if you needed anything. That's all I did."

His voice held an annoying high pitch.

"Out here on the road, folks should look out for each other. Don't you agree?" he went on. "I do have plenty of food available. Might you be wanting a bite to eat, perhaps?"

"No." Kishin attempted to move past him.

The merchant put out a hand. "Now, now. No need to rush on our ways here. I would at least be interested in a bit of news from Varioch. Perhaps you could tell me some in exchange for some dried pork?"

"No." That voice grated on him, scraping against his nerves.

"Well, now. I'd expect more from a fellow traveler like yourself. Returning to Ch'olan, are you? I just want to know about where you've been, which happens to be where I'm going. I've made offers, and you've refused them. Not much else to say, I suppose."

Kishin growled and tried to step past him again.

"But wait. That's a mighty fine sword you have at your side there. Don't see many weapons like that on the road. Some bows for killing game, to be sure, and knives. Everyone needs a good knife. I have a dozen or so on my cart. But no swords. I don't suppose you'd be interested in selling it? Might I see it?"

Kishin grabbed the merchant by his collar and shoved him up against the cart, whipping out his sword at the same time. "You want to see this sword?" He held the blade up against the merchant's neck.

"Mercy!" he cried. "I meant no harm!"

"Tell me your curse." The words spilled out of Kishin's mouth before he even thought them. He always said those words. He always wanted to know the answer.

"I'm not cursed!" The high-pitched voice took on an even more annoying tone with its indignation.

"All men are cursed."

"I'm not, I tell you! But you will be if you keep this up!"

Kishin stopped himself. The merchant spoke the truth. He himself had no curse right now. But if he killed this man...

Part of him wanted to do it. Kill him. Not only because he enjoyed the killing, but because it might return his curse to him. He wanted it back. It defined him.

His hand shook and the sword blade vibrated against the merchant's neck. "Please! Spare me!"

Yet he might not get the same curse again. What if he killed this man and Theon or the magic gave him a different curse? One that did not set him free like his old curse? He could not take that risk. Could he? He pushed forward with the blade, ever so slightly. The merchant squealed.

Do it! Kill him!

Kishin pulled back the sword, screamed incoherently, and spun in a circle, taking hold of the sword hilt with both hands. He slammed it into the cart, a hair's breadth from the merchant's neck.

No words now. The merchant shook, gasping and trying to control his breathing, having already lost control of other bodily functions. A puddle formed at his feet.

Kishin yanked his sword back and glared. The merchant whimpered and sank to his knees in his own urine. Pathetic. He needed to die. He...

The sword slid back into its sheath. Kishin spun and walked on down the road. The merchant began to sob behind him.

He didn't know why he hadn't killed the man. He tried to tell himself the merchant wasn't worth it. This warpsteel blade should not be sullied with the likes of his blood. Yet he had wanted to kill him. Wanted it so much.

Life did not make sense any more. Nothing did.

(((22)))

Otioch entered Volraag's command tent in a hurry. "Your lordship! The Rasnians are doing something!"

Volraag looked up from his map. "And what would that be?"

"General Cassian wants you to see it for yourself."

Intrigued, Volraag followed him outside. The elevated platform had been constructed to Cassian's specifications to gain a better visual of the wide, flat land. Otioch and Volraag climbed the ladder to join the general at its top.

"What are the Rasnians doing?"

In response, Cassian handed Volraag a spyglass. "See for yourself."

Volraag gave his general a raised eyebrow, but took the glass. He focused on the Rasnian lines.

"Look to the middle," Cassian said.

Volraag moved the glass. Several squads of Rasnian soldiers had advanced into the disputed land. But they weren't advancing to fight, it appeared.

"They're... building?"

"I think they're trying to build a barrier wall."

Volraag lowered the glass. "How do you propose we disrupt this? Cavalry?"

"It would be the easiest, but I hesitate to commit them for this," Cassian said. "It's hard to see from here, but the Rasnians may have archers at ready in case we try that. I don't want to lose good men and horses for this."

"Conscripts then."

Cassian nodded. "I've given the preparation order. Just waiting for you to confirm it. I'll send two centuries in, and have the cavalry standing ready."

(((23)))

Victor took a deep breath and looked sideways at Marshal. "This is it, I guess."

Marshal only nodded. They stood at the front lines, waiting for the command to advance.

Victor looked over his shoulder. The rest of the curse squad stood behind them. He tried to read their expressions. Topleb's downturned face spoke of resignation. The twins and Rufus kept shifting their feet and looking around. The others, surprisingly, didn't appear very nervous. Wolf's face held no discernible emotion. Albus stood quiet and still, while Gnaeus tried to position himself properly with the shield. Merish smiled, as he always did when someone put a sword in his hand.

Marshal, Victor noticed, did not look back at the others. He felt a brief flash of anger. A leader should be encouraging the men, preparing them for what was to come, not ignoring them.

"Are you going to say something to them?"

"What?" Marshal blinked.

Victor leaned in. "We're about to go into battle. Shouldn't you say something to your squad?"

Marshal glanced back. "I..." He looked down. "I don't know what I would say."

"You're their leader! They need to hear from you!"

"I didn't want this! I tried... to tell you!"

"Hailstones!" Victor spun on his heel and took a step back. He looked over the squad again.

"Curse squad!" he called, loud enough the other conscripts around them could hear. "Curse squad! They expect you to die today!" He pointed left and right with his weapons. "All of them do! At best, they hope you distract the enemy for a few precious moments. At worst, they expect you to just lie down or run away."

"Is that an option?" Topleb's question inspired a few nervous chuckles.

"I say no! Today, we defy their expectations! Today, we show them that a curse doesn't define a man!"

"Then what does?" Marshal whispered, low enough that only Victor heard.

"A man is defined by what he fights for!"

"Varioch?" Callus said.

"We fight not just for Varioch! We fight for all! We fight to be known for who we truly are!" Victor met Marshal's eyes and lifted his sword high. "We fight for a world without curses!"

"I don't think this is going to help with that," Marshal said in an aside as he drew his sword and held it up.

"Does it matter if it inspires them?" Victor whispered back.

"No curses!" Marshal yelled.

"No curses!" Victor and several of the squad responded.

"No curses!" Marshal yelled again.

"No curses!" A much louder shout. Victor swore conscripts all around them joined in.

"Conscripts!" Another loud voice shouted from horseback nearby. "Advance!"

Marshal and Victor turned as one and started forward.

A shallow branch of the Amnis flowed here, marking the boundary of the disputed region. The conscripts, two hundred strong, splashed across it, looking ahead in dread and anticipation. Only a few hundred yards away, Rasnian soldiers worked to erect a crude barrier of wood and dirt.

Victor could hear the shouts from the enemy soldiers, warning of their advance. Some of them began to scramble about, but others kept on with their tasks, continuing to build.

The vibration began to build in his hands again. Victor glanced at Marshal. Could he feel it too? Was it like this for him all the time? Marshal only stared toward the enemy. His scars pulsed red.

As they drew nearer, Victor saw the barrier had already grown much larger than he expected. At least three feet tall, taller in some spots, it stretched in a line for dozens of yards in both directions. Even if the Rasnian soldiers ran away, it would take some time for them to tear all of that down, as they had been commanded.

Only a hundred yards now. A centurion rode by, ordering several squads to peel off and circle to the right. Victor assumed more did the same on the left. The Rasnians, seeing their progress, finally abandoned their work and began to disappear behind the wall.

They were hiding? What good would that do?

Fifty yards. Still they marched at a steady pace.

"This is insane," Gallus said.

"Quiet!" Victor ordered.

Twenty yards.

"Weapons ready!" the centurion bellowed. "Take them down!"

The conscripts broke into a run for the last stretch. Why were the Rasnians hiding? Would they have to cut them down while they lay on the ground?

Ten yards away, the wall itself shook. Victor's steps faltered, as did dozens of others.

The wall, every last inch of it, rose off the ground, trailing dirt. One man stood at the center, his arms raised high. The wall reached a height of six feet off the ground as the charging conscripts stumbled to a halt. Many of them cried out against the magic.

Around the central figure, the Rasnian troops jumped to their feet. This close, Victor saw them all drawing back on bows. "Shields!" he screamed.

Arrows launched from dozens of short bows at such a close range, Victor knew they would all die. He ducked behind Marshal's shield as best as he could. Arrows splintered against it, and some splintered in the air around it. Marshal's power. It must be growing.

Behind him, he heard shouts of pain, but he couldn't spare a moment to look back. The magician threw his arms forward, and the entire wall came hurtling at them, falling into pieces as it flew.

In the midst of the chaos, Topleb stepped next to him and grunted with effort as his arm swept forward. One of his spear-darts left the atlatl and punched into the center of the magician's chest. He dropped, even as the wall crashed down on top of the conscripts.

Again, Marshal's shield and power protected them. Topleb fell beside them as a chunk of rock smacked his head. Looking up through the dust cloud and debris, Victor saw the Rasnians preparing to launch arrows again. A rage unlike he had ever known filled his chest. The vibration in his hands grew so strong, he almost dropped his weapons.

Instead, he launched forward, feet digging into the loose dirt still falling around him. The vibrations spread down to his toes. His left hand spun his flail. Once again, the magic seemed not to diminish his movements, but enhance them. His eyes tightened. He could see two Rasnian soldiers directly ahead, both releasing their bows at the same time. Two arrows. Coming right at him. Only feet away.

His Eldanim-forged sword swept up, cutting through both arrows in the air. One broken piece struck his face, slicing his cheek. The other three missed him entirely, their trajectory thrown off by the sword.

The Rasnian's mouths were open in screams, but he couldn't hear them. A whooshing sound filled his ears, the rapid beat of his own heart. The enemy's eyes were wide. They dropped their bows and grabbed at spears.

But Victor was there. His flail caught the first soldier on the side of his chest, shattering ribs. Victor spun with the flail's movement, bringing his sword around and back to slash across the second soldier's spine. He continued his spin, the flail starting to twirl up again, and moved toward the next enemy soldier.

The whooshing filled his ears. The enemy filled his vision. The rage and the magic that tightened his grip and sped his movements filled his body.

Somewhere in his mind, he knew he screamed. He knew he killed. And killed again. Yet his conscious mind seemed to have no part in his actions. He existed. He fought.

And then he stopped. Not because he wanted to, but because he could see no more of the enemy.

Victor looked about him and saw devastation. The magician's attack and the Rasnian arrows had killed dozens. Death reigned here.

And Victor had served him.

• • • • •

"We didn't anticipate a wild magician," Cassian said.

"No," Volraag agreed. "I thought Lord Tyrr had used them all up already."

"Sir?"

"He brought many with him to Zes Sivas. They... did not return."

Volraag lifted the spyglass again and surveyed the remains of the battle. Several centurions were trying to coordinate the withdrawal of the conscripts from the field. Cassian at first suggested keeping troops there, laying claim to the area. But the openness of the terrain would leave them too vulnerable to counter-attack.

"Unusually powerful for a wild mage," Volraag mused.

"Indeed. I've never known one to be able to do… that."

"Lord Tyrr seems to have quite a collection of wild mages."

"Perhaps we should have been collecting them ourselves, sir."

"Perhaps. Still. He should not have been that powerful."

"As you say."

"How many did we lose?"

"Between the magician and the archers, we lost 30-40 conscripts. There are many wounded, as well," Otioch said.

"It would have been higher if not for that one man," Cassian said.

"What man is that?" Volraag lowered the spyglass.

"One of the conscripts," Otioch said. "He went into a battle frenzy and took out most of the archers on his own."

"A conscript did this?"

"Even stranger: they say he's a member of the curse squad."

Volraag turned to descend from the platform. "I must meet this hero. Bring him to the command tent as soon as you can."

(((24)))

Victor staggered across the battlefield. Where was his squad? Everywhere he looked, he saw dead and dying men. A cloud of still-settling dust hung over all. The men of Varioch lay pierced with arrows or crushed by fallen debris. The men of Rasna lay dead of other means. The conscripts still standing stared at Victor as he moved past them. Their looks... he had never seen those expressions before. Awe? Or was it fear?

At last he saw Marshal standing alone, sword still drawn, looking around. For him? Confirming his guess, Marshal spotted him and approached.

"Are you hurt?"

Victor shook his head. Somehow, he had remained untouched during his rampage. His cheek throbbed from the arrow's scratch earlier, but it seemed inconsequential in light of all he saw around him.

"How... did you do that?"

"I don't know. I really don't. I just... lost myself."

Marshal nodded like he understood. His own face held none of the awe and fear of the others. Instead, he looked miserable. His shoulders slumped, his mouth turned down. He ran a hand through his hair and dirt rained down.

"The others?" Victor asked.

In response, Marshal pointed with his sword.

Victor turned. One of the twins knelt beside the still body of his brother. Victor's guts twisted, both from the death and the fact that even now he couldn't tell the twins apart.

"Gallus," Marshal whispered, as if knowing his mind.

Victor looked about. Albus lay nearby, three arrows protruding from his chest, his eyes wide and unmoving. Had his curse released him at the moment of death? Had he seen one last time, one brief second of light, one look at the face of death itself? What a horrible thought.

Wolf sat nearby, looking more withdrawn than ever. His arm rested around the shoulders of Gnaeus, whose body shook with sobs.

"We're lucky," Marshal said. "We only lost three. Most squads lost more." He gestured weakly around them.

"Three?"

"It will be three. Topleb is… hurt bad. I had Rufus and Merish carry him to the medics, but I don't see…" He trailed off.

No. Not Topleb. Victor recalled, almost like remembering a dream, seeing him go down after killing the mage. He looked around again. They had been standing… not far from here. He took a few steps, then broke into a short run. Marshal followed.

Topleb's atlatl lay on the ground where he had fallen. The fragments of two of his spears lay around it. Victor sheathed his sword and hung his flail on his belt. He bent and gathered Topleb's fallen gear into his arms. He looked up at Marshal.

"Starshine," he said. "It saved me. Maybe they can use it to save him."

Marshal's eyes lit up with a strange light, one Victor couldn't identify. Not that it mattered. He clambered to his feet. "Let's go find him."

It took longer than he expected for them to make their way back from the battlefield into the camp and then find the medics. Three times, dirty conscripts rushed up to him and threw their arms around him, whispering thanks. Others just looked at him with tears in their eyes.

"Why are they doing this?" he asked Marshal.

Marshal raised his eyebrows and looked at him askance. "You don't know?" Victor shook his head. "You fought the Rasnians. Alone."

"But… but we all charged after they fired, didn't we?"

Marshal shook his head. "You charged. No one else."

"I didn't—I couldn't have killed them all by myself."

Marshal shrugged. "You did the most. We followed after you, but you did most of it."

Victor didn't know what to say. He tried to remember his charge. The Rasnian soldiers. Hadn't there been dozens of them? He couldn't have. Marshal must not have seen the other conscripts that also attacked. And yet… he could not remember anyone fighting at his side.

The wails of the wounded led them to their destination. Victor tried not to look too closely as they moved between the hurt and dying. His foot slipped on wet ground and he almost fell, catching himself by grabbing Marshal's arm. His other hand dropped Topleb's weapons and hit the ground to push himself back up. Only then did he realize the wetness came from blood.

Lifting up his eyes, he saw Merish standing with a vacant expression and smile. At the same time, Rufus came running up to them.

"Have they... helped him?" Marshal asked.

"A doctor looked at him," Rufus said. He glanced at Victor and flinched. "He muttered something about it being too late and went to the next man."

Victor saw Topleb then, lying on a mat beside Merish. A single arrow jutted out from his left thigh. But his head and neck looked horrible. The entire right side was a mass of blood. His chest moved up and down with a wheezing that did not sound natural at all.

Marshal grabbed a man who tried to hurry past. "Are you a doctor?" he demanded.

"Yes..." He glanced at Marshal's insignia. "...decanus. Is there a problem?"

"This man. Can you help him?"

The doctor looked to Topleb, then shook his head. "We haven't the tools or skill to deal with something like that. I'm sorry."

"What about starshine?" Victor said.

The doctor snorted. "Is he an elite? We have very little starshine and it's only for them."

Victor grabbed the doctor's tunic. "This man saved us out there! He killed the mage. You need to save him!"

"I'm sorry. It's out of my hands."

"There he is!" Several regular soldiers hurried up, followed by a taller man in a Remavian Guard uniform. He looked them over and addressed himself to Victor.

"You're the one who charged the enemy?"

"Yes, but—"

"You need to come with me. Lord Volraag wishes to see you."

Victor looked to Marshal, their eyes wide. The Guard followed his gaze. "Your decanus is not summoned. Just you."

Victor swallowed his protest. "Yes, sir."

• • • • •

Victor hesitated at the entrance to the command tent. Volraag would not remember him, of course. When he visited Drusa's Crossing, he had spoken only with the town leaders, Aelia, and Marshal. Even so, Victor could not restrain a shudder of trepidation as the Remavian Guard gestured him inside. He stepped out of the early twilight and into the large tent, lit by a pair of lanterns.

Volraag looked up from a map spread across a small table. It had been months, but Victor easily recognized Marshal's half-brother, the new Lord of Varioch. If anything, he looked taller and stronger than he had that day. Try as he might, Victor could not see any resemblance between this man and his friend.

"Is this him?" Volraag asked.

"Yes, sir."

The Lord stepped out from behind the table and put his hands behind his back. "I'm told that you're the hero of the battle today," he said to Victor.

"No, sir." Victor shook his head.

"No?" Volraag looked back to the Guard. "Otioch, did you find the wrong man?"

"No, your lordship. The other conscripts had no doubt. This is the man."

Volraag turned back to Victor. "So. Humility then. Did you not charge the enemy and defeat most of them alone?"

"They say I did, sir. But I did not kill the mage. My friend did that."

"Then we should honor him as well," Volraag said. "Otioch, find this friend and—"

"He's dying," Victor interrupted. "Please, sir. If you want to honor someone, do so by saving his life. Starshine can save him. I know it."

Volraag cocked his head. "You are acquainted with the effects of starshine?"

Victor nodded. "It saved my life once."

Volraag stepped closer and reached out. He pulled aside a piece of Victor's tunic, exposing the long scar across his chest. Until that moment, Victor hadn't even noticed that his tunic hung in tatters. How had that happened?

"So I see. Very well. Otioch, find this injured man and make sure they make every effort to save his life, including starshine if necessary."

"As you command, sir." The Guard ducked and left the tent.

Victor found himself alone with Lord Volraag. The thought crossed his mind that he could draw his sword and end all of this with one quick thrust. Yet even as he thought it, he dismissed the idea. He had no concept of how well Volraag could use his powers.

"You have fought before."

Victor jumped, as the raspy voice did not come from Volraag, but from behind him. He could have sworn they were alone in the tent. He turned as another Remavian Guard stepped out of the tent's shadows, looking him over. Victor took in a sharp breath. The leper assassin! But... no. This man looked very like him, but not quite the same. How could there be two of them?

The Guard moved past him. "He has a scar on his back even larger," he told Volraag. "Not fully healed."

"The time you were saved by starshine?" Volraag asked.

Victor nodded.

"Who were you fighting?"

"It was... an insane man."

"No doubt." Volraag nodded in approval. "Otherwise, you'd be cursed yourself, I suppose. Which raises another question. I'm told you're part of a curse squad."

"What is your curse?" the leprous-looking Guard asked. Victor tried to keep himself from shivering.

"I am not cursed. I am there because of a friend."

"The same friend who killed the mage?"

"No. Another friend."

"Loyalty is commendable. But sacrificing your own future and achievements for someone who can never return the favor? That's going a bit far, don't you think?"

"It wouldn't be called sacrifice then." Victor wasn't sure where that response had come from. It just felt right.

The Guard hissed. What a strange reaction.

"Rathri, there's no need to traumatize our brave soldier." Volraag waved the Guard away. Victor couldn't help noticing a brief look of annoyance on the Lord's face.

Volraag took a deep breath. He stepped forward and placed a hand on Victor's shoulder. "We've gotten sidetracked. I invited you here to see you for myself and to honor you. What you did today took great courage and skill. If you like, I would be proud to have you move up to the regular army, out of the conscripts. In time, if you continue to prove yourself, you would be a prime candidate for my Remavian Guard."

It was everything Victor ever wanted. All he had to do was say yes. It wouldn't even be a problem with his Bond to Marshal. While this war lasted, Bonds were overruled. In the midst of the battle today, he had experienced no sense of Marshal, even though he had been in grave danger.

All he had to do was say yes. All he had to do was abandon his friend.

"Thank you, sir. But I'd rather stay where I am." They were the right words, but he could not help the regret that flooded him upon saying them.

Volraag nodded as if he expected that answer. He removed his hand and walked back to his table. "Your friend will be saved, if it is at all possible. And your squad will receive double rations for the next three days."

"Thank you, sir."

"You may go."

Victor started toward the entrance.

"Should you change your mind..." Volraag said.

Victor paused.

"The offer remains open."

Victor nodded and left the tent.

• • • • •

"He has been around a magic user."

Volraag looked up as Rathri's voice disturbed his thoughts. The assassin's behavior during his meeting with the conscript hero had been disturbing. Volraag hadn't even noticed his return. "What are you talking about?"

"The conscript. He has been around someone with power."

"The Rasnian mage? He was close, at least."

"No." Rathri pulled his helmet off, revealing his hairless, decaying skin. "Not a brief encounter. He has been in close proximity to magic for a lengthy time. He's absorbed it."

"I've never heard of such a thing."

"It is why I asked to be by your side. Those who stay close to a Lord for the longest are transformed by their magic."

"If that were true, I would have heard it," Volraag argued. "More, that would mean my mother…"

"Your mother?"

Memories flooded back into Volraag's head, memories of his childhood. His mother's hands shaking. The doctor never understood. The treatment…

"She died," Volraag said. "She died because of it."

Rathri scratched his head and flakes of skin tumbled off. Volraag tried not to let his revulsion show. "I have made a long study of this," he said. "Most of the time, it is the Lord's wife who absorbs excess power. Sometimes, they can cope with it, even use it. Sometimes… not."

The revelation upended much of what Volraag thought he knew of his mother. But that could not be the focus of his thoughts right now. He considered the immediate implications.

"Are you suggesting that conscript is actually a close confidante of Lord Tyrr?"

"I don't know who it is. But it is someone with great power."

"Recent, you say?"

"Recent and prolonged."

"In the curse squad."

A long silence followed.

"Your brother is cursed, is he not?" Rathri asked.

Volraag leaned on his table. "I learned… recently… that my half-brother's curse was lifted."

"That is not possible."

"The mages on Zes Sivas disagree with you. And so does… my source."

"Not. Possible." Rathri's scowl transformed his repulsive face into something downright horrifying.

"Regardless. Why am I even discussing this with you? Otioch!"

The tent door pushed open and Volraag's right hand entered. "Your lordship?"

"The hero you brought in earlier. I have reason to believe he may be in contact with… someone of power."

"You need a spy."

Volraag nodded. "I promised double rations for the squad for three days. See to it. And find one of them willing to be your spy. I want to know everything there is to know about this Victor. And who his friends are."

(((25)))

Victor returned to the diminished curse squad's camp area. The darkness of night enveloped the camp, broken only by each squad's fire. Callus and Gnaeus sat by their own. He didn't see anyone else around.

"Where's Marshal?"

Callus pointed toward the tents.

Victor found the tent he shared with his friend and lifted the flap. "Marshal?"

Marshal sat inside, his knees pulled up to his chest. He glanced up when Victor peered in, but did not move.

"Are you all right?"

Marshal hugged his knees. "Is he coming for me?"

"Volraag? No. I didn't mention you at all."

"Then why did he want to see you?"

"Uh, the battle? He offered me a transfer to the regular army. I turned him down." Victor crawled into the tent and let the flap close. "But good news! He sent someone to bring Topleb some starshine."

Marshal nodded, but did not look at him. "That's good," he whispered.

"What's wrong with you?"

Marshal finally looked at him, his face twisted. "How can you ask that? After... that battle? Two of our men died, Victor!" He looked away again. "Two of my men."

"A lot of men died." Victor crossed his legs and settled into a more comfortable position. "But... yeah, it's horrible. This is war."

"I never wanted this."

"Can't change it now. But you could do something good."

115

"What's that?"

Victor pointed outside the tent. "Callus and Gnaeus are grieving. You should go talk to them."

"Why? What good would that do?"

"You're their leader!"

"No." Marshal seemed to pull himself even smaller. "No, I'm not. You are."

"We already talked about this."

"You talked about it. I'm still not a leader. I'm worthless."

"Worthless? Don't be ridiculous. You—you're practically a Lord! Your mother died for you!"

"And what good did it do?" Marshal lashed out. "She died! Nian died! Gallus and Albus died! Everyone around me dies! And it's all for nothing!"

Victor grabbed Marshal's tunic and forced him to look him in the face. "You don't know how important you are. You're—"

Vibration tossed Victor away from Marshal into the side of the tent. For a moment, he remained still, stunned that Marshal would do such a thing.

"Well, look at that," he said at last. "I guess your power is coming back after all."

"What difference does it make?"

"You're upset that Gallus and Albus died? Then next time, don't hold back. Protect them all. You have the power."

"And then Volraag will find me and we'll all be dead, anyway."

"Not if you do it right! You can change things here. You can make a difference!"

"I'll just fail again. It's hopeless."

Victor's own emotions threatened to overwhelm him. After everything they had been through today... His voice shook. "I just turned down everything I ever wanted. For you."

"I didn't ask you to do that. I don't want that."

"And you didn't want Aelia to die, either, but she did! For you! Because you're worth it! She—she would have told you. That you have a purpose, right?"

"She was wrong. And so are you."

"You're pathetic." Victor clambered out of the tent.

•••••

The air outside the tent felt cool through Victor's tattered tunic. He shivered, but whether from the chill or from the turmoil he felt inside, he didn't know. What was wrong with Marshal? How could he possibly feel that way after all they had been through? It made no sense.

He turned down Volraag's offer, only to be treated like this? It stung. Volraag said the offer remained open, though. For a moment, he considered it. But only for a moment.

He worked his way back to the fire where Gnaeus and Callus still sat. He warmed himself for a minute or so, knowing he needed to say something to these two. If Marshal wouldn't help them, someone had to. Callus sat with one knee pulled up to his chest, staring into the fire. Gnaeus held his twisted hand with his other, staring as if it were the cause of all his problems. He probably believed that. Victor took a deep breath.

"Callus, your brother was a good man. Will you—will you be all right?"

The young man did not respond.

"Callus?"

"We've always been together," he said, still staring at the fire. "We never left each other's side."

"I noticed that," Victor said, trying to keep his voice calm and soothing. He had no idea if he were succeeding.

"That's part of why people think we're strange. Even cursed. Not just because we look the same, but because we stay together." Callus shrugged. "We just enjoyed each other's company more than anyone else."

"Nothing wrong with that," Victor said. "You grew up together."

"And now he's gone."

Victor nodded. They sat in silence for a while again. Now for Gnaeus.

"I don't want to sleep alone," Callus said just as Victor opened his mouth.

"Uh, all right."

"I don't want to be alone in that tent."

"Right. All right. Well…" Victor thought for a moment. "I'll talk to Rufus. I'm sure he'd be glad to get out of the tent with Wolf. I think you two will… get along. Is that all right?"

Callus nodded. "Thanks," he whispered.

"If you want to encourage me, it's pointless," Gnaeus growled.

"Is that right?"

"I'm not in shock."

"I believe you."

"I just got someone killed, that's all."

"You didn't—"

"I did. I was supposed to be his shield. And he died. From arrows. No getting around that. It's my fault."

"No one was prepared for what happened. A lot of soldiers died today."

"You prepared us. You and the decanus, wherever he's hiding."

Victor winced.

"You gave me a job," Gnaeus went on. "Protect Albus with the shield. And I didn't. He's dead."

"It's not your fault."

"You know why Merish is cursed?"

Victor blinked. He hadn't expected that turn in the conversation. Even Callus turned to look at Gnaeus.

"That's my fault, too. I had this big plan to steal something so valuable it wouldn't matter if we got cursed for it. Except we got caught in the act. And Merish killed a man. So I got this." He held up his twisted hand. "And he got his head messed up."

Something popped in the fire and a few sparks sprayed out near Victor's foot.

"What were you trying to steal?" Callus asked.

Gnaeus snorted. "The only thing that got Merish's interest. A sword. The most beautiful sword anyone's ever seen."

Gnaeus got to his feet. "So keep your sympathy. My real curse is messing up other people's lives. I'm good at that." He left the fire.

So that hadn't gone the way Victor expected or hoped. Still, he tried.

After finding Rufus and explaining the situation to him, Victor returned to the fire alone. He didn't want to see Marshal again just yet.

Lost. That's what he felt. Through their entire journey from Drusa's Crossing, he had followed Aelia and Talinir. With both of them gone, he had looked to Marshal for guidance. But Marshal rejected the idea of leadership. Of course, why would Marshal have any idea what to do next? His power didn't grant him wisdom.

So what should he do? They had gone along with the whole conscript thing to get to this location. Nian suggested it might be a way to the Otherworld, a way to find Talinir. Victor looked out toward the battlefield. If a gateway to the Otherworld were out there somewhere, he certainly hadn't seen it today.

Guidance. He needed someone to tell him what to do. Marshal wasn't making any decisions, not that he knew any better. But who did that leave? No one else even knew about Marshal and his power. Except Volraag. And the Eldanim.

"Now that's an idea," he whispered.

He checked to see if the pouch was still attached to his belt. After that crazy battle, it wouldn't surprise him if he had lost it. But no. He felt the shape of the pouch and almost smiled. He got to his feet. He needed to get away from everyone else. Unfortunately, that meant either wandering out onto the battlefield again, where Rasnian archers might spot him, or crossing the entire camp. Well, if that's what it took, that's what it took.

He crossed the camp in the dark easily. No one recognized him as the "hero" of the battle. Most people ignored him entirely. The walk took less time than he expected.

Beyond the edge of the conscript camp, he hesitated. He knew regular soldiers patrolled the edges of the camp to keep any conscripts from trying to run away. He didn't want to run away; he just needed some space. He moved on.

Darkness kept him concealed once he found some trees and brush. When the conscripts had arrived, they passed by on the eastern side of the town of Kanna, coming south. By now, he must be quite a bit further to the east.

Victor tripped on a tree root and stumbled. Regaining his balance, he looked ahead. The ground looked darker not far away. He glanced up at the nearly full moon and then looked down again. He took a cautious step forward. Then he realized: the darker area was a ravine. He couldn't tell how deep it might be in the dark. That tree root might have saved his life.

This was probably far enough, anyway. No one should be able to hear him, unless he were unlucky enough to attract the attention of one of those patrols. Maybe they didn't come this way because the ravine provided enough of an obstacle. Maybe.

He untied the pouch and removed the Ranir Stone. To his eyes, it looked like an ordinary grayish-white rock. Its smoothness made it attractive, he supposed, but nothing about it seemed magical or anything. How did this work, exactly? Aelia hadn't told him much. She only said you could call the Eldanim while holding it, and they would hear you. At least, if any of them were nearby. Or something like that.

He held up the stone. "Eldanim!" he called. "I need your help!"

Silence.

"Eldanim! Can you hear me?" He rapped on the stone with his knuckle. "Anyone?"

More silence.

"This stupid rock doesn't work," he grumbled. He almost turned to go back. But he had come this far. May as well stick with it.

"I'm friends with Talinir!" he tried. "I've visited your city! Um... Looking for some help here now."

Nothing happened. Or did it? Victor scrutinized the stone. For a moment, it glowed a faint orange. Maybe.

Victor brushed off a spot near the ravine's edge and sat down.

"I'll, uh, just wait right here, then. I guess."

Silence.

"Stupid rock."

(((26)))

Kishin slowed as he came down the hill. The creek at its base flowed a little more swiftly than he anticipated. Strange. This late in the Spring, it should have diminished by now. Still, his path led across it, and crossing it would be only an inconvenience, not a true hazard.

He had almost reached the water before he noticed the old man, leaning on a walking stick. He almost backed away, but he had already been noticed.

"Ah, good day, young sir!" the elderly man called. "Theon's blessings on you this fine morning!"

"And to you, sir," Kishin answered. Why would a man of such obvious frailty be out on the road? He looked as if a strong wind might blow him away. His skin tone implied a Ch'olanese background, but Ch'olan was still many miles away. And his accent sounded wrong. Kishin couldn't place it.

The aged one wiped at his scraggly beard. "I wonder if I might, perchance, persuade you to help such a one as I across this formidable stream."

Kishin resisted a sigh. At his first sight of the old man, he suspected as much. Words rose up in his throat and he almost let them out. The urge to ask for the old man's curse pulled at him. But what good did it do now? He was not that person any more. His outward appearance had changed; should not his behavior change as well? All these thoughts and more wrestled their way through his mind.

"I seem to have dumbfounded you. Was my request that startling?"

Kishin shook his head. "No, no. Not at all. I just..." He paused, words continuing to wrestle their way to his lips. "I was just thinking of something else. I will help you, father."

Kishin waded into the edge of the steam and bent down so the old man could clamber onto his back. It took three tries, with quite a few friendly grumbles, before the old man succeeded. He handed Kishin his walking stick, a sturdy staff polished and worn smooth over years of use.

As Kishin expected, the old man weighed very little and caused hardly any difficulty as he began making his way through the flowing water. The creek itself caused him much more of a struggle. In a few steps, Kishin found himself almost waist deep with a swift current pulling at his legs.

"What smooth skin you still have!" the old man said. "Enjoy it while you can."

Kishin stumbled. Such an unusual comment. Why choose that particular observation?

"Sorry for distracting you. Use the staff. It does wonders for me."

Kishin leaned harder on the staff. It did make a significant difference. Step by step, he made it through the deepest part of the creek. As he neared the shore, he heard the old man let out a relieved sigh.

"Time was I could walk right through one of these," he said. "Just my staff and I."

"Old age comes for all of us," Kishin said. He bent down and let his rider off. He turned around and found the old man holding a sword and gazing at it admiringly. Kishin grabbed at his sheath. Empty.

"A warpsteel blade," the old man said. "In the right hands, it can do amazing things in two worlds. Even crossing the worlds." His eyes narrowed. "Yours are not the right hands."

In Kishin's mind, he gave the old man a swift blow to the chin with his own staff, killing him instantly. Instead, he offered the staff back and said, "Shall we trade?" What was wrong with him?

The old man snorted and proffered the sword back to Kishin hilt first. He took it and handed the staff back. He returned the sword to its proper place.

"Good day to you, sir," Kishin said, tired of this encounter. He turned and started down the road.

To his annoyance, though not great surprise, the old man fell into pace beside him. "We seem to be going the same way."

Kishin grunted.

"I've been away from Woqan for quite some time," his unwelcome companion said after a few moments. "I look forward to seeing how it's grown."

Kishin nodded, but increased his walking speed. Somehow, the old man kept up with him without showing any signs of difficulty.

"Come, Kishin. Why do you keep trying to run?"

Kishin came to a complete halt and stared at the old man. "Who are you?" he whispered.

"Why do you ask?"

"You spoke my name."

"Did I? You haven't spoken mine."

"I don't know your name."

"Don't you?"

Kishin growled in frustration and his hand instinctively slipped toward his sword hilt. The old man noticed and sighed.

"And still your instinct is to resort to violence. Even now."

"How do you know so much about me?"

"I know you've been given an unbelievable gift." The old man found a large rock next to the path and settled back against it. "I must say: I'm quite intrigued to see how you handle it."

"I don't understand."

"Yes, you do." He pointed his staff at Kishin's face. "Don't lie. It won't get you a curse, but it is a commandment, all the same."

Kishin blinked. He had no idea what to say next.

"Ah, I've rendered you speechless at last. You keep asking questions of me, yet you never ask me the one question you always asked everyone else."

The words tumbled out, without conscious thought allowing them: "Tell me your curse."

"That's the one. And yet... I have no answer to that one."

"All men are cursed." Again the words came automatically.

"Yet we two sit here—or rather I sit and you stand—without a curse between us. How is that possible? Have neither of us done anything deserving of punishment?"

To open his mouth again would condemn him. Kishin fought to keep from doing so.

"Ah." The old man sighed again. He looked down and scratched in the dirt with his staff. "Afraid to say the truth even now."

"I am afraid." Not. He had meant to say "not afraid." Why had it come out wrong?

"You should be. Grace is terrifying."

Trembling. He was actually trembling.

"You have been given much. You should expect that much will be required from you."

The old man stood. He shook his staff and looked down the road. "I have traveled so far, for so long," he said. "Perhaps my journey nears its end." He looked back to Kishin. "Your journey is just beginning. You get to decide which direction it takes. Look!"

With his staff, he pointed to a beetle careening wildly across the path. Kishin watched it run into a stone, hesitate, then turn around and run the other direction.

"Your choices will decide. Will you fall that low? Or rise as high as that mountain?" He pointed the staff behind Kishin's back.

The former assassin turned and looked up at the mountain in the distance. Marshal and his mother had come from that mountain, or near it, anyway. Coincidence? He licked his lips. He felt confident enough to speak his mind now, to ask the old man the direct questions. He turned around.

The old man was gone. Only his staff remained, leaning against the rock.

(((27)))

Victor woke up in pain and wondered why he saw trees. What happened to the tent? Then he noticed the edge of the ravine. He had fallen asleep waiting with the Ranir Stone. It took him a moment to find it a couple of feet away. He didn't remember leaving it that far away, but he also didn't remember falling asleep out here.

He glanced over the edge of the ravine, then took a longer look. Far deeper than he had anticipated. While most of the ravine's floor looked smooth, the area immediately below him sported dozens of large rocks. It seemed an unusual formation for this flat region of land.

"Victor?"

The voice caught him by surprise. He whirled, reaching for his flail. Only Marshal stood there. He looked even more miserable than usual. The dark circles under his eyes clashed with his scars. Victor relaxed.

"You... didn't come back."

"Yeah, I slept out here." Victor chuckled. "I didn't plan to."

"I'm... sorry."

Victor waved dismissively. "Don't worry about it. Everyone felt strange last night. I guess war affects people in different ways."

Marshal moved to the ravine's edge and looked down. "This is... strange."

"I know. I've never seen anything like it. Ravines aren't so smooth at the bottom."

"It's not natural."

"No, it's not. Wait. What do you mean?"

"This was dug by magic."

Victor frowned. "Are you sure?"

Marshal nodded. He stepped back from the ravine, bent down and

125

pointed. Victor couldn't see the magic being released, but he saw the effects. As Marshal drew his finger across the dirt, dust erupted and a narrow ditch formed.

"So someone with a lot of power did this? Volraag?" Even as he said it, he knew that wasn't right. "No, if he had done this, there would be soldiers here keeping an eye on it."

"Lord Tyrr."

Victor leaned as far as he dared and looked down the ravine. "This might reach all the way to Rasna's side. It's the perfect way to sneak some troops around behind us." He looked around on the surface. Varioch's scouts probably assumed they could see any troops moving through this region, but not if they were moving below...

"You should tell the centurion."

Marshal nodded. He moved back to the ravine's edge and looked down again.

"If we position some archers along the edge," Victor said, illustrating with his hands, "properly concealed, of course, we could take out any soldiers that try to come through." He jogged several yards along the edge and took another look. "Yeah, there's a good spot right over there. That would work."

He turned back. Marshal still stood in the same place, staring down. Victor returned to his side, and glanced down at the rocks.

"Why the pile of rocks, do you suppose?"

Marshal started, as if he hadn't noticed Victor's approach. He hesitated before answering. "Lord Tyrr probably pushed all the rocks he uncovered to one side or the other as he dug this."

Victor cocked his head. "I wonder. Could you just collapse this whole thing by yourself?"

"Maybe. But why?"

Victor shrugged. "To save trouble."

"He'd just dig it out again... I think."

"You're probably right."

Victor turned to go, but Marshal continued to look down. Victor put his hand on his friend's shoulder. "Let's go find the centurion, huh?"

Marshal blinked and nodded. As they both headed back to camp, Victor couldn't help but wonder. Marshal's expression at the end had been odd. He seemed sad. Over what? Lord Tyrr's scheming? The soldiers who would die for it? Or something else?

●●●●●

The centurion thanked Marshal and promised to look into it, though he seemed suspicious about why they had been so far from camp. Victor grumbled, but he knew their status didn't demand much better.

They returned to their squad. To Victor's delight, Topleb returned, healed by the starshine. He moved stiffly and would take a few days to fully recover, as Victor well knew. But just seeing his smile was enough to make him forget Marshal's odd behavior and the magic-carved ravine.

Victor wanted to resume training, but Marshal rejected the idea. The men needed a day off after the battle, he argued. Some were mourning. Victor suggested a good workout would help get their minds off of it, but Marshal stood firm. Today was a day off. Victor accepted the decision and sought out the company of the rest of the squad, to see how they were doing.

"Where did you disappear to last night?" Rufus asked as he approached.

"I needed to get away from these tents," Victor said. "Everyone stinks around here."

"You're no better," Callus said. "You haven't even washed the blood of your face."

Victor touched his cheek. He had completely forgotten about the arrow scratch.

"Hope that doesn't leave a scar," he said.

"You'll still have a long way to go to match the decanus," Topleb said.

"Yeah, how did he get those scars, anyway?" Rufus said. "Never seen anything like them."

"Curse-stalker," Victor said without thinking.

"What?" "Now you have to tell us!" "How?" The squad erupted with questions. Victor lifted both hands until they quieted.

"All right. I'll tell you." He related the story of the curse-stalker's attack, leaving out the reasons for their travel or any mention of Marshal's actual curse. He enhanced Marshal's part in the battle, but did not leave out Aelia, especially since Rufus had met her.

"Why did it attack you, anyway?" Callus asked. "I thought you two weren't cursed."

Victor shrugged. "The monster was crazy. Who knows why it did anything? Any other questions?"

"Why am I here?" Wolf said. He looked around in surprise when everyone laughed.

Topleb patted him on the back. "We don't know why we're here, little Wolf, so how can we answer that?"

"No matter how many times he asks it," Gnaeus muttered.

(((28)))

"He's still asleep?" Seri asked.

Ixchel nodded. "I insisted on seeing him myself. They no longer attempt to stop me. He sleeps quite soundly."

Seri sighed. "He absorbed a lot of magic and then had it pulled back out of him. I expected him to be exhausted, but two days? I'm worried."

"I could try to wake him."

"No, he probably does need the rest. But if he's not awake by this evening's meal, I'll go wake him up myself."

"The white robes will not appreciate that. But I will make sure you can get in."

Seri snorted. That might be entertaining. She got up from the chair in the sun. Forerunner's sanctuary was a nice place, but she felt idle. The last two days had passed in boredom, impatience, and homesickness. Seri found herself thinking of her parents more and more often. Forerunner himself proved elusive, though she hadn't tried too hard to find him.

"I suppose we should look for Forerunner again. I want to talk with him... and I don't want to talk with him."

"You're afraid he will gain influence over you again."

"I'm not afraid!" Seri's initial irritation faded almost immediately. "Well... maybe I am. I don't want to fall back into what I was before you woke me up."

"Like everyone else around here."

"No doubt." In her boredom, Seri tried talking with numerous residents of the sanctuary, including several of the white-robed women. Without exception, they all expressed awe and delight at being in Forerunner's presence. None of them could find anything negative to say about him.

They made their way into Forerunner's pavilion. Seri looked about and spotted a single white-robed woman, sitting alone and strumming on a lyre. "Lucia?" she called. The young woman looked up and smiled, recognizing Seri from an earlier conversation.

"Seri. Have you had any musical training? I'm looking for someone to join me in a duet this evening."

"Uh, no. I am sorry to say that my university schooling did not include any formal music education." As a matter of fact, the university had offered numerous musical opportunities, but Seri had never taken advantage of any of them. Her desire to become a mage overrode everything else.

"We are looking for Forerunner," Ixchel said. "Do you know where he is?"

"If only." Lucia sighed. "He came through around an hour ago, but hurried on before I could speak to him."

"Which way did he go?"

Lucia gestured vaguely toward the western doors. "He left through those doors, I believe. I wanted to follow, but then I had this idea for a performance. Have you had any training, maybe?" She directed the last question toward Ixchel.

"I have. But I will not be able to join you this evening. I wish you success in finding another partner."

Ixchel hurried toward the doors before anything else could be said. Seri followed, delighted in this information. Once they left the pavilion, she grabbed Ixchel by the arm.

"What training?"

"My Lady?"

"What musical training have you had? You've never told me about that!"

"It is not relevant to—to my protection of you."

"What difference does that make? We're friends too, you know! Tell me!"

"I think Forerunner must have gone down this trail."

Seri looked in the direction Ixchel pointed. A well-worn trail wound down from the pavilion then up another small hill before disappearing into a circular grove.

"All right. But we'll talk more about this later."

The two women followed the trail. The grove itself opened up in a wide circular clearing surrounded by tall pines. Forerunner stood in the center of the clearing, surrounded by a group of shadowy figures.

Seri caught her breath. "Gidim," she whispered. It had to be. Each of the six figures appeared man-size, perhaps a little taller. Everything about them appeared fuzzy and indistinct, almost like they were made of shadow and smoke.

"He consults with tzitzimitl," Ixchel said. She drew her sword.

At the sound of her voice, Forerunner and his companions turned to see them. Almost in unison, the shadow figures left in different directions and all vanished. Forerunner strode to meet them.

"Ah, Seri. Ixchel. So good to see you. I'm afraid my companions were a bit shy about staying to chat, but I am available in whatever capacity you desire." As usual, Seri could tell that magic vibrated through the words.

Ixchel held her sword in a defensive pose. "You speak with evil ones, deceiver!" Though she intended to sound angry, Seri noticed a tremble in her voice.

Forerunner raised his hands, palms outward. "I speak no deceit, Ixchel of the Holcan. And those you saw are not evil, merely visitors from a different realm."

A different realm? "The Otherworld?" Seri asked.

"You have called it that, yes. When its inhabitants wish to interact with those of us in this realm, this is how they appear. There is nothing sinister about it."

"No," Ixchel said, her voice barely above a whisper. Her sword hand shook.

"Stop it!" Seri insisted.

Forerunner spread his open hands further. "Stop what?"

"Stop channeling magic through your voice! I can tell you're doing it!"

"Ah, that." Forerunner closed his eyes and gave a single nod. He opened his eyes and smiled again. When he resumed speaking, he spoke without vibration. "I apologize. It's a natural part of who I am. I have to focus in order not to do it."

"If the Gidim are the same as the Eldanim that live in the Otherworld, I see no reason to trust them," Seri said. "The last visitor I knew from there was a murderer."

"How horrible. Still, you wouldn't judge an entire world by the actions of one, would you? Is that fair?"

"I, uh…"

"Of course not. Let's put that behind us and move on. You were looking for me?"

"Yes…" In that moment, Seri's mind went blank. Why had she been searching for him? Something important. Something vital. But what? Forerunner tilted his head ever so slightly, and she stared at his eyes. Four stars. What did that do to his vision? Could he see both worlds, like the Eldanim? Or… more than two worlds?

"Why are you breaking our Bonds?" Ixchel's voice broke into her thoughts like metal scraping on metal. The harshness of it made her wince, and yet Ixchel sounded like she might burst into tears.

"I am not," Forerunner said.

"Liar. My Lady's Bond to me is gone. All of our Bindings are gone." Ixchel's sword arm shook. "I cannot even tell where home is!"

"It must be a side effect." Forerunner ran his hand over his smooth chin, as if stroking a beard. "My own power must somehow be negating these things."

"The Laws of Cursings and Bindings are inviolable," Seri said. "They're bound into the very land itself. You cannot negate them."

Forerunner's eyebrows went up. "Can I not?" He bent and pulled up a handful of dirt. He held it up and watched as pieces fell through his fingers. "I will admit that I had not anticipated this, but it is not a surprise."

"How?" Seri demanded. "It's the most powerful magic we know! You cannot be that strong!"

"Ordinarily, I'm not. But for my task at the present, I have been gifted more power than I am used to handling." He dropped the rest of the dirt, and brushed his hands together. "The Bindings, as you call them, are the weakest of Antises's magic. It makes sense that they would be submerged."

"Submerged?"

"Yes. They're not gone. Once you leave and travel far enough away from me, I imagine they'll snap back into place at full power. It might be an unpleasant experience."

"One that I will risk," Ixchel said. She half-turned. "Let us leave this place, my Lady."

"No, I can't."

Ixchel stopped.

Seri stared at Forerunner. "If there's any chance he can do what he says he can do… I have to stay."

"He lies."

"You need proof, I suppose," Forerunner said. "Very well. Where is Junia?"

Seri glanced at the trail. "I haven't seen her in a couple of days."

"That's because she is on her way home, where she will find her brother restored to her, just as I promised."

"But you had nothing to do with that."

Forerunner tilted his head to the side. "I did, but I can see how that would not convince you. Tell me, have you spoken with Lucia?"

"Yes..."

"And did she tell you what I did for her?"

Seri thought for a moment, recalling the various conversations she had experienced in the last few days. "No, I don't think so."

"Why is she so intent on her music now?" Forerunner let the question hang in the air for a moment before continuing. "Because when she arrived here, she was deaf. A childhood illness stole her hearing from her three years ago. I restored it."

Could it be true? On the road, Junia and Cato spoke of healing miracles.

"Words!" Ixchel snapped. "Just words. You have no real proof!"

"Very well." With an abruptness that took them both by surprise, Forerunner lunged forward and grabbed Seri by the head. He placed one hand over her left eye and cried out, "See!"

Seri's head exploded in pain. She would have staggered back, but Forerunner held her. At first, she could see nothing but light. Blinding, painful light. Ixchel screamed something and Seri felt her moving beside her, but couldn't see or otherwise perceive anything but the light.

Then her vision cleared. For a moment, she saw Forerunner pulling away from her. With his left hand, he blocked an attack from Ixchel with a sword that appeared to be made of literal fire. Yet his eyes continued to study her. "Blink," he said.

Seri did. And immediately, she saw the Otherworld. The blazing, beautiful stars called to her from above the broken landscape. But her view focused instead on a group of six individuals who stood a few dozen yards away. They turned toward her, perceiving her presence.

All six were human-shaped, not the stretched proportions of the Eldanim. Yet they all stood at least seven feet tall, each one stunningly beautiful. Seri blushed at her own thoughts of the four males, so muscular they might have been sculpted to look like the peak of masculinity. The beauty of the two females made her want to hide her own face. Standing in their presence, even at this distance, made her feel tiny and insignificant. But they continued to stare at her. Their skin glowed like burnished bronze and lightning seemed to radiate from their eyes. She had no clear idea of their clothing, so struck was she by their raw beauty, sexuality, and magical presence.

She found herself trembling. All six of them projected such an immense aura of magic it dwarfed Forerunner or even the Lords. Her mouth filled with saliva in the time it took to recognize their appearance.

Against her own desires, she closed her eyes. When she re-opened them, she stood in the clearing again with Forerunner and Ixchel. The latter looked prepared to launch herself at Seri's presumed attacker, sword at ready.

"No, don't," Seri said weakly. Ixchel paused, literally on her tiptoes, and looked at her in concern.

At that moment, Seri's star-sight activated. A light blue ray of magic erupted from the ground right at her feet. She grabbed at it and absorbed it. The power felt so good. As she looked around, she saw numerous other small bursts of magic coming from the ground. Zes Sivas had many times the magic output, but this was significant. This location must be a strong source for wild magic. And then she looked at Forerunner.

He blazed with a fiery magic unlike any she had seen. Instinctively, she knew it to be similar to Lady Lilitu's power, and even more closely related to the six strangers in the Otherworld.

"Are you all right, Seri?" Forerunner asked. As he spoke, Seri saw beams of orange light launch from his mouth and shoot into her own and Ixchel's ears. As suddenly as it had all started, the star-sight stopped and Seri's vision returned to normal.

"I, I think so." Seri sank to her knees and put her hands on the ground.

"I am sorry that the restoration is only temporary at this point," Forerunner said. "I need to draw more power to finish the job. This is why I ask you to stay. I need time."

Ixchel knelt beside Seri and put a hand on her shoulder. "My Lady?"

"I'll be all right." She looked up at Forerunner. "Who were they?"

"What?"

"The six people in the Otherworld. Who were they?" Her mind whirled with the impact of what she had seen. Six unbelievably powerful individuals. Six.

"Who do you think they are?"

"I don't know. They were like no one I've ever seen. They—" Seri could not think of the right words to say.

Forerunner reached down and took Seri's arm. With Ixchel, he lifted her back to her feet. "You will learn," he said. "You will learn. It is your heritage, after all."

(((29)))

Talinir groaned. Keeping his eyes down at all times turned out to be extremely difficult. Janaab rescued him on frequent occasions.

"If only the terrain were more interesting to watch," he grumbled.

"About that..."

Talinir looked at his companion. "About what? This is the Starlit Realm. It has been this way for hundreds of years."

"Hmm."

"What does that mean?"

Janaab cocked his head. "How old are you, Talinir? How long have you been a warden?"

"I am forty-seven years, as you measure them in the primary world. I have been a warden for twenty-three."

"And in all those years, how far have you wandered in this world?"

"I wandered some distance in my younger years, but since becoming a warden, my duties keep me within a day's journey of Intal Eldanir... until I promised to help Marshal."

"Have you ever been in the mountains?"

"I've... been in the foothills. I've never gone very high or deep."

"Then I would like to suggest a detour on our journey north."

"Into the mountains?"

"You wanted a change of scenery."

"But isn't time of the essence? For both of us?"

"I think we can afford a few days."

"But why? What purpose would it serve?"

Janaab tapped his spear against a rock and looked ahead. "I've been here less time than you've been a warden. But in that time, I've traveled further than you have. I've been to the mountains."

"And?"

"And there is something there that you need to see."

Talinir did not know what to think. He could not believe a human knew more about the Starlit Realm than he did. And yet… he never had been to the mountains. He considered it a time or two before his appointment as warden. But then his time had been spent more in the joy of the stars. When he held no worries about the future. Before he even heard the name Durunim.

(((30)))

"I had it back." Seri pulled her pillow toward her and squeezed it. "It was glorious." Forerunner had dismissed them without further explaining anything. Yet Seri still luxuriated in the afterglow of having her power back.

"So you have said." Ixchel straightened the mattress on the floor, looked it over with a critical eye, then sat on it. She reached for her braided hair.

"Oh, let me help," Seri said. She climbed off the bed and hurried to Ixchel's side. She carefully removed the two green feathers that Ixchel valued so highly, and set them aside. Then she set to work on the braid itself.

"How do you get this so tight?" she asked. "I've never been able to get my hair to behave this way."

"It is… my grandmother taught me."

"Grandmother? Not your mother?"

"I never knew my mother. She died when I was born."

"Oh."

Seri remained quiet for a few minutes while she worked on the braid.

"So… musical training?"

Ixchel sighed. "You will not let this go, will you?"

"Not a chance."

Ixchel gestured. "Bring me my pack."

Seri heaved Ixchel's pack and handed it to her. She grinned in anticipation. Ixchel rolled her eyes and opened the pack. From within, she drew a long item, wrapped tightly in multiple layers of cloth and bound with twine. She untied the twine and removed the cloth in

138

precise movements. Seri almost reached out to help out of impatience.

With a gentle touch so different from her usual brusqueness, Ixchel lifted out a wooden device around a foot and a half long. Carved primarily from black walnut, the instrument boasted a wide mouthpiece at one end and two rounded chambers, one much shorter than the other. Ixchel positioned her fingers on either side, placing three fingers of each hand over corresponding holes.

"It's like a flute?" Seri asked. She had seen a number of flute players back home in Arazu.

Ixchel nodded. She tossed her head to get some loose hair out of her face, then brought the mouthpiece to her lips. She blew a few notes through one chamber, then adjusted an odd device up near the mouthpiece. It looked like two additional pieces of polished, carved wood couple inches long. They were strapped to the flute with lengths of leather running through a pair of drilled holes. Seri could just make out that they covered an additional set of air holes in the flute itself. A tiny turquoise decorated each of the pieces, along with a third gem mounted just below them.

This time, when Ixchel began to play, she blew through both chambers. Seri had never heard anything like it. The effect was astounding. Ixchel moved her fingers steadily, playing a series of notes that blended together in amazing harmony.

"It's like you're playing a duet with yourself!" Seri exclaimed.

Ixchel's face twitched in amusement, but she continued to play. The tones, much lower than the flutes Seri knew, swelled in a haunting melody that seemed vaguely familiar. Ixchel hit a couple of notes out of tune and winced at each.

The curtains moved and two other young women peeked inside, attracted by the music. Seri smiled at them, but surreptitiously gestured for them to remain hidden. They nodded and pulled back.

Ixchel completed her song and set the flute down. Seri realized she had been holding her breath for the last part of the song. She gasped and clapped. Ixchel blushed. "I did not do it justice," she said.

"That was beautiful!" Seri said. "You were fantastic!"

"I missed five notes."

"That's impressive! I mean, I've never heard you practice, so it must be some time since you tried it last!"

Ixchel shrugged.

"What was the song?"

"It is the tale of a woman who loses her love. The sipak, the great beast of the sea, takes him in a storm. In response, she learns the way of the spear. She tries to hunt the beast down, but never finds it again."

"That's what sounded familiar!" Seri exclaimed. "Some of it sounded like the waves of the sea!"

Ixchel nodded.

Seri sat back. "You just continue to amaze me, Ixchel. You are so full of talents and—and I can't even compare. You're a warrior, a musician, and I don't even know what!"

Ixchel's mouth twisted. "I'm not very good at any of them," she said. "But you! You can see into other worlds! And work great magic!"

Seri frowned. "I can't see into other worlds right now. He said it was temporary, but he can restore it all. If he has time."

"And so you want to stay."

"I have to! I need it back, Ixchel. I need it."

She nodded. "Then I will do what I can to protect you, even from yourself."

"You do a good job at that, you know."

"Today I learned that I cannot protect you from Forerunner. Did you see his magic? A sword of fire! How can I stand against that?"

"You shouldn't have to." Seri got up and moved back to her bed. "I don't think he means us genuine harm."

"I am not sure of that."

Seri sat in silence as Ixchel carefully put the flute away. She wanted to ask her to play again, but just getting the one song had been amazing. She didn't dare push further.

"Who do you think they were?" Ixchel asked. "The ones you saw in the other world?"

"I don't know." Seri looked up at the ceiling. "Before I met Lady Lilitu on Zes Sivas, I thought I understood magic. It came from the Lords and the land. But she had something different. And now Forerunner has it too. And these strangers... they were unbelievably powerful."

"Didn't your Master know the Lady?"

Seri cocked her head. "Master Hain? Of course he did."

"Then he knew of her power, also? He did not speak of this to you?"

"He didn't." Seri sucked in a breath, amazed at the pain that statement brought her. Not only had her mentor died, he kept a secret from her, a secret that seemed vitally important to the world itself. Or worlds, for that matter.

Ixchel completed her preparations and blew out the lantern.

"Tomorrow, we should wake Dravid," she suggested.

"Yes."

Seri rolled to face the back wall and wiped a pair of tears from her cheeks. In all her despair over losing her star-sight, she had not really mourned for Master Hain. What would he have thought of Forerunner? What advice would he have offered? Seri felt a hole inside. To whom could she go for advice now? Her friends were all her age; they knew some things she did not, but they possessed limited wisdom.

Her loss pulled her thoughts down a spiral of sadness until sleep finally silenced them.

•••••

"You should wake up."

Dravid's eyelids felt like each one carried a heavy weight, but he forced them open. His mind took a few moments to process what he saw.

Ixchel stood above him, looking down. Still unsure whether he dreamed or woke, Dravid said the first thing that came into his head.

"You're so beautiful when you're not frowning."

The slap woke him up completely.

"I'm sorry, Ixchel. Sorry." Dravid called as she stalked away. "I was dreaming."

"Clearly."

"No, you don't understand." Dravid reached for his crutch and missed. He fell from the bed and rolled on the ground.

Ixchel turned with a sigh. "Are you all right?"

"No. I'm not all right. I'm missing a leg. Have you seen it?"

Ixchel rolled her eyes.

"That's what I was dreaming." Dravid grabbed the side of the bed and pulled himself into a sitting position. "That my leg wasn't gone. I was walking." He lowered his head. "I was walking."

Ixchel stood still. Dravid didn't know what effect, if any, his words might have had on her. She wasn't the one he wanted to confide in, but she was here at this moment.

"Seri needs to see you," she said at last. "We'll be outside. Clean up and get dressed."

Dravid nodded. Ixchel spun on her heel and left the room.

He closed his eyes and thought. What was the last thing he

remembered? Oh, yes. Trying to absorb some of Forerunner's magic, and failing. Just like everything else he tried to do.

Seri. He needed to tell her about Forerunner's power, about what he had felt. Maybe she would understand better.

He found his crutch and pulled himself up.

• • • • •

Dravid found Seri and Ixchel not far from the men's lodgings. His heart leaped when he saw the look of delight on Seri's face upon seeing him approaching. It pushed all his depressing thoughts away.

"Dravid! So good to see you up again!" She hurried to meet him, then came to an awkward stop a couple of feet away. Dravid would have welcomed a hug, but her smile would have to be enough.

"Thanks, Seri." He looked around. "Is there somewhere we can sit? I still feel drained."

"The pavilion contains many seats," Ixchel said.

Dravid agreed. Seri wanted to launch right into something, he could tell, but she held it back while they walked. He smiled as he watched her trying not to say anything.

Only two followers of Forerunner sat talking on one side of the otherwise empty pavilion. Dravid and the girls found seats with a table on the opposite side.

"Forerunner restored my star-sight!" Seri exclaimed.

Dravid jerked back. "Really?"

"For a few moments," Ixchel said.

"It was temporary," Seri said, "but he proved he can do it. He just needs time to gain enough power to do it permanently."

"All that power he has, and it's not enough?"

Seri frowned. "If… if you had seen… the creature that took it from me. I can't imagine the power it held. To overcome it… until yesterday, I wouldn't think it was even possible."

"All right. So… I'm guessing you want to stay here."

"Tell him the rest of it," Ixchel said.

"The rest?"

"The other powerful ones."

"Oh, right." Seri explained about the Gidim, and how they looked in the Otherworld.

Dravid felt questions bubble up inside of him.

"Wait, wait, wait. You said the creature that took your star-sight was unimaginably powerful. And we both know Forerunner is full of power. And now you say these beings in the Otherworld are also insanely powerful. So… which one is the most?"

"That's… uh… hard to say. Let me think. Forerunner is at least as powerful as one of the Lords. Do you think so?"

"Definitely." After trying to absorb some of his power, Dravid had no doubt of that. "But his power is different."

"They all are! It's like everything we learned on Zes Sivas only told half the story!"

"I know. My head is spinning. And you said the, uh, people in the Otherworld were more powerful still?"

"Yes. And their power was something else entirely. Like Forerunner's but higher? And it made me feel…"

"Made you feel what?"

Seri blushed. "I, uh…"

Dravid waited.

"Desire." Seri's voice was so low, he barely heard it.

"Oh." Dravid had no idea how to respond to that. In the silence that followed, Dravid reached out for magic, more to occupy his mind than anything else. To his surprise, he found some right away and pulled it in. Seri remained quiet, so he looked around. Finding a small crack in the table's surface, he channeled the magic into it slowly. With precision control, he widened and lengthened the crack, twisting it as he did.

"It—It's just a different kind of power. So strange!" Seri said all in a rush. "I don't know what it means. And the creature that took my star-sight was another thing entirely. It was like it was made of magic or something. I don't know how to explain it."

"So more or less powerful?" Dravid ignored the disapproving look Ixchel gave him. He focused on the crack, twisting it again.

"I just don't know."

Dravid looked over the letter he had carved into the table, the first letter of his name. "Everything we thought we knew has been upended. What do we do now?" He looked up at Seri.

"We have no one else to ask for guidance. No Masters out here."

"We have to blunder along on our own."

"Why?" Ixchel asked. "Why must we even stay? This is not our quest."

Seri lifted her hands in exasperation. "We've been over this!"

At that moment, the ground began to shake.

(((31)))

Victor thought he heard a rumble just before the ground itself began to shake. Not again.

"Marshal?" He felt a familiar twitch from their Bond. But that shouldn't be working during war, should it?

Rufus stumbled and fell next to him. "What's happening?"

All around him, the other curse squad members reacted, trying to stay on their feet.

"Not again!" Callus wailed.

Wolf slumped onto the ground. "Dying," he said.

"Marshal!"

"He went that way!" Gnaeus said, pointing across the camp, even as the Bond pulled Victor in that direction.

He started running. Or at least he tried. One step, everything seemed normal; the next step, he couldn't find the ground. By the time his foot hit solid ground, his entire body had gone parallel to it. He hit the dirt hard and slid.

As he lifted himself up, his hand began to vibrate. But it felt wrong. The vibrations did not radiate outward as they usually did. Instead, his hand vibrated only toward the ground itself, as if the ground pulled the vibrations into it.

Victor considered this for only a moment, before scrambling back to his feet and continuing to run. The pull of the Bond compelled him. During their journey, the Bond yanked him toward Marshal many times. This felt the same way. It wasn't the strongest he had ever felt it, but that didn't change his urgency.

Around him, shouts and cries of both fear and command echoed. Out of the corner of his eye, he saw Volraag's command tent collapse.

If not him, then the shaking might be coming from Lord Tyrr, which meant this could be the precursor to a full-scale assault. But what did Marshal have to do with all this?

He fell five or six times, scraping his knees and palms bloody. But the Bond would not let up, forcing him to keep getting back up and running on and on. He might be imagining it, but it felt like he began to anticipate the ground's movements and time his steps to match it. At the very least, he stopped falling.

The Bond led him in a familiar direction. The ravine!

The ground's shaking subsided and he picked up speed. Then it erupted again and threw him to the ground once more.

Victor spit dirt from his mouth and pulled himself up. Marshal knelt on the ground a few feet away, at the edge of the ravine, palms in the dirt.

"Marshal?" He approached with careful steps. The Bond seemed not to be pulling at him any more, now that he had arrived.

Marshal looked up. Even through the scars, Victor could see his fear.

A quick glance at the ravine revealed much of it had collapsed. Lord Tyrr's troops would not be using this unless he came back and dug it out again. Still, enough of it remained to make it a danger to ignorant travelers. The rocks stayed exposed just below.

"Did you do all this?"

"No, I..." Marshal seemed at a loss for words. He looked back at the ravine, then down at his own hands. He lifted them from the ground and stared at them. "It... it pulled me, Victor."

"What do you mean?"

"When the ground began to shake, it... it pulled at me. It wanted my magic."

The vibrations went toward the ground. Same thing, perhaps.

"Did you, I don't know, give it to the, uh, ground?"

Marshal shook his head. "It was already shaking. How could I add to it? But it pulled. It pulled."

Victor bent down and helped Marshal stand. "We need to get back to the squad. Lord Tyrr might have done this to shake us up before attacking."

"No. It wasn't him."

"You're sure?"

Marshal nodded. "This was like before. I think the earth itself is... breaking?"

"Well, that's frightening."

Louder yells came from the camp. Yells of command, not fright. Lord Tyrr might take advantage of the chaos, even if he didn't cause it.

"We've got to get back to our squad. Come on!"

Marshal took a last look at the ravine, then hurried after him. They both began to run.

Only when they reached the borders of the camp did Victor realize Marshal hadn't explained why he had been at the ravine in the first place.

(((32)))

Seri's eyes widened. They were many miles from Zes Sivas. If the ground were shaking this far away, then the situation had grown worse since they left. This quake must be far worse on the island. Would Jamana be all right? All of this passed through her mind before she even considered the danger to herself.

The ground rumbled. Chairs toppled. The pillars holding up the ceiling rocked. Curtains fluttered. Wood paneling buckled. One of Forerunner's followers screamed.

"Get out of the building!" Ixchel yelled.

"No!" Forerunner's magic-enhanced voice boomed throughout the pavilion. Somehow, he appeared in the center of the room, arms spread wide. "To me! I will protect you!"

Seri didn't hesitate. "Come on!" she said. She started toward Forerunner.

Ixchel grabbed her by her robe. "My Lady!"

Seri glanced back at her. "Whether we trust him or not, his power can protect us!" she argued.

Dravid put his hand on Ixchel's arm. "This time," he said, looking into her eyes. She hesitated, then nodded.

They hurried to Forerunner's side. A dozen or more of his followers, the women in white and others, came rushing in from all directions. "Hurry! My power can protect you!" he called.

Even as he spoke, Seri saw a crack open up on the east side of the pavilion. It moved toward them with frightening speed, widening to a couple feet, swallowing a few chairs and half a table. The ground continued to shake. Dravid sat down hard, unable to maintain his balance.

"Forerunner!" Lucia screamed, pointing at the crack.

"Fear not!" Forerunner brought his arms down in separate arcs, then swept them back up. As he did, a translucent golden dome formed in the air around the crowd of people. Seri stared. The dome reminded her of the way she beheld magic with her star-sight: as beams of colored light. The dome appeared similar, though she had never seen magic in this exact color range.

"Are you seeing this?" she asked Dravid.

"The dome? Yeah."

Interesting. She wondered if the dome's visual manifestation was a necessary part of the magic, or something Forerunner added to impress his people. It fit within his character.

The crack reached the dome's edge and stopped, inches away from where Dravid sat. How could that be, unless the dome extended into the ground itself? Dravid raised his hand to touch it.

"The roof!" someone cried.

Seri looked up and saw the pavilion's ceiling collapse. Though not much of a solid construction, no one would want to be under it as it fell. But again, the dome protected them. Pieces of lumber of varying sizes and shapes plummeted all around them. Yet where they struck the dome, they were deflected and slid to the ground outside the protective region.

The rumbling stopped. Forerunner did not move, holding his hands - and by implication, the dome - aloft.

"Is it over?" a woman asked.

The ground shook again, answering her question. But it only lasted a few seconds this time and stopped again.

"Now it's over," Forerunner said. He lowered his arms, and the dome dissipated into the air.

The crowd erupted in nervous discussion. Seri looked around. About half of the pavilion's roof had fallen. Many of the chairs and tables had been damaged or outright destroyed, especially those around the crack that still stood open before them.

Dravid bent to examine where the crack met the dome. "It's like it hit a wall too strong for it," he said, pointing.

Seri looked at it briefly, but didn't see much. Just dirt. She looked up to find Forerunner gazing at her, a smile of contentment on his face. When he realized she saw him, his smile grew larger and he turned away.

"My friends! We are all right! Let us spread out and check the other buildings. There may be others who did not make it here in time. Find them, if you can. And then we will begin the work of rebuilding. This will not stop us!"

The followers offered a few nervous cheers, and then dispersed to follow his instructions. Seri and Ixchel helped Dravid get back up.

"Maybe we should go back to looking for the lost King," Dravid said. "If Antises is this unstable…"

"Or maybe there's another option," Seri said. She strode directly up to Forerunner until he looked down at her.

"Yes?"

"Forerunner. You say you're here to restore things. Can you restore stability to Antises?"

(((33)))

Victor and Marshal raced across the army's camp. A decanus yelled at them, but Marshal showed his own insignia to keep moving. Everywhere they passed conscripts getting into formation, centurions riding by shouting orders, civilians scrambling to get out of the way.

Victor craned his neck trying to get a view of the battlefield, but he had no success. Whatever might happen remained a mystery.

They found the curse squad at the front lines, as expected.

"Oh, good. We have a leader," Topleb said.

"You shouldn't be out here," Marshal said.

Topleb shrugged. "I'm able to throw my darts, so here I am."

Victor looked ahead. The Rasnians had already taken the field, as before, though they showed no signs of trying to build anything. Row after row of spearmen led the way. He couldn't see them, but Victor knew archers waited behind the spears.

"They're going to send us into that?"

"Time for the rest of us to die," Gnaeus said.

"No one is dying!" Marshal's voice carried over them. He looked over his squad. "Do you all hear me? No one else!"

"May Theon hear you," Topleb said after a moment of silence.

The order came to advance. Victor drew his sword and readied his flail. The vibration in his hands grew with each step. Whatever magic he now possessed, absorbed from Marshal or something else, it seemed to ache for battle. His breathing quickened.

As they splashed across the Amnis, the first wave of arrows descended on them. "Shields!" Marshal yelled, along with every decanus along the front. Victor ducked under Marshal's and Merish's shields. He caught glimpses of conscripts falling around them, some screaming, some silent. The shallow muck of the Amnis turned red. Somehow, none of the curse squad fell.

"Charge!" screamed a centurion on horseback.

Victor made sure he had room on his left and began to swing his flail. The Rasnian front line knelt and held their spears at waist level. Behind them, another line aimed theirs just above. The intimidation factor caused many conscripts to falter as the charge drew close.

Why did Volraag use these tactics? Were the lives of the conscripts so easily expendable to him? Victor gritted his teeth. He had made the right decision in rejecting the Lord's offer, even if he died here and now. Better to die than to serve someone like that.

As if in answer, the power exploded through his arms and legs. He picked up speed, outdistancing Marshal and everyone else. He screamed and began to swing his flail in an arc in front of him, holding his sword back. Only a few feet separated him from the spearmen now.

One of Topleb's spear-darts caught a kneeling spearman in the throat. As he toppled, Victor charged into the hole, sweeping away the second spear with his flail. He stabbed forward, his sword impaling the Rasnian through the stomach. For a moment, everything seemed frozen. Victor stared into the eyes of the man he killed. They were blue. And young. And dead.

The rest of the army caught up to him and smashed against the wall of spearmen with a thunderous cacophony of screams and splintering wood. For a moment, chaos reigned over all.

Victor pulled his sword back and the Rasnian fell. Soldiers of both nations surrounded him, leaving him no room to maneuver, no room to swing his flail. Merish appeared beside him, swinging his sword in deadly arcs that cut through enemy spears and bodies equally. Victor fought beside him, though he felt little of the battle rage from before. He fought for his own life and those around him, but he heard no whooshing, felt no desire to let loose. The vibrations seemed barely there.

"Cavalry!" someone shouted. Victor looked up and saw mounted Rasnian soldiers bearing down on them. Another of Topleb's spear-darts bounced off the shield of the nearest rider. And then their spears came down. Victor stared at his own death: an experienced soldier and over a thousand pounds of his steed about to trample him if the spear didn't get him first.

Marshal shoved past him, leveling his sword at the oncoming storm of riders. He screamed, the first time Victor had heard him do so. The ground erupted in front of them. Horses and riders cascaded back, colliding with each other in a chaotic mess. Marshal's power blew apart an entire squad of cavalry, shattering bones in horse and rider alike. The screams of the horses drowned out the screams of men.

The rage took over then. Victor charged through the opening Marshal created, flail swinging, bloody sword held high. The whooshing of his heart filled his ears once more. He fought with his body, but also fought to reclaim his own mind, to keep some understanding of what took place around him.

He saw Marshal and Merish fighting side-by-side. Gnaeus, Callus and Rufus bunched up, using their spears for defense, but not pursuing any enemies who came near. A Rasnian stumbled past, impaled by one of his own comrade's spears, yet still on his feet somehow.

Victor felt the ground pulse beneath him, a roll of magic that upended dozens of soldiers on both sides. If he hadn't been moving so fast, he would have fallen himself. But where did that magic come from? Not Marshal. He had been knocked down as well. In fact, he saw no one on their feet anywhere nearby. Wolf knelt in the midst of a pile of corpses, a silent scream elevated at the sky. Topleb, only a few feet away from him, scrambled up, grabbing his atlatl and one final spear.

Desperate, Victor spun. It had to be Lord Tyrr. Or another wild mage. But he saw no sign of anyone who could have done this. The upending magic seemed to have been confined to a small area near them. The battle still raged and now began to close in on them again.

"Get up!" he screamed and charged at the nearest enemy soldiers. A spear sliced a short gash on the side of his chest beneath his left arm. Another one, destined for his face, shattered into splinters, no doubt from Marshal helping again.

Already this battle had lasted far longer than the last one. And he saw no end in sight. Dimly, he became aware of a much larger cavalry group battling beyond their reach, horses rearing and pawing at each other. Regular soldiers, not conscripts, also fought now, mingling with the rest of them.

The frenzy overtook him once more and he struggled to keep track of anything else. Was that Topleb lifting a Rasnian soldier and throwing him into the spears of his oncoming friends? Was that Rufus stumbling, too late to stop a spear from reaching someone beside him? Callus? Did Marshal unleash another blast that took down half a dozen more of the enemy? Victor could not be sure of anything now.

When he finally came to himself and stopped, the battle seemed all but over. The only Rasnians he could see were running away as fast as they could. The whooshing faded. For a brief moment, he heard nothing. And then his ears filled with the moans and screams of the wounded and dying of both sides.

Fatigue struck him like a physical force, staggering him and almost bringing him to his knees. How long had he been fighting? How much death had he given out? How much death had he avoided somehow?

He had roamed far from his squad once again. He stumbled in the direction he thought he could find them, his steps made more difficult by the bodies and gore covering the ground everywhere. How? How had so many died? So many. For their homelands? Or for their Lords?

He spied Merish and Topleb standing together, covered in dust and grime. Topleb saw him and lifted his atlatl in silent greeting. Then he stepped aside and Victor saw the others.

Marshal sat on the ground, surrounded by Gnaeus, Wolf and Rufus.

And in his arms lay Callus.

The twins were united again.

• • • • •

Volraag lowered the spyglass. The high platform had somehow withstood the earthquake, but it rocked a little beneath his feet.

"Victory," General Cassian said. "Well done, your Lordship. The Rasnians have been thoroughly routed."

Volraag nodded.

"The cavalry on their flanks while the conscripts fought in the center proved too much for them," Otioch said.

"Another assault, perhaps tomorrow, will probably end this," Cassian added.

No doubt. He couldn't see how Lord Tyrr could possibly stop it now, aside from direct intervention. In which case, he would have to interfere as well. But something else bothered him now.

"Someone used magic in the fight."

Rathri climbed onto the platform. "Two someones, if I felt it right."

"Two?"

"Someone used power in the battle several times, but then a wave went out." Rathri gestured expansively. "The ground is broken up all over the place from it."

"You don't think it was the same person?"

Rathri shook his head. "It was... a different kind of power."

Volraag considered. He had felt the wave also. And it had definitely "felt" different from the power he possessed or any he encountered among the mages and other Lords.

"Otioch! You did find a spy in the conscripts, didn't you?"

"Yes, your Lordship. Only too eager to tell me everything."

"Find him tonight. Find out everything you can about this fight. What Victor did. And anyone else in their squad."

"It shall be done."

Volraag nodded. If his half-brother were truly out there, he needed something else.

"Rathri. Fetch Tezan. I need him by my side for the next few days."

"It shall be done."

When Rathri said it, it didn't have the same ring.

(((34)))

"He died in my arms, Victor."

After all these weeks, Marshal's voice had finally started sounding normal. But now, brokenness filled it with new anguish. Sobs damaged his throat. Victor winced to hear it.

"I know." There didn't seem much else he could say. He went back to cleaning his sword.

"He... he couldn't see... at the end."

Victor gritted his teeth. Marshal wouldn't stop talking about Callus. The battle ended hours ago. The rest of the curse squad now slept, exhausted. Like Victor wished he could do. Every muscle in his body ached. A large wad of an old tunic under his armpit kept his arm out away from the gash on his chest. He would need to change that dressing in the morning.

"He asked me... to describe something beautiful. For him to think about. As he died."

Victor paused. "What did you say?"

Marshal looked up. Tears made their way through his scars, glistening in the campfire's glow. "I... I told him about the stars. In the Otherworld."

Victor nodded. Those stars had made quite an impact on Marshal. Victor hadn't seen them himself.

"Stars. Of all colors and sizes. So beautiful. So perfect."

Victor frowned at a dark spot on his sword. Why wouldn't it come off? He spit on the piece of cloth and rubbed harder.

"I told him. Callus. I told him. And then..."

The darker stain started to come off. Victor spit on the cloth again.

"He said... he hoped Theon would take him somewhere like that."

"Maybe he did."

"And, and then he died, Victor. He died."

Victor set the sword aside. "I know, Marshal. I know. It's horrible."

"I couldn't save him."

"You saved me. And Merish. And probably a lot of others."

"You told me not to hold back. I tried. I used my power."

"And you made a difference!"

"No. Callus still died."

"But I didn't. Doesn't that count for something?"

"It's not enough. It's never enough, Victor. They keep dying. Why do they keep dying?"

"Because we're at war, Marshal. That's what happens. I'm sorry, but it's true. Tomorrow, we might fight again. And more will die. I don't know what else to tell you."

Marshal lowered his head again. "So it's all worthless."

"I didn't say that."

"They died for nothing."

"No, they—"

"Aelia died for nothing."

"She did not! She lifted your curse!"

"What good did it do? It's hopeless. I'm hopeless."

Victor ran his hand through his hair. His fingers caught in tangles and blood clots. He jerked at it and couldn't repress an "ow!" Marshal didn't say anything for a while.

"It's not hopeless," Victor said. "Nothing is ever completely hopeless."

"Then tell me. Tell me something about... hope."

"Ah, well... remember the Eldanim city? How beautiful it was? And that girl we stayed with? What was her name?"

"Eniri."

"Right. Her. She was something else, wasn't she? And that domed building? And..."

"Why are you talking about this?"

"You wanted hope. I'm trying to remember good things. I don't... I'm not sure what else to say."

"That's not hope."

"Talinir. Talinir will come back and help us."

"He can't."

"You don't know that."

"Aelia's dead. Talinir's gone. Nian's dead. And my soldiers are dying. Hopeless."

"That's..."

"I can't stop it. I'm worthless."

"No, you're... you're Marshal. You're so much more. You..."

Marshal got to his feet. Victor looked up at him. When Marshal had disappeared into the Otherworld, he had felt helpless, because he couldn't do anything. This was worse. Marshal stood right here, and he didn't have the words to help him.

"It's all right, Victor. You... you're a good friend."

Victor blinked. Whether from the exhaustion, the smoke, or the emotion, a tear slipped out.

"We should go to bed."

"I need to walk first."

"Do you want me to come?"

"No."

Victor nodded, relieved. He wasn't sure he could even stand back up right now, let alone take a walk.

"Goodbye, Victor."

"Goodnight."

The sword seemed clean enough. Victor picked up the flail. What a mess. Blood and rust. He sighed. Maybe he could find a new flail somewhere around here.

(((35)))

Dravid stared at Seri and Forerunner. He had not considered that angle. Trust Seri to connect Forerunner's powers with the earthquakes.

"You'll have to be more specific, my dear," Forerunner said.

"You know exactly what I mean," Seri said. "If you really know as much as you claim to know, then you know that Antises is breaking apart, because of the lost King. Without his power at The Passing, the land cannot hold together."

"I have heard this."

Dravid noticed Forerunner continued to use magic in his voice.

"So can you do it? Can you restore the power the land needs to be stable?"

Forerunner hesitated only briefly. "You know the King's power is greater than that of any Lord's."

"Your power is greater than that of any Lord's," Seri countered.

Forerunner nodded. "And yet, as you've no doubt noticed, my power differs from theirs. It is not what Antises needs to heal itself."

"Are you sure?"

"Even if it were, I have no way of passing my power into the land, as your Lords do. It is a part of me and cannot be removed, even temporarily."

"Is that so?"

"It is."

Dravid stepped closer. "Maybe you just need a little help," he said. "I absorbed some of your power. That proves it can leave you." He looked at Seri. "Remember the false king and his ability?"

"Tezan! Of course! He could pull powers from others and transfer them… maybe he could do the same with you!"

Forerunner shook his head and exhaled. "You are not understanding me. If what you suggest were indeed possible, that this Tezan could pull my power from me and restore it to Antises... then it would kill me. I am not willing to do that at this time. Would you do that?"

"Would I do what?"

"Sacrifice yourself to save Antises?"

Seri glanced at Dravid. "I... I'd like to say I would, of course. But I don't know. Who can really know what they'd do in that kind of situation?"

That surprised him. He would have expected her to immediately say she would, without question. Then again, her answer sounded more... mature. Seri was growing, changing. She wasn't quite the naive acolyte any more.

Dravid's left hand grew warm. He glanced down, then shifted so his body kept his hand from view by Seri and Forerunner. It wouldn't do to let them see it glowing with the same tone as the protective dome.

•••••

Dravid wanted to confide in Seri about the changes he felt inside, but... he couldn't be completely sure she wasn't under Forerunner's influence. She ran when Forerunner called, and she argued a little too emotionally about staying here.

He looked around his room and saw little earthquake damage. Seri and Ixchel had gone to check on their own quarters, giving him time alone again. He needed it.

From the moment Ixchel awakened him, he felt something odd inside. He had ignored it, pushed it aside, while dealing with the aftermath of his dream, and then all of Seri's revelations. And then the earthquake and Forerunner used his power...

He took a deep breath and held up his left hand. Focus. He closed his eyes and concentrated. It was a different feeling from seeking out magic and channeling it, like Master Hain taught him back on Zes Sivas. He knew that feeling quite well, knew how to seek it out and draw it in, knew how to use it for various purposes. He possessed nowhere near the ability of Seri, of course, but he flattered himself he wasn't all that bad. But this...

There. The power pulsed, just like Forerunner's. Except this power came from within him. Had he kept some of Forerunner's power for himself somehow? Or awakened an ability unlike anyone else? Either way, the prospects made him shiver. Perhaps, just perhaps, with this power, he would not be a failure any more.

He opened himself up to the pulse and let it flow through him. The effects felt similar to his absorption of Forerunner, but nowhere near that intensity. He felt a slight tightness in his chest, followed by a dry heat that rushed up his throat and glowed behind his eyes. He concentrated and focused on his hand. The power flowed to it, obeying his thoughts. He opened his eyes.

His hand glowed again, that same glow which Forerunner's protective dome had showcased. Curious, he attempted to release some of it, while tracing his hand through the air. To his delight, he created a round disc of light in the air. He took hold of it and moved it around. The disc had substance; it felt solid. Yet it also felt almost completely weightless.

"That could come in handy."

Dravid jumped and looked up. "Ixchel! Don't you ever let someone know before you barge into his room?"

Her expression, as usual, did not change. "Why should I? When I have a task, I do it."

"Fine." He sighed. "Just don't tell Seri about this yet, please."

"Why not?"

"Because… because I'm not sure about it, and I'm honestly not sure about her." He turned the disc sideways and moved it back and forth.

"You think she might tell Forerunner."

Dravid nodded. "I'm worried about her."

"I understand. I am concerned as well." Ixchel stepped closer and looked at his disc. "How solid is it?"

"I don't know." Dravid tapped the disc against the paving stone near his pool. The disc cut smoothly through the stone with a spray of tiny sparks. Shocked, Dravid dropped it. The disc fell and lay still without a sound.

"Impressive," Ixchel said. She drew her sword and struck the disc. Her sword bounced back. "Both shield and weapon."

"Is everything about fighting with you?" Dravid picked the disc back up and turned it back and forth in his hands.

"Almost everything." She knelt next to him, her presence a warmth not unlike the magic that still burned within him. He swallowed, and realized his throat had grown drier still. That might not be good.

"Can you throw it?" Ixchel asked.

In response, Dravid tossed the disc across his room with a flick of his wrist. It flew a few feet and came to a rest near his bed.

The heat began to bother him. He closed his eyes against it and focused on releasing the power. Usually, he would just let it go, toss it out in a vibratory burst. But this power needed to go back inside him, didn't it? He pushed down mentally. After a few moments, he felt it diminish. He bent to the pool, scooped up some water and swallowed.

"It disappeared," Ixchel said. "Did you mean to do that?"

"I turned the power off," Dravid said, "so I guess anything I made with it goes away when I do that."

"How much can you do?"

"I have no idea. I don't even know if this is a permanent thing, or if I only absorbed a small portion from Forerunner. So I might use it all up if I keep doing it." He took another swallow of water. "I just don't know."

Ixchel sheathed her sword. "I encourage you to discover what you can. It may give us insight into Forerunner's powers."

"You think we need more insight?"

She nodded. "I do not trust him. His promises are false. But the hope he offers keeps my Lady here. I cannot dissuade her."

"Then we'll have to protect her."

"Yes. And that is why we need the insight." She stood, long bare legs brushing against him. "I will go find her now. You should rest some more. Afterward, we can both talk with her again."

"Yeah, sure." Dravid watched her leave, then shook his head. What was he thinking? After a moment, he realized he felt ravenously hungry. He pulled his crutch to him, got up, and set out to find something to eat.

(((36)))

The Bond yanked Victor around, nearly throwing his legs into the campfire. How? Marshal left him only a few minutes ago. How could he be in danger already? And weren't Bindings supposed to be negated by war? Second time today!

He gasped as an invisible force pulled him several inches along the ground. The Bond had never been that strong! He scrambled to his feet, heart in his throat. He took several steps, then broke into a run.

The sword! He left his sword. He paused to turn back, but the Bond wouldn't let him. The flail would have to be enough.

Where was Marshal? He hadn't been gone long. Volraag! Did he find him?

Victor stumbled. A haze of exhaustion nearly collapsed him, but the Bond pulled him on. He staggered on, one foot in front of the other, each step a victory somehow.

He knew now. He ran this path hours ago, this morning. Across the camp, toward… the ravine. Why there? Why did Marshal go back there? And what was the danger?

The Bond knew when Marshal faced life-threatening danger. Victor had experienced it multiple times over the past year. The curse-stalker. The assassin. The eidolon. Each time, he had been summoned. Each time, desperation consumed him, the magic enhancing his emotions.

But none of them compared to this. His heart raced. Chills swept his body, followed by a sudden burst of sweat. Worse than monsters or killers. What could it be? Victor's breaths came short and fast. He couldn't catch it. The Bond might kill him if this kept up. But… it also might kill him if he were too late to help Marshal. He gritted his teeth and kept moving.

The heavy flail weighed on him. Maybe he should drop it to move faster. What good would it do, anyway? He should have gone back for the sword. Too late now.

The ravine drew near.

"Marshal!" He coughed and lost his balance. The ground, the solid ground, met him and drove the air from his lungs. He gasped for more air, trying to ignore the pain that wracked his body. Aching, bruised muscles impacting everything. Yet still the compulsion dragged at him. He reached out and dug fingers into the dirt, pulling himself forward.

The flail. He lost it. Leave it! No. He might need a weapon. Unable to turn his head back, he scrambled around with his other hand until it touched the chain. He grabbed hold and pulled it along.

Knees. He got to his knees and crawled a few feet. The scabs formed from his earlier scrapings tore off in the dirt. His blood mixed with the dust.

Feet. He wavered, staggered, but kept moving. His legs felt like immense weights to lift with each and every step. But he kept moving.

"Marshal!" Why did he call? He needed that breath.

No answer again. The ravine. Where was it? There. The darker region. The light of the moon showed it.

And the single figure standing at its edge.

"Marshal!"

The Bond let him stop at last.

"What... what are you doing?"

"It's no use, Victor."

"What is?" Victor almost fell again, put one hand on a bloody knee and held himself up. The flail dangled from his other hand. Useless piece of junk. He let it fall so he could lean on both hands.

"I told you goodbye already. I... I can't do it any more."

The truth started to take hold in Victor's mind. "You can't do what?" But he knew.

Marshal turned toward him. In the moonlight, Victor could barely make out his face. "This is the only way. Blades still don't work." He held up the dagger Volraag had given him so long ago. Before Victor could react, he stabbed it at his own chest. It bounced off. The protection spell from the Eldanim.

Marshal tossed the dagger aside and pointed down the ravine. "The rocks, though. They're not blades."

"Stop."

Marshal shook his head. "It's too much. Goodbye again, Victor." He turned back and stepped to the very edge of the ravine.

No. This could not happen.

The flail. The only thing he brought with him. He grabbed it from the ground and lunged forward.

Marshal leaned forward, falling into darkness.

As he landed in the dirt once more, Victor swept the flail forward. Marshall's feet came up as he fell. The ball of the flail wrapped around Marshal's left leg. Victor grabbed it with his other hand and yanked his arms apart. The chain wrapped around Marshal's ankle.

Marshal struck the side of the ravine and yelled. Victor's arms felt almost yanked from their sockets. The flail's handle slid in his hand, but he gripped tighter. Was it the Bond or the vibrating magic that helped him? No way to know. The wound on the side of his chest re-opened. Blood stained the front of his tunic.

"Let go!" Marshal shouted.

"Never!" Victor screamed.

Marshal pounded the side of the ravine, raining dirt down toward the rocks. "Let go!"

"I won't." Victor found himself crying.

Marshal grew still. His weight hung from the flail's chain wrapped around his ankle. With one hand, Victor held the flail's handle. With the other, its chain. The immense strain made his arms shake.

"Let me go, Victor." Marshal's voice shifted to pleading. "It's no use."

"I won't."

"I, I know the Bond compels you, but it's all right. You... don't have to do this."

"Yes, I do."

"No. I want to go. Please."

"You can't. You're needed here, Marshal. Antises needs you!"

"Antises? Antises cursed me for my father's sins. Antises sent a curse-stalker to destroy my face. Antises... Antises killed my mother!"

Victor let out a moan from his effort and closed his eyes. "The curses. Remember the curses. You can help."

"I can't help! I'm worthless!"

Victor struggled to breathe. His position, arms outstretched above his head, held his chest against the ground. Each time he inhaled, he had to push his entire body upward. And each time, it felt as though he slipped forward ever so slightly.

"You. Are not worthless. You. Are the one. Who can change.

Everything."

"How? I'm nothing! I'm a scarred, broken little boy who can't save anyone!" He slammed his fist into the side of the ravine again. The impact jarred against Victor's hands.

"You have a Lord's power," Victor groaned. If this wasn't the time, it never would be. "And more."

Marshal did not respond.

"Your mother told me. About your grandfather. The one Varion killed. He was… he was the King. Of Antises."

Marshal hung silent and still. Victor took a deep breath, pushing against the ground.

"You don't just have a Lord's power. You have a King's power. Both, I guess. If anyone can change things, it's you." Victor took another deep breath. "It's you."

"Why… why didn't she tell me?" Marshal's voice sounded even more broken. Had he done right in telling him?

"I don't know. She wanted me to tell you. At the right time. She said. I don't know."

"Then I'm even more of a failure!" Broken switched to vicious. "I have all this power and it's useless!"

Victor didn't answer. His muscles trembled from the burden.

Silence stretched out for several moments.

"Victor."

"Still here."

"I could use this power right now. I could force you to let go."

"Don't."

"Why? Because of the Bond? It's the only reason you're here."

"No."

"I'll do it, Victor."

"No."

"I will."

"Your mother begged me!"

"What?"

"Before she died. She begged me to watch out for you. She knew about the Bond and still she begged me. I told her I would."

"She… she wanted to die. And now I do. I want to be with her. Let me go."

"NO!"

Marshal began to sob. Each of his movements pulled on the chain, pulled on Victor's bloody, aching, exhausted hands.

"Why… why won't you… let go?"

"It's not the Bond." As he said it, Victor knew the truth. "It's not my word to Aelia." He fought for another breath to speak again. "You are my friend, Marshal." His voice cracked. "My friend." He swallowed and struggled to find air. "You are."

In the stillness that followed, in the quiet below the moon's radiance, the Bond slipped away. Victor felt it leaving him with a caress, a soft touch of gentle vibration that swept over his body, and a warm glow within his heart that gave him the strength for one more breath.

"Nnnnyaaarrgh!" Marshal screamed. Victor felt heavy vibrations run up the flail's chain into his arms.

And Marshal threw himself with the force of his power—not down, but up, up over Victor, pulling his ankle out of the twisted chain, and landing on the ground behind him, where he rolled over and over before finally coming to a stop.

Victor wanted to run to his side, but he couldn't move. It took all his effort just to let go of the flail.

He did it. He saved Marshal's life. The Bond was broken. Or fulfilled. Or whatever you wanted to call it. He was free.

He rolled onto his side and managed to twist enough to see Marshal. His friend also rolled onto his side and looked back at him. In that moment, he knew.

Some bonds should last a lifetime.

(((37)))

Jamana moved another large rock, then wiped his forehead. The latest earthquake had been the worst yet. Even with the diminished populace here on Zes Sivas, the quake killed three people. An entire tower collapsed on top of them. At least the remaining Masters and acolytes had managed to escape major injury so far.

Unfortunately, that also meant more work for Jamana. Master Korda sent the acolyte to help clear out some of the fallen tower's ruins. The Masters still held out hope that everything could be rebuilt once the earthquakes stopped. If they ever stopped.

"Jamana!" called a nearby voice. "Come here."

Jamana climbed over part of the tower's debris and saw Adhi, the only other acolyte on the island. He looked curiously into an opening between several fallen stones.

"What is it, little Adhi?"

He glanced up and then pointed down into the opening. "There's a chamber down here."

Jamana looked around, considering their location between the citadels. He prided himself on a thorough knowledge of every passage in both the King's and Mage's Citadels. He had already known them well, but after Seri and Dravid left, he had worked hard to learn more. He had more time to himself now. Adhi could be decent company occasionally, but he was not Dravid.

"There should not be a chamber below here," he said at last. "It does not make sense."

"Yet there it is." Adhi pointed again.

Jamana bent and looked. He did not like close spaces, but only the initial opening seemed small. The chamber below looked quite large.

"Shall we, then?"

Adhi climbed over a rock and slid down inside. Jamana followed slow and careful, only after moving a few more rocks out of the way.

From the opening, he dropped a few feet down to the floor. The cave-in broke through one wall near the ceiling. The late afternoon sunlight shone almost directly through the hole, providing ample illumination, though the beams were filled with dust.

Adhi approached what looked like a set of shelves not far from the opening. He looked back at Jamana, his face dirty from the dust. "Jamana, these are… books!"

"Truly?" He joined the other acolyte and looked. Heavy volumes lined the shelf at eye level. He carefully grasped one and pulled. It came apart in his hand. The cover remained almost intact, but very little remained of the pages within.

"Too old, I guess."

Adhi moved further into the room. "More of the shelves," he said. "I think this might have been a library."

Jamana frowned. "The Masters have a library," he said. "It's upstairs." Again, he tried to figure out how this room might connect somehow. Looking around the room, he spotted a door against the leftmost wall.

"Now we'll see," he said to himself. He went to the door, found it unlocked, and pulled. It came open to reveal a solid wall of stone.

"Not a very useful door, is it?" Adhi asked.

Jamana touched the stones. "They walled this room up," he said. "Why? If there is a hallway beyond this wall, then…"

"Wouldn't that be in the King's Citadel?"

"I am thinking you are right." Jamana felt a slight irritation that Adhi calculated it before him. But even Seri had noticed how smart the little acolyte seemed to be.

He concentrated, absorbed some of Zes Sivas' magic, and channeled it against one stone in the wall behind the door. After two more attempts, he managed to break it down enough to open a hole into the hallway beyond. Now he could find this spot from the other side.

"Hailstones!" Adhi exclaimed. He had tried a different book on another shelf. It had come apart in his hands also.

Jamana turned back and looked around. "This library wasn't for the mages, then," he said. "If it was a part of the King's Citadel, then it was for someone that worked there."

"Do you think it belonged to the King himself?"

"I doubt it. Not all the way down here. It probably belonged to someone who worked for the King."

Adhi moved between the shelves. "I guess we'll never know. Nothing seems to have survived."

Jamana found the remains of a desk near the door. Empty, save for something he assumed to be a dried-up feather pen. Next to the desk, however, he found something better.

"Come here," he called. Adhi joined him and they both examined a stone encasement.

"It looks like a coffin for a small child," Adhi said.

"In a library?"

Adhi shrugged. "Just saying what it looks like. We buried one of my sisters in a coffin this size."

Jamana did not know how to respond. "I..."

"It is all right. I come from a very large family."

"I'm not sure that makes it better."

"It doesn't. Not really. Death is still death. But I had a happy and busy childhood."

Jamana nodded. He moved to one side of the encasement and gestured to Adhi. "We should be able to lift this lid."

"Should we? Maybe we should call one of the Masters."

"To show them what? Decayed books? We'll look in here and then tell them."

Adhi seemed reluctant, but he took hold of the other end of the lid. Jamana found it easy to lift, but Adhi struggled. Together, they managed to get the lid off and onto the floor. Jamana peered anxiously into the box.

Several large books lay inside, looking much more preserved than those on the shelves. Adhi reached in and dusted off the cover of one of them. "It's just a book of the Law," he said, disappointment evident in his voice.

Jamana pushed that one aside and looked at the next book. It appeared to be an older copy of one of their primary magic texts. Interesting, but not of major importance.

The cover of the third book made him catch his breath. Slightly smaller than the others, the cover looked etched in gold. But the title!

"A History of the Lords' Betrayal," Adhi read out loud.

With trembling fingers, Jamana opened the book. "It's written by Aharu! Do you know what this means?"

"Aharu? The founder of the priesthood?"

"He was there!" Jamana said. "There at the beginning with Akhenadom! He was actually there!"

"Wasn't he a mage, also? One of the Masters?"

Jamana nodded. "I've read other histories of those days, but none by someone who was there. And a mage! This might even tell us how they created the Laws of Bindings and Cursings!"

"That knowledge is lost."

"Maybe not any more." Jamana turned a page. "We can now learn from a man who saw it happen…" He broke off, stunned by the words before him.

"What is it?"

"Not a man who saw it happen, after all." Jamana looked up. "Aharu was a woman!"

(((38)))

Kishin arrived at his home unnoticed and unacknowledged by anyone in the streets. Those few who did know him - more accurately, knew *of* him - were used to him taking long trips and returning at any time afterward. But why would even those few notice him? He looked nothing like himself any more.

He paused at the door. He remembered being so proud when he purchased this home on the edge of Woqan. The vaulted masonry roof, such a symbol of wealth in this city, never failed to make him smile. Before the curse, before his change of profession, he never could have afforded such a home. But his smile faded. What was he to do now? What was he to become?

Before entering, Kishin pulled his hood up and hid his exposed skin as best he could. His clothes, at least, should be recognizable. He opened the door and walked in. He shut the door behind him quickly, keeping out as much light as possible. His servants expected that of him.

Aapo hurried into the foyer, hearing him enter. Kishin decided it was a good thing he hadn't killed this servant before leaving... assuming he had done well in taking care of the house. If not, he would have to... No. He couldn't kill any more. Getting used to this would be difficult.

"Master! You've returned."

Ah yes. The other reason he considered killing this one. So intelligent.

"Fetch me Inkil," Kishin ordered. His voice had always been under his control, so that would sound familiar to Aapo, also. Inkil was his eyes and ears, the one he depended on to keep him informed of anything that might be relevant to his work, or the world at large.

"At once, sir. Will there be anything else?"

"Bring food and drink to my room. It's been a long road."

Aapo nodded and hurried away.

Kishin walked down the hall and pushed aside the curtain covering the door to his room. Once inside, he fumbled around until he found a candle to light. He looked around at his possessions. All of them seemed so pointless now.

He moved to the wall that held his weapons. So many he had collected over the years, most from people he had killed. He put a hand on the sword hilt at his side. All of these weapons combined did not equal the value of the warpsteel blade, the one the Eldani warden left in his gut.

The door opened and Aapo entered, carrying a tray. "Inkil is on his way," he said. He looked at the lit candle, clearly perplexed, but did not say anything. Kishin stayed in the shadows while Aapo set the tray on his desk. "Anything else?"

"Not now," Kishin said. "You may go." Aapo did not wait for another order.

With the servant gone, Kishin ate and drank, considering his next moves. Once he heard from Inkil, he probably needed to find Blademaster Kuch. He would be the one who would know about his daughter, if Inkil didn't.

It took longer than he hoped for Inkil to show up. When at last Aapo let him in, Kishin waited on the opposite side of the room, back turned.

"Welcome back, Kishin," Inkil said. "I trust your latest trip was a success?"

"That depends on how you define success." Kishin let his hood fall back and picked up the candle. The light fell across his perfectly smooth skin.

Inkil took a step backward. "I—I don't understand." He stared, mouth agape.

"Neither do I." Kishin set the candle down again. "But it's real, Inkil. My curse is gone."

"What magic could do this? It—it defies reason. It defies Theon!"

Kishin snorted. "Since when do you care about Theon?" He pulled out his desk chair and sat down.

Inkil could not stop staring. "Have you... that is... are you still immune to further curses?"

"I am not inclined to test that possibility."

"No, I would imagine not."

Kishin rolled his eyes. "You can stop staring now. Do what I pay you for. Tell me the news. I've been on the road for weeks."

"You've felt the earth shake, I assume?"

Kishin nodded.

"It seems to have started, or at least be centered on, the island of Zes Sivas. All of the Lords were gathered there some weeks ago, for the annual Passing."

"I was in Reman at that point."

Inkil nodded and tried to look away from Kishin's face. "Ah, something happened there. Both Lords Varion of Varioch and Sundinka of Mandiata were killed. Lord Sundinka's heirs blame the new Lord Volraag for it. One rumor claims that Volraag also stole Sundinka's power. I would have said that was impossible, but... seeing you here is making me re-evaluate what is impossible."

Kishin waved him on impatiently.

"If you were in Reman, perhaps you also heard their temple was destroyed?"

"I was there. And no, I did not do it."

"Interesting. I would like to know who did."

"I pay for you to give me information, not for me to give it out."

"Of course. As his first act as Lord, Volraag declared war on Rasna. There has been fighting along their border, but nothing of specificity as yet."

War with Rasna. What could Volraag be thinking? And what did it have to do with the scar-faced one, whose mother had lifted their curses? Kishin ground his teeth.

"Those are the most significant events. Beyond that, we have seen unusual activity in Kuktarma regarding—"

"Enough. What about here?"

"Here? I have no major news about Ch'olan. Things are, ah, normal."

"Lord Rajwir returned from Zes Sivas?"

"Yes, he and the Lady Ajaw."

Kishin leaned forward. "The Lady went, as well? Then she took the full complement of Holcan with her?"

"Yes, now that you mention it, but... two did not return. I believe they perished in the earthquake or the same incident that took the lives of the two Lords."

Kishin felt a coldness steal over him.

(((39)))

Talinir glanced up as Janaab approached. He congratulated himself on not getting lost in the stars while his companion had been away. A small victory, but significant.

"What do you have there?" he asked.

Janaab held up the bodies of two moderately-sized rodents. "A good dinner," he said. "Honestly, I'm surprised at how much life still exists here, with much of the land so dead. The tunaldi, for instance. They're huge! And they're not the largest creatures here. How do they survive?"

Talinir began pulling wood together for a fire. The Starlit Realm had no shortage of dead branches, at least. Water, on the other hand, would always be hard to find. "There are multiple answers to your questions," he said.

"I'd love to hear them."

"First, you can find life below the surface. That's where we find water, obviously. You have to dig. And sometimes, you find plant life in caves. Some older Eldanim have also told me that there is plant life aplenty here... but beyond the borders of Antises."

"But you've never traveled that far."

"I'm a warden. I have a duty to stay within a certain range."

"So why would the animals leave that and come here?"

Talinir took out his flint and struck sparks. "You know as well as I do."

"Pretend that I don't."

"All life here is different from life in your world. Each living thing draws sustenance, not just from food and drink, but from what you call magic."

"You have a different name for it?"

"There are many names for it," Talinir said, irritated. Janaab should know these things, if he had been here this long.

"Have you ever noticed that this world doesn't seem to have any birds?" Janaab said. "No, don't look up. But I've never seen one in all the time I've been here."

"It is... different." Talinir had wondered the same thing as a young man.

"So why do the animals usually stay away from Zes Sivas?" Janaab shifted the topic again. "It seems they would be flocking there, since it's such a strong source of magic."

"Zes Sivas both attracts and repels. Animals desire its magic, but it frightens them as well."

"Frightens how?"

"The sheer vastness of its power overwhelms them. Many are drawn there, but quickly leave. They can't handle it."

Janaab nodded. "I wonder if your people feel the same way about the mountains."

"We do not fear the mountains!"

"Then why don't you go there?"

"Some do!"

"And what have they told you about what's there?"

Talinir stopped and considered. He actually did not know of anyone who had been to the mountains. At least not recently. Or at the very least, no one had told him about it. Why was that?

Janaab smiled. "Oh, there is so much you don't know. And you need to, Talinir. You need to know."

"Why?" The question escaped his lips instinctively.

"Because it all matters. And you'll need to tell Marshal. And the girl. Before they fall."

Talinir wondered why Marshal and the girl would fall, but then he realized Janaab looked up when he said it. Looked up at...

He was lost again.

(((40)))

Dravid stretched the glowing magic as far as he could reach. A beam of golden light floated in the air in front of him like a levitating quarterstaff. He began adding more and more to it, seeing how large of a construct he could create. It felt good to manipulate the strange power.

But at the same time, the negative effects grew the more he created and the longer he let it exist. The tightness in his chest and heat within built up far too rapidly for his tastes. In fact, the heat and pressure behind his eyes grew especially painful this time. He needed to let the power go.

He pushed down within, but nothing happened. Wasn't that how he had released it before? He struggled to take a breath against the tightness. His lungs did not want to expand. He had to let the power go!

He focused and pushed back. Darkness began to gather on the edges of his vision. He couldn't breathe! At last, the edges of his construct began to dissolve. But it was taking too long!

He clapped his hands together. The construct exploded outward. Several shards cut through the curtains on either side of his room, while three of them pierced through the ceiling, letting tiny beams of sunlight in.

Dravid collapsed, gasping for air. The heat and tightness subsided, and he recovered himself in short order.

What if he hadn't been able to release it? He needed help, or someone could get hurt. Unfortunately, Dravid realized he knew only one person he could talk to about this power. When needing advice, he knew to seek out someone with knowledge, wisdom, and trust.

Forerunner had the first, might have some of the second, but none of the third. But no other options presented themselves, and Dravid needed to know something, anything. Even a clue would be helpful.

Forerunner immediately recognized the change in him. "What is this?" he asked as Dravid approached. He leaped to his feet, sleeves fluttering, and dismissed two of his white-robed women with a wave. He walked in a quick circle around Dravid, who turned awkwardly on his crutch to follow him.

"Remarkable. Totally unforeseen."

"I'm guessing you can tell what's going on with me, then," Dravid said.

"My dear boy, I can sense what is within you, and it is absolutely unprecedented. To my knowledge—and it is quite extensive—no human has ever absorbed any of the... any power like this."

"Power like what?"

"Like mine. Tell me, have you experimented with this?"

In response, Dravid repeated his experiment from back in his room. In a few moments, his hand began to glow.

"Delightful! Extraordinary." Forerunner actually clapped his hands. "But enough. Please, have a seat." He gestured, and Dravid sat as instructed. He closed his fist and stopped the glow.

"Is this permanent?"

"A very good question." Forerunner sat down across from him. "As you are the first with this... capability, I cannot answer that question for certain. However..." He hesitated and closed his eyes. "I do not sense a diminishing of the power since you used it. That may be instructive." He opened his eyes. "It's hard to tell, of course."

"Of course." Dravid felt ridiculous. Maybe this had been a stupid idea.

"When you all arrived, I understood Seri and her amazing capabilities immediately," Forerunner said. "I could see the cause both of her power, and her current lack thereof. You, on the other hand... I did not see anything special about you."

"I thought you were going to restore my great purpose in life," Dravid said, unable to keep the sarcasm from his voice.

Forerunner sat back and steepled his fingers in front of him. "Let us be open with each other, shall we? When you first arrived, I had full intentions of restoring either your leg or your purpose. After your ill-advised attempt to absorb my power, and your continual poisoning of Seri against me, I had decided to find a way to remove you from my sanctuary. In fact, I was just discussing that method with my friends when you entered. But now?"

Forerunner leaned forward. "This is truly amazing, Dravid. I renew my promise to you. You may choose what I restore."

"My leg or my purpose?"

"Glorious purpose. Especially now."

"And you want me to choose now?"

"No, not at all. But there will come a turning point, a place where you must make the decision once and for all."

"All right. But I need answers about what's happening to me. Tell me about this power."

Forerunner tapped his chin with his steepled fingers. "I will do all I can, under one condition."

"What is that?"

"That you stop trying to convince Seri to leave."

Twice now, Forerunner referenced Seri. He wanted her to stay. But why? She didn't even have her power right now. What made her so important to him?

"Do you intend any harm toward her?"

"Far from it," Forerunner said. "I want to help her. And you. And Ixchel, who resists me most of all."

Dravid considered for a moment. Learning how to use this power could be of vital importance, especially since it seemed to guard against Antises' current problems. Was it worth staying around Forerunner? He swore good intentions toward Seri, but…

"Have you told Seri about this yet?"

Dravid looked up. "I have not."

"And why not?"

Dravid didn't answer. He hadn't told Seri because he didn't trust Forerunner. Yet here he stood, telling him anyway. It didn't make a lot of sense.

"Sometimes, we don't tell those closest to us about things, because we want to protect them," Forerunner said for him. "Despite your misgivings about me, I feel the same way. I only want to help. To protect. And to restore. I am here for all the lost children of Antises."

And yet a few moments earlier, Forerunner willingly admitted to plotting to kick him out. His intentions still did not add up.

"Well, then. Shall we have an agreement, Dravid?" Forerunner stood and held out his hand.

Dravid hesitated for a moment, then held out his own hand.

Forerunner took it and pulled him up onto his foot. He wavered, but Forerunner grabbed his shoulder with his other hand. He found himself looking into those extraordinary, starry eyes.

"Together, Dravid. Together we will help you. And Seri. And all of Antises will be restored."

(((41)))

Marshal looked out over the battlefield from the edge of their camp. After a few moments, he sat on the ground, setting his sword beside him. He needed to think things through here.

For the longest time, his thoughts had been only darkness. When Nian died, it felt like something else died within him, changing him. The death of Aelia had been horrible, devastating. But it had been in the midst of so many other events: his curse being lifted, the Lord's power coming, fighting in the Otherworld. Nian's death came out of nowhere. So pointless.

Perhaps most important, Nian had been the last wise counselor left to him. Aelia dead. Talinir missing. Who could he turn to now?

For a time, he tried leaning on Victor. But Victor wanted to lean on him! Wanted him to be some great leader of men. He glanced up as Merish walked by with a silly grin on his face. Marshal snorted. The curse squad hardly seemed the place to begin great leadership.

No. Marshal had lived his whole life without aspirations. It was vain to imagine he could have them now, just because he no longer bore a curse. No.

And yet depending on his own counsel led him only to the edge of that ravine. In retrospect, he felt foolish over that. Killing himself would not solve anything. Where would his power have gone, anyway, since he had no children? To Volraag? But he already had power. Would it only make him stronger?

Stupid. He should have thought of that.

Victor saved him. The Bond was broken. And yet Victor was still here, sleeping in the tent after that ordeal. Victor, his friend. His true friend.

The dark side of his thoughts tried to warn him of Victor's death. Everyone else kept dying. Why not him? Marshal fought back against those thoughts.

Blessings. Nian's final word. How to fight curses? Blessings. Marshal possessed great power. Greater than he imagined, if Victor had relayed Aelia's words correctly. A King's power. Somehow he should be using that power to bless people, to help them instead of hurting them.

Nian also spoke of lifting all curses, an impossible task. Yet one he should be exploring, not sitting on a battlefield. He needed someone who could advise him, someone who understood magic.

His eyes wandered to Volraag's command tent. For a moment, he considered going to his half-brother and asking him to work together. But Volraag wanted him dead. Somehow, Marshal didn't think he would have abandoned that idea, even though he now held the Lordship.

The decanus from the next squad over, a man whose name Marshal had never bothered to learn, approached. Marshal waved in greeting, but did not get up.

"Word's come down," the decanus said. "We fight again this afternoon."

"That soon?"

He shrugged. "The centurion says his Lordship expects us to finish off the Rasnians this time. Then maybe we can all go home. In any case, have your squad ready."

Marshal agreed and the decanus left in a hurry. He never wanted to stay near the curse squad.

So. This is what it came down to. Another battle. Marshal's own muscles still ached from yesterday's exertions. He knew everyone else felt as bad or worse, Victor most of all.

"Enough of this."

He got to his feet and began to walk.

• • • • •

Volraag looked across his table at the spy. Such a pathetic man. He would never waste time with someone like this if he didn't need him. Such a worthless individual outside his nearness to his half-brother.

"Marshal. You're sure his name is Marshal?" Volraag hated repeating himself.

The spy nodded. "I've heard him called that by Victor any number of times."

"But he speaks."

"Why wouldn't he?"

Volraag rolled his eyes. "Because the man I'm looking for was cursed. He could not speak."

"Oh, he's cursed all right. I mean, look at him! He says he's not, but Victor says he got the scars from a curse-stalker! Why else would it come after him?"

Volraag looked to Otioch. "A curse-stalker."

"It would make sense, sire. And don't forget the scar-faced man at the temple."

"I haven't."

His brother's moves did not make much sense. Somewhere after that peasant village, he had encountered a curse-stalker and received the scars. Then he somehow eluded Kishin, one of the greatest assassins in Antises, came to Reman, of all places, and destroyed the temple when he gained his father's power. Then, after supposedly being freed from his curse, he... ended up a conscript in the army? Something did not add up.

"Pay the man and send him back," Volraag told Otioch. He glared at the spy. "And keep your mouth shut about this."

"Yes, your Lordship. They never pay attention to me, anyway."

Volraag left the command tent and strolled outside. Rathri slithered up beside him.

"Shall I bring you his head?"

"Not yet. There's something I don't understand here, if it is him. It doesn't make sense."

"What better place for him to hide?"

Volraag gestured as he spoke, playing with the vibratory power at his command. He did that more and more lately. It felt right. It felt good.

"No. We're not dealing with some schemer here. He's an uneducated peasant! We should not attribute brilliant plans to him."

"Never underestimate a target," Rathri said. "I always take that into consideration. And thus, I'm never surprised."

Volraag climbed up onto his viewing platform. "We should not overestimate, either. No. There is still something I'm missing. I need to think before I act."

He looked out over the army's camp and the battlefield. His spies told him the Rasnian forces were all but broken, held together only by the threats of their commanders now. One solid push should end this. The order had already gone out. But should he try to deal with this Marshal first? Was it really his half-brother?

Otioch climbed up beside them. "I've done as you said. The spy will go back to the curse squad and stay with them." He hesitated. "We've been putting the conscripts at the front lines so far. If you wish to keep this one alive, it might be best to hold them back this time."

"And risk our regular soldiers? No. Lord Tyrr might be desperate now. And desperate men do desperate things."

"If that's true, this could be a bloodbath." After a moment of silence, Otioch added, "Curious."

"What is?"

Otioch pointed. "It appears we have one man walking out onto the battlefield."

"What?"

Volraag leveled his spyglass and looked. "A conscript by his clothing, but he has some insignia on his shoulder. A decanus, probably."

Rathri sneered. "Military control at its finest."

"No…" Volraag continued to stare at the lone figure walking with slow, steady steps toward the center of the disputed land.

"Sire?"

The figure's face turned, looking straight at him. Scars.

"It's him. Marshal."

•••••

Simple, really. If another battle happened, many more would die. If the other decanus spoke true, and the Rasnians were broken, then many of them would die. Otherwise, many on both sides would die.

Either way, Marshal had enough of death.

He began summoning the power, letting it build up within him, filling his arms until his hands ached with the vibrations. He had not attempted using his powers this much since the temple and the battle in the Otherworld.

By now, he knew he had been noticed. If he didn't start, some centurion on a horse would be on top of him in short order, commanding him back. He didn't want to hurt even one of them unless necessary.

He turned and looked toward Volraag's tent and platform. What would his brother think? What would he do? Ultimately, it didn't matter. He made his choice. This battle would end. Now.

Marshal pulled his hands in to his chest, then pushed outwards. The ground erupted in front of him. Really, Lord Tyrr had given him the idea with his little wall and that trench. Time to create one of his own, of a sort.

The power flowed out. A deep channel began to form in front of him. Marshal spread his arms apart. He didn't want just a big hole. He wanted a trench, a ravine. And more than that. The channel expanded in both directions, tearing apart the ground, throwing cascades of dirt into the air. To his surprise, the dirt beneath the topsoil turned out to be red. He wondered if those back at the camp could even see him any more, with all the dust clouds he created.

Marshal laughed. He strained to use this much power, but even that seemed remarkably simple. He had expected this to be much harder. How much power did he have?

Deeper. Wider. He kept the power flowing. The barrier needed to be large enough to stop conscripts, regular army, cavalry, everything. Even a trench would not be enough. He began to push forward at the same time. The red earth piled itself high on the other side of his trench. Higher and higher.

He walked now, side to side, continuing to release his power. The trench grew deeper, the barrier higher. He could only guess at how much earth he moved. On the edges of the battlefield, he uprooted a handful of trees. That took more strain.

In fact, the strain was becoming serious now. His arms hurt. He had broken his finger bones the last time he unleashed this much power. But that had been in uncontrolled blasts. Here, he considered each motion carefully, expending what he needed for the job at hand.

At last, he let his arms fall to his sides. As the crimson dust began to settle, he surveyed his work.

A trench at least twenty feet deep ran in a jagged line across the battlefield. The Amnis River already flowed down into it, stirring up the mud and making it even more of a hazard. On the other side, he had piled the dirt, every bit of what he had dug into one long barrier that barred the way.

Marshal knew Volraag or Lord Tyrr could probably undo all of this work just as easily as he had done it. But it would serve, at least for now.

Victor appeared at his side. "Ahhh… let's get you out of here before they all come for you."

Marshal nodded. "I'm done with war."

(((42)))

The spyglass exploded in Volraag's hand. He didn't even glance at it. His chest tightened as fury rose within.

"That was impressive," Otioch said. He noticed the spyglass pieces falling to the platform. "I, uh, meant the display on the battlefield."

"Send as many troops as it takes," Volraag ordered. "Take him."

"I will give the order, but I suspect it will be difficult to enforce."

"Do it. I will come myself, as soon as Rathri here brings Tezan. We will put an end to this."

Both of his Guards hastened off the platform to obey.

Volraag ground his teeth. Marshal. Here all along. The reasons no longer mattered. Even the reasons for his current actions, impressive though they were. Volraag had not attempted anything on that scale. Surely, he had the capability now. Lord Tyrr had done something similar with the trench the soldiers discovered. Volraag knew his power equaled either of them. Didn't it?

A whisper of power fluttered to his left. He whirled, hand instinctively going to his sword hilt. Curasir stood beside him. His normal eye flicked to the hand on hilt, then back to Volraag's face.

"I think you'd find your power a slightly more effective defense," the Eldani said. "Though, if a sword is well-made, you can use it channel your power. Have you discovered that yet?"

Volraag ignored the question. "Why are you here? I need to go after my brother. He's here."

Curasir cocked his head. "Really? That's who did that? Fascinating."

"I don't have time for idle talk." Volraag started to the ladder.

"The way to the portal is open."

Curasir's words brought him to a halt. He turned back. "What are you saying?"

Curasir pointed out to the battlefield. "Your brother dug it up. You can reach the portal now."

"Where?" Volraag looked out toward Marshal's handiwork.

"Near the eastern end of that new trench. A short descent, and you can be there."

Volraag nodded. "Excellent. I will deal with my brother and then come."

"You may not have time for that."

"Why?"

Curasir pointed further south. "Lord Tyrr knows. Why do you think he's fought so hard here? Brought in the last of his wild magicians? He wants the portal. If you don't go now, he may bury the entrance, undoing your brother's work, or... more likely, he will attempt to sneak in himself and discover its secrets. Its power."

"But you promised it to me."

Curasir lifted his hands. "I told you I cannot stand against the power of a Lord. If he comes first, I may have no choice."

"If he comes, I'll deal with him."

Curasir smiled. "A battle of Lords. Beneath the ground. That would be something to see."

Volraag glanced down and saw Rathri approaching with Tezan.

"A battle may not be necessary."

"As you say." Curasir noted the approach of the other two. "Be careful of that assassin. His goals may not align with yours in the end."

"He does everything I ask of him." Volraag wasn't sure why he argued. He never trusted Rathri himself.

"Do not mistake obedience for loyalty. At any rate, I will see you when you open the portal."

"And how do I do that? You never told me."

"I'm sure it will be no trouble for you." Curasir took a step to the right and vanished.

Volraag wanted to break something. Everything happening at once, and out of his control. Not at all how he had foreseen this day progressing. Still, he would adapt. One could never anticipate everything. He took one more look in the direction he had last seen Marshal. Otioch would have to handle him, for now.

He vaulted over the railing of the platform and dropped to the ground, unleashing a short burst of power to slow his impact. Rathri nodded in approval at his landing.

"Shall we find the whelp?"

"No. We have a more important job."

• • • • •

Volraag led Rathri and Tezan toward the new trench. Around them, the after-effects of Marshal's power continued: slight tremors in the ground, red dust clouds sometimes whipped up into small whirlwinds. Nature itself seemed angry at the abuse it had suffered.

Abuse seemed a good word for it. Volraag had taken a look at Lord Tyrr's trench, before the earthquake collapsed much of it. Tyrr carved it with care and precision, for its intended purpose. Marshal, however, tore the ground apart with reckless abandon.

"A magical temper tantrum," Volraag said under his breath. He coughed and pulled his tunic up over his mouth and nostrils to keep out some of the dust.

"Who did all this?" Tezan asked. The other two ignored him.

They reached the edge of the trench and looked down. Everything about the new gorge looked rough and unnatural. Rocks, roots, and odd shaped combinations of brown and red dirt formed an endless variety of protrusions, holes, and a generally uneven landscape.

Volraag surveyed it all. "There." He pointed. Nearly hidden in a lower portion of the trench, he spotted an opening larger than most. A cave. He started down over the edge.

Rathri took his arm. "Wait. Look over there."

Volraag looked. The Amnis had been trickling into the new gorge since Marshal finished. Where Rathri pointed, the water pooled up, encountering a significant barrier in the uneven surface. Given enough time, the water pressure would break down the barrier and send a significant mudslide cascading down the ravine... and into the cave entrance.

"We'll just have to hurry," Volraag said. He resumed his descent.

"Seriously?" Tezan said. "This is insane, even for you." Rathri gave him a shove and he started to follow.

In his youth, Volraag roamed the hills surrounding Reman for miles in every direction. Much to his guardians' worry, he descended into a number of caves. Some had been huge disappointments, reaching only a few dozen yards beneath the surface. But twice he found caverns much larger and more extensive. As he continued the difficult climb down, he kept an eye on this cave entrance. Something about it seemed different from the others he had explored. It looked too symmetrical, too even.

Tezan slipped and slid almost past him. Volraag stopped him, but the impact almost knocked him off the side of the gorge. He channeled a small burst of power behind to push himself back against the wall. More dirt crumbled around him, sliding down into the trench. If he weren't careful, he could create a substantial landslide.

Near the bottom, Volraag jumped the final few feet. His feet landed in soft red dirt and sank. He shook his way free and took a few steps toward the cave. While they were at the top, he heard constant shouts from both sides's armies as commanders sought to determine new courses of action, and soldiers demanded explanations. Here at the base of the gorge, those shouts could no longer be heard. The silence added to the unnatural feel of everything.

Tezan stumbled beside him. "I assume we have a reason for this."

Volraag pointed into the cave. "As always, Tezan, it's about power. Finding it and taking control of it."

"In there?"

In answer, Volraag resumed his route to the cave entrance. He shoved a root out of his way, only to have it swing back. He stepped over it instead.

Shattered pieces of rock lay all about the cave entrance, torn apart by Marshal's power. He hadn't just happened to uncover the exact entrance to the cave, but actually blasted part of it into piles of debris. That made this last bit the most difficult to traverse.

"Ahh!" Tezan pulled a hand back, blood trickling from a cut across his palm. The shards were sharp in places.

Nothing would stop him now. Volraag ignored several cuts the rocks gave him and continued. At last, he stood in the cave entrance.

As he surmised, the symmetrical shape of the cave was not natural. Someone had carved it. He could see tool marks in the walls. Had they cut the entire thing out of solid rock by hand? Or was magic involved? He suspected the latter.

Tezan and Rathri joined him. Together, they looked down. The cave formed a tunnel about ten feet wide and tall, stretching down at a slight angle and curving to the right. Wherever it led could not be seen from here.

"I don't suppose you can generate light with your magic?" Tezan asked. Volraag shook his head. As far as he knew, he could only vibrate things.

Tezan sighed, glanced up at the walls, then snapped his fingers. A glowing orb of pale light appeared in his palm.

Volraag admitted surprise. "I didn't think you had any power left."

"Not enough for anything significant, or you wouldn't have been able to keep me caged this long. But light? That I can do. And now I'm curious. I want to see what's down here now."

Rathri put his crudely-wrapped hands against the wall of the tunnel. "We are near," he said. "Magic flows through these walls. Can you feel it?"

Now that he mentioned it, Volraag could feel something, a disturbance in the air. He reached out and brushed the tips of his fingers against the wall. Rathri was right. He felt movement within the rock, as if something flowed just beyond it. Flowed up. Out of the cave. Which meant it came from below. He began walking.

Tezan's light orb provided just enough guidance, not that they needed much. Once past the ruin Marshal had made of the entrance, the tunnel floor became smooth and clear of obstacles, almost like an underground hallway. And hallways led to doors.

"They used to call these spots high places," Tezan said. His voice breaking the silence almost made Volraag jump. "Who came down this tunnel and decided to proclaim it 'high'?"

"How do you know these things?" Volraag asked.

"I worked with Lord Tyrr, studying all things related to magic. You know he wanted this place."

"What else do you know?"

Tezan shrugged. "Myths and legends. All I know for certain is that wild magic proliferates near here." After a moment's silence, he added, "My home was only ten miles from here."

Volraag listened, but kept his focus on what he could see and feel. The tunnel had not changed in the slightest. The walls looked exactly the same as they had upon first entering. But even as he thought it, he realized the tunnel was growing wider, taller. The air grew cool once they left the sun behind.

"Something ahead," Rathri said.

How could eyes in that corrupted body see things better than he could? Volraag saw it one moment later. As they drew nearer and Tezan's light orb expanded its glow, more and more became visible.

The tunnel ended in what Volraag could only think of as some kind of round door. Its size surprised him. Without being asked, Tezan increased the power of his orb so they could see the entire thing. The door stretched up to the height of three men, with equal width.

Volraag put a hand on the door's surface. It appeared to be made of... iron? No. Steel. What manner of forge could have produced something of this size and intricacy?

The door bulged outward from the rock, creating a rounded surface, like the outer edge of an enormous ball. Deep into its surface Volraag saw detailed carvings, inscriptions of some kind. He saw text in places, formed of letters he could not read. Other areas contained drawings of some kind, but drawings of such detail he could not imagine how they could be carved into a steel surface.

He stepped further back to try to understand the drawings. In the exact center of the door he saw three overlapping circles. Inside each circle stood three figures. The central circle's figures were tall with odd proportions that did not look right.

"Eldanim," he whispered.

The other two circles held more human-proportioned figures. But the figures on the left seemed larger and more powerful than the ones on the right. Circling around all three groups cascaded a wide variety of animals, many he knew but some he did not recognize. The creature at the very top looked like a winged lizard or...

"What do you suppose it all means?" Tezan said. His voice echoed against the stillness of the tunnel.

Rathri went to the edge of the door, where it met the rock. He scraped at it with a sword tip. "I see no way through this," he said. "Perhaps you could break it?"

"He said only the power of a Lord could open the portal," Volraag said, "but I don't think that meant to destroy it."

"Who said?"

Volraag ran his hands along the steel surface again, amazed at the smoothness. "The Eldanim."

"You've spoken with the Eldanim?" Tezan asked.

Volraag pressed against the steel and released a short burst of power. Nothing happened. The door absorbed the vibrations without any shaking itself. Ordinary steel would not do that. Could that be how it worked? Just channel enough power into the door itself? It seemed a dangerous idea. There must be something else.

"Keep looking," he said.

The three of them spread out and examined the door from all angles. Volraag grew restless. Why didn't Curasir show up and just tell him what to do? They were wasting time.

"Here," the assassin's voice rasped. He pointed to a section of the door near the center.

Volraag approached and examined the area Rathri indicated. Right at eye level, he saw two slots in the door's surface. He slid his hand up inside one of them and found grooves matching his fingers. He repeated the action with the other hand.

"This must be it!" Tezan even sounded excited.

Volraag concentrated. He released a small burst of magic through both hands again. This time, he received an answer in the form of a distant rumble. Tezan and Rathri both took a few steps back.

Volraag took a deep breath and channeled more power, then even more. As he did, the door itself began to shake. Dust and tiny pieces of rock rained down around the door's edges. To his surprise, the door began to move backward, pulling him with it. He yanked his hands out of the slots.

The door continued to recede. Around the edges, the parts furthest back, something else began to appear. At first, Volraag thought it looked like water, but it did not flow down or behave like water in any other way. The door slid back and back, revealing more and more of the watery substance. It shimmered, reflecting Tezan's light orb. The entire process took at least ten minutes. At last, the central inscription with the connected rings and figures vanished within. Nothing remained of the door. Instead, they stared at a massive circle of the unknown.

"The gateway to the Otherworld," Rathri said. Volraag could sense awe even in the assassin's abrasive voice. Or was it desire?

A crackle echoed in the chamber. Light glimmered briefly, light not from the orb. Volraag stepped further back to get a better look. Another crackle. Multi-colored light danced around a spot toward the top right of the circle. Then another appeared near the bottom left. Each burst of light exploded with a crackling sound. The watery substance turned dark, no longer reflecting any of the light. The multi-colored crackles expanded, becoming more rapid and larger, spreading over the entire outer edge.

A blast of cool air, colder than the tunnel's chill, gusted out from the circle. Volraag's hair swept backward and he blinked against the force of it.

The darkness of the circle swirled with the multi-colored lights and became translucent. Volraag could make out figures moving around beyond it, human-shaped but ridiculously tall. He knew now that he stared into another world, though he could see nothing distinct.

Rathri stepped toward the portal, as if he wanted to enter it. He probably did. "Don't touch it!" Volraag ordered.

Rathri stretched out his hand in defiance. "We didn't come down here just to look at it!"

One of the moving figures on the other side approached the portal, then stepped through. As he did, he seemed to shrink in size, appearing almost human as he came across into this world. Curasir.

"I knew you could do it, son of Varion. Well done!"

Rathri whipped out one of his short blades, but backed away from the Eldani. Tezan only stared.

"Does this lead to your world, then?" Volraag gestured at the portal.

"It leads to the Starlit Realm, a world like and unlike your own," Curasir said.

Rathri took another step toward it. Curasir put out a hand. "The Starlit Realm is not for you, assassin."

"You do not command me, Eldani."

"In this case, I do. And if you do not listen to me, you will face them." He waved to the portal and two more figures emerged, dragging something behind them.

Volraag took a step back. In form, the figures appeared similar to Curasir, though taller. Each looked to be at least eight feet. Their skin, on the other hand, looked like nothing he had ever seen. Black, but not black. As if their skin absorbed all color. Dark energy crackled around them, creating a menacing glow around their exposed skin. Through it, Volraag saw only shades of gray, the color removed from everything they eclipsed.

Each held a curved sword in one hand, and dragged their burden with the other. They wore dark armor in composite pieces across their bodies, including tall helmets that served to exaggerate their height even more.

"Am I supposed to be impressed?" Rathri asked.

Tezan stepped up next to Volraag. "Look down!" he whispered. Volraag glanced down and saw a trickle of water passing between his feet.

One of the dark Eldanim pointed his sword at Rathri. "I have killed more than you've ever dreamed of, human," he said.

Rathri stepped toward him, drawing his second blade. "You know noth—"

"Rathri! Stand down!" Volraag said.

"Fourteen more of the Durunim wait on the other side of the portal," Curasir said. "If you are truly determined, you can try your blades against them. I do not think it will end well for you."

Rathri stood still for a long moment, then sheathed his blades and stepped back. But he held a stiffness to his posture Volraag had never seen in him. Anger? Disappointment?

Volraag spared the trickle of water another glance, then turned to Curasir. "You promised me power."

"I did. And here it is."

The Durunim pulled their burden forward and deposited it at Volraag's feet. He looked down at another Eldani, not dissimilar from Curasir, bound and gagged. "What is this?"

"As you humans are fond of saying, we Eldanim are creatures of magic. Have your pet wild mage absorb this one's magic and give it to you."

"Can this be done, Tezan?"

"I, I don't know. I've never…"

"It can be done," Curasir said. "I am certain."

"But… if the magic is part of your being," Tezan said, "then what will happen to him if I take it?"

Curasir shrugged. "He will die. Or not. I'm not entirely sure."

"No." Tezan backed away. "You're the killers. Not me. This is too far, Volraag."

"I told you my goals, Tezan. You understood them."

"Not like this. You don't even need this."

Volraag's mind raced with the possibilities. Already, he wielded the power of a Lord. But Eldanim magic was different. If he possessed it, it would give him another advantage over the other Lords, maybe enough to give him what he needed to defeat them.

"Rathri."

The assassin's blade appeared next to Tezan's neck. "Do as you're told, mage."

"I will not. You'll have to kill me."

Rathri pressed the blade a little harder.

"Wait."

Curasir stepped up and placed a hand on Tezan's shoulder. "Let me help you begin," he said. "Once it starts, I don't think you'll stop."

"What? No, I don't want…"

Curasir took Tezan's hand and held it out. He made another small gesture and the bound Eldani shivered. Tezan gasped.

"What is it?" Volraag said. His own anticipation escalated.

"I… didn't know…" Tezan said.

"Intoxicating, isn't it?"

Tezan's breath shuddered.

"Give it to me!" Volraag demanded.

Tezan stretched out his other hand toward Volraag. He clenched his fist, then opened it.

A burst of power exploded within Volraag, unlike his existing power. It began in his chest, a feeling of strength, of invincibility. As Tezan continued, it spread outward throughout his body. A warm glow invigorated him. He held up his arm and looked at his skin, surprised to see it wasn't glowing. Strangely, he tasted salt and found he craved something sweet in response.

Tezan threw his head back as Curasir stepped away. Even as the pleasure of the power continued to spread through him, Volraag wondered at that. Did it feel the same for him? Or better somehow?

His vision shifted. Everything seemed slightly off-kilter, the light not hitting things quite right. For a moment, he saw the other side of the portal, the Durunim lined up and waiting, as Curasir had mentioned. And behind them, in the sky: stars. Amazing stars. He barely had time to register that before his vision snapped back to normal.

Tezan dropped his arms and sagged. He stumbled back a few steps and sat down hard. Still, his face held a smile, a look of ecstasy.

Volraag looked down at the Eldani whose power he now possessed. He lay still, both eyes staring without life. Both eyes. It took him a moment to register why that was wrong. One of them should be black. It took him a moment longer to notice that the body lay in a puddle of water.

"What was his name?"

Curasir looked up. "Ruitel. Why do you ask?"

"I like to know the names of those who have given their lives in my cause."

At that precise moment, a blast of magical power struck Volraag from behind.

(((43)))

Victor didn't see anyone rushing toward them at the moment, but that could change. Marshal moved quickly enough, even with a slight limp, but it couldn't last. He had expended immense magic power, and that never ended well. He might collapse at any second. They needed to move fast.

They both had their weapons, and Victor had the Ranir Stone. Anything else… they could survive without. No time to go visit their tent.

The dust clouds gave them some cover until they reached the trees. But even here, they remained in danger. The trees weren't dense enough to hide them.

"Keep moving," Victor said. "Our only chance is distance."

They were running away from the army. Running away from Victor's dreams. Except the dreams hadn't quite worked out the way he thought they would. He could fight far better than he ever expected… but he worried about what it did to him.

"I could move faster if my ankle hadn't been torn ragged by your flail," Marshal said between gasps for air.

"I'm not apologizing for that."

"You don't need to."

Pounding hooves approached from the right. Victor swept out his sword and turned to face the approaching centurion. He reined to a halt and looked down at them.

"Conscript, I think you had better put that sword away," he said.

"We're not going back," Marshal said.

"Desertion can be punishable by death."

"You saw what I just did to the battlefield, didn't you? Do you need

196

another demonstration?" Marshal waved his hand over the ground and a tremor ran through it. The horse snorted and pawed at the earth.

The centurion stared. "You did all that? What are you?"

"You should get out of his way. That's all you need to know," Victor said. He sheathed his sword. He inclined his head to Marshal and they both began walking again.

"I... I'll have to report this," the centurion said.

"You do that."

Marshal stumbled a little and Victor caught his arm. "I was worried about that. Are you all right?"

"I'll manage."

They kept moving for a while, leaving the camp behind. Once they were far enough out, Victor tried to turn north. He couldn't be completely sure he had it right, but at this point any direction would do.

"I need to rest," Marshal said after another couple of minutes. He stumbled and sat down at the foot of a large pine.

"Sure." Despite his concerns, Victor appreciated the break himself. He hadn't gotten enough rest after yesterday's exertions. And the gash on his side had begun to bleed again.

"They're coming," Marshal said. A moment later, Victor also heard the hoofbeats again. More than one this time.

"Can you take them?"

"I don't know."

Since it would be futile to run, they waited. A few moments later, their pursuers arrived. A dozen Remavian Guards, led by Lord Volraag's right-hand man, Otioch. Victor recognized him from a few nights earlier. The horsemen encircled them. Several leveled spears, while the others held bows at ready. Otioch dismounted and approached.

"Lord Volraag requires your presence," he said, looking at Marshal.

"And I require that you leave me alone."

Otioch spread his hands. "You are powerful. No one here questions that. But Lord Volraag himself will be here shortly."

"I do not fear him."

"Listen... you did... that..." Otioch waved back toward the battlefield. "To stop the fighting, yes?"

Marshal nodded.

"So now you'll start another fight here?"

"It won't be much of a fight," Victor said. "Just let us go."

"I have no desire to hurt you or your men," Marshal said. "But I will not wait for your Lord, either."

"You'll come with us, or..."

"Or what? You can't hurt me."

Otioch whipped out his sword and aimed it at Victor. "But I can hurt him. Archers!"

Victor found himself looking up at four or five arrows aimed at him. He looked to Marshal. "Don't worry about me."

Marshal looked unsure for the first time this morning.

"What will it be?" Otioch asked. "Will you come with us to Lord Volraag now or shall we wait for him here?"

A swish-thunk sounded and Victor winced, expecting one of the archers had loosed early. Instead, he saw a thin spear quivering in the ground between himself and Otioch.

"How about you let the heroes go?" a voice called. Victor smiled. He knew that accent. Topleb.

Otioch turned, as did half of the Remavian Guard horsemen. A couple dozen yards away stood the curse squad, along with around a hundred other conscripts.

"Return to camp at once!" Otioch commanded.

"I don't think we will," said Topleb.

"This is ridiculous! I could have you all executed!"

"But you won't," said the decanus whose name they had never learned. "Let it go, Commander. Let these men go."

Otioch's face grew red and his sword-arm shook. "Idiots! Even a hundred conscripts cannot stand against a dozen of the Remavian Guard!"

Topleb chuckled at that. "How about a hundred conscripts, plus the Hero of Varioch and the Scarred Magician?" He gestured with his atlatl.

Otioch looked back. Victor let his flail hang loose and drew his sword. Marshal stood up next to him and held his arms out to his sides, palms upward.

"You can't win, Commander," Marshal said.

"Once Lord Volraag arrives, this will all be pointless!"

At the mention of Volraag, the conscripts murmured and several began to back off.

"Yes, see? Your Lord is coming. You cannot stand against his power! No one can!"

At that moment, a massive rumble sounded somewhere behind

them, back toward the battlefield.

"I think your Lordship found something else to occupy him," Marshal said.

All eyes looked back and saw a cloud of red dust rolling toward them. "Devouring fire!" Otioch snarled. He swung up into his saddle and waved at the rest of the Guards. They obediently followed him as he charged back into the dust.

Victor let out his breath, then immediately sucked in another one and closed his eyes. The dust cloud struck them.

• • • • •

When the dust cleared, the conscripts gathered around Marshal and Victor. To a man, they expressed gratitude for their actions.

"Theon bless you, sir."

"You ended the war all on your own!"

"If it weren't for you, we'd be fighting and dying even now, for certain!"

Marshal lifted his hands until they finally hushed.

"I'm just trying to help," Marshal said, loud enough for all to hear. "I'm sorry that I didn't act sooner. If I had, maybe more would be alive now."

The crowd started to protest, but he lifted his hands again. "Listen, the Commander wasn't wrong. Once Volraag finishes with whatever he's doing now, he's probably coming after me. You should all go now."

"We'll stay with you!" someone shouted, followed by echoes of agreement.

Marshal shook his head. "No, no. We'll do better in small groups, all of us. Go home. You're not obligated to fight any more." He took hold of the insignia on his shoulder and tore it off. "We're not part of Volraag's army any more!" He tossed the insignia to the ground.

After a few more arguments countered by encouraging words from Marshal and Victor, the crowd finally agreed. One by one and in small groups, the conscripts split off in every direction. At last, Marshal and Victor were left alone with only the five remaining members of the curse squad: Topleb, Gnaeus, Merish, Wolf, and Rufus.

"You should go too," Marshal said.

"Where we gonna go?" Gnaeus said. "I think we're better off with you."

"Wherever I go, there will be danger," Marshal said. "I can't take you."

Topleb snorted. "Danger? Your whole land is danger. I want to go home, but I figure I'm safer with you two. Full of k'uh you are."

Marshal considered him for a moment. "Then we'll take you home," he said.

"We will?" Victor said.

"Isn't the next closest magic site in Ch'olan? I don't think we'll get close to this one again."

"Ha!" Topleb laughed. "I will take you there! Let you all see what real civilization looks like."

"What about the rest of you?" Marshal asked, looking at them.

"I think we're coming with you," Rufus said, glancing at the others around him. "Gnaeus is right. We're better off that way."

"Most of us don't have anywhere else to go," Gnaeus said.

"All right then." Marshal took a deep breath, bowed his head a moment, then looked back up. "I haven't been a good leader to you all. I was lost. I didn't know what I was doing."

"I've had worse," Topleb said.

"But now… we're away from the war. We can get back to what I should be doing, what I'm destined to do."

"What's that?"

"We're going to lift all the curses."

As the squad erupted with questions, Victor took a step back and watched. He couldn't remove the smile from his face. Now things could get moving again. They had a mission, a purpose. And finally, a leader.

(((44)))

Volraag felt the air move just before the blast of power struck him. In that split second, he tried to throw up his own power in defense. Whether it helped or not, he wasn't sure. The blast lifted him off his feet and threw him at the portal.

One of the Durunim snatched him out of mid-air and brought him back to the ground. To his surprise, Volraag still felt the invigoration of his new power. He looked down the tunnel and found he could see much further in the dark than he expected.

Lord Tyrr stood around a hundred feet away, flanked by two strangers. He looked no different from when Volraag met him on Zes Sivas, though he had traded his diplomatic clothes for armor and a warrior's cape. The strangers, one male and one female, wore gray clothing that told nothing of their status.

"This is foolish, Lord Tyrr!" Volraag called. "I expected better of you." He glanced around. Tezan stared at his former master, still holding up his light orb. Rathri had vanished into the shadows.

"It's time for a reckoning, boy!" Rasna's Lord bellowed. "You have cost me dearly."

"This is your battle," Curasir said. "I hope to see you at the next portal."

"What? Curasir!" But he and the two Durunim retreated through the portal, leaving only the body of Ruitel behind.

Volraag lunged to grab at him, but as his hand struck the portal, it turned dark again and returned to its original watery appearance. His hand bounced off solid rock.

"Diabol take you!" Volraag whirled back to see that Lord Tyrr and his companions had advanced another dozen feet. "Devouring fire and hailstones!" He unleashed a blast of his own at the trio.

The two strangers beside Tyrr waved their arms in opposite directions. Though he couldn't see it, Volraag knew they had diverted his blast. The tunnel walls shook with the impact. Wild magicians. Still more of them. How had Tyrr found so many? Varion should have been doing the same over the past few years. Volraag should have been doing it, for that matter!

"Tezan!" Lord Tyrr exclaimed. "So wonderful to see you again!" He pointed at the man he had set up as king.

"Get down!" Volraag shouted. He rushed toward Tezan and tried to throw up more of his own power to deflect Tyrr's. He succeeded, but the clashing power knocked Tezan off his feet and against the wall. He struck hard and slid to the floor, unconscious. His light orb went out, plunging the tunnel into darkness.

Something changed within Volraag. His insides churned. The salty taste in his mouth grew. Part of him knew the Eldanim power now within him interacted somehow with his own power. But he had no time to consider it.

He retaliated at Lord Tyrr and the wild mages deflected it again. Tyrr laughed. "You're outmatched, boy! Trying to wield power not even your own! Your death comes soon."

Volraag didn't answer. He felt the power growing inside him, building up like the very first time he tasted it. Regardless of what Lord Tyrr did or didn't do, in a few moments, he knew he would unleash more power than ever. He had no choice.

And then Rathri struck. The assassin launched himself out of the darkness and landed beside the female wild mage. His blade punctured straight through her neck, then tore out the front. Before her body fell, Rathri ducked and rolled past Lord Tyrr. As he came to his feet, he stabbed the other mage up through his chest.

Lord Tyrr roared with inarticulate rage, releasing his power in all directions. Rathri had nowhere to dodge. The blast threw him against the tunnel's roof and slammed him against it four or five times before letting him fall. The assassin hit the ground and did not move.

The power within Volraag reached a point of no return. He knew he had to choose: strike directly at Lord Tyrr, killing Rathri (if he still lived) and collapsing the entire tunnel, or…

Volraag fell to his knees and threw his arms up. Power unimaginable erupted out of him. It smashed its way through the ceiling and kept going, straight up, spreading out. Volraag began to scream as the power continued to pour out of him, pulverizing stone and dirt, shoving everything up, up, up and out. Sunlight shot back at him, through the dust that remained, clouding the new upward passage at least a dozen feet in diameter.

Volraag suspected both armies would be thrown into even more chaos now. First Marshal built a wall and a ditch, now the earth erupted somewhere in the middle of it all. Lords waged war and the common soldiers paid the price if they were not careful.

"What was the point of that?" Lord Tyrr asked.

"Just creating another exit," Volraag said. "I'll need another way out."

"You really think you can beat me alone?"

Volraag listened for the rumbles he knew would follow. There.

"I don't need to. You'll be busy enough."

Lord Tyrr turned in time to see a wall of water coming at him. Volraag's blast shook everything enough to break apart the fragile dam that had formed in the gorge above. The trapped waters of the Amnis flooded down the tunnel.

Volraag lifted Tezan onto his shoulder and blasted power downward, launching himself up the new passage. He slammed into the side of it and used more power to ricochet himself and his burden off that point and to a higher one. Two more of those rough impacts and he threw himself out into the open air in the middle of the former battlefield.

Lord Tyrr's roars of fury echoed below.

(((45)))

"Tell me about the Durunim."

Talinir blinked in surprise. Janaab had brought up many topics of conversation throughout their Otherworld travels. He had especially been interested in Talinir's stories of his travels with Marshal and Aelia. But this was a new one.

"I would think you would know all about that by now."

"Tell me anyway. Everything I know comes mostly from my own deductions."

Arriving at the mountains' foothills slowed their travel. The ground became even more uneven as they ascended.

"Their existence is why my present condition is so threatening," Talinir said. "I risk becoming one of them."

"How, exactly?"

"The exact reasons and process are unknown, but it comes from spending too much time here."

"Yet you bring your entire city here."

"It's not the same." Talinir struggled to find the right words. "We Eldanim exist in both worlds. We see them both with our eyes, every minute of every day. Normally, when we walk in one world, we also partially exist in the other. We forge our warpsteel blades to pierce through both worlds as well."

"But that's not you right now."

"Exactly. Marshal pulled my entire essence through a portal. But some Eldanim have done this on purpose, choosing only to walk in the Starlit Realm, forsaking the primary world."

"And they are the Durunim?"

"They become the Durunim," Talinir clarified. "Our bodies are not made to stay within only one world. Too much time here and we begin to change. It is some kind of interaction between the magic of our bodies and the magic of this world."

Janaab pushed aside his tattered sleeve and pointed to the dark splotches on his own skin. "Like this."

Talinir nodded. "I would not have thought it could happen to a human, but here you are."

"Can you do the same in my world? Bring yourself completely into it?"

"Yes, but it is not a pleasant experience. We call it 'unfolding.' We take our entire bodies, as you see us here, and bring it into the primary world. It does not feel right at all. It is difficult to move. The only reason one would do it is to intimidate humans, I suppose."

"So… you seem to be at war with these Durunim. Does the process change them in other ways, then? Does it make them evil or something?"

"I do not know if I would say 'evil.' But it does change them in their minds. They become… more violent. Driven by darker desires. The person they once were ceases to exist."

"Do you know that for sure, or is that just what you tell yourself?"

"What do you mean?"

"Have you studied them? Tried to turn them back?"

"Of course we have! Do you think we would give up on our own people that easily?"

"I don't know. That's why I ask."

"They attacked Intal Eldanir," Talinir said. "They killed over a dozen innocents before we even realized what was happening."

"Yet they don't all seem exactly the same. That Curasir, for example, is very different."

Talinir didn't answer. The problem of Curasir had bothered him greatly since their meeting. He had been able to appear as a normal Eldani, without the Durunim's skin distinction. And then he had shifted into the darkness. How? It made no sense, and contradicted everything he thought he knew about his enemy.

"Let me state some obvious things, then," Janaab said. He stopped walking and held up two fingers. "There are two worlds."

"Yes. And the world beyond."

"The afterlife."

"Correct."

"Yeah, let's save that one for another discussion. Two worlds."

Talinir chuckled and nodded.

Janaab pointed to one finger. "Humans live in this world." He pointed to the space between the two fingers. "And Eldanim live between the worlds. Or in both. Sort of."

He pointed to the second finger. "And this world..."

Talinir frowned. "What are you saying?"

"Let us assume that everything was created by Theon in the beginning, as the Law says. Your beliefs are not far from that, correct?"

"It's... more complicated than that, but go on."

"Then humans were created for the primary world. Eldanim were created to bridge the gap between worlds. Who was created for this world?"

"No one. Why should there be?"

"Doesn't it make sense?"

"It's a flawed premise. Just because a world exists doesn't mean a people also exist for it." Talinir gestured at the stars, making sure not to look up at them. "Our wisest ones say there are other worlds out there. By your argument, a new race must exist for each one of them."

Janaab shrugged. "Maybe they do. It just seems odd to me."

Talinir tried not to give Janaab's theory any further consideration, but it weighed on him. During his training to become a warden, one of the eldest of their order once told him about a group of strangers who wandered the Starlit Realm. "Not us, not them," he said. Talinir had been fascinated by the idea, but the other wardens dismissed it as the imagination of an elderly mind.

Now he wasn't so sure.

(((46)))

Seri frowned. "He didn't want to come?"

"I was unable to find him. One of the women told me he was... busy." Ixchel didn't seem pleased in sharing the words.

"Busy." How could Dravid be busy? They literally had nothing to do here. "So he wasn't in his room?"

"I looked. They did not want me to, but I looked anyway. He was not there."

Seri ran her hands through her hair. After everything that happened with the earthquake yesterday, she would have thought Dravid would be more determined than ever to convince her to leave. She almost wanted him to. But where had he gone?

She hopped to her feet. "Come on. We'll find him together."

Ixchel didn't move. "Do we have to speak with Forerunner again?"

"Possibly. He's the one most likely to know where Dravid is."

Ixchel sighed and followed Seri.

They could search the entire sanctuary in a short time. Dravid wasn't in his room or anywhere else in the men's quarters. The women's quarters were not an option. That left only Forerunner's pavilion and the outdoors. Ixchel insisted on doing a sweep of the road before returning to the pavilion.

Inside, they found repairs still underway from the earthquake. No one had seen Dravid, but one of the workers thought he had seen Forerunner pass through the western doors.

Seri and Ixchel exited and found a familiar path. "The clearing in the grove?" Seri suggested. Ixchel nodded.

Sure enough, they found Forerunner sitting on the edge of the clearing. He glanced up as they approached, smiled, and pointed. Seri looked and her mouth fell open.

Dravid stood in the center of the clearing. Face red, he leaned on his crutch with one hand and held the other out as if grasping at the air. Beside him, Lucia stood, balancing on top of a disk of light that floated a foot off the ground. She appeared delighted.

"Dravid?"

He looked up, saw Seri and gasped. The disk of light dissolved and Lucia fell. She tumbled against Dravid, and both of them collapsed to the ground.

Lucia giggled, brushing her long blonde hair back as she rolled off Dravid. "That was fun!"

"Concentration!" Forerunner called. "You know this, Dravid."

Dravid scrambled up into a sitting position. "Seri! I, uh, need to tell you something."

"I guess you do." She put her hands on her hips and shook her head. "What are you doing?"

Lucia helped Dravid get up on his crutch. "He's been chosen to receive power!" she said in a far-too-cheery voice.

"Chosen?"

"No, no. Lucia, let me explain it." He turned back to Seri. "I didn't want to tell you yet, but, uh, something has happened to me."

"And what would that be?"

Dravid's face drew in, concentrating. He gestured in the air with a glowing hand. Using some kind of golden light, he formed a ball. He grabbed it and tossed it to Seri. She caught it and looked it over. Somewhat lopsided, it appeared to be formed of the same substance Forerunner used to protect them during the quake.

She looked back at Dravid. "How?"

He took a breath. "I'm not entirely sure, but—"

"He absorbed some of my power," Forerunner interrupted. He walked up beside the group. "And now it is his to wield. It really is quite remarkable, Seri. I would not have been surprised if you did it, of course, given your... well, anyway, I am instead very surprised."

"Given her what?" Lucia asked.

"Ah, our Seri is very special," Forerunner said. He patted Seri on the shoulder. "Once she is restored, she will be amazing."

Dravid's face grew red again, though from embarrassment or something else, Seri couldn't tell. He gasped and the golden ball in Seri's hands dissolved. "Sorry. Using the power has some side effects, and I've been pushing myself a lot today."

"This is... crazy. You gained this, this new power, and you didn't even tell me? You told... him?"

"Also me," Lucia chimed in.

"Because we needed an assistant," Dravid said quickly. "It's not... I didn't..."

"Didn't what?"

"I was going to show you once I learned more about how to use it."

"Why? I thought we were friends. Why would..."

"Because of him!" Ixchel interrupted, pointing at Forerunner. "He confuses all of us! He clouds our thoughts and motivations with every word he speaks. You've both said he uses magic in his voice. Have you forgotten?"

Seri had forgotten. She had gotten so used to Forerunner's voice, the magic content had slipped her mind. And why did Lucia still have her hands on Dravid?

"I've been confused," Dravid said. "Maybe. I don't know."

"Oh, now that's interesting!" Forerunner's exclamation drew everyone's attention. He had moved away from the conversation and now stood facing south.

Lucia let go of Dravid and moved next to him. "What is it, Forerunner?"

He ignored her and tilted his head, as if listening. "Well. Who would have thought?"

"No one here," Dravid said. "What are you talking about?"

Forerunner lifted his head and smiled at them. "Something has come to my attention," he said. "I will call everyone together shortly. Thank you all."

He turned and hurried down the path back toward the pavilion. The others all looked at each other.

"Do any of you know what he meant?" Lucia asked. Dravid and Seri shook their heads. Ixchel ignored her and stepped to where she could continue to watch Forerunner's progress.

Seri looked back to Dravid. She didn't fully understand why she was so upset. She should be thrilled. Dravid possessing a special power would only make things better in their search for the lost King. Wouldn't it?

"Seri, I..."

"Not now." She turned and hastened down the path herself. Betrayal. That's what she felt. And she didn't even know why.

(((47)))

Kishin smeared the mud across his face and rubbed down his forearms. For tonight's visit, he did not want to waste time with questions about his appearance. In the dark, the mud would be enough of a disguise.

He slipped out of his home through his usual route and made his way across the city. The streets and shadows of Woqan were as familiar to him as his own house. For years, he had passed unseen through these buildings. Visiting those who desired his services. Killing those for whom he was paid. And sometimes, if he were lucky, taking an invisible look at his daughter, the one who had not seen him in return for somewhere around twenty years. He couldn't be sure, exactly. During the early days of his curse, he had given up keeping track of the months and years. It hadn't seemed important any longer.

He vaulted a garden wall and approached a house that dwarfed even his own. He remembered the day Kuch upgraded to this, after being appointed Blademaster of Ch'olan. He would not have that position if Kishin had not killed his predecessor for him. Kuch knew well how useful Kishin could be. Or had been.

Kishin entered the bedroom and looked down at his target. For a moment, the circle of his life amused him. Once long ago, he had stood at Kuch's bed—in his previous house—and that visit had truly started his life as an assassin. It also concerned the topic which brought him here now.

He stretched out his sword and placed the cold flat against Kuch's neck until he woke. He nearly sliced open his own neck when he jerked. Kishin wondered if that would have counted as a murder.

Kuch looked up and saw Kishin's silhouette. He froze, but then relaxed as he recognized the appearance. "Kishin!" he whispered, so as not to wake his wife.

Kishin gestured with his sword and moved out to the garden. Kuch joined him in a moment, wrapping a robe around his body. Kishin noted Kuch had gained a few pounds in the last few months. Perhaps he had given up doing the weapons training himself now. That would make him an easier target if… Again no. He did not kill anymore.

"To what do I owe the pleasure of this visit?" Kuch asked, stifling a yawn.

"Lady Ajaw went to the Passing. She took the Holcan with her, but two did not return. What happened to them?"

To his credit, Kuch's eyes widened only slightly. He knew the significance of what Kishin asked.

"One of them died on Zes Sivas," he said. "They tell me she fought against a leper who killed without fear. I was sure it was you."

Kishin blinked. He had not expected that, nor had Inkil mentioned it. Another leper assassin? How? He was—had been the only one. He was unique and always had been.

"It was not," he said. "And the other?"

"Lady Ajaw assigned her to another Lady," Kuch said. "She did not see fit to share her identity with me. But one of the other Holcan told me that it was not one of the great Ladies, but a mage of some kind."

How did that happen? Holcan guardians were occasionally gifted or assigned to another Lady, usually as part of a ceremony celebrating an agreement between two lands. Kishin could not recall one ever being assigned to a woman other than the wife of one of the six Lords.

"Which land?"

"I'm sorry?"

"Which land is this Lady, this mage, from?"

"I don't know. As often happens at The Passing, Lord Rajwir made new trade agreements with several lands. Kuktarma, Arazu, and Mandiata, I believe. I do not know that this assignment was tied to any of them in particular."

"It's her, isn't it?"

"What's her?"

Kishin lashed out, his sword stopping just short of Kuch's eye. "Stop being a fool, Kuch. I gave you your position. Do not think for an instant that I cannot take it away. Or something else you value even more." He traced down Kuch's body with his sword's tip.

"Of course it was her," Kuch said. His voice did not tremble.

Perhaps the years as Blademaster had toughened him up.

Kishin lowered his blade and turned away.

"Are you all right, Kishin? There's something... different about you."

"You are not the one I would confide in, if things had changed."

Kishin took a step and leaped up onto the garden wall. He glanced back at Kuch for a moment, then jumped out into the night again.

(((48)))

"Any sign of him?" Volraag rolled up the map and tucked it into his bag.

"No, your Lordship," Otioch said. "If Lord Tyrr escaped the ruin you left behind, then he is well and truly gone."

"I meant my brother." Volraag scowled and Otioch winced.

"I told you what happened. We came back to find you, and—"

"You should have obeyed my orders and stayed with him."

"You did not come as you said you would."

Volraag turned and looked his Guard leader in the eyes. "You defy me, Otioch?"

"No, my Lord. Merely stating the facts."

"Send twenty Guardsmen under your best leader and track him down."

"I will handle it myself."

"No." Volraag turned back to his packing. "I have another task for you."

Otioch stood stiff, waiting.

"Cassian will keep a watch on Rasna, but I doubt we have anything to fear from them. Between my brother's... creative efforts, and my defeat of Lord Tyrr, I don't think they will want to fight any more."

Otioch nodded.

"At the bottom of that hole is a gate, a portal. I need it to be more accessible."

"What did you have in mind?"

"Take as many men as you need. Dig it out. Divert the stream. Build a path down to it. Whatever it takes."

"It shall be done. Anything else, my Lord?"

"That will be all." As he turned to go, Volraag stopped him. "Otioch."

"My Lord?"

"I do not blame you for not succeeding. If my brother had chosen, he could have obliterated all of you. You've seen the power he wields. And yet you went, anyway. You are my most loyal, valued friend."

"Thank you, my Lord."

"Varioch will be in good hands while I'm gone."

"I still think it's a bad time to leave."

"I know. But if I do not act quickly, I will miss out on the opportunity to achieve all that I've planned for."

"As you say."

Volraag frowned. "Nothing new in the messages? From Mandiata?"

"No, my Lord."

"That is troubling. I would expect more of a response by now. At any rate, it doesn't change anything. Fetch Tezan and we'll go."

"As you command."

"Oh, and if Rathri somehow shows up, send him after us."

• • • • •

Victor looked about at the curse squad setting up a camp. So different from when he and Marshal were alone. So much more... laughter. Camaraderie. Even when Talinir and Aelia had been with them, it hadn't been this jovial.

There sat Gnaeus trying to build a fire with Merish. Topleb helped Wolf sort through a big pile of gear. Apparently, when the squad rushed out to help Marshal, they grabbed everything they could. Victor smiled to see that his and Marshal's bedrolls had been included. He hadn't been looking forward to sleeping on the ground.

Marshal stepped up next to him. "This is nice," he said.

Victor nodded. "I was just thinking that. So... you know our path?"

"North is all I know. I'm trusting Topleb with the rest. We're heading toward his home, after all."

Rufus approached, spear in hand. "Where have you been?" Victor asked.

The redhead pointed back. "Backtracking a bit. Trying to hide our trail."

"Good thought," Marshal said. "You know they won't have given up on us."

"Do you think Lord Volraag will follow us?" Rufus asked.

"I don't know. I don't know what happened back at the battlefield. If Lord Tyrr got involved, that may have kept him busy. But he'll at least send troops after us again. Probably his best."

"Oh, uh, did I mention he has another assassin with him?" Victor said.

"What?"

"Looked a lot like the other guy. Leper. Ugly."

Marshal rolled his eyes. "Great. We've got to deal with one of those again?"

"You mean... like the man who killed my friends?" Rufus said.

"Yeah, but not the same one. We dealt with him. I think."

"We did?" Victor raised his eyebrows.

"The last time I saw him was in the temple," Marshal said. "Before it came down. Either that killed him, or he gave up."

"That doesn't seem likely. Maybe he's just healing somewhere."

"So... we might have two of them after us?" Rufus asked.

"Theon's pillars. I hope not," Victor said. "One was enough."

Gnaeus looked up. "Wait. Scar-faced man. Temple. That was you?"

Topleb chuckled. "You hadn't figured that out yet?"

"You had?"

Topleb tapped his skull. "Ch'olan brains work twice as fast as Varioch. Also larger."

"Larger doesn't always mean better."

"Name me one area of life in which this is true."

"Noses," said Wolf, and appeared delighted at the laughter that followed.

"Feet," said Rufus.

"Not so!" said Topleb. "Large feet can be very helpful!"

The conversation degraded rapidly from that point. Everyone offered multiple suggestions, all of which Topleb argued. The idea of pursuit faded from their minds.

Some time later, Victor sat next to Topleb near the now-blazing fire. "You know our route from here?" he asked.

"Most certainly." Topleb picked up a stick and drew in the dirt. "We are here, near the border of Rasna. If we head almost directly northeast, we should cut across the center of Varioch. That will avoid your city of Reman and its surroundings. Then we arrive in Theon's own country, Ch'olan."

"And you know where this place of power is?"

Topleb drew another spot on his dirt map. "Is here. Northeast of Woqan, greatest city of Antises."

Victor tried not to smile. Topleb had been boastful before, but escaping the army seemed to have triggered more exaggeration. Victor couldn't blame him. Everything did seem better now.

He glanced around at the others. "Where's Gnaeus?"

"He was here a minute ago," Marshal said, looking around.

"I'm right here!" Gnaeus stumbled out of the darkness. "Had to relieve myself. Do you need to know all the details?"

"Just making sure you're all right," Marshal said.

"I don't belong here," Wolf announced, staring into the fire.

Marshal put a hand on his shoulder. "Yes, you do, Wolf. Yes, you do."

(((49)))

"Is this everyone?" Forerunner asked. His three primary assistants all nodded.

Seri looked around. All the residents of the sanctuary crowded together in the pavilion. All in all, she only counted around twenty-five people. A few days ago, it had seemed like so many more. She knew some, like Junia, had left, but hadn't others come? Nothing about this place ever made sense.

Dravid approached and opened his mouth to say something, but she turned away. Not yet.

"Very well. Listen, my friends!" Forerunner's voice projected throughout the chamber. Reminded by Ixchel, Seri paid attention to how the magic reverberated through every word he said.

"It has come to my attention that an old friend of mine is in need of help. I must go to him."

Murmurs of disappointment arose. Forerunner lifted his hands.

"It can't be helped, I'm afraid. This friend cannot come to me. I don't think he fully understands the situation in which he finds himself. So I will have to go to him. Once I do, we will doubtlessly return to this wonderful place."

"Are you going alone?" someone asked.

"No, no. I don't think I'll ever travel alone again. But I cannot take all of you with me. Some must remain here to take care of our sanctuary, and welcome any others who come to us with their needs."

A clamor arose as most of the followers offered themselves as Forerunner's traveling companions. He assured them he would choose carefully, and would be departing on the following morning. With that, he dismissed the crowd.

As Forerunner moved through, talking individually with various followers, Seri pondered. An old friend? If Forerunner came from the Otherworld as he said, what kind of old friends would he possess? Eldanim? Gidim? She thought of the glowing beings she had seen there.

"Seri. You and your friends should definitely come along," Forerunner said. She jerked. She hadn't noticed him drawing so close.

"Why should we?"

"Because I have not yet restored what you each desire," he said. "And... because I think this trip will help you in your quest."

"My quest?"

"The reason you're here in Varion?"

Before she could say anything else, he moved on, addressing another follower. Seri didn't remember telling him about her mission. But Forerunner always seemed to know things. Frustrating.

"Can we talk? Please?" Dravid.

•••••

Seri watched Dravid lead the way through the eastern doors of the pavilion. Was he trying to get as far away from the spot where she had found him last? Outside, he turned to face her.

"Listen, I was wrong not to tell you about this right away," he said. "I'm sorry."

Hailstones. She couldn't get too upset at an unconditional apology. "All right," she said.

"I was scared, and, and I didn't know what to do."

"That's why you should have come to me."

"I know! I was wrong. I did say that."

"All right."

Dravid glanced nervously around. "I guess I was worried, because you've lost your star-sight. I didn't want to tell you that I had suddenly got this new power when you lost yours. And it was all my fault, anyway."

Seri tried to take a few calming breaths. "You thought I might be jealous?"

"Yes. No. I mean, I just didn't want to make you feel bad in any way." He took an awkward step closer. "I care about you, Seri. I never want to do anything that would cause you pain."

He said everything she wanted to hear. Starting with a complete apology, telling her he cared. So sweet. So...

"Wait. Did Ixchel tell you what to say?"

"What?"

She frowned. "Did Ixchel give you advice on apologizing to me?"

"Uh, she helped some. That is, I wanted to know how to, um..."

"And did she do this in your room?"

"Uh... yes?"

"She visits your room a lot."

"But... you send her to find me. Don't you?"

"How many other girls come to your room?"

"What?"

"Has Lucia been there? Maybe Junia, before she left?"

Dravid shook his head. "No, no. What is this? What are you—"

Seri trembled. "Maybe you should stay here when we leave with Forerunner. Then you can have all the pretty girls all to yourself. You can show off your magic and make them giggle, and, and..."

"No!"

"Not enough for you? You want to be around the girls that come on the trip too?"

"I want to be around you!"

Silence.

Dravid sighed and leaned hard against his crutch. "I just told you that I care about you. I meant that."

Seri sniffed. "I'm... I know you do. You came with me, Dravid. That meant a lot."

He shrugged. "I didn't have much else to do."

She pushed him. "Stop it. You could have gone back to Kuktarma, to —what was it? All the broken female hearts you left behind?"

He chuckled, a weak little thing. "I... may have exaggerated that."

"Stop." She put a hand up to his face. That gorgeous skin that had given her those totally improper thoughts the first time she met him. "All the girls like you. And they can't help it."

He looked into her eyes. Had she ever noticed they were practically the same height? "But what about you?" he asked.

"I like you." His smile dazzled. "You're... my best friend." The smile faded ever so slightly.

"And you're mine." He put his arm out and she stepped into the hug. The crutch was in the way. She knocked it aside so she could put both arms around him, and he could do the same. He laughed. "Don't let me fall now!"

"I won't."

Dravid held her close. His hands moved across her robe, rubbing her back and shoulders. It was nice.

And then her mind flashed to an unwanted memory. Lord Varion's hands. Touching her. Through her robe.

She broke away from Dravid with a gasp. He wavered, but caught hold of her hands to keep from falling. "Hey, I said don't let me fall!" He sounded jovial, but his eyes looked confused.

"I'm sorry. It's not your fault. I'm sorry." She bent and picked up his crutch. Once he took it, she hurried away, calling herself a coward, but still unable to erase Lord Varion's face from her mind.

(((50)))

Marshal knelt with his palm flat against the dirt. He closed his eyes and concentrated. Back at the battlefield, he had been able to sense Volraag's presence, or at least that's what he assumed he sensed. He hoped the same held true now.

Nothing. No disturbances. No vibrations. No mouth watering. Either Volraag remained far away, or Marshal couldn't sense him after all.

Wait. He felt something... but no. It came from the opposite direction of where he would expect to find his half-brother, and it... wasn't the same. Power, maybe, but very faint. And not at all like his own. Rather than vibrations, it felt like a weak pulse. Regular, but slow. Strange.

"Anything?" Victor asked.

"I don't think so," Marshal said. "No sign of Volraag, anyway."

"Well, that's good. But I can't imagine why he's not coming after us full speed."

"We have to expect that someone is coming."

"Either the assassin, or soldiers, or both."

"Any idea on what to do about it?"

"To do about what?" Topleb strolled up beside them.

"Pursuit," Victor said. "You know, Rufus thought about trying to hide our trail. Maybe we should do that every time we travel?"

Topleb snorted. "Rufus knows nothing of tracking and trails. What can he do? Scuff up a few footprints?"

"We don't know much, either," Marshal said.

"We are big group," Topleb said. "If someone wants to follow us, it will not be hard."

"Should we try to find a defensive position or keep moving?" Victor asked.

"Since we have no idea who is coming or when they might catch up, I say keep moving," Topleb said.

Marshal nodded. "I agree. Tell the others to pack up so we can start."

As Topleb obeyed, Victor toyed with his flail. "I could hang back, keep an eye out, then catch up to let you know."

"And if it's the assassin and he finds you alone?"

"I've gotten better since the last time." Victor grinned. "But not that much better. You're right."

Marshal frowned and looked back the way they had come yesterday. The inevitable pursuit would come. And then he would have to choose: use his power to save his squad, probably by killing the enemy, or... let someone else die for him. Both prospects involved death. There had to be another way. He just couldn't see it.

He and Victor rejoined the squad, finished packing up the gear, and headed out.

•••••

While Victor found it more pleasant traveling in the company of the squad, he realized they would never be able to travel as fast as when Talinir led them. Topleb knew the direction he wanted to go, but very little about Varioch's actual landscape. He sometimes led them into dead ends which led to backtracking and trying different paths. The men grumbled good-naturedly, but they followed.

Rufus often lagged behind due to his twisted foot. Victor sometimes dropped back to walk with him, which seemed to cheer him up.

Once, Gnaeus lagged instead. Curious, Victor joined him and asked if he needed help.

Gnaeus shook his head. "Nah, I just... sometimes I gotta get away from Merish, ya know?"

Victor frowned. "But he never even talks."

"Were you listening that night at the fire? I told you it's my fault he's cursed."

"Oh."

They walked in silence for a while. Victor wondered at the guilt that could keep a man committed to a friend, yet want to escape his company. He imagined he would do the same in Gnaeus' shoes.

The thoughts consumed him so deeply, he didn't notice the sound until Gnaeus turned to look behind them. Horses!

"Go! Tell Marshal and the others!" Victor ordered. As Gnaeus broke into a run, Victor took out his flail and drew his sword. He was committed too. No Bindings this time. Just doing the right thing.

He drew a deep breath. The pounding of hooves grew louder. More this time. And no army of conscripts to help. In the distance, he caught glimpses of the red cloaks moving through the hills. Very little undergrowth to slow their path. Plenty of riding room between the scattered trees. They should have caught up much sooner. Were they being cautious?

A shout. One of them had seen him. As they came within sight, he counted. Ten… fifteen… twenty. That's a lot. He began to spin the flail. He still didn't know what activated his battle rage, but now would be a very good time for it. So far, he only felt nervous.

"You think you can take them all?" Marshal appeared beside him, gasping from running.

Victor grinned. "Thought I'd leave a few for you."

"Why are men of Varioch such braggarts?" Topleb said, joining them. "Is not like this in Ch'olan. Humble we are."

Marshal pointed. "I'll blast the ground in the middle there. That should give some of them pause. The rest will have to split to either side."

"Do it quickly!" The horsemen were less than a hundred yards away.

Marshal clapped his hands together. Though Victor couldn't see it, he knew waves of power must have erupted from those hands. The ground ahead of them tore itself apart, rippling out in either direction and straight ahead. As expected, the charge of the horsemen broke apart. Some of the horses reared, stalling their drive. Others swept around to either side. Victor whooped and charged to the right. Vaguely, he knew the rest of the squad had come up behind them also.

"Victor, wait! I can't—"

"Take the ones on the left!" Topleb shouted.

Victor barely heard them. The whooshing in his ears started again. The magic was at work, tightening his grip through the vibrations, speeding his feet as they pounded around a tree and rushed at the first horse and rider.

This one had broken well ahead of the others. His red Remavian Guard cloak fluttering, he swung his own flail out and down. In the back of his mind, Victor recalled a day when one of these Guards armed just like this had come to his own village, escorting a Lord-to-be. The day everything changed.

His own flail swept forward in an arc at his side. Forward and up, backward and down, as he ran. The rider turned his mount ever so slightly to come at Victor on his right. Perfect.

At the last moment, as his flail came up from its lower arc, Victor swept it across his body instead of directly forward. He twisted to his right, ducking his head back. He sidestepped and swept the flail upward now in a rotation that intersected with the enemy's flail. The two chains collided and wrapped around each other. Victor continued his spin to the right, yanking down as hard as he could.

One supposed advantage the Guard's flail had over Victor's old piece was a strap to help keep its user from dropping it. Victor had been counting on that. The Guard flipped off his horse in full gallop, smashing into the ground. Victor lost hold of his own flail, but it didn't matter now.

"Well done!" Topleb called. He flung a spear from his atlatl, striking the next oncoming horse. It made an awful scream and veered just enough for its rider to miss Victor with the sweep of a sword.

Dimly, he knew Marshal was using his power again on the other side. He could feel the vibrations in the ground. But it meant little. Another dozen riders came toward him, more cautious than the first two. He stood armed with only his sword, Topleb behind him with the atlatl. This might not end well.

An arrow passed by his head. He forgot some of the Guard also carried bows. Back in the battle, he could spin and charge through Rasna's hapless troops, but that was a far cry from mounted elite warriors. You couldn't shove your way through 1,000-pound horses while dodging the attacks of their riders.

But that didn't mean he wouldn't try. The rage, the magic, the whooshing of his heartbeat… it took over, driving him into a run toward the enemy. Topleb shouted something at him, but he couldn't hear it.

And then he was among them. Dodging, weaving, slashing, ducking, running. He understood little of what he did, only that it felt right in the moment. He knew he moved far faster than he ever had before. How else could he dance in the midst of charging horses without being run down?

Did Marshal feel this way when using his power? Did he hear the whooshing, experience the heightened awareness, feel the thrill?

He came to a stop and spun back around. He had come all the way through the charge. Blood dripped from his sword, whether human or horse he didn't know. The Remavian Guard pulled their horses into turns. Out of the dozen that had charged, he saw two empty saddles.

The lead rider shouted something to the others and they spun their horses away. Victor didn't know and didn't care where they were going. His attention focused on the leader, who dismounted and approached on foot, sword at the ready. A large man, his rough look and handful of small scars implied he had been fighting for many years.

Victor charged him, sweeping in with a crossing slash that immediately came back in a downward stroke Talinir taught him. The Guard dodged the first and parried the second. His sword looked like good steel, the best Varioch had to offer. But it didn't compare to Victor's Eldani-forged blade.

For a few moments, they exchanged attack after attack, moving back and forth, circling each other. Neither scored a hit. Victor knew this to be the most skilled opponent he had faced since Talinir or the assassin. But he couldn't figure out why the Guard seemed to grow slower with each move.

Victor dodged back and to his own right, using the momentum to spin entirely around, sidestepping as he did to tag the guard in a scratch across his side. From that moment, it became almost too easy.

The Guard yelled something, but Victor couldn't understand it. He parried a thrust downward, then brought his own sword up in another scratch across the Guard's leather breastplate. Another yell he couldn't hear. The Guard's facial expression looked desperate.

The Guard's low slash seemed almost in slow motion. Victor jumped over it, then stabbed up and under the breastplate. He pulled back and the Guard collapsed, his lips still moving.

A strange sight caught Victor's attention. A ripple in the ground came toward him. The earth crumbled upward, then settled as it moved on, like a ripple in the water. He easily jumped over it as it passed by and kept going.

Victor looked around in every direction. Horses scattered about, riderless and unsure. Five Guards lay unmoving on the ground. Topleb pulled one of his spears out of a body and looked at him.

The whooshing faded almost as swiftly as it had come. Victor's hands shook.

"—you hear me?" He realized Topleb had been speaking to him.
"What?"

"Oh, so you can hear. You just didn't want to answer him?"

"What was he saying?"

Topleb cocked his head. "So you couldn't hear while fighting? Strange."

"What was he saying?"

"He kept screaming, 'How are you so fast?'"

• • • • •

Victor wondered what could be happening to him. He thrilled to the battle, but it frightened him. He seemed to lose control of almost everything while fighting.

Marshal scrambled into view. "What happened over here?"

Topleb gestured. "Victor happened. He charged them all by himself, so their leader sent everyone to go after you. He stayed to deal with Victor. It did not end well for him. It was like watching one of the ancient heroes of Ch'olan."

"Did you take care of the rest?" Victor asked.

Marshal nodded. "After some more demonstrations of power, they took off. I don't think they'll be bothering us any more."

"The ones who survived," Topleb said. He bent over the Guard's body at his feet and struggled with something.

Victor felt fatigue sweep over him, and he stumbled. "What do we do now?"

"As crude as it sounds, we scavenge the dead," Topleb said. He stood, holding a leather breastplate, and walked to Victor. "For starters, if you're going to keep imitating a wild bull, you should wear some more protection." He held up the breastplate to gauge its fit and nodded.

"Why? I don't..." He trailed off as he realized that his tunic was shredded in multiple places. Again. At the same moment, twinges of pain pierced his consciousness. Apparently, his opponents had scored a few shots on him. None of them appeared serious, but Topleb had a point.

"It seems wrong to take from the dead," Marshal said. Gnaeus and Merish came up behind him.

"You would rather steal from the living?" Topleb pointed at the bodies. "They have good weapons, better than most of ours. Good clothes too, if Victor hasn't cut them all to pieces."

"What about the horses?" Gnaeus asked.

"Do you know how to ride?"

"Not well."

"They didn't leave enough for all of us, and I don't think most of us would be very comfortable," Topleb said. "Too bad we can't sell them." He paused. "We could eat one."

"We can't eat a horse!" Gnaeus protested.

"If we get hungry enough, we can."

Marshal stepped away from the others. He pointed his hands at the ground and it exploded in front of him. He worked at it for a few moments, then stepped back. He left behind a large ditch a few feet wide and twice as long.

"Take what we can from them," he ordered, "then put their bodies here. We'll bury them together. I won't leave them for the animals. They're still our countrymen, even if they worked for horrible men."

"Your countrymen," Topleb muttered.

Victor started to help, but found he could barely move. He sat down hard. Marshal approached. "Are you all right?"

"Just exhausted," he said. His own voice sounded strange to him, distorted somehow.

Marshal nodded. "I don't know what's happening exactly, but you've got your own magic somehow. Maybe you get it from hanging around me all the time? Or it came through our Bond?"

"I don't know, either," Victor said. "It comes on me and I can't stop. I can't hear or anything. I just keep fighting. And getting faster, I guess."

"He moves like spinning top, the children's toy," Topleb said.

Rufus limped up. "I found your flail," he said, offering it. "And one of theirs. Maybe you would like a new one?"

Victor took both flails and compared them. The Guard's flail was newer, obviously, not coated in rust like his own. The chain might be a link or two shorter. The ball might be the same size, but it had multiple spikes protruding from its surface. It certainly looked like a deadlier weapon, crafted for elite warriors. Yet he couldn't decide. The old one had been with him for so long.

"Keep both," Marshal said, watching him. "Practice with the new one. See if you like it or not. It's good to have a backup, right?"

Victor nodded. He took a deep breath and closed his eyes for a moment. Feeling a little more like himself, he opened his eyes and looked around.

"What did you mean by 'demonstrations of power'?"

"There may be fewer trees around than were here earlier," Marshal said.

"You uprooted trees?"

"A few."

"No wonder they gave up. That ripple you created came all the way over here, by the way."

"What ripple?"

"In the ground. Came through toward the end of the fight."

"I didn't do that." Marshal furrowed his brow.

"It wasn't the after effects of something else you did?"

Marshal shook his head. "No. It wasn't me."

"Then who was it?"

"I don't know."

During the last big battle with Rasna, he felt a similar pulse, Victor remembered. "I think it's someone in our squad," he said. "It happened in the battle too."

"You're right. I remember."

They both looked around. Topleb. Gnaeus. Merish. Wolf. Rufus. Did one of them possess power? Did he even know it?

"Unless..." Marshal said, "someone else has been near us all along. Following us, maybe. A spy for Volraag."

"Then why intervene in the fight?"

Marshal shrugged. "To protect himself? I don't know. If it was one of these guys, wouldn't he have told us?"

Victor had no answers. He set the two flails down and lowered his head. The exhaustion came right back. Maybe he had imagined it letting up.

"The Hero of Varioch needs a nap," Rufus said with a grin.

Topleb came up behind Victor and draped something over his shoulders. "If hero, he should at least look respectable doing it." Victor touched the soft material. One of the Remavian Guard's cloaks. Red with gold trim. He had never owned anything this fine.

"That one at least has no blood on it," Topleb said. "Try to keep it that way." He stepped around Victor and saluted. The other five, including Marshal, followed his example.

Victor swallowed. All his life, he had wanted to be a soldier. The Remavian Guard were the best, so naturally he had dreamed of joining them. But this... this was better. He was a soldier, a real soldier with soldier companions who fought by his side. More than that, they were his friends.

He straightened his head and saluted back.

(((51)))

Kishin knew more about most people in Woqan than anyone else. One of the side effects of spying out targets as an assassin. As it applied to this morning, he knew which priests of Theon genuinely believed what they taught, and which ones served for other reasons.

The temple of Woqan was not so different from the one destroyed in Reman. They possessed the same basic layout, but the builders of Ch'olan made this temple their own, with touches of their own architectural style, the most obvious being a vaulted rather than flat roof. While he waited for the priest he sought, Kishin idly wondered if a god cared about the shape of a roof. He chuckled without sound. He had once considered himself a god, and he had cared. What did that say?

The priest he wanted emerged from the temple at last and unlocked the main gates to allow petitioners to enter. Kishin had never been able to determine Chimon's exact age. He had been here as long as he could remember. He moved so slow as to defy patience, step by painful step, bent over with age... yet he appeared the same way when Kishin was a child.

Kishin waited until Chimon continued his morning habits and made his way around behind the temple. He began to clean up the remains of the food he left out the night before for stray animals.

"You've always watched out for the strays, haven't you, Chimon?"

The priest looked up without surprise and smiled, the early morning sun playing across his wizened skin. "Always, my son. Your voice... it's familiar, but I don't recognize the face."

Kishin stepped close and let himself be seen fully. "Perhaps it's because the last time you saw this face, it was ravaged by a curse of

230

leprosy."

Chimon lifted a trembling hand toward Kishin's face. "You... you claim to be healed of leprosy? The Law does contain instructions for that. I must examine you and—"

"I am Kishin, Chimon. Kishin the Untouchable. Pariah. Leper. Outcast."

Chimon tilted his head, then turned Kishin so the sun shone in his face. "Can it be?"

"My curse is gone, Chimon. I have come to you to find out what that means."

Kishin caught the old priest as he fainted. Well, what did he expect?

A short time later, Kishin waited inside Chimon's humble dwelling, a chamber built into the outer wall of the temple courtyard. Chimon drank a sip of his tea and gazed at Kishin with a peaceful smile. His stare became uncomfortable.

"I need to understand this," he said. "Tell me what you think."

Chimon set down his cup on a crude wooden table. "First tell me how this took place."

Kishin hesitated. "You know who I am, old man. You know what I have done all these years."

"Somehow I doubt you were healed by killing someone else."

"No, I... failed to kill someone."

"Ah."

"I tried to kill him. A young man in Varioch. Cursed. But his mother..." Kishin shook his head at the memory of Aelia. "She insisted there was a way to lift a curse. I thought it blasphemy."

"An amusing thought, coming from one such as you."

Kishin snorted. "I have had... my own theology, priest. My own beliefs."

"And have those beliefs done you any good?"

"They made me stronger!" Yet even as he said the words, Kishin felt the lie.

"So. This mother took your curse away?"

"She... died to take away her son's curse. At least, that is what she said she was doing. I'm not entirely sure. I don't even know what happened to him. But when it was over, my skin was as you see me now." Kishin displayed his bare arms as further evidence.

Chimon nodded. "And what will you do now?"

"I do not know. I am... undone."

"Undone. By a miracle. How ironic."

Kishin slammed his fist against the stone wall. "I have not served Theon in over twenty years. I've wanted nothing to do with him or his followers. Yet if this is from him, I must know. Why? What does it mean?"

Chimon sat silent for a moment. Kishin considered leaving. Maybe this hadn't been a good idea.

"Tell me, why did you come to me?"

"I just told you. I'm looking for answers."

"But why me?" Chimon pointed a crooked finger at himself. "Why Chimon in particular?"

"Because..."

"Yes?"

"Because unlike many of your fellow priests, you seem to really believe all of this." Kishin gestured toward the temple.

Chimon nodded. "Because you've watched us. Despite not wanting anything to do with us, you've watched us."

"I watched you because I had a job. I killed one of your fellows six years ago."

Chimon sat silent again. "Payr," he said at last. "I thought he had come to an untimely end."

"He did not truly believe," Kishin said. "He told me so after the first three fingers I removed from his hand." Chimon's slow reactions angered him, making him give out more details than he had intended.

Chimon did not display shock or horror. Instead, he picked up his tea and took another sip. He put the cup down and took a long breath. "Tell me," he said. "Will you kill again?"

"I... do not plan to."

"Ah."

When the priest did not say anything else, Kishin could not stand it. "What do you want from me?"

At last, he looked surprised. "I? I do not want anything from you, my boy. You came to me. So the question should be directed at you, I suppose. What do you want from me?"

"Tell me..."

"Yes?"

"Tell me what I should do."

"You know the Law. Perhaps now, you should give some heed to following it, lest you be cursed again."

"The Law." Kishin scoffed. "The Law does nothing except force people to find creative ways to do what they want to do without breaking it."

Chimon leaned forward. "Precisely."

Kishin blinked.

"The Law does one thing, and one thing only. It shows our wrongdoing. Theon cares less for the Law than he does for this." That crooked finger tapped at the old man's chest.

Kishin did not know what to say.

Chimon leaned back again. "You have lived long under a horrible curse. You have committed many grave sins. These cannot be denied. Yet we all live under curses. We all commit grave sins."

"What did you say?"

"You have lived long—"

"No. You said all men are cursed."

"Yes. All men are cursed."

Kishin found himself shaking. He had said the words himself for years. To hear a priest repeat them shook everything. "If we are all cursed, then what is our hope?"

"Our only hope is in Theon. But that is the answer you expect from me, no doubt. Tell me true: will you kill again?"

"I do not want to."

"Yet you come to me still wearing a sword."

The warpsteel blade seemed much heavier all of a sudden.

Chimon sighed. "You are prepared to kill, but you say you don't want to. Is it merely fear that holds you back now? Fear of another curse?"

"Of course I'm afraid, old man! Why wouldn't I be?"

"As long as that is the only reason that holds you back, then you will never escape cursings. To be truly free, your heart must change. Not just your skin."

"This is ridiculous." Kishin moved to the door.

"How is your daughter, Kishin?"

He froze. "What do you know of her?"

"I know her well. Such a beautiful child she was. Now grown. And like her father, she knows how to kill. Yet she is different."

"How so?"

That ugly, old finger tapped at the heart again. "She will not do it, unless she must. She serves a higher cause."

Kishin looked away. He could not answer.

"Perhaps you should seek out such a cause yourself."

Kishin laughed at that. "You think I should go the Lord Rajwir?

Offer my sword in his service?"

"No." Chimon shook his head. "I'm saying you need a cause. If you must fight, if you must carry a sword, then you need a reason to do so. If you have no cause, no reason… then all I can see for your future is a return to what you were. And while Theon's mercy is great, I would not dare to test it."

(((52)))

What just happened? Dravid stared after Seri's swiftly-departing back. What had he said wrong? What had he done?

Dravid was no stranger to romantic relationships. He told jokes about leaving girls behind in Kuktarma. When pressed, he passed it off as an exaggeration. But not by much. Girls truly were drawn to him. His looks. His smile. And he encouraged it, of course. Now, if he really wanted it, he could entice any one of the women here at the sanctuary, especially if he stayed behind when Forerunner left.

But Seri.

No other girl affected him the way she did. Everything about her amazed him. Even her naiveté, her innocence, was tantalizing. And cute.

"Best friend." Well, it was better than "just friends." Best friends could mean something more. At least he had hope.

What made her break off, though? Was she scared he wanted more than a hug?

He did want more. But he could wait. She was worth it.

He sighed and adjusted his crutch. A couple of hours remained until lunch. May as well return to his room and begin packing.

At that moment, Dravid heard a hiss. He spun on his crutch. A curse-stalker watched him from only a few feet away, its tail moving side to side.

Lord Meluhha of Kuktarma kept a pair of curse-stalkers in one of his palace gardens, visible for guests to observe these strange creatures. Dravid had seen them several times. But this one seemed much larger.

"I'm not cursed," Dravid said, as if the creature could understand him. But he knew curse-stalkers didn't actually stalk only the cursed.

They were drawn to magic. And his body now held a new and powerful magic.

He opened himself to the pulse and felt the heat rush up inside him. It grew easier every time. His hand began to glow.

The curse-stalker moved toward him. It seemed cautious, perhaps thinking his crutch a weapon. Dravid drew in the air and created one of the now-familiar discs.

That seemed to antagonize it. The creature opened its mouth and twin tongues shot out at Dravid. He managed to block them with the disc and crutch, but one brushed against his left hand, burning him with some kind of acidic substance.

Dravid yelled, hoping to attract the attention of anyone else in the vicinity. Maybe Seri hadn't gone far. Maybe Ixchel could see him.

Off-balance from blocking the tongues, Dravid almost fell as the curse-stalker lumbered closer. He managed to move another step back, but that didn't do much good. The creature was upon him.

Dravid whacked at it with his crutch and cursed himself for the disc. Why hadn't he shaped a more useful device, like a sword? Then an enormous mouth rushed right at his chest. He slammed the disc into the monster's mouth, shattering at least two teeth, but the impact knocked him down.

Three hundred pounds of reptilian muscle landed on top of him. He screamed as a claw tore into his right bicep, and his arm fell useless. The disc in its mouth kept the curse-stalker from biting at him without hurting itself, but it had other weapons. Another claw scraped skin from Dravid's shin.

Dravid had never formed two items of the magic at the same time. He didn't know if the disc would stay intact while he created something else, but he had to risk it. Already, the heat inside him was building up.

He couldn't see. He tried to shape with his left hand. He only needed something sharp. He grabbed on to whatever he had formed and slammed it into the creature's side.

It worked. The monster squealed and bit down. Dravid couldn't maintain the disc any more, and it dissolved. He hoped it took out some more teeth in those last seconds.

He stabbed again and again. With the strength of the magic, it felt like stabbing into butter.

Despite its wounds, the creature did not give up. It reared up, opening its mouth. Dravid looked up into the enormous maw, lined with serrated teeth. In another moment, those teeth would close around his head and he could do nothing to stop it.

As the jaws descended, a round shield appeared in front of Dravid's face. The curse-stalker's mouth slammed into it, smashing it into Dravid's nose, cheek, and forehead.

Something else hit the creature and its weight rolled off of him. He gasped and tried to lift himself up on his elbow, shoving the shield away.

Ixchel rolled with the curse-stalker down a slight hill. Somehow, she came out on top. She lifted her sword and plunged it down into the creature's head. If her sword had been longer, she would have pinned it to the ground. As it was, the monster threw her off and thrashed about, still moving even though a sword protruded from its brain.

What did it take to kill this thing? Dravid tried to throw his makeshift dagger, only to find it had also dissolved.

Ixchel got to her feet, disheveled and dirty, bleeding from a gash in her side. From somewhere on her back, she pulled out a dagger. She approached the creature and stabbed it in the eye. At the same time, she grabbed her sword hilt and yanked it back out. With both weapons, she stabbed again and again until it finally lay still.

She pulled her weapons free and looked all around, even taking a few steps away. Satisfied at last, she approached Dravid.

"What were you looking for?" he couldn't help asking.

"These creatures often hunt in pairs, with their mate," Ixchel said. She knelt beside him and looked over his wounds. "Your leg is bleeding, but it looks superficial. That arm wound is serious."

"And my head hurts." Dravid tried to get up, but his right arm couldn't help much. Great. Crippled in multiple ways now.

Ixchel assisted him in sitting up. "Your nose might be broken. But I don't think so. I'm sorry that my shield injured you."

"Are you serious? You saved my life! Thank you!"

Ixchel nodded. "My job is to protect the Lady Seri. It doesn't prevent me from protecting those she cares for, when necessary."

"Those she… how about just because we're friends?"

Ixchel inclined her head. "I suppose that is true also."

"You suppose." Dravid snorted. "Ow!" That hurt.

"We should take care of your injuries," Ixchel said. She took hold of his left arm and lifted him upright.

"What about you?" Dravid asked. "Didn't it get you too?"

Ixchel touched her side, and her hand came back bloody. "It's not bad."

With her help, Dravid began to hobble back toward the pavilion. "I suppose I'm Bonded to you now."

"No doubt, though you won't be able to feel it."

"What do you mean?"

"My Lady didn't tell you? Forerunner's power here is blocking our Bindings."

"Blocking?"

"He says we will feel them again once we leave him. Which cannot happen soon enough."

Dravid considered. He now possessed some of Forerunner's power. Did it make him immune to Bindings also? He couldn't know until they left Forerunner behind. He wasn't sure he wanted to do that as soon as Ixchel did.

"I need more training," he muttered.

"Yes, you do," Ixchel said. "But not from Forerunner. You need to learn how to defend yourself." She stopped their progress just before entering the pavilion, and looked into his eyes. "This will not be the last time you might have to fight. I can teach you that."

"Well…" Bruises were swelling on Dravid's face, making it difficult to speak. "That sounds fun."

• • • • •

Seri found she couldn't close her mouth. Both her friends looked like they had escaped from a war, or at least how she imagined a war would look like.

"A curse-stalker did this?"

Ixchel nodded. "Dravid may have trouble answering you. His face is damaged."

"I can see that." Several huge bruises marred Dravid's beautiful skin. His nose looked swollen too. In addition, a bloody bandage covered his right upper arm, while his pant leg hung in tatters, showing badly-scraped skin all over his shin. Ixchel bore a bandage on her left side also.

Seri knelt beside Dravid. She wanted to touch him, but was afraid of putting her hand on another injury. "You could have been killed."

"Almost was," he said through thick slips, slurring a bit. "Ixchel saved me."

"She's good at that." She glanced up at Ixchel to see her smiling.

"My mentor would be pleased. Defeating one of those beasts is significant," she said.

"Your mentor?"

"The assistant blademaster. Primary trainer of the Holcan. He hated curse-stalkers. There are many of them in Ch'olan."

"Then let's not go there," Dravid mumbled.

At that moment, Forerunner hurried into the pavilion, followed by his three assistants. "What is this?" he exclaimed. "They told me one of those creatures made it into our sanctuary. Is this true?"

"Your magic didn't tell you?" Ixchel said.

"Contrary to some reports, I am not all-knowing," he said, giving her a quick look over. He focused on her bandaged side before turning to examine Dravid.

"Oh, my. Your face will take some time to return to its usual handsome self," he said. "The leg looks like it will be fine, but this..." He began to remove the bandage around Dravid's bicep.

"That is not necessary!" Ixchel said, starting forward.

Forerunner held up a hand. "I need to see the wound."

Ixchel frowned, but did not intervene.

Seri gasped as the bandage came away. The tear in Dravid's skin looked deep. She knew little of such injuries, but she had never seen one this bad. The muscle looked nearly torn in half. Blood oozed from it in a sluggish flow. How could it ever return to normal?

Forerunner looked it over and made an unintelligible sound in the back of his throat. He pushed the sides of the wound together. Dravid jerked and cried out. "If left to itself, this would never heal properly," Forerunner said. "You might regain use of the arm, but never to the degree you had before."

It wasn't fair. Dravid already lost a leg. Now he might lose the use of an arm too?

Forerunner looked into Dravid's face. "If you will allow me?" Dravid didn't say anything, but something seemed to pass between them. Forerunner nodded.

He closed his eyes and tilted his head back. Seri thought she heard him murmuring something, but couldn't make out the words. His hands began to glow, like when he erected the shield to protect them from the earthquake.

Forerunner placed his hands on Dravid's upper arm. While blood began to seep out between his fingers, the glow spread around the wound. It grew brighter and brighter until Seri had to turn her eyes away. Dravid cried out, but it sounded more out of surprise than pain.

The glow subsided and Seri looked back. Everything looked the same until Forerunner pulled his hands away, wiping blood off Dravid's arm as he did.

"It's gone!" one of Forerunner's assistants exclaimed. Seri had forgotten they were even here.

But she was right. As Forerunner wiped away the rest of the blood, Seri saw no sign of Dravid's injury. The skin looked smooth and unbroken. Dravid flexed the arm and moved it back and forth, his mouth agape.

"This cannot be," Ixchel said.

"You say 'cannot' many times, Ixchel," Forerunner said. "Perhaps you should focus more on 'can.'" He looked at her side. "Your wound is not as severe, but I can heal it as well, if you will permit me."

"I will not."

Forerunner nodded. "It is your choice."

"Ixchel, why not let him?" Seri said. "He has the power, and no reason to hurt you."

Ixchel shook her head.

"Battle scars are important to the Holcan," Forerunner said. "Once it heals naturally, she will look at the scar it leaves behind with pride. I understand."

"You do not. You can not."

"Do you think I have never seen battle? Speak to me when you have glimpsed the endless war that rages in the third world. Tell me when you have slain one of the tunaldi, who stalk the curse-stalkers. Regale me when you have wielded weapons that would devastate your entire order. I understand far more than you can imagine." As he spoke, Forerunner's voice vibrated with magic, growing louder and deeper.

Ixchel took a step back and her hand went to her sword hilt.

"Stop it! You said you wouldn't use magic in your voice again!" Seri shouted.

Forerunner lifted his hands, still dripping from Dravid's blood. "I apologize. I grew agitated and overreached myself." He turned away "If I am no longer needed here, I will go. I need to clean up, after all."

"Thank you," Dravid managed to say through his swollen mouth.

Forerunner nodded. "You are quite welcome."

Seri watched him leave with his assistants. Almost every encounter with Forerunner led to some new mystery about his powers and origins. She needed answers. Maybe getting away from this place would help.

(((53)))

Traveling with Forerunner turned out to be quite the experience. He didn't seem to be in any kind of a hurry. Instead, he stopped for any number of reasons: an early lunch, a beautiful landscape to survey, or because one of his followers wanted to discuss something. While it seemed strange, Seri did learn more about their mysterious leader from listening to his conversations. He never ventured into outright blasphemy or even criticism, but she detected an overriding disapproval of the Laws of Cursings and Bindings. At times, she thought that disapproval carried over to Theon himself, but she might be imagining it.

On the other hand, he seemed exceptionally interested in hearing people tell their own stories. And it wasn't just the dramatic stories, like Seri's, that intrigued him. He appeared fascinated by stories of simple lives, simple needs. Almost as if he had never heard them before, or experienced anything similar.

In addition to Seri, Ixchel, and Dravid, Forerunner brought along seven other followers, all female. Two of them were part of his trio of primary assistants. The others had all been present at the sanctuary for differing times. Seri could see no particular reason for this specific group, save that they all seemed willing and eager to engage Forerunner in the conversations he sought. They also brought along a single donkey loaded down with many bags. It allowed most of the company to walk unencumbered.

"Can you tell where we're going?" she asked Ixchel after two days.

Ixchel made a noise Seri took to be disgust. "We started out heading south, but then shifted west. Today has been mostly southeast. We have made little progress."

"We're not sticking to the roads. That's for sure."

"I am not convinced he knows where we are going."

Seri's eyes trailed to the bandage on Ixchel's ribs. "How is your side?"

"It heals well."

"Was Forerunner right? Do you truly prefer to have a scar?"

Ixchel considered for a moment. "It is… a memory. When I notice the scar in years to come, I will remember fighting that creature."

"And that's a good thing?"

Ixchel nodded. She pulled up the side of her skirt much higher than usual. Seri's eyes darted around to see if either of the men were nearby. "Look," Ixchel said. Seri looked back and saw her indicating a small scar near the top of her thigh. "This is from the fight on Zes Sivas, against Volraag and his assassin."

"Oh. I didn't even know you had been hurt then."

"If one is not hurt, is it truly a battle?"

Seri wrinkled her brow. "I'd rather avoid battles altogether, myself."

"That is why you have me."

Seri stifled a laugh. "I guess so."

"My friends!" Forerunner called. "Let us move on!" He pointed forward and set out, expecting everyone to follow.

"Which way is he heading now?" Seri asked.

Ixchel sighed loudly. "Northeast."

• • • • •

"Dravid, I need your help." Seri knelt on the ground next to her friend.

He raised his eyebrows. "You've barely spoken to me since we left the sanctuary. But as always, whatever you need, I'm here."

Seri winced. She had been avoiding him since their hug. She wanted to say more, to try to explain herself, but she couldn't. She didn't know how.

"I'm sorry. I shouldn't have done that."

He nodded. "I forgive you, of course. What's going on?"

"You remember when we first arrived in Varioch and we both tried to sense which way to go?"

Dravid nodded.

"We need to do that again. I think I'm sensing something." She held out her hand.

Dravid hesitated only a moment before taking her hand in his. She

tried not to think of it as anything other than uniting their magic
senses. Not uniting anything else. Except now that she tried not to
think of it, it filled her thoughts. Great.

She let go of his hand. "Let's... try without that." A bit of confusion
and maybe hurt flashed across his face. Seri tried to ignore that. She
closed her eyes and took a deep breath. Reach out. Feel the vibrations.

"I haven't used these senses much lately," Dravid muttered. Of
course. He had the new power to focus on.

There. She found it. "Um, that way," she pointed, then opened one
eye to see. Dravid opened his eyes, noted her direction, and closed
them again.

She focused again. Yes, definitely. A strong power, not very far away
at all. She could feel it even over the strangeness of Forerunner's
power behind her.

"I feel it," Dravid said. "I think it's the direction we're going. Not
far."

"Yes." She opened her eyes and looked at him. "It's not Volraag.
He's too far away, or I'd feel the Bond. So who is it? The boy I'm
looking for? Or Forerunner's friend?"

Dravid frowned. "Could be either of them. Or maybe they're the
same person. But I don't think so. This feels more like Antises magic.
Not... his." He gestured toward Forerunner.

"Good point." Seri licked her lips. The brush against the new power
source actually made her thirsty. "Maybe we're back on track."

"We'll know soon enough, I think."

• • • • •

Marshal knelt again and put his hand in the dirt. This time, he felt
more than he expected, and almost immediately.

"That's different."

"What is it?" Victor asked. He stood next to his friend while the rest
of the squad packed up their camp.

"It's not Volraag... or anyone like him. I'm sensing someone or
something not far away. Very powerful. But not the same."

"What does that mean?"

"I don't know. When we were near Volraag, I could feel his power. It
was like mine. But this isn't."

"A wild magician?" Victor suggested. "Or even a regular magician, I
guess."

Marshal stood and dusted off his hands. "I don't think so. I think magicians use the same kind of power that I do. This is… not like it at all."

Victor held out his hand and wiggled his fingers. "So not shaking?"

"No, not exactly. More like a large release, followed by nothing, then another release."

"Release?"

"Of power. I think."

"Which direction?"

Marshal thought for a moment, then pointed northwest. Somewhere else, he heard a distant howl. Wolves?

"Huh. Well, we're going northeast. Unless you think we should go that way?"

"I don't think we'll have to."

"Why not?"

"I think it's moving. And coming toward us."

(((54)))

Dravid scowled. What good was all this new power if he still had to use this crutch? He hated traveling again, especially now that Forerunner led them. Admittedly, he didn't mind very much being the only other man in a group of eleven. Everywhere he turned, he saw something to admire.

Yet his thoughts remained focused on Seri. Helping her with the magic detection yesterday had only reminded him of the awkwardness between them. There had to be something he could do or say to fix things.

Ixchel dropped back to walk beside him. "My Lady suggested I ask you a question. Are we closer to the magic source you two found yesterday?"

"Why doesn't she ask me, or check for herself?"

"She has. She just wants confirmation."

"Is she afraid to talk with me?"

"Afraid? Why would she be afraid?"

Dravid sighed. "I don't know. I think she's worried I might hurt her."

"Then I would have to hurt you."

"Ha. I know. I meant emotionally."

Ixchel grunted.

"You do know what I mean, right? I mean, even with your warrior training, surely you had some time for…"

"For what?"

"Romance?"

"I… never had time for…"

"Ixchel!" Forerunner swept up next to them with a flourish of his

246

sleeves. "I must ask something of you."

"The answer is no."

Dravid stifled a laugh. This should be interesting.

"I need you to protect me," Forerunner said, ignoring her response.

"Protect you?" Ixchel stopped walking. This time Dravid couldn't stop his laugh. He and Forerunner paused and turned back to her.

Forerunner nodded and gestured in the direction they walked. "It's not far now. When I see my friend, I will have to help him."

"Help him with what?" Dravid asked.

Forerunner spared him a glance. "Help him to wake up, you could call it. At any rate, his... companions will not understand what I am doing. They may try to stop me. I want you to protect me from them."

"And why would I do that?"

"Because you know." Forerunner pointed at her. "You know what it looked like when I helped Seri with her star-sight."

"You protected yourself from me then."

"But I may not be able to do so this time. There will be more than one of them. But you know that I meant no harm to Seri." He waved at Dravid. "And when I healed him. This is the same kind of thing."

"I can't believe you want help from me. I don't trust you."

He held up a finger. "But you know what I am doing. You know that I do not mean to harm this man. All I ask is that you let me finish helping him. Then they will all see. They will understand. Just like you did when I helped Seri."

Ixchel did not answer. Dravid found himself very curious about all this, knowing what he and Seri had sensed.

"Maybe we should let this play out, Ixchel," he said. "I want to see what happens."

"I will not kill for you," Ixchel said.

"I would not ask," Forerunner said. "Just hold them back." He turned his gaze toward Dravid. "You might want to be ready as well. This is going to be... fascinating."

• • • • •

Seri saw them before anyone else. They had entered a more open area of Varioch's countryside, a large plain that opened up without any trees before rising up into a new line of hills. The opening let her catch a glimpse of high mountains off toward the north. But as her eyes came back down, she saw a small group of men walking together.

Their paths looked to intersect in moments.

"Hello over there!" Forerunner called.

The men, hearing him, stopped walking and turned to face their group. As they drew closer, Seri noticed they all carried weapons. They looked rough and dangerous. A large Ch'olanese man held some kind of spear. Four others around him carried swords and spears. But the two that broke off and came toward them demanded Seri's attention.

The tallest of the two looked quite handsome for a pale-skinned Varioch resident. His blond hair reached to his shoulders. His face held a short beard, but he looked no older than Seri and her friends. His muscles bulged out of some kind of leather shirt with a beautiful gold-trimmed red cloak on his shoulders. A sword hung on one side of his belt, and some other odd device with a chain hung on the other.

Seri's attention turned to the second young man. He also wore a sword at his side, but otherwise dressed in a simple tunic and trousers. Ugly scars like ropes criss-crossed his face. His hair mirrored his companions, but brown like Seri's own.

"It's him," Seri gasped aloud.

"Who's him?" Dravid said.

Seri pointed. "The one with the scars. He's the one I saw in the Otherworld! The one who fought Curasir!"

"Him? That's your 'boy'?" Dravid paused. "You must be right. I can sense his power. Like a Lord himself."

The other five men followed the first two, looking curiously at all of them.

No. The young man's power was not like a Lord; it was stronger. Stronger than any of the Lords or Masters. He might be more powerful than Forerunner, though his power could be hard to measure. And yet, she felt something else as well. She couldn't grasp it. For a moment, his power had seemed even greater, but now it didn't. So strange.

The young man opened his mouth to speak, but Forerunner cried out first.

"There you are!"

• • • • •

"This might be the last thing I expected," Marshal whispered to Victor as they approached the strange group of travelers.

Most of this group were women, and almost all of them wore simple white robes. It seemed an unusual choice for traveling apparel. Their leader, a man, boasted even stranger clothing: beige trousers and a multi-colored tunic with long sleeves that hung from his wrists. A crimson-trimmed purple cloak hung from his broad shoulders. Long, pale hair framed a face whose skin tone looked darker than the others', but not by much. Or did it? Marshal blinked.

"Who are these people?" Victor said.

Marshal's eyes flickered to the last three members of the group, the only others not dressed in white robes. They all seemed to be around his age with dark skin, like Topleb. Ch'olan, maybe? The one other male dressed in more casual clothes, but leaned on a crutch. Was he missing part of a leg? His face also looked bruised.

One of the remaining two women wore robes, but blue not white. Did that make her some kind of leader to the others? He thought her long brown hair quite... lovely. She said something to the young man beside her, but kept her eyes focused on Marshal. Her attention made him uncomfortable. He wouldn't have noticed her other companion if she hadn't been so extraordinary.

She wore a calf-length skirt, but no shirt. Instead, she had cloth wrapped around her upper chest, leaving her stomach bare. Two green feathers hung from a tight braid on the left side of her rounded face, which had twin black stripes painted on either cheek. She carried a round shield, painted orange with three green stripes, and had drawn a short sword from her belt.

"Is she barefoot?" Victor whispered. The other members of the curse squad came up behind them. Marshal opened his mouth to suggest they wait when the strangely-clad man cried out in a voice that sent tiny vibrations across Marshal's skin: "There you are!"

The man rushed forward. Marshal held out his hand in greeting, but the man shoved past him. Victor instinctively drew his sword.

"My friend! I've missed you so much!" the strange man said, again with the strange voice.

He placed his hands on Wolf's shoulders.

"Wolf?" Marshal stared at the two of them.

Wolf lifted his face and looked up at the strange man. "Do... do you know me?" he asked.

"Know you? I've been searching everywhere for you! But I need you to do something right away."

"Wait just a minute—" Marshal started.

"Wake up!" The strange man placed one of his hands on top of Wolf's head. Power and light erupted from him. The other squad members were thrown back several feet. Marshal and Victor managed to stay upright, but both took a couple of steps backward.

Marshal's mind struggled to comprehend the turn of events. This man was using some sort of magic, far different from his own, a magic made of heat and light. A magic against which Marshal had no defense.

And neither did Wolf. He screamed.

• • • • •

"What are you doing?" Victor shouted. He took a step toward Wolf and his attacker.

The flat of a sword blade rested against his chest. "Do not interfere." It was the barefoot warrior girl.

Wolf's scream flailed against his ears, painful in its volume. He almost believed more than one person—or animal—was screaming.

"Out of my way." Victor pushed the sword blade away. It came back, this time pointed at him.

He lifted his own sword. The girl raised an eyebrow, but did not back down. They stood for a moment, Wolf still screaming, looking at each other.

The white-robed women streamed down, all coming between Wolf and the other squad members.

"I do not want to fight you," Victor said. He feinted a stab at her exposed stomach. For the first time, he noticed she wore a bandage on her side.

She dodged easily, then took a simple slash at him. "Then don't."

"Your friend is hurting my friend. I have to stop it."

"This must happen."

"Woman, stand aside!" He made a more aggressive attack. She caught it on her shield, then countered, forcing him to dodge back.

"Man, I will not." Yet she cast a quick glance back at Wolf and the other man. She didn't seem to have convinced herself.

"I do not want to hurt you!" Victor spun and found himself blocked again.

"You would not be able to." This time, Victor used his own sword to block hers. He tried to slip up under it to attack again, but her shield came down just in time to stop him.

"You're that sure, huh?" A vibration ran through his hand. He didn't know what was going on here, and desperately wanted to help Wolf.

But at the same time, he didn't want his battle rage to take over with so many potential innocents around.

They exchanged several more thrusts, blocks, parries. She fought well. Very well. At least the equal of the Remavian Guard he had fought, if not better. He almost didn't notice that she kept trying to maneuver him further away from Wolf.

He stepped back and took his flail from his belt. The old one. He still hadn't made up his mind.

"Interesting weapon choice," she said. "Are you any better with it than you are with a sword?"

"Let's find out." The flail began to spin and Victor moved forward.

• • • • •

At Wolf's scream, Marshal started forward.

"Wait," said a voice, and the one-legged man hobbled in front of him. "Let it happen."

"Get out of my way."

He shook his head. "No, you don't understand. He's helping him."

"You call that help?" Out of the corner of his eye, Marshal saw Victor engage with the warrior girl. And the other women rushed down into the way too.

"Please. Just wait a moment."

Marshal let his power flow out of his feet, rumbling through the ground around them. "Move."

His opponent's hand began to glow. What was this? "You aren't the only one with power," he said. He drew in the air and created a kind of shield between them. It appeared almost made of golden light. In any other circumstance, Marshal would be fascinated.

But now it only made him angry. Wolf was in danger, hurting. He would not lose another squad member. Not one more.

Marshal grabbed the shield and let his own power escape. The glowing disc shattered into thousands of pieces that dissolved in the air as they fell. His opponent looked stunned.

Marshal shoved him out of the way. He staggered and fell, leaving the path open to Wolf.

But it was too late.

(((55)))

Dravid lost his balance from the shove and hit the ground. He tried to grab at the scar-faced man's ankle as he stepped past, but missed.

Then Seri. Beautiful Seri. She came out of nowhere, rushing in front of Forerunner, hands out.

"Stop, all of you!" she cried. "This is not what it looks like!" Dravid heard her, but he doubted very many others did, over Wolf's screaming, the clash of swords (Ixchel?), and all the other voices from both sides yelling at each other.

And then Dravid's worst nightmare unfolded in front of him. One of the ragged warriors, the Ch'olanese one, shoved one of the women aside, bellowed a war cry, and used some kind of tool to launch a spear straight at Forerunner.

Except Seri was there. In the way. He didn't see her until too late. Dravid could see the horror on his face as his spear struck this beautiful woman in the gut.

Her mouth and eyes went wide. She clutched at the spear and went down. No. No. No!

Dravid screamed. The scar-faced man caught Seri as she fell, holding her gently.

Ixchel dropped her own sword and ran.

Forerunner let the strange man fall in the same moment, his hands still glowing.

Dravid scrambled to Seri's side as the scar-faced man knelt down, still holding her. So much blood! Her robes turned purple with it. How could this be? Not Seri. She gasped, over and over, struggling to breathe.

"Seri! Seri!"

The scar-faced man looked up at Dravid, tears in his eyes. "This wound is mortal," he said.

Ixchel seized Forerunner by his tunic and yanked him toward Seri. "Heal her!" she shouted at him.

Forerunner looked drained, but horrified. "I cannot," he said. "My power is exhausted."

"Then show me!" Dravid said. "Maybe my power can do it!"

Forerunner shook his head. "No, you're not ready."

Dravid's hand glowed and he reached out, but hesitated. Without knowing what to do, he might only make it worse. But he couldn't lose her!

"You cannot do it," Forerunner said. "But he can." He pointed.

Dravid looked up. The man Forerunner came to find stood up. At first, he looked the same as he had before: a disheveled, skinny man with long gray-streaked hair. But then he began to change. His eyes glowed, and his entire body began to shift, to grow. Muscles expanded, splitting his already-torn clothing in multiple places. He rose several inches taller. His hair, so ragged and tangled before, grew even longer, smoothing and transforming into a beautiful mix of brown, gray, and white.

"Wolf?" said one of the other warriors.

The one who had thrown the spear stood ashen-faced, wringing his hands. "She got in the way," he murmured. "I didn't mean…"

"My friend!" Forerunner called to the one called Wolf. "Your power is needed, right away!"

Seri's whole body shook. "I think it's too late," said the scar-faced man.

"No!" Dravid tried to take her away from him. "It can't be!"

The Wolf approached slowly. Too slowly. Ixchel reached out to grab him, but pulled back immediately, holding her hand as if it burned. He looked down at Seri, the scarred man, and Dravid. His eyes seemed made of the same substance as Forerunner's magic, glowing and golden. They were too bright to look at for long, and Dravid turned his attention back to Seri. Her breath came out in one long exhale, and her hand started to fall away.

Wolf bent down and reached out his hands. One touched Seri's head and the other her stomach where the spear still protruded and blood continued to flow. "I will permit this," he said in a voice resonating with strange power. "But there will be a cost later." He turned to look at Dravid.

"I will pay it! Help her!"

Wolf's hands glowed. "Remove the spear," he said. The blond warrior stepped over, grasped the spear's shaft, and yanked it free. More blood exploded from the wound, but Seri did not react. Was she already gone?

The glow spread around Seri's wound. It grew brighter until Dravid had to close his eyes. Just like when Forerunner healed him. But would it be enough?

• • • • •

Seri opened her eyes. What a strange dream she had... And then the memory of pain rushed back. The impact in her stomach like a powerful kick. The unbelievable agony that spread out from it. Losing her breath. And then... nothing. The pain vanished. And...

She looked up into glowing eyes. This was the man Forerunner had come to find. A beautiful man, but something more than that. As she stared, she understood. He wasn't a man. He resembled those six beings she had seen in the Otherworld.

And in that moment, she saw everything. Her vision exploded with light. Everywhere light. Overwhelming. Intoxicating. Glorious. Her star-sight had returned.

The man standing above her glowed with power, incredible power like the ones in the Otherworld. She found herself drawn to him in ways she couldn't explain. Behind him, Forerunner stood, his power diminished greatly, but still there. And Dravid, dear Dravid, kneeling beside her, power glowing inside of him as well.

She turned her head, realizing someone else held her. Someone with power. She looked up into brown eyes surrounded by horrible scars. Eyes that stared at her with almost as much concern as Dravid. But behind them... she saw power. Power like the Masters and Lords, yet more. Power that drew her even more than the strange man who had healed her. It was the power of Antises. She had found him. For in that moment, she knew. He wasn't just the boy she saw in the Otherworld. He was the lost King. He had to be.

"You..." she whispered. Both Dravid and the young man bent down to hear her. "You're the one. The one I've been looking for." At his look of confusion, she added, "You fought Curasir."

With those words, she felt drained beyond understanding. She heard Dravid say her name. But she could not reply. Her eyes drifted back and she lost herself again.

(((56)))

Talinir reached for the next ledge, but kept his eyes low. The steeper their path grew, the harder it became to avoid looking at the stars.

"Shouldn't be far now," Janaab called from above.

"What shouldn't?" Talinir couldn't keep the annoyance from his voice. His human companion continued to be vague about their destination.

He pulled himself up and found Janaab waiting for him. They stood on a relatively flat surface high above the wastelands. About a dozen feet away, another sharp incline rose another eight feet before leveling out again. Janaab pointed toward it.

"I think we can get a look just over that ridge," he said, his voice lower. "We might want to keep it quiet now."

Talinir raised an eyebrow, then strode to the next ridge. In the primary world, he would have had to climb it. Here, he could look directly over the top. Height had its advantages. He bent and helped Janaab clamber up to sufficient height to see as well.

At first, he saw nothing unusual. The mountains opened into a much larger flat area here. In the distance, they resumed climbing higher than Talinir cared to climb. But then he noticed the base of the next ascension. Were those... buildings?

A simple bit of Eldanim magic let him focus his eyes for a longer distance. Definitely buildings. The architecture made him think of a blend of Intal Eldanir's decorative flourishes and the strength of Ch'olan's masonry. The buildings appeared well lit and he could see figures moving about between them.

"Is this where the Durunim live?" But even as he asked the question, he knew the answer. Those people, whoever they were, could not be

Durunim or Eldanim. They lacked the lengthened proportions all his people possessed here in the Starlit Realm. They seemed closer to humans, though still taller and stronger.

"The third race," Janaab said. "Or at least that's my belief. Humans live in one world. These people live here. And you live in between." He continued to keep his voice quiet.

"But who are they?"

Janaab shrugged. "I know they are not to be trifled with. Their magic is innate, like yours, but far more powerful. At least the ones I've seen are."

"I must learn more."

Janaab shook his head. He let himself slide down the incline to the previous surface. "They're dangerous, I tell you. We're probably already tempting trouble by staying here this long."

Talinir opened his mouth to ask why. At that moment, a pair of heavy feet landed hard right in front of him, kicking up dust into his eyes. He took a moment to refocus and looked up.

A man looked down at him. But not a man. He stood at least seven and a half feet tall. His clothes, strangely enough, resembled the nobility of Mandiata: a bright, full-length tunic topped with colorful beaded necklaces. His musculature rippled beneath his shirt, his skin glowing with a golden power Talinir had never seen.

"Come to spy on us, Eldani?" The stranger's voice boomed around him, vibrating with power. He projected magic through his voice? "You would do better to bow at our feet!"

Before Talinir could react, the stranger grabbed his forearm and yanked him up onto the upper surface. His skin burned where the hand contacted it. He pulled away and stared in horror. Most of his forearm had turned into the color-absorbing blackness of the Durunim.

The stranger laughed at his reaction. "Now you know the truth. Welcome!" He spread his arms wide. "Come. Worship us. It is what you were made for!"

"Talinir! Dive backwards. Now!" Janaab's voice broke through to him, also vibrating with magic, with command. Talinir launched himself backward without hesitation.

Below, he saw Janaab thrust one hand forward. The cliff edge below the stranger exploded in rock and debris, knocking him off his feet. At the same time, he threw the other hand up toward Talinir. The warden felt waves of vibrational power rolling over his body, slowing his descent. With plenty of time, he twisted into a ball, then straightened out with his feet facing down. Janaab released him, and he landed with no more impact than if he had hopped a few feet.

"They know we're here now. Run!"

Once again, Talinir did not question his companion. They slid down the next ridge and hurried down the mountain as fast as they could. Behind them, Talinir heard the booming laughter again, followed by shouts he couldn't make out.

Janaab released another vibratory shockwave behind them. It might make a temporary solution, but if he did that too much, he might bring the whole mountain down on top of them. Talinir doubted whether his companion's fearsome power could daunt their pursuers. That probably explained why he had struck at the cliff instead of the stranger himself.

Janaab said something, but Talinir couldn't make it out over the sounds of rocks falling. It might have included the word "hide."

He risked a glance back. He could see glowing figures in the distance, but couldn't tell how close they followed.

Janaab scrambled down another incline, nearly plunging over a steep cliff. "Over there!" he shouted and pointed. Talinir looked and saw a cave mouth. He rushed to it, followed by Janaab.

It could barely be called a cave. The opening extended no more than a dozen feet back. "It'll have to do." Janaab pushed him, and they both reached the far wall and turned back. Janaab lifted his hands, pointing toward the cave mouth.

"Wait!" Talinir exclaimed. But Janaab unleashed his power and brought down the ceiling in another avalanche. In a moment, they were trapped.

"I have to hide my power." Janaab dropped to the floor and rolled into a fetal position. He closed his eyes and lay completely still.

Talinir slid down and sat against the back wall. He could see a few tiny gaps in the rocks. At least they wouldn't suffocate. But they had trapped themselves with no way to escape.

(((57)))

Marshal looked up in confusion. "What did she mean? Who are you people?"

The warrior girl stepped in. "Give her to me. Now."

Marshal saw no reason to disobey. She took the young woman from his arms and stepped back. The other young man joined her as they looked over their friend. Marshal stood and looked around.

The squad stood behind him, clearly uneasy and not sure what to do. Topleb's face had drained of all color and he trembled. "It'll be all right," Marshal said to them, lifting a hand for a moment. "We'll figure this out."

Victor stood holding Topleb's spear-dart, covered in the girl's blood. She had died in his arms, hadn't she? Or come as close to death as someone might go without reaching it. And Wolf...

He looked up at Wolf. The man he knew had changed in so many ways. No longer skinny or morose. He fairly crackled with mysterious power now, power he had used to heal—to heal! How was that possible?

"Wolf?" Victor said. "Are you all right?"

"You call him Wolf? How utterly delightful," said the man in the colorful outfit.

"I don't belong here," Wolf said. He turned and walked away.

• • • • •

Victor watched Wolf walk away, followed by the man who had changed him, and the women in white. He looked down at the spear in his hands, still dripping blood. What had just happened here?

The rest of the squad gathered around him and Marshal, full of their own questions.

"Who are these people?"

"What did he do to Wolf?"

"Is the girl all right?" Topleb.

Victor put a hand on Topleb's shoulder. "It was an accident," he said. "And it looks like she'll be fine."

Topleb still shook. "In all my days, I never hurt a woman. Never." His eyes widened even further. "Do you think I'll be cursed for this?"

In the heat of the moment, Victor hadn't even considered that. What if he had hurt the warrior girl? Would he have been cursed?

"I think it would have happened already," Marshal said to Topleb, "if it were going to happen."

Topleb nodded, but did not look comforted.

"What in Theon's crumbling pillars is going on?" Rufus demanded.

"I don't know," Victor said. "But we're going to find out. Marshal?"

Marshal looked at the new people and considered. "You see what you can find out from Wolf and his new friend. I'll talk to the others."

Victor nodded and headed to the crowd around Wolf. The man who had changed him noticed his approach and came out to meet him.

"Ah, you are the one called Victor, yes? I am Forerunner."

"How do you know my name?"

"I know many things. I am Forerunner."

"What does that mean?"

He shrugged. "It is who I am. It is what I am. That is all." He cocked his head and looked Victor over. "You are the unique one, aren't you?"

"What do you mean? And what did you do to Wolf?"

"I restored him. As for you... this is very strange. I don't see that you've lost much of anything. That is, you've lost dreams and purpose, but found them anew. Fascinating. I'm not sure I can help you."

"I didn't ask for your help."

He spread his arms wide, those ridiculous sleeves dangling. "Yet that is what I do. I restore that which was lost. And I prepare the way."

"Prepare the way for what?"

"Ah, that would be telling."

Victor shook his head. Pointless. "Edin Na Zu." He hadn't found much use for his favorite phrase in a while. "I want to speak with Wolf."

"I'm not sure he wants to speak with you."

"Why not? I'm his friend."

"Are you? Did you ever try to help him?"

"Of course I did! And I fought to protect him!"

Forerunner snorted. "As if he needed protection from you."

Victor glanced at the muscular being who stood apart from them. "Maybe not now, but before... he was a sad little man. I did what I could for him. We all did." He gestured back to the rest of the squad. "We're all his friends."

"A sad little man." Forerunner spat out the words as if they tasted bad in his mouth. "So little you know. So little all of you know."

"Then educate me." Victor's eyes narrowed. Mystical power or not, if this man didn't get out of his way soon...

"I will do that, but not you alone. It will be all of you together. For we are going with you."

"You're what?"

Forerunner chuckled. "You're on your way to the portal in Ch'olan, are you not? That is where your 'Wolf' and I need to go next."

Victor tried to keep his mouth from dropping open. "I, ah, don't know if bringing all these women along is such a good idea. We've had soldiers chasing us, and—"

Forerunner waved a hand. "I will send them away. Do not worry." He looked at Marshal talking with the others. "Now those three will do as they will. But I suspect they're coming too."

Victor looked around. "At this rate, we may as well be a caravan."

• • • • •

Marshal approached the sleeping young woman and her two friends. As he drew near, neither of them looked pleased to see him. The warrior girl reached for her sword.

He lifted his hands. "I mean no harm," he said. "I want to apologize for all the misunderstanding here."

The young man pointed at his friend's bloody robes. "You call this a misunderstanding?"

"No, I call it a tragedy. My friend over there is devastated about it."

"He should be."

"To be fair, he thought your friend was attacking ours. You have to admit it looked like it."

"We tried to tell you."

"And how would you have reacted if I had appeared suddenly and done something like that to one of your friends?"

"I would have attacked you," the warrior girl said. "He is correct, Dravid."

Dravid snorted. Marshal suspected he was not being reasonable because of who had gotten hurt, not the circumstances themselves.

"Dravid? My name is Marshal. We have recently come from Lord Volraag's army and are on our way north to Ch'olan. We've been attacked several times in the last few days, so this naturally felt like another one. Again, I'm sorry for all of it."

The warrior girl stood and gave a short bow. "I am Ixchel, Holcan to my Lady here."

"Who is she? How did she know me? She said she was looking for me."

"This is my Lady Seri, mage of Arazu. I will let her explain anything beyond that."

"A mage? That explains her robes, then? What about those over there?" Marshal pointed at the other women.

"They are... followers of the other man. Forerunner. We are not like them."

"I see. Do you know what he did to my friend Wolf?"

"I do not."

Dravid sighed. "I think he awoke some power in him that he didn't know he had. Or maybe he forgot it. I'm not sure."

Marshal nodded. "I knew someone else nearby was using magic of some kind. I never guessed it was him."

Seri stirred. "I think she's waking up," Marshal noted.

•••••

Seri heard voices, but something else awakened her. The magic. The power so close she could taste it. How could he stand it? How could he contain all of it?

She opened her eyes. She lay on the ground, Dravid kneeling beside her. Ixchel and the scarred boy stood at her feet. All eyes turned to her.

"You're already awake?" Dravid asked. "Are you all right?"

"I'm exhausted, but I'll be fine," she said. She looked up at the boy. Man, really. "Who are you?"

He knelt beside her. "My name is Marshal. Your friends told me yours. You were... looking for me?"

"I saw you. Fighting Curasir. I helped cut off his power."

Marshal blinked, a look of surprise crossing his face. "That was in the Otherworld! You were there?"

She nodded and pulled herself into a sitting position. Only then did she realize the spear and her subsequent healing had ripped open her robe, leaving her stomach almost as exposed as Ixchel's. She gasped and flipped several folds over it. Marshal, to his credit, looked away momentarily.

"Yes, uh, in the Otherworld. I ran there to escape Volraag when he attacked the other Lords."

"Wait, wait, wait." Marshal held up a hand. "Volraag? I can see we have a lot to tell each other."

"You know him?"

"He's my half-brother."

Silence.

"What a family," Dravid muttered.

"Listen," Marshal said. "I think we should tell each other everything."

Seri nodded, but Dravid frowned.

"Let me get my friend. He needs to hear this too." Marshal stood and called, "Victor!"

The blond warrior disengaged from Forerunner and strode over to them.

"Are you getting anywhere?" he asked. "That guy... he makes my head spin."

"Welcome to the club." Seri laughed.

"I'm Victor. You are?"

Everyone introduced themselves again.

Victor bowed to Ixchel. "You're good with a sword," he said, smiling. "I am impressed. Are you from Ch'olan too?"

She nodded. "You are skilled as well," she said. She did not smile. Oh, Ixchel.

"Tell the squad to start setting up camp," Marshal told Victor. "I don't think we're going further today. And then come back here. We need to talk."

Victor nodded, and went back to the other warriors. When he came back, the large Ch'olanese man who had thrown the spear came with him. He looked absolutely distraught, his head hung low, wringing a piece of cloth in his hands.

"Topleb here would like to say something," Victor said.

"I... I am nothing, my lady. I tried to help a friend, and I hurt you. For that, I will never forgive myself, and I don't expect you to, either. It was a terrible thing. Terrible. If Theon doesn't curse me, I curse myself."

"No, no." Seri shook her head. Even that little movement gave her more fatigue. "It wasn't your fault. It's all right."

Topleb looked up, not at Seri, but at Ixchel. "Does she mean it, Holcan? If not, you may strike my head from my body right here."

Ixchel rolled her eyes. "She means it. My Lady is nothing if not forgiving."

Topleb took a deep breath. "Then you have my thanks, and my servitude, great lady. If ever you come to Ch'olan, I will show you all the greatness you can find there. I will serve you in any way you desire. I am in your debt."

"We might just be on our way to Ch'olan," Seri said.

"Really? That would be outstanding! I can—"

"Not now, Topleb," Marshal interrupted. "For now, let's get the camp set up. I need to talk with the great lady now."

"Of course, of course." Topleb bowed and backed away several steps, bowed again, then finally turned and hurried away.

Victor laughed. "I don't think I've ever seen his mood change that fast!"

"He's a good man," Marshal said. He looked back at Seri. "Thank you for treating him that way."

"Of course. How else would I treat him?"

Marshal settled on the ground. Victor and Ixchel joined them.

"Now. Which of us should go first?"

(((58)))

Kishin sat in his dark room, the staff resting across his knees. He did not need it to be dark, but it felt comforting nonetheless. He had grown used to sitting in the dark over the years. And he still felt no desire to let Aapo know of his change.

His daughter, the sole reason he returned to Woqan, was not here, and would probably not return. He could seek her out. He should seek her out. It would not be too difficult.

But would that give him the cause Chimon claimed he needed? Being a father seemed a good cause, but not much of one for a child already grown to adulthood. As much as his heart desired to find her, that might not be the best course of action just yet.

His curse had been lifted. Everything came back to that, over and over again. Because of Marshal. Whose curse had also been lifted, if he understood correctly.

"Until all curses are lifted," he whispered. That was how the old saying went, wasn't it? The words those in the cursed village outside of town used to encourage each other. Empty words, which no one really believed, but repeated all the same. Just in case.

Could all curses be undone? He was living proof that some could. But who would know? Who could tell him more of this? Chimon? The Eldanim? The mages of Zes Sivas?

Connection. His daughter might still be on Zes Sivas. He could go seek the mages' wisdom and look for her at the same time.

But would they believe him? He needed to be sure. Perhaps...

He reached a resolution. Knew what he had to do.

"Aapo!"

A few moments later, his servant entered, squinting at the darkness.

"What is it, sir?"

"I need a message sent to all of my contacts. I am searching for someone. Tell them I seek a young man of Varioch with horrible facial scars. He possesses great k'uh. He may be traveling in the company of others, possibly even one of the Eldanim."

Aapo's eyes widened, even in the dark. "Will that be all, sir?"

"Double my usual reward offer. I want to know where this man is. And I want to know as soon as possible."

(((59)))

"I'm not the lost King," Marshal said.

"Yes, you are," Victor said.

Marshal pointed at Seri. "She just said the guy in the Otherworld is the King."

"No, I said he claimed to be the King," Seri said. "I don't know if he actually was."

"There can't be two Kings."

"Your mother said that your grandfather was King," Victor insisted. "That makes you the next King."

"Then who's the other guy?"

"I don't know!"

"Why do you think he's the King?" Dravid asked.

"It's his power," Seri said, gesturing. "It's different."

"Different how? He feels like one of the Lords to me."

"It's more than that."

"You say you can see magic with this star-sight of yours," Marshal said. "Can you explain what that looks like?"

Seri blinked and her vision changed. How glorious to have it back! She luxuriated in it for a moment before speaking.

"Most of the time, I see the magic of Antises as beams of colored light. There aren't very many out here, far from Zes Sivas, but there are a few. Here's a light blue beam right now." She reached out to the beam that came from the ground near Ixchel's bare feet. "Got it." She picked up a clod of dirt and let the magic vibrate it apart in her hand. "And then I release it."

She turned to Marshal. "But when I look at someone like you who possesses magic within them, it's different. You're like a glowing bundle of light."

"What color is it?"

"All colors, all mixed up together. But mostly just pure light without color. The Masters on Zes Sivas had brightness to them, strong power they had absorbed over the years. But they were nothing compared to the Lords. I saw all of them, and they all shone with tremendous brightness. Like you."

"Isn't that the way it should be, since I have Varion's power?"

"There's more to it, though." She leaned forward, staring at him. Marshal shifted under the intensity of her gaze. He wasn't used to girls looking at him for very long.

"It's like there is a brightness behind the brightness," Seri said at last.

"A what?"

"I don't know how else to explain it." She sat back. "There's just more. I know it."

"And my Lady does not lie," Ixchel said.

"No one is saying she does," Marshal said. "Just trying to understand."

"What about me?" Victor asked. "What do I look like?"

"You? Why would—oh!" Seri actually stood up and looked down at Victor. "Stand up!" she ordered. He glanced at Marshal and scrambled to his feet.

"What is it?"

Seri walked in a circle around him, forgetting about the hole in her robe again. "I've never seen this. This is… fascinating. Dravid, do you detect anything from him?"

Dravid frowned and closed his eyes. He reached out toward Victor. "Not really," he said at last. "But the lost King here is kind of dominating things in this area."

"I'm not the lost King."

Seri pointed from Marshal to Victor. "There are threads of light connecting you two. I didn't notice them before because I was so focused on Marshal's power."

"Connections?" Marshal and Victor looked at each other with raised eyebrows. "You don't mean a Binding, do you?"

"No, I've never been able to see Bindings before," Seri said. "This is something else." She traced something through the air with her fingers. "It's like… the threads come from Marshal, then wrap themselves around Victor's arms and legs. Amazing."

Victor looked at his hands. "I guess that explains what's been happening to me during battle."

Seri cocked her head. "So you must be absorbing it from him because you've been so close together for so long."

"But I'm not a mage or anything."

"I guess it's just the magic needing more space, since Marshal can't contain it all. I wonder how often this happens."

"And what about those two?" Marshal thumbed over his shoulder at Forerunner and Wolf.

"Different. Very different. Their magic is not of Antises like yours. I think it's from the Otherworld. It's more like a fire than light. Blazing. Pulsing. I've gotten used to it from Forerunner over the last couple of weeks, but the other man—Wolf—is more powerful than he is. I think he's like the others I saw in the Otherworld."

Marshal got to his feet. "It's about time I met this Forerunner, don't you think?"

"Be careful," Ixchel said. "He lies."

Marshal nodded. "I've met a few like that."

He crossed the open space toward Forerunner and his coterie. Off to the right, the curse squad had erected their camp and were talking together, casting occasional looks toward the white-robed women.

Forerunner saw Marshal approaching and came out to meet him, his arms spread. "Oh!" he cried. "Your loss is so great! It is too much for one man to bear!"

Before Marshal could react, Forerunner grabbed him by the shoulders and pulled him in close, resting his forehead against Marshal's. As they did, a low voice vibrated into Marshal's left ear, barely discernible.

"I am speaking so that only you can hear me. Listen well. As Forerunner, I am charged with restoring. Your new friends will have told you this. In a moment, I will tell you this out loud and say that I can help you."

Marshal opened his mouth to respond, but a touch of magic vibrated against his lips. "Do not speak yet. Let me finish. I can help you, but I must not. For the sake of this world, for the sake of your people, I must not! Your losses are horrible, but you need them to become who you must."

Forerunner pulled back, looking Marshal in the eyes. "For the sake of Antises, your world. It is not mine, but I have come to understand your people better. Seri and Dravid have shown me how amazing humans can be. I do not wish them harm."

"I am Forerunner!" he said, now in a louder voice that could be heard by his own people and by Victor and the others. "I am here to restore that which was lost. What was lost can be found. What was taken can be returned. Do not let these losses define you!"

Marshal pushed Forerunner's arms away. "I have lost nothing that you can restore," he said. "You cannot bring the dead back."

"That is not all you have lost," Forerunner said. He reached a finger toward Marshal's face.

Marshal grabbed the finger and twisted it away. "No games. No mysteries. And no more about my losses. Tell me what has happened to my friend Wolf." He spun Forerunner around and pointed.

"His name is Calu," Forerunner said. "I'm not sure how he came to this sad state, but he's been missing for quite some time. He is a friend of mine who forgot who and what he is."

"And what is that? Does he come from the Otherworld?"

"It is as you have said. I merely restored to him his memories and true form. I told you that I restore."

"I want to talk to him."

"You may try. I do not know if he will answer. He is remembering many things right now."

Marshal pushed past Forerunner and approached the man he had known as Wolf. The white-robed women moved out of his way. "Wolf? Can you hear me?"

"Forerunner has told you my name is Calu," he answered, his voice deep and resonant, nothing like the man Marshal knew. He turned and looked down at Marshal. "But you and the other squad members may call me Wolf for now... for the sake of the friendship you offered me."

"What has happened to you, Wolf?"

"I do not think I can explain, decanus. But I am remembering who I am."

Marshal nodded. "I'm not your decanus. But I'm glad this is a good thing. We all thought you were being attacked."

"Yes, well, you can't help your ignorance. Humans never have been very bright."

"Humans? So... you're not human?"

"I do not claim that any longer. No. In time, you will understand."

"I'm not sure about that."

Wolf lifted a hand, then lowered it. "I need more time. Please. Tell everyone to leave me alone for a while. I am remembering so much right now. It… is a lot to go through."

"I'll tell them," Marshal said. "Just know that we're still your friends. If you need anything, we will be there for you."

"Thank you."

Marshal turned to go, but Wolf caught his arm. "Marshal… Forerunner serves me and those like me. Do not mistake the hierarchy."

"I'll keep that in mind."

Wolf released his arm and Marshal walked back toward Victor and the others. He knew only one thing for certain: he didn't trust Wolf or Forerunner, despite their promises of friendship. Something seemed very wrong here.

• • • • •

Victor watched as everyone took a seat. Marshal and the curse squad on one side, Forerunner and two of his women to their right, and Seri with her friends to the left. Wolf remained standing off by himself. The other women gathered behind Forerunner.

Marshal glanced at Victor, then began speaking. "I think we've finally discussed all that needs to be straightened out," he said. "Now we need to figure out what happens next."

"We should go to Zes Sivas!" Seri said. "I need to bring you back to meet the Masters."

"I can't do that right now," Marshal said. "I have promises to keep. I told Topleb I would take him home. And my friend Talinir is trapped by my doing. So we're traveling to the, uh, place of magic in Ch'olan."

"High place," Forerunner said. "That's what it used to be called."

"All right. The high place. That's where I have to go."

"And that is where we must go as well," Forerunner said. "Calu desires to return to the Otherworld."

"Who's Calu?" Rufus asked.

"He means Wolf," Victor said.

"Wolf's from another world?"

"That explains some things," Topleb said. "He always seemed too smart to be Varioch."

"This is a very large group to travel with," Marshal said. "I don't think that's a good idea."

"You are correct," Forerunner said. "My followers will return to the sanctuary and await my return. I have already spoken with them about this."

"Your followers?" Victor said. "You're sending the women back? By themselves?"

Forerunner spread his hands out. "Is there danger in this land of curses? Who would harm them?"

Victor exchanged a look with Marshal. "Yes, there is danger. We've… learned that very well."

Marshal stood and looked at his squad. "Men. Victor, Topleb and I are going to Ch'olan. The rest of you do not need to come with us. And here is an opportunity for you to do some good. These women need an escort. I'd like you to go with them."

Gnaeus scratched his chin. "I think Merish and I are willin' to take on that task. Rufus?"

Rufus looked over at the women then back at Marshal. "I, I'd rather stay with you, sir. I've never seen Ch'olan."

"It's going to be a long walk, Rufus. Are you up for that?"

Rufus flushed. "Begging your pardon, sir, but don't you have one man over there without a leg? I think I can keep up as well as he can!"

"Just making the offer, Rufus." Marshal turned back to Forerunner. "I have two men willing to be your ladies' escorts. Is that acceptable?"

Forerunner looked to his two assistants, who nodded. "Thank you for your assistance," he said. "I'm sure your men will find an enthusiastic welcome at my sanctuary."

Gnaeus brightened. Victor nudged him. "You'd better behave," he whispered.

"I'm a good man!" Gnaeus protested.

"Of course you are."

"Fine. But after this, we should go to Zes Sivas!" Seri said.

Marshal sat down again. "I'm not promising, but I think that can happen."

Victor frowned. Going to Zes Sivas sounded all right, but everything had changed with these new arrivals. And how did this fit in with the goal of ending curses?

(((60)))

Volraag stood by the ship's rail and watched his hand as he rotated it. The fact that it didn't glow still surprised him. The glow within continued, giving him strength and warmth. Or at least it felt that way. The salty taste in his mouth had not diminished, either.

He had no idea how much this new power would enhance his own, or if it just strengthened his body. It seemed to interact with his other power somehow during his fight with Lord Tyrr, but just how he couldn't tell. It would have helped if Curasir had stuck around long enough to discuss this. Who else could he ask?

Tezan came to his side. The wild mage had been much more conciliatory since the portal. Perhaps the taste of power had convinced him where Volraag's words had not.

"What is our course, then?" Tezan asked.

Volraag pointed along the coastline. "We'll stay near the coast until we pass the border with Ch'olan. Then we'll swing out to avoid coming anywhere near Woqan. Somewhere to the east, we'll make landfall and then move north to the portal."

"As long as we don't go too far east. I can't imagine we'd get a warm welcome in Mandiata."

Volraag snorted. He squeezed the railing and felt disappointed when his fingers didn't break through it. Did he have more strength or was it nothing more than a feeling?

"Salt," Tezan said. "Do you taste salt?"

Volraag turned to look at him. "I wondered. So you do retain some of the power that flows through you."

Tezan shrugged. "A little here and there. I… It feels good."

"It does."

Tezan looked down at his own hands. "It's changing us, Volraag. And I don't just mean getting stronger. Do you sense it?"

"What do you mean?"

"I'm feeling… I don't know. I want more of it. More of the power. It's like a hunger."

Volraag agreed, but didn't reply. Rathri appeared on his other side. For a moment, Volraag didn't consider the significance of this. Tezan reacted first.

"Where did you come from?"

Rathri inclined his head. "That's a subject of much debate," he said in his usual rasp.

Volraag frowned at him. "When last I saw you, you were unconscious on the floor of a tunnel, about to be drowned. How did you get here?"

"If I told you all my secrets, Lord, I would not be as much use to you."

"You try my patience, assassin."

"He's like the tailless monkey of Lord Sakouna," Tezan muttered.

"My loss of consciousness was temporary," Rathri said. "I escaped the water, though I did get trapped for quite a while when the rest of the tunnel collapsed."

"Did you see what happened to Lord Tyrr?"

"By the time I escaped, there was no sign of him. He may have been buried. He may have escaped."

Volraag eyed the assassin. With the beating he took from Lord Tyrr, he should not even be able to walk. That kind of abuse would have broken most of the bones in a normal man's body. From all he knew of Rathri, he could think of no reason why he should have more endurance than anyone else. Yet Rathri stood here as if he had only returned from a casual walk.

"How did you get on the ship?" Tezan asked.

"Magic."

Volraag scowled. "I'll need a better answer than that."

"I met with Otioch, long enough to learn that your Remavian Guard was unable to stop your brother. After that, I hired a small and fast sailing vessel, caught up to you, and boarded this ship in the rear. I don't believe the captain even knows I'm here now."

"Is our spy still in place with them?"

"At last report, he was. I'm not sure how much you can depend on a conscript, though."

Volraag recalled the small man. "He might surprise us. You never know."

The three stood in silence. Volraag watched the waves.

"What is the result of your new powers?" Rathri asked.

"I don't know. I feel stronger, but I don't know if it means anything. I can feel it within me, though."

"Perhaps we can find a way to test it."

Volraag looked down at the corrupted skin of his assassin and considered the suggestion. "Perhaps," he said. But the longer he spent in Rathri's presence, the less he wanted to continue. Beyond the curse, something else disturbed him about the assassin.

(((61)))

"Did you see where they went?"

Talinir jerked at the sound of the voice. One of their pursuers must be standing directly outside their shelter. He glanced at Janaab. The man hadn't moved, still curled up.

Talinir drew his sword without a sound. If they were found, he would fight. He didn't quite understand the identity of these strange beings, but the marks on his forearm told him all he needed to know about them.

"Why can't we sense the magic-user?"

Another voice answered. "He must have cloaked himself. How else could he survive here? He looked human."

The first voice snorted. "I want to find the Eldani. I touched him, but didn't complete the process."

Talinir shivered, looking at his forearm. It had burned at the stranger's touch, but the feeling faded. Now it felt cold, cold and vibrating with a dull ache. What did it mean?

One of the voices outside said something about "downhill." Talinir heard the sounds of footsteps moving away. He rested his sword across his knees and waited. But as he did, anger built up inside. What nonsense was this? He was Talinir, warden of the Eldanim! Why should he fear these beings, whatever they were? He almost stood up before a saner part of his mind prevailed.

Instead, he waited. Janaab remained unmoving. Once, he thought he heard movement outside again, but it faded as soon as he tried to focus on it. Time crawled by. He looked up at the rock ceiling and smiled to himself. At least here he didn't have to worry about being caught by the stars.

Janaab uncurled and sat up, brushing himself off. "I think they're far enough away now," he said. "But we'll wait a while longer before trying to get out of here, just to be sure."

"Are you all right?"

Janaab shrugged. "I'm fine. What about you? How much did he touch you?"

Talinir displayed his forearm. "Ugh." Janaab sighed. "Well, now you know. It's not from spending too much time here, after all. Or at least, that's not the only reason."

"You mean...?"

"Yeah. They created the Durunim. And the Durunim serve them."

Talinir's gaze wandered to the dark spots on Janaab's own skin. "Then you've had other encounters with them."

Janaab nodded. "Barely escaped with my life the first time. Some of them know me now. But they don't seem interested in hunting too far from the mountains. Either they don't like to leave home, or..."

"Or what?"

"Or they're too busy to waste time with me. They didn't create the Durunim and send them to attack you just for fun, you know. I think they've got big plans. I've seen them moving entire armies around. And they're not moving toward Intal Eldanir either. I haven't been able to follow them, but they're definitely up to something."

Talinir felt reluctant to speak of the next thing on his mind. "The one we met spoke of... worship."

"That was the biggest surprise to me. They think of themselves as gods, it seems."

"They do not resemble any deity my people have ever worshipped, to my knowledge."

"But they do look like humanity's old gods. Before the Great Cataclysm and Akhenadom. Before Theon."

"Is that who you think they are?"

Janaab shrugged again. "Whether they are, or just believe they are, it doesn't make much difference. They have immense power, and they're not afraid to use it. My fear is that they'll cross over into my world. Who knows what will happen then?" He shifted to look more directly at Talinir. "This is what I wanted you to see. So you can tell Marshal and the girl about it."

"Why can't you tell them?"

"I don't know if I'll survive that long. But I have confidence in you."

That felt odd.

Talinir recalled something else from the encounter. "You commanded me."

"What?"

"When that thing had me, you ordered me to dive backwards."

"It worked, didn't it?"

"But you used magic in your voice. Like they're doing. I felt compelled to obey you."

Janaab scratched at the cave floor with his spear tip. "Over the years, I've learned some new tricks with my powers. That's one of them. You could have disobeyed me if you had wanted to. The command only works on someone that trusts you, or is inclined to trust you, I guess."

"How do I know you haven't been using it on me all along?"

Janaab lifted his brows. "Have I?"

No. He would have felt that, sensed it like he did this time.

"Get some rest," Janaab suggested. "We'll wait a couple more hours and then try to dig our way out without using magic, if possible. Then we head straight for the high place."

Talinir agreed. Time to get back to the primary world where he belonged.

(((62)))

Seri and Ixchel helped the other women hang up some curtains taken from the donkey's saddlebags. Seri was pleased to have some privacy, at least for this one evening. After the women and the donkey left tomorrow, she and Ixchel would be the only women left in a party of men. She couldn't help feeling a little nervous about that.

"What do you think of them?" she asked Ixchel as she tied one of the cords to a tree branch.

"They're acceptable," Ixchel said. "For those of you who care about privacy."

Seri giggled. "Not the curtains. I meant the men."

"Oh." Ixchel didn't answer for a moment. "The one I fought is a capable warrior."

"Victor? The magic he's drawing from Marshal is fascinating. It binds them together."

"They're Bonded?"

"No, I don't think so. I mean, I can't see Bindings. But it might have practically the same effect on them. I wonder if they know that."

"They seem to be good friends." Ixchel paused. "What about you, my Lady? Do you feel all right?"

"I'm tired, but that's all. Why?"

Ixchel gave another tug on a knot, then lowered her hands and looked at Seri. "You almost died. I was certain you *had* died. Yet you stand here as if nothing happened."

Seri looked down. "I, I'm trying not to think about that."

"It seems somewhat important."

"I don't know." Seri took a deep breath. "It hurt so much. And then I just... fell asleep, I guess. I started to dream something about the stars of the Otherworld… and then I was back. And it didn't hurt any more."

Ixchel frowned, but did not answer.

With the curtains completed, they moved to prepare their own bedrolls. Forerunner's assistants had already started a fire nearby. This far into Spring, the nights no longer felt frigid, but could still be cool.

Seri looked over the tear in her robe. The spear itself had not made a large hole, but someone had torn it open further to remove the spear or try to help her some other way. She looked at the ragged edges and fought back a lump in her throat. The blue robes meant so much to her, the symbol of her rank as a full mage. If she couldn't wear them, she might have to resort to her old orange acolyte robes. Ugh.

"I'll mend it for you," Ixchel said.

Seri looked up. "You can sew?"

Ixchel almost shrugged. "I can do some basic mending. Nothing very well."

"Ixchel, that would be fantastic!"

"Get them off and I'll see what I can do."

After Seri changed into her sleep clothes, Ixchel sat and began manipulating a needle and thread. She seemed frustrated with the robe. Seri watched for a few moments, but couldn't keep silent.

"This is so exciting! We've found him, Ixchel! Marshal. The one with the power. He can save Antises. I just know it!"

"I am pleased." She didn't look it.

"So. We let him finish this trip to Ch'olan. That shouldn't take long, should it? I don't know how far we are from Ch'olan, but I can't imagine it being that far. And then we can return to Zes Sivas. Jamana will be so excited. We call the Lords back, we have a new Passing, and then Marshal will heal the land. And be the new King!"

Ixchel grunted. She yanked at her thread. It didn't pull as far as she wanted it to. She yanked harder.

Malena, Forerunner's blonde assistant, came up behind her. "I would be happy to fix that for you," she offered. "I spent two years as a seamstress in Raeton."

"You're from Rasna?" Seri said. "I thought all of you were from Varioch."

"Most are," she answered with a smile. "But there are a few of us."

"The war didn't stop you, I guess."

"No. May I?" she offered to Ixchel again.

Ixchel threw the robe into her arms. "Do what you can."

"We all have our skills," Malena said. She left them alone.

Ixchel glared at her hands. Seri considered leaving her alone, but then who could she talk to?

"I wonder if I can get a message to Master Korda somehow. Maybe we can travel near the coast on our way to Ch'olan."

"Aren't you forgetting something?"

Seri looked up. "What?" She could not ever remember Ixchel looking at her that way.

Ixchel shook her head. "Volraag. He stole power from one of the Lords. Why would they return? You need his power to be part of the Passing. But he won't come. And if he did, who would trust him?"

Seri felt like a bucket of cold water had been poured on her head. Of course. They had to solve the problem of Volraag before anything else could happen.

She jumped to her feet. "I'll talk to Marshal about this. Maybe together we can find Volraag." She started toward the curtains.

"My Lady."

"Yes?"

"Perhaps you would like to wait until morning? Or at least until you have gotten dressed again."

Seri stopped. She really had been about to walk over to the men's camp in only her sleep clothes. She turned back and sat down.

"Ixchel. If I didn't have you with me, I don't know what I'd do."

"If you didn't have me with you, you'd be dead."

"Of embarrassment."

Ixchel actually chuckled. "You can laugh!" Seri gasped.

"Of course I can laugh."

"But you never do!"

"Does that displease you?"

"It's not about what I think. You should laugh more often. It's... good for you."

"I'll consider it, then."

Seri snorted.

•••••

Marshal found the curse squad around the fire, plying Dravid with questions about his traveling companions. It seemed only natural for them to be curious, but some of the talk bothered him.

"It'll be strange to have so many foreigners," Rufus mused.

"How do you think I feel?" Dravid asked. "I haven't seen another native of Kuktarma in months!"

"Welcome to my world," Topleb said. "Being only proper-colored man around all these Variochs."

"People are people," Dravid said, shrugging. "I saw all kinds on Zes Sivas."

The reference to Zes Sivas inspired multiple new lines of conversation, before Gnaeus brought it back to traveling arrangements. "What's it like being around so many women?"

"You're about to find out!" Dravid gestured toward the area where the women hung curtains for privacy.

"Do they do that every night?"

"Forerunner's women do."

"The other two don't?"

Marshal stepped up. "That's enough, men. Whichever group you travel with, you will treat the women with respect. Is that understood?"

The soldiers mumbled their assent. Marshal glanced at Victor, who nodded. He didn't want to be harsh with the men. But knowledge of what his mother had been through made him want to be careful about such things. He thought he knew all of them, but they faced a new situation. All of his experience with them came from war and travel. They grew close through circumstances, but what did he really know about them?

•••••

Marshal finished putting his pack together and tightened the strap. A new morning awaited, with new traveling companions and all sorts of new possibilities. One of them approached right now.

Seri strode up to him. Someone had done an expert job in repairing her robe. He couldn't even see where it had been torn. It struck him that he felt slightly disappointed he wouldn't be able to catch glimpses of her stomach any longer. He shook that thought off, though it did make him smile.

"We need to find Volraag!" she said without any other greeting.

"Um, good morning. I slept well, thank you."

Seri actually blushed a little. It was… cute. Her darker skin took on a funny tint in her cheeks. "I'm sorry. I get ideas in my head and I just talk too much, especially if I'm excited about something, and I sometimes can't stop myself."

"I... can't say I've ever had that problem."

"Most people say that. You... oh. That's right. You literally couldn't talk."

Marshal nodded. "Until just a few weeks ago."

"What was that like?"

Marshal wrinkled his brow. "What was it like? I... don't know how to answer that. I couldn't talk. Or anything. It took effort just to remember what nodding and shaking my head meant."

"You were trapped inside your own head," she said. "How horrible."

"What were you saying about Volraag?" Sympathy was the last thing he wanted from Seri. But as that thought went by, his mind quickly followed it with further consideration of what he did want from her. He pushed those thoughts back. Focus, Marshal!

"Oh, yes. Volraag. We need to find him."

"Did you miss the part of my story yesterday about leaving him behind at the battlefield? That's the last we know of him. And why would we want to find him, anyway?" He stood up to face her.

"He has one of the Lord's powers. We need him."

"Oh. You mean on Zes Sivas."

"Yes. To save Antises."

"Somehow, I don't think my half-brother is interested in saving Antises."

Seri tilted her head. "You know, you don't look like him at all."

"Volraag? No, I don't think I do, either."

"Except maybe in the facial structure. It's hard to tell for sure, with the..." She stopped herself, but reached a hand out toward Marshal's face. He didn't move. Sympathy it might be, but he wouldn't turn down a touch from her. Her fingers brushed ever so lightly against the largest scar on his cheek. She pulled her hand back abruptly. "Sorry. I'm sorry."

"It's all right."

"So, um, anyway. We need to find Volraag and persuade him to come. It's the only way."

"You really believe that all of Antises is in danger from this?"

"You've felt the earthquakes, haven't you? Everything might tear apart."

"I don't think I can form this 'heart of fire' thing you talked about."

"You won't know that unless you come."

Marshal nodded. With just the two of them talking, he found he wanted to do whatever she asked, if only to see her continue to smile and talk.

"I can... I can try to detect Volraag's power. When he's near, I can feel him."

"Oh! Yes, I can do that too. Shall we try it together?"

Marshal blinked. "I'm not sure how that would work."

Seri held out her hand. "Give me your hand." Marshal took it, surprised by how soft it felt. "I think it will work better if you close your eyes," she said. "I'll use my star-sight to help focus my senses."

Marshal did as she told him, but he peeked out to observe Seri's actions. She waved her hand in the air as if trying to find something. He closed his eyes and focused himself again. He could immediately sense the power of Forerunner and Wolf behind him. He ignored them and reached out in his mind toward the south.

"I've only been able to sense him when we were very close," he said. "Unless he's been chasing us, I'm not sure this will work."

"Just try," Seri said. "You didn't have me with you before. Open yourself up."

"How?"

"Picture your power as closed inside a sealed room within you."

"All right..."

"Then open that door."

Marshal frowned. The analogy felt off, but he could try it. He formed the image in his mind and opened the door. At the same time, he willed himself to let Seri do whatever she wanted.

Almost at once, he felt something flow from him into her hand. "Oh!" she exclaimed.

"What is it?"

She took a deep breath and let it out. "I did this once with Master Hain, but it was nothing like this. This is... incredible."

Marshal felt something flowing from her into his arm as well. But she had no power of her own, did she? What could that be? He opened his eyes and gasped.

Multi-colored beams of light swirled around both of them. He saw every color in the spectrum sweeping around him, crossing over the other beams, intersecting them, creating new shades, then splitting back up. Everything beyond the beams looked dull and fuzzy. His hand began to loosen from Seri's. She grabbed it tighter. "Don't let go!"

"I can... see the colors!"

"And I can feel your power. I think I'm going to explode! It's so much!"

"Are you all right?" Anxiety instantly replaced wonder.

"I can handle it. This is fantastic! I don't... whoa. Is that my voice?" As she spoke, her tones began to vibrate. Marshal recognized it as similar to Forerunner's voice. He looked to Seri's face. Her eyes shone bright, with a gleaming point of light in the left eye outshining everything else. Thin beams of purple light escaped from her mouth when she spoke again. "I can't... I don't know what's happening."

"I don't, either." All he knew was that he never wanted it to stop. The spectacular colors danced across his view, while the rush of power through their arms vibrated throughout his body.

"It's too much!" Seri's hand released his. The colors faded in seconds. His arm jerked as their connection broke. It felt sore.

Seri bent over, then fell to her knees.

"Seri!" He fell beside her, reaching for her.

She put her hands up, but they shook. "I'll be all right. Just a moment." She clenched her hands into fists, then released them. The shaking came to a stop.

Ixchel appeared out of nowhere next to her. "My Lady?"

"I'm fine. I'm fine." She looked up at Marshal. "I'm sorry for breaking it off. That was... spectacular! We need to do it again!"

"Not if it hurts you," he said. Ixchel shot him a look.

"It's all right. I'll learn how to control it." Seri got to her feet with Ixchel's help.

"We should, uh, get ready to move out for the day," Marshal said.

Seri nodded. "I need to finish packing."

As the two girls moved away, Victor approached. Marshal remained sitting on the ground. He chuckled.

"Victor, I think I'm going to love that girl."

Victor snorted. "Too obvious."

$$\bullet \bullet \bullet \bullet \bullet$$

Dravid created a palm-sized disc of golden light. He closed his eyes, focused for a moment, and found the magic of Antises calling to him. He absorbed it, opened his eyes, and released it as a vibratory wave against the disc.

Nothing happened.

Frustrated, he released the magic that held the disc intact and watched it dissolve. How had Marshal blown apart his shield? He couldn't generate enough power to even damage a tiny bit of the gold magic. Forerunner's barrier had held off the power of an earthquake. How much power did Marshal have?

If Seri were right, and he truly possessed the power of the King, it would be something like three times that of a Lord. Dravid had a hard time comprehending it. How could a person contain that much power? Marshal wasn't even a big man. He was... average in size, at best. Ordinary. It seemed impossible.

He felt the presence before he looked up to see who had approached him. Wolf. Or Calu. Or whatever he called himself.

"When will you be ready to pay the price?" he asked. His voice resonated with magic like Forerunner's.

"The price?"

"For the healing."

In all the tumult, Dravid had forgotten that detail. "You haven't told me what the price is."

"When will you be ready?"

"I don't know. How can I know if I don't know what it is?"

"I will require it when I leave this realm." With that, Wolf turned and walked away with heavy strides. Now there went a body able to contain power. And yet he had been smaller before, and still held it somehow. Or had he? Forerunner hadn't exactly explained what happened there.

Dravid got up and moved toward the others. Everyone seemed ready to set out for the day. He looked around at the group and smiled without humor. Yesterday morning, he had been one of two males in a group with nine females. Now he was one of seven males in a group with only two females.

Yet one of those was the only female that mattered.

Forerunner stepped up beside him. Great. "Ah, Dravid, my friend. I wanted to assure you that I haven't forgotten you." He paused. "Unlike some people." He looked in the direction of Seri, who seemed to be in quite a conversation with Marshal.

"What do you want, Forerunner?"

"To assure you I still intend to keep my word to you. Of course, one could argue that I've already restored a purpose to your life. You can be a mage again, in a different way than you planned."

"You didn't do that!"

"Didn't I? Ah, well. I don't count it, either. I will restore to you what you choose. Once you choose."

"Can you restore to me whatever it is that your friend takes from me?"

"My friend?"

Dravid pointed at the tall figure of Calu.

Forerunner seemed uncertain. "He... wants to take something from you?"

"He says I must pay the price for Seri's healing."

"Oh. Oh, dear."

"What?"

"If someone like Calu requires a price, you can be sure that it will be significant. I don't believe I can help you there."

"Then what good are you?" Dravid growled the words with more savagery than he actually felt.

"I apologize. I will... leave you to your own thoughts. I'm sure they will keep you in good company."

Forerunner hurried away to Calu's side. At that moment, Marshal called for everyone to set out. Led by Topleb, the group began walking. For a very brief moment, Dravid wondered what would happen if he simply didn't follow. But that path led to complete insignificance and failure. He had enough of that. He began walking.

(((63)))

Victor took a deep breath and approached the girls. They seemed engrossed in a detailed examination of Seri's pack. "Excuse me?"

Seri looked up. "Oh, Victor. What is it?"

"Actually, I was hoping to speak with, uh, Ix..." He paused, struggling to remember how to say her name.

"Ixchel," Seri finished.

The girl in question stood. Victor found himself unable to remember what he had been going to say. He still had trouble understanding how this woman went about in bare feet. Her soles must be incredibly tough.

"You wanted something?" she asked.

"Ah, right. I, uh, was working out this morning and remembered our first meeting a couple of days ago..." Why did he feel so awkward? He toyed with the two practice swords he had cut from a sturdy branch.

"Yes."

"I, yes... what?"

"You wish to spar. I accept."

"Right, spar. Right." The reason he had sought her out. It had just slipped his mind for some reason.

The two of them moved away from Seri to an open area. Victor noticed Rufus watching with a grin. Great. An audience. He wanted to test himself against Ixchel again, because she seemed far more capable than anyone else here. But he didn't want anyone else to see him get embarrassed. As he handed Ixchel one of the practice swords, he considered it a distinct possibility.

She bent the branch to test its strength. It snapped back into shape.

288

Victor had chosen well.

"Rules?" he asked.

Ixchel looked him over. "Arm and leg tags do not count. We stop if someone simulates a killing blow."

Victor agreed. He felt nervous, more nervous than he had since his first training sessions with Talinir. Based on their first encounter, Ixchel fought like a highly trained warrior.

He dropped into his defensive stance and held his practice sword at ready. He wished he could use his flail, but that would be too dangerous.

Ixchel observed him for a moment, then slid smoothly into a stance of her own, shield up and practice sword hovering just behind it. The shield, though small, concealed some of her movements from his immediate view. Interesting. She didn't conceal much of anything else, of course, and that...

He almost didn't see the sword coming. He ducked his head to the right and down. It flashed over him. How had she backhanded a blow from that position? He needed to stop getting distracted. He resumed his stance and focused on the movements, not his opponent's appearance.

They traded feints back and forth for a while. Victor took note of Ixchel's swift foot movements. She moved much faster than anyone he had seen since Talinir. And she had a very different style from the Eldanim or the soldiers of Varioch. Her movements were flexible, graceful even.

"Graceful but deadly," he said aloud.

"Excuse me?"

"Your style," he answered. His sword swept upward from ground level, but Ixchel caught it on her shield. "It's very... different than I'm used to."

"Thank you."

They continued their dance for some time. Victor managed only once to tag Ixchel's leg. She tagged him three times, once in the ribs. It felt hard enough to leave a bruise. It might not have been a killing blow, but it was close.

Victor took a step back and lifted his sword. "Take a break?" Ixchel nodded and they both seated themselves, sweating and breathing hard.

Victor rubbed his side. "Good stroke. That one hurt," he complained.

"You are skilled yourself. I haven't sparred like this in months. Since I joined my Lady."

"And I haven't sparred since we lost Talinir. He was my trainer. A, uh, warden of the Eldanim."

Ixchel cocked her head. "That explains it. I did not recognize some of your moves. The Eldanim is not a style I was taught."

"Where were you taught?"

Ixchel hesitated, then explained her upbringing as one of the Holcan, traditional warriors in Ch'olan. Victor found her vocal style just as fascinating as her fighting style. She spoke only in short sentences, and her voice seemed to rise ever so slightly through each word.

"Before I met Talinir, all I had was an open field outside my village," Victor said. "And this flail." He picked it up.

"What made you choose that weapon?"

"I didn't choose it, really." Victor toyed with the chain. "I found it one day, and I guess I just thought it was special. I started practicing right away." He looked up and smiled. "And almost broke my leg on the first day."

Ixchel smiled, but did not laugh. "You are self-taught with it, then?"

"Pretty much. Talinir gave me a few pointers, but he mostly taught me the sword."

"You are... surprisingly effective." Seeing his facial reaction, she added, "For being self-taught."

"Heh. Thanks." Victor paused. "I do have a question."

She looked at him without responding.

"Why, uh, why do you and Topleb sound so different? I mean, you don't have the same accent he does."

Ixchel cocked her head. "Topleb is from the country. I grew up in the city of Woqan."

"And that's it?"

She shrugged.

"Huh."

Ixchel stood abruptly. "I need to clean up. We will travel again shortly. Perhaps we will spar another day?"

"Uh, yeah. Definitely."

Victor watched her leave. He noticed Rufus and Topleb both watching him now, and scowled at them. He got to his feet and braced himself for the teasing he knew would come.

• • • • •

Seri frowned at Marshal. "I'm not sure I understand." She looked back at the trail to make sure she didn't stumble. Topleb wasn't as careful as Ixchel had been about finding the smoothest roads.

"What do you mean?" Marshal asked. "I want to end the curses."

"You want to erase the Laws of Cursings and Bindings? The foundation of all magic in Antises?"

Marshal actually stumbled. He shot a look at the road ahead, and then back at Seri. "I... don't know about the Bindings. But the curses are wrong."

"Well, I mean, you grew up cursed for something you didn't do, so I can see that point of view," Seri said. "But what about those who deserve it?"

Marshal pointed toward the back of their small group. Seri looked back. Rufus limped along next to Dravid. "Rufus stole some corn from his neighbor five years ago. Does he deserve to have a twisted foot for the rest of his life?"

"I don't know." What could she say to that? "But what about those who commit real crimes, like murder? Don't they deserve it?"

Marshal shrugged. "I don't know. Maybe they do. But should we leave that up to... to the magic? How do we know it even works? We see the results of curses, but we don't see every crime."

"Then how..." Seri ducked under a tree branch and glared at Topleb. "How would we discover the crimes in the first place? How would they get punished?"

"Maybe we could have some kind of special warriors, like Ixchel and, and Victor, who would have that job," Marshal suggested.

Seri shook her head. "I don't see how that would work. You would take the job away from unbiased magic and give it to people? How would you know you could trust them?"

"They would have to be good people."

"Who decides who is good?"

Marshal waved his arms. "I don't know! I just know what we have now is wrong."

"I don't even know how we would do such a thing," Seri said. "No one knows quite how the first mages created the Laws. It's beyond anything the current Masters can do."

"My mother died to lift my curse. Nian died telling me that Theon wants to give us blessings, not curses. I won't let them die in vain."

Seri didn't answer. Marshal obviously believed all of this, but his arguments were based on his personal experiences. She couldn't argue with that.

After a few more minutes, Marshal spoke up again. "We knew that we needed more power and knowledge," he said slowly. "Nian suggested that someone from the Conclave could help us, but you don't sound like you really want to."

"That's—"

"Which is why I need to find Talinir. I trust him, and he'll know more."

"The Masters on Zes Sivas will know more too."

"I'm not going to Zes Sivas until I find Talinir and get Topleb home."

"Yes, you said that. I'm just trying to explain."

"You haven't explained very much so far."

"But that—you—"

Seri almost ran into Victor. She and Marshal both stopped as he smiled at them.

"I'm not sure if the two of you are about to fight or kiss," Victor observed.

"What?"

Victor pointed ahead. "Topleb says we should go ahead and make camp here. There's a village nearby where we can get some supplies."

"Works for me," Marshal said. He pushed past Victor and went to speak with Topleb.

Seri sighed. "I'm not very good at persuading people," she admitted.

Victor glanced over his shoulder at Marshal. "Don't worry about it. You have to remember that up until recently, Marshal couldn't even talk. He's not used to it. And definitely not used to people responding to what he says." He paused and chuckled. "It took me a while to figure that out."

The other travelers caught up with them. "Let's make camp," Victor called.

As everyone relaxed, Seri watched Marshal talking with Topleb. She had to get through to him somehow. It wasn't just her opinion. The fate of Antises depended on it.

(((64)))

Victor looked down the hill at the small town. "Reminds me of Efesun," he told Topleb. When he got no reaction, he added, "It's a town we traveled through a long time ago. Maybe a little bigger than this one, actually."

The two of them started down the road. Marshal had decided only they two would enter the town and gather a few supplies. Victor agreed with keeping Forerunner and Wolf out of sight, at the least.

"We are so close to Ch'olan," Topleb said. "There may be as many of my people in this town as yours."

"I don't see any people yet."

"Perhaps they are all indoors for lunch. I am hungry myself."

"Nothing to stop us from getting a meal for ourselves while we're here." Victor grinned. "It's got to be better than your cooking!"

"Ha! I make do with what we have. When we visit my home, I will show you real cooking."

"That... would be nice."

They had almost reached the first homes on the outskirts of the town, and still no one appeared. "Where is everyone?" Victor asked. This time, Topleb did not answer.

They passed by the first houses without seeing anyone. But Victor couldn't help feeling someone watched them from inside one or more of the homes.

"That looks like an inn," Topleb said, pointing. Victor nodded. Maybe they could find some answers there.

The door was closed. Not necessarily unusual, but taken with the absence of any people, it gave Victor an odd feeling. He looked at Topleb. The other man shrugged and reached for the door.

Before he could grasp the handle, the door flew open. A short man with a scraggly beard stood trembling in the opening, a crude crossbow in his hands. When he saw the two of them, he lowered the weapon and breathed a sigh of relief.

"Ah, forgive me. You look human enough," he said, his voice weak and tremulous.

Victor and Topleb exchanged glances. "Yes, we are," Victor said. "You were expecting something else?"

"Aye. You haven't seen them, then?"

"Seen what?"

He looked up and down the street, his hands nervously moving around the crossbow.

"Eidolons," he whispered.

"Oh. Them again?" Victor couldn't help his response.

The man at the door eyed him with a bit of confusion. "You'd best come in," he said. "They could appear at any time. Come on." He gestured and stood aside.

Topleb and Victor glanced at each other again, then entered. Inside, they found the inn's common room populated by what they took to be the innkeeper's family and a couple of other families all sitting quietly together. As he looked around, Victor guessed few of them had slept much recently. He saw dark circles under eyes, unkempt hair, and nervous looks to and fro. He also noticed as everyone looked over the two newcomers, their eyes kept being drawn to the weapons at their belts.

"Not a smile in the house," Topleb whispered.

"What brings you to Tungrorum?" the innkeeper asked after closing the door behind them.

"We're with a caravan camped not far from here," Victor said. "We just stopped in for some supplies. What's going on here?"

"First explain what you meant outside," the innkeeper said. "You've seen eidolons before?"

"I've fought them," Victor said. "They were after one of my friends."

"You know how to fight them?" a woman spoke up. Several others murmured in response.

Victor glanced around the room again. "I, uh, I've fought them, but never, um, killed one or anything."

"But can they be stopped?" the innkeeper asked, stepping closer.

"I don't know. My friend back at the caravan might know more than I do. But first I need to know what's going on?"

Several more glances and whispers were exchanged before a tall woman who looked less fearful than the rest stood up. "My sister saw the first one over a week ago," she said. "It wandered around their house in the twilight hours, then disappeared as it grew dark."

"It was marking them!" someone else added.

"Two days later," the tall woman went on, with a hitch in her voice, "my sister and her whole family... vanished. We looked everywhere for them. But all we saw was the eidolon." She paused. "I swear it was laughing at us!" Murmurs of agreement followed her words.

"Since then, we've all seen them," the innkeeper broke in. "Sometimes just one. Sometimes it's three or four."

"I saw six!" A few other voices argued with that one for a moment.

Topleb leaned in to Victor. "These are ghosts, yes? Spirits?"

"That's what people think," Victor said. "They look like shadows. They're actually Eldanim or something like them, crossing over from the Otherworld. At least, I think so. I never did fully understand that."

"We call them tzitzimitl," Topleb said. "They are rare, but have been seen near the high place."

"What are you saying?" the innkeeper asked. "The eidolons are Eldanim?"

"Something like them," Victor said. "Not exactly."

"Then why would they take my sister?" the tall woman demanded.

"I don't know. Have they taken anyone else since then?"

Several people tried to talk at once. Eventually, Victor determined two other families had vanished without a trace. Someone suggested a local merchant had also disappeared, but others argued he just left on his own. He wasn't the only one. At least three other families had fled the town.

"What should we do?" Topleb asked.

"We should get this information back to Marshal," Victor said. "Between him and our new mage friends, someone will know what to do about this." He frowned. "It's such strange behavior, though. I've never heard of them taking people away."

"You told me a curse was lifted," Topleb said. "Did you think the natural order of things wouldn't change after that?"

Victor couldn't see the connection, but didn't argue. He explained his intentions to the people, promising to return as soon as he could. The people responded with equal parts gratitude and skepticism.

Victor opened the door and Topleb followed him. They both stopped right outside.

Four eidola stood in the road, swords drawn.

• • • • •

Seri concentrated and tried again. This time, she felt certain.

"Volraag is on the move," she said. "I think he's on a ship. Or at least near the water."

She opened her eyes and looked up at Marshal watching her. "You can tell that much?"

"I'm pretty sure," she said, getting to her feet. The two of them stood at the summit of a small hill. Ixchel waited a few feet away.

Marshal shook his head. "I'm amazed at how much you can determine. All I can tell is when he's close."

"You haven't had any training," Seri said. "How much do you know about your power?"

"All I know how to do is let it out." A tremor ran through the ground to illustrate his words.

"There are so many more things you can do besides destroy! I can teach you! Maybe that's one of the reasons I needed to find you."

"I would… appreciate that."

Marshal turned away. Seri had trouble understanding his moods. The scars made reading his facial expressions difficult if not impossible. And a lifetime without speaking had left him reticent to explain himself. It frustrated her more than she wanted to admit. Understanding Marshal might be the key to saving Antises itself. She could not fail. And beyond that, she found him intriguing. He wasn't handsome like Dravid, but his strength—magical and physical—was undeniable.

"Listen," she called. Marshal turned back. "Our magic is based on vibration, the Masters taught me. And everything vibrates, to some extent. When you can find the vibration of something, you can learn how to do more with it—control it, even."

Marshal's brow furrowed. He gestured to the nearest tree. "So if I learn the… vibration of this tree, I could… what? Make it grow more or something?"

"Well, living things are different. You should start with something less complicated."

"Of course." Marshal turned, as if looking for something else to use as an example. Seri clenched her fist. Why had it been so easy for Master Hain? Because she had been an eager student. Marshal wasn't.

He had doubts. How could she change that?

She heard a sharp intake of breath. Marshal drew his sword. "What is it?" she asked, then turned in the direction he faced. "Oh."

Six of the Gidim stood nearby, all of them with shadowy swords in their hands.

"Stay back!" Marshal warned. "I've dealt with these before."

"You're not the only one." Men always resorted to weapons. And Marshal with so much power! What use did he have for a sword? Seri stepped forward and waved at the nearest shadow figure. "Greetings! Welcome to Antises! Are you looking for someone?"

The figure lunged at her, sword lifted. She barely had time to gasp and take a step back when Marshal shoved her aside and lifted his own sword to block the attack. To both their surprise, the shadow sword passed right through his.

Marshal stood with mouth open. "It worked the last time."

Ixchel knelt beside her, shield and sword at the ready. "I suggest you retreat, my Lady."

Seri scrambled back to her feet and backed away. Why had it attacked her? Where was Forerunner, anyway? He should be talking to these things.

The shadow warriors moved closer, spreading around Marshal and Ixchel.

"Are our weapons of any use against them?" Ixchel asked.

"I think I get it," Marshal said. "The last one I fought must have had a warpsteel sword that could fight in both worlds. They don't all have those, so our weapons don't interact with them."

"What about their bodies?"

"No idea."

"Let's test it, then."

Ixchel dashed forward, ducked under a swing and slashed through one of the warrior's legs. Her sword passed through, but seemed to have no impact. As she danced back, it continued to advance.

"We don't have warpsteel blades, either, and they're not fully here. Still, I expected some kind of reaction."

"But can they hurt us?" Seri asked.

"I'm not inclined to test that one."

Seri looked around, but none of the others were close. Dravid and Rufus waited with the gear downhill somewhere, and she had no idea where Forerunner and Calu had gone.

She blinked and her vision changed. Marshal became the glowing beacon of power she had grown used to, and a few beams of light exploded from the ground in various places. The shadow warriors grew more distinct, their outlines more solid. Their appearance became more elongated and sharp, much more like Curasir than the golden-skinned people she had seen recently.

They charged from both sides. Ixchel and Marshal tried to stand between her and them.

Ixchel instinctively tried to block an attack with her shield. The shadow sword passed right through it and through her forearm.

Ixchel screamed.

(((65)))

Victor drew his sword and dropped into a defensive position.

"I am guessing this is not good," Topleb said behind him.

"No, not good at all. I can handle one, or maybe two. Four is not good."

"Then let us cut down the numbers."

Victor felt the rush of air as Topleb's atlatl hurled a spear past his head. He struck true into the chest of an eidolon. But the spear passed straight through the shadowy being without any obvious effect. The spear struck another building across the street and fell to the ground.

"Perhaps we should back into the building."

"I'm pretty sure walls aren't going to stop them," Victor said. But his mind raced. Why hadn't the spear hurt them? The last time, when he and Talinir had fought side-by-side against them, it had been like fighting humans. Hadn't it?

"Come with us." The whisper floated on the air. That was also new. Victor never heard them whisper before.

"Come. You will serve us beneath the stars."

That didn't sound pleasant.

"Only one thing to do," he said mostly to himself. He unleashed his flail and let it hang by his side. Then he started forward and began to swing it.

"Try to protect those people inside!" he said over his shoulder. Then he pivoted to the right and rushed the nearest eidolon. Right before he reached it, he spun. Both flail and sword passed through the creature, neither having any impact.

Victor felt his battle rage, as he now thought of it, begin to take effect. The tingling in his hands and feet began to swell as he approached the second eidolon. Maybe that would help his weapons have more of an effect?

With his next spin, he took off the eidolon's head with his sword. Or would have, if it had been solid. As his flail came around, the eidolon struck with its sword, slashing down through Victor's upper left arm.

Pain like he'd never experienced erupted through Victor's arm. The pain rushed down his arm into his hand, following unknown paths beneath his skin. The flail fell from his hand without any conscious thought on his part. At the same time, the pain shot up his shoulder and into his chest. He lost control of his legs and tumbled, nearly cutting himself in half with his own sword. For a moment, he couldn't breathe, couldn't do anything.

Air rushed back into his lungs, and he gulped it in and tried to control the rest of his body. He managed to come to a stop, still holding his sword. He looked up and saw the four shadow warriors had followed his progress and now watched him instead of the inn. At least he could distract them. Maybe Topleb would take the villagers out the back.

He held up his sword, his hand shaking, not from magic. He felt nothing from his left arm. It was still attached to his body, but only as a weight he couldn't control. Again the difference. The last eidolon he fought cut his thigh, and it had bled like a normal sword wound.

"That's... not very fair," he managed. He tried to get to his feet, but stumbled, unable to lean on his left arm. Since they hadn't charged him yet, he let his sword hand drop and used it to help himself get up. He held the sword up again and took a few steps backward.

"Come and get me."

• • • • •

Seri's star-sight showed strange flickers of darkness running up Ixchel's arm. She had never seen anything like it.

Light exploded behind her. She turned in time to see one of the Gidim dissolve completely, leaving behind only Marshal's shining sword. Shining?

"You channeled your power through the sword? That's brilliant!"

"They're vulnerable to magic!" he shouted. He pointed his palm at the others. Spiraling beams of every color of light erupted from his hand, expanding outward and slamming into all of his attackers. So that is what it looked like when a Lord used his powers! Spectacular colors filled her vision.

The light beams shredded through the Gidim, tearing them apart. The shadowy pieces left behind dissolved in the air and faded away.

Seri stood, mouth open in awe. "That was fantastic!" she exclaimed.

Ixchel moaned. Seri gasped. How had she forgotten? She whirled and knelt by her friend. Her sight gave her one last glimpse of darkness in Ixchel's left hand before that too faded away.

Ixchel untied her shield and let it fall. "I can't move my hand," she said. "I can't feel it at all!"

Seri took Ixchel's hand. It felt cool and stiff. She pressed against the palm. "Can you feel that?"

Ixchel shook her head.

"A group of shadow warriors. Eidolon," Marshal said. Seri looked back, and saw him talking to Rufus and Dravid. They must have just arrived.

"I don't know what to do," Seri said to Ixchel. "I can't see anything wrong with it. Maybe I can get Forerunner to look at it."

"No." Ixchel shook her head again.

"Oh, come on. You know he can heal. We don't even know if this will heal naturally at all!"

"What is it?" Dravid asked, coming up next to them.

"One of them cut through Ixchel's arm," Seri said. "She's lost all feeling in it."

"They don't like our magic," Marshal said. "It's good that we have so many magic-users in this group. We don't..." He stopped. "Victor!"

Marshal spun and raced down the hill, leaving the others behind. Seri understood. The two men sent into town had no magic of their own. They were defenseless against these creatures.

• • • • •

Marshal raced toward the town. If they made it through this, no one should ever split off from the group without at least one magic-wielder with them. Why hadn't he thought of that before?

Because he didn't know, none of them had known, that this kind of thing would happen. The eidola hadn't shown any interest in them since the battle at the temple. What had changed?

He tried to channel some magic through his legs to speed his run, but didn't notice any difference. He needed to ask Seri if that was even possible. She knew so much more than he did. He needed her help.

But right now, Victor needed his.

He almost fell when he reached the bottom of the hill and the ground leveled out. He stumbled and waved his arms before regaining his balance and rushing on. He found the main road and followed it into the town itself.

Victor lay on the ground, but with head lifted up. He still held his sword in the air, pointed at four eidola only a few feet away, all moving toward him. He seemed to be trying to say something, but a trickle of blood ran from his mouth. No words came with it.

Marshal couldn't blast at the attackers from here without hitting Victor. He yelled to get their attention. They stopped their movement and at least seemed to be looking toward him.

He dropped his sword. He needed a wider burst right now. He vaulted over Victor, dropped to his knees and spread his arms wide, letting the power explode outward. The four shadow warriors dissolved. Did he hear screams? He thought so back at the hill, but maybe he only wanted to hear it.

Breathing heavily, he turned back to Victor. "How you doing?"

Victor let his own sword drop and fell back onto the road. "Did you just Bind me to you again?" His voice slurred.

Marshal chuckled. "Come on. You know we're stuck with each other."

"Best thing... ever happened to me."

Topleb emerged from between two buildings. Behind him, the townsfolk from the inn waited, not ready to come out in the open yet.

"That was impressive," Topleb said. "Next time, you go to the village, and we'll wait in the camp."

"They attacked us there too."

"Ah." Topleb pointed back at the villagers. "They say people have been taken."

"Taken? That doesn't seem right." Marshal knelt beside Victor. "Where did they get you?"

With gestures and a few muttered words, Victor managed to explain. He had been slashed twice on his left arm, once on his right ankle, and stabbed twice in both thighs. Both legs and arm were useless now. Marshal had never seen anything like it, even while watching his mother work as a healer.

"Watch out!" someone called from the watching crowd.

Marshal looked up. The villagers all stared down the road. He turned. A lone eidolon stood in the center of the village, sword drawn.

"Only one now?" Topleb said. "They insult you."

Marshal stood and retrieved his own sword. Somehow, he knew this one would be different. "You're not welcome here!" he called. "These people are now under my protection!"

In response, the eidolon lifted its sword and drew it down. It looked like the blade cut from one world to the other, leaving a dark gash floating in mid-air. Hands emerged through the gash, pulling it apart. And then the eidolon stepped through, transforming into one of the Eldanim.

"Curasir?" But no. Marshal had never seen this Eldani before, though his white hair made him similar to the last one he fought.

"Warpsteel," Victor slurred. Marshal nodded. This one carried a different sort of sword, very powerful, like Talinir always carried. Perhaps that explained how he cut through the worlds' barriers. Except Talinir had never shown or mentioned any such ability. It also meant Marshal couldn't count on his blade ward to protect him.

The Eldani spread his arms wide. "This village is mine," he announced. "Why do you get in my way?"

"These people are innocent," Marshal said. "Why are you attacking them?"

"They are human. They are not innocent."

Marshal took a few steps forward. "You should leave while you can. And you should return those you have taken."

"You do not frighten me, Marshal, son of Varion. I know who you are."

At the Eldani's words, murmurs erupted among the villagers. That might be a problem.

"Then you know I will fight you. Where are the people you took?" Marshal pointed at his foe, letting his power build up.

"They are beyond your reach now. We needed slaves in our realm. And now that you have weakened the barriers, we can come for them any time we wish."

"Me?" What was he talking about?

"You understand so little, not even the consequences of your own actions."

Marshal had enough of cryptic hints and taunts. He let his power flow, blasting full force at this arrogant Eldani. The ground erupted between them.

The warpsteel sword came up, either blocking or absorbing Marshal's attack. The torn ground came to a stop, at any rate. Curasir had done something similar in the Otherworld, now that he thought of it. How many capabilities did those swords possess?

"It appears you do not wish to talk any longer. Then my steel will have to speak." The Eldani rushed forward.

Marshal dropped into his defensive stance and readied himself. Aside from some practices with Victor, he had not fought against a single opponent in weeks. But he always found the sword to be natural in his hand. He had a skill that seemed more innate than taught, though both Aelia and Talinir had drilled many lessons into his head.

He easily shifted on his back leg and dodged the Eldani's first swing. He hoped to immediately retaliate, but this opponent gave him no time. In fact, it only took a few more thrusts, dodges, and parries to realize he was seriously outmatched.

Marshal wanted to use his power again, since the Eldani would not be able to block it if he kept the sword busy. But he had to focus entirely on keeping himself alive, watching the Eldani's movement and countering them. The attacks came so fast and so frequent that defending himself took everything he had.

Just when he thought he might not be able to prevent one more strike, one of Topleb's spears flew in from the side and struck the Eldani in the hip. He cried out and stumbled back. Marshal took immediate advantage of the breather to unleash a burst of magic at his opponent's other leg. The combination of attacks knocked him down.

Topleb stepped up, atlatl ready to launch again. "Drop the sword!" he ordered. The Eldani glared at him.

"Behind you!" Marshal cried. Another eidolon materialized behind Topleb, about to strike. Marshal blasted it apart without a thought.

He whirled back to the Eldani. He pointed and let his power flow in repeated bursts at the enemy's arm until the warpsteel sword fell from his hand. Marshal pointed his own sword at the Eldani's neck.

"You are trapped. If more of you continue to show up, I will continue to destroy them. I don't know what that's doing to them on the other side, but it can't be pleasant."

"And you have no honor. We were engaged in single combat and—"

"You have no place to talk of honor!" Topleb shouted. "You terrify these people and kidnap them? This is not honor!"

"Kill me then. Let us see how your Laws react to that. What curse will you receive, I wonder?"

Topleb leaned forward, but Marshal put a hand out. "He's right. Now that he's helpless, we can't kill him."

"Then what should we do with him?"

Marshal smiled. "We'll tie him up, take care of that spear he's got stuck in him... and then let Seri talk with him."

Victor, still on the ground behind them, snorted.

Marshal bent and picked up the warpsteel sword. "But I am taking this."

(((66)))

Seri's mouth dropped open. "Why me?"

"Trust me on this," Marshal said. "I think you'll be able to get more out of him than any of the rest of us."

Seri looked to Dravid. "Is that a compliment?"

He chuckled. "Kind of. I think Marshal respects your ability to gain information from other people."

Seri frowned. "All right. I'll try. But I think Forerunner—"

"Don't tell Forerunner about this prisoner just yet," Marshal interrupted. "They both come from the Otherworld. I want to see what we can learn from one before we let them together."

Seri looked around the village. Its people now moved freely through the streets, though many stopped and stared at their party. She and Dravid followed after Marshal, leaving the injured Ixchel with Rufus. So far, Forerunner and Calu had remained apart. She wondered what they would think once they discovered what had been going on… or if they already knew.

"We're going to help these people as much as we can," Marshal said. "Topleb and I are going to carry Victor back to our camp. I'm hoping Forerunner can help him. Dravid, can you stay on top of things here until I get back?"

Dravid looked surprised that Marshal even spoke to him. "Uh, sure. I guess."

"Just keep an eye on Seri and the prisoner. And if anyone asks for anything, tell them to wait for me. I'll be back as soon as I can."

Dravid nodded.

Marshal hurried back to Victor. Topleb gave a slow laugh. "So much the leader he becomes now," he said. "It is… entertaining to watch."

306

He followed.

Seri watched them go for a moment, then turned to Dravid. "All right. Well, no use putting this off, I guess."

"Do you want me to come with you?"

"No, but stay close, just in case." She paused. "In fact, if you feel me use magic in any way, that's a signal for you to come join me."

"I'll be there."

Seri took a deep breath and approached the empty home Marshal used to house the prisoner. She pushed open the door and entered, not sure what to expect.

The Eldani lay on a crude bed, propped up with some pillows, hands tied in front of him. A makeshift bandage covered an injury on his hip.

His similarity to Curasir made Seri swallow in nervousness. The sharp features, the strange eye, the white hair... and the always-there feeling he was somehow taller than he actually appeared. Unnerving.

"And who are you that they send to question me?" he asked. His voice even had the same commanding tone like Curasir's.

"I am Seri-Belit, mage of Arazu," she answered, then winced. Why had she used her full name? Ugh.

"A mage?" The Eldani laughed. "You are one of those who camps on Zes Sivas and plays with things you can never understand."

"And what is your name?"

He watched her face with a condescending smile on his own. "Hanirel. I tell you only for the sake of conversation. I wish to see how your tiny mind handles anything you hear from me, so why let names get in the way?" The mockery in his voice grated on her, but she ignored it.

"Hanirel. All right, Hanirel." Seri looked around and found a stool. She pulled it over near the bed and sat. The stool wobbled, and she shifted her position.

"My first question is..." She hesitated, because she actually hadn't decided until then what she to ask. But Marshal had suggested a couple of ideas, so she went with one. "Who are the Durunim?"

She might have imagined it, but it looked like a flicker of surprise crossed Hanirel's normal eye. "The Durunim? It is the name of one of the factions of our people in the Starlit Realm."

"Are you Durunim?"

"I might be. What difference does that make to you?"

"Do you know the name Calu?"

Again that flicker. These were definitely not the questions he had been expecting. "I don't know anyone by that name."

"I think you're lying, but I'll let that one go for now." She smiled. By starting with those questions, she had established that she knew more than he expected. It might make things go smoother with the questions she really wanted answered.

"Why have you been kidnapping people from this village?"

"We needed some slaves. They were available."

"Why this village in particular?"

He shrugged. "It's an isolated spot. It's not the only one. Our people are numerous. We can always use more slaves."

"So you're doing this in other parts of Antises?"

He gave a non-committal grunt.

Seri intwined her fingers together. She flipped her thumbs back and forth without thinking about it. "You crossed over here using that sword of yours. Is that how your people have been able to come in and kidnap humans?"

"The barriers are weakened. A warpsteel blade can pierce them now, if you know how."

"I crossed the barrier myself, without a sword of any kind," Seri said.

He snorted. "I find that hard to believe."

"It doesn't matter whether you believe it or not. It happened. I traveled into your world from Zes Sivas. I watched Curasir battle Marshal and changed the outcome. And I never needed a sword."

"What fanciful tales you weave."

Seri frowned. It really wasn't important whether he believed her or not. She just wanted to see how he reacted. The fact he thought she lied confirmed the uniqueness of what she had done that day.

"What about Forerunner?" she asked, the idea just then popping into her head.

"Who?"

"Oh, don't tell me you don't know that name, either. He's from your world too. Uses a strange magic that involves a kind of golden light."

Hanirel's face took on a strange look for such a brief moment she thought she might have imagined it. What was that? Fear? Confusion? Whatever it might be, she had made a connection. With a quick wave of her hand, she released a tiny burst of magic at the door.

A moment later, the door swung open and Dravid entered.

"Now you bring in a cripple?" the Eldani asked.

"Dravid," Seri said, without looking up from the prisoner, "this is Hanirel. Please show him what you learned from Forerunner."

For a moment, she didn't think Dravid understood her. Then she heard him take in a few deep breaths. She did not turn to watch, but knew he was creating something like one of his discs again. Hanirel's expression told her as much.

"That is impossible!"

Seri leaned forward, putting her hands on her knees. "Why is it impossible?"

"A human cannot channel that power! What is this?" He shifted in agitation, and Seri noticed the bandage on his hip turning red.

"Why not?" Seri asked. "He clearly does have that power. Your eyes don't lie. Or eye, I suppose."

He glared at her. "That power is reserved."

"For who?"

He didn't answer.

"Do you serve the golden people?"

He continued to glare.

"Are Calu and Forerunner part of those golden people?"

Nothing.

"Since you won't tell me, let me put it together on my own. You are Durunim. The Durunim serve the golden people. I call them that because that's how they looked when I saw them. I don't know what else to call them now. I know the Durunim are also at war with the Eldanim. What I don't know is what all this has to do with our world."

Hanirel did not answer at first, his face down. When he lifted it up and looked at Seri, she resisted a shiver. A new coldness seemed to have come over him. When he spoke again, his voice had lost the mocking sneer. "Your world destroyed ours. It is only just that we return the favor."

A chill ran down Seri's back and she glanced around the room without thinking. Death threats were one thing, but hearing a threat to an entire world…

"I don't like your tone," Dravid said, stepping closer. "You need to show more respect."

"Do you show respect for the beetle you grind beneath your shoe?"

Dravid flipped his disc forward, lodging it in the wall a few inches away from the prisoner. "I can always throw one lower—" he began.

In one fluid motion, Hanirel brought his tied hands up to the disc, used its edge to slice through the rope, and pushed off at Seri. He knocked her off the stool and rolled onto the floor. Seri tried to push him off, but he rolled one more time and landed on top of her. He whipped a dagger out of a hidden sheath in his bracer and held it to her throat.

"Now, cripple," he said, his voice still low and cold. "Bring me my sword. Or you will find yourself without one mage of Arazu."

"All right," Dravid said, backing up. "I'll see what I can do. Seri, are you all right?"

"Do not answer," Hanirel said, "or I will make sure you never speak again."

Seri's eyes widened, but she did not attempt to speak.

"Go, cripple!"

Dravid hurried out of the door with one last desperate glance at Seri.

Seri looked up at her captor. Hanirel smiled, a cruel thing that did not reach his eyes. He held the dagger steady against her neck, but his labored breathing pointed to his pain. Seri tried to look down to his wounded hip, but couldn't see it from her trapped position.

"Marshal will not give you the sword," she said, hoping she sounded more confident than she felt.

"Of course he will. He's already shown an inclination to protect those in danger. And you're someone he knows. If he was willing to fight for these simple peasants, what will he be willing to do for his 'mage of Arazu'?"

"He might just give you the sword through your heart!"

"He's welcome to try." Hanirel bent over, his white hair hanging down on either side of both their faces. "But will he be faster than my dagger? Are you that eager to test it?"

Seri blinked, activating her star-sight. She saw the magic of the Eldanim glowing throughout Hanirel's body. He didn't possess the same power as Curasir, but it still looked impressive. Her eyes darted back and forth, searching for any other magic she could channel. One dim beam of green light flickered near the doorway, then faded. Nothing else appeared.

"You have a star in your eye," Hanirel said, apparently just noticing it. "Fascinating. No wonder you're so interested in people like Calu."

"You do know him!"

"I know enough. Tell me: what have they told you about your eye?"

Despite her perilous position, Seri's curiosity overtook her. "Do you know Curasir?"

"Curasir? I know him, but we've never met. What does he have to do with this?"

"He told me it was wild magic."

"Did he now?"

"Are you saying it's not?"

"Curasir loves to mislead humans."

That much Seri knew to be true.

Hanirel shifted and winced. Seri stared at him. His glow, his magic, seemed to be fading, ever so slightly. Or was that wishful thinking?

"If it's not wild magic, then what is it?" she asked. She really wanted to know, but also figured keeping him talking would drain his energy faster.

"You might call it your heritage."

Heritage. Forerunner had used that word, but in reference to the golden people. Was she connected to them somehow?

"No more talking," Hanirel said. "We'll wait now."

"All right, but you should—" Seri stopped as the dagger blade pressed against her neck. For now, she would stop talking.

•••••

Forerunner looked down at Victor. "How did he obtain these injuries?"

Marshal tried to be patient, but his thoughts were with Seri and the prisoner. "Eidolon. Durunim. Whatever you call them. They attacked the village, and Victor defended the people."

Forerunner nodded. He knelt and touched Victor's left arm. "Not long ago, I assume?"

"Not very long. Does that matter?"

Forerunner stood back up. "These should heal on their own, within a day or so," he said. "Rest is all that he needs."

"I can do that," Victor murmured, his eyes half-closed.

Marshal frowned. "I guess we can wait a day or two. We can help the villagers in the meantime. Topleb, you stay with Victor and Ixchel. I'll take Rufus with me this time. We'll see what needs to be done to get them back on their feet."

"What about the prisoner?"

Forerunner, about to depart, turned back. "What prisoner?"

"We'll deal with him," Marshal said, ignoring Forerunner.

Despite Marshal's attempts to put him off, Forerunner insisted on accompanying them back to the village. Marshal couldn't quite figure out where Wolf had gone, but he found Rufus. The three of them took the now-familiar path back toward the village.

They were getting close when Dravid came toward them, moving as fast as his crutch allowed. Marshal immediately tensed. What now?

"Marshal!" Dravid gasped as he came to a stop. "He got loose. He has a knife to Seri's throat. He's demanding his sword back."

Marshal drew the sword and broke into a run. Surprisingly, Forerunner kept pace with him all the way to the house.

"You aren't really going to surrender that sword, are you?" Forerunner asked. "Do you know what it's worth?"

"I'll do whatever I have to do to protect Seri," Marshal said.

Forerunner nodded. "Then might I make a suggestion?"

Marshal listened to what Forerunner had to say. It made sense. And it might work.

Rufus and Dravid caught up to them as Marshal reached for the door. He nodded and smiled to reassure them, then opened the door and stepped inside.

Hanirel straddled Seri on the floor. He held a small dagger against her neck. But his left thigh looked soaked in blood from his hip. He couldn't keep losing that much blood for long.

"Where is the sword?" the Eldani demanded.

Marshal held up the warpsteel blade. "It's right here. You may have it if you let her go."

"Do you think me a fool? Give me the sword, and then she goes free."

"How do I know you won't kill her?"

"I am not the one who has demonstrated a lack of honor today. If I say I will release her, I will."

Marshal nodded. He also noted what Hanirel had not said: what would happen after he released Seri. "Here's what I will do." He moved to the other side of the room. "I will place the sword here on this table." He set it down and moved back to his starting point, hands held open. "Now you can release her and get the sword. I won't stop you." The sword vibrated, but Hanirel couldn't see that from his position.

"Then get on your knees!"

Marshal complied. Hanirel eyed him for a moment. Marshal looked to Seri. Her eyes were wide. Maybe she understood.

Hanirel stood, fighting back a grunt of pain. He kept the dagger aimed down at Seri. He watched Marshal for another moment, then lunged across the room. He grabbed the sword and whirled to face them.

"Marshal, what are—" Seri began, pulling up on her elbows.

"Get down!" He dove on top of her, pushing her back against the floor. He closed his eyes and triggered his power, hoping it would be enough.

A tsunami of magic erupted from the sword itself. Hanirel's scream could not be heard over the sound of the house exploding around them. Marshal closes his eyes and continued letting his power flow outward, shielding him and Seri from the cataclysm.

When the force pounding against him faded away, he stopped pushing back. He lifted up on his hands and opened his eyes. He found himself looking down into Seri's face.

"Are you—" he started.

"That was amazing!" Seri exclaimed. "You charged the sword up with power before giving it to him, didn't you? How did you trigger it to release, though?"

"It was Forerunner's idea," Marshal said. "He told me how to do it, and that if I charged it enough, it would explode once Hanirel picked it up and his own magic interacted with it."

"I could see it glowing so bright the moment you entered! I couldn't believe he couldn't tell! Maybe the Eldanim can't detect magic as well as we can?"

Marshal laughed. Even in this situation, she had to keep talking.

"I think you can let her up now!" Dravid called.

Marshal blinked. He hadn't even thought about their position. Seri realized it at the same time, face flushing in embarrassment. He scrambled off and looked around.

Everything in the house, its walls and roof, had all been obliterated by the explosion. A few chunks of debris fell here and there. The ground around them, except where he and Seri had been laying, had been torn apart. No sign of Hanirel could be seen anywhere.

Forerunner, Rufus, and Dravid had kept everyone back when it happened, but now they and a crowd of villagers rushed forward. Marshal found himself surrounded, congratulated, and hugged repeatedly, while others helped Seri to her feet and made sure she wasn't hurt. Out of the corner of his eye, Marshal saw Forerunner bend over and pick something up.

"I'll take that!" he called. He pushed away from the villagers, with a little help from Rufus, and strode to Forerunner. He held out his hand.

Forerunner nodded with a smile and placed the warpsteel sword into his hand. "The spoils of war."

Marshal looked over the sword. He had to admit surprise it still looked the same. He looked over it to Forerunner. "Thank you for your help."

"Of course. That is why I am here, is it not?"

Marshal looked him in the eyes, considering. Forerunner's private words to him at their first meeting still resonated within him. He doubted he would ever forget that. But he still couldn't tell how much of it had been true. Did he trust Forerunner's private words or his public words? And why must they be different?

For now, Forerunner's suggestion had saved Seri. Nothing else mattered. He reached out his hand, offering. Forerunner took it. Marshal nodded. "Stronger together," he said. Forerunner's eyes sparkled with their four stars, and he nodded in return.

(((67)))

Jamana entered Master Korda's chamber and found him poring over the book they had found in the hidden room. He waited for a moment before clearing his throat.

"You sent for me, Master?"

"This changes so many things," Master Korda said without looking up form the book. His thick voice rumbled in the small room. "We thought we knew everything that happened at the Lords' Betrayal. We were so blind. For Theon's sake, we didn't even know Aharu was a woman!" He paused. "Or that she was the first High Master Mage."

"High Master Mage?"

"Of course. Just as the Lords had a King, the mages had a High Master Mage. Aharu's son, Nehesy, followed in her footsteps as the second of that title."

"Then... why don't we have one now?"

Master Korda sighed and leaned back from the book. "Sometime after the death of the third or fourth High Master Mage, there was an extreme argument among the Masters. They could not agree on a new High Master, so there hasn't been one since. Again, so much of this information is lost because of poor record-keeping."

Jamana opened his mouth, but stopped himself. He had almost said something about how precise the Masters were about copying the names of the dead, compared to their actual history. At the same time, he realized: Seri would have said it out loud. He smiled to himself.

Master Korda reached out and turned another page. "So much has been lost," he said in a low tone. "So much."

Jamana waited. This would not be the first time he had been summoned to listen to Master Korda share his thoughts at length.

Sometimes, he seemed surprised to discover Jamana still there at the end of a soliloquy.

"Do you know why the magic beneath Zes Sivas never runs out?" Master Korda punched one enormous hand into the palm of the other. "The first Masters drew all of the magic of Antises through Zes Sivas itself before binding it into the bloodlines of the Lords and King. If I am right, their action has never stopped. The magic is still being drawn here, from the very edges of Antises, perhaps even beyond."

"From the Otherworld?"

Master Korda looked up sharply. "Who said our magic came from the Otherworld?"

Jamana shifted his weight nervously. "I believe the Eldani who was here said that. I could be mistaken."

"Of course he would say that." The Master nodded. "But as your friend Seri pointed out, we cannot exactly trust his word for anything."

"Has there been any news from her, Master?"

"None." He shook his head. "But neither do I expect any, unless she fulfills her quest or gives up entirely. In either case, I expect it to be some time."

Jamana agreed. He could not imagine Seri giving up. He waited a few more moments before asking his next question. "Does the book explain how the Laws of Cursings and Bindings were created?"

Master Korda tilted his head and fixed Jamana with a curious stare. "Why do you ask of this?"

"I..." Jamana swallowed. "You have spoken of the end of all curses. And Seri asked me to learn what I could of that time while she was gone. If the curses are to end, would we not need to find out how they began?"

Master Korda folded his hands together. "I do not think that will be our task, acolyte. A curse has been lifted; that we know." He gestured to the book. "Aharu said that when one curse was lifted, it would signal the end of all curses. But this is a thing that Theon will do, not we ourselves."

"But... the Laws were enacted by the mages. Shouldn't they be the ones to end them?"

"The Law was given by Theon. The mages merely enforced it."

"The curses came from the mages, then."

Korda nodded. "So it is."

"Then we should end them."

"Your stubbornness has not lessened, acolyte." Master Korda raised a finger. "I have been trying to remove this negative trait from you since you arrived here. You do not seem to be learning."

"I am sorry, Master." It still made sense to him. If the original mages had been the ones to enact the curses, then it would require mages to end them. Master Korda seemed to be implying that if Theon didn't like the curses, he would end them himself. Then why hadn't he done so years ago?

Master Korda looked at the book in silence for a moment. "The book does speak of this," he said at last.

Jamana felt a vibration run through him, as if the magic of Zes Sivas reacted to the words.

"Aharu seemed reluctant to speak of it. I think she regretted the action, though she was a part of it."

"She regretted the Lords' Betrayal, or the Laws themselves?"

"That is difficult to make out. But I suspect she regretted all of it. The Lords' Betrayal is the worst of it, of course."

Of course. While the Laws of Cursings and Bindings had been intended for good, what the Lords had done twisted it in a perverse way. Such selfishness.

Master Korda closed the book and stood. "I did summon you, acolyte. You should pack your things."

Jamana blinked. "Pack, Master?"

"I have received a summons to return home at once. You will come with me."

Jamana frowned. Master Mages rarely returned home, unless they were needed to help with a serious problem. "Is it about the succession, Master?"

"No, that is not at issue. Despite the horrendous actions of Volraag of Varioch, there is no question of the Lordship. Bakari has assumed his father's place." It went without saying that Bakari now possessed the distinction of being the first Lord of Antises without any magical power.

"Then...?"

"Ours is not to question." Master Korda placed one hand on the book. "At the very least, I can inform him of what we have learned here. And what we continue to learn." He looked up. "What are you waiting for? Go pack! We leave in the morning!" He looked back down at the book. "And we will take this with us."

(((68)))

Dravid focused and held his hands above his head. He spread them in slow arcs out and down. Golden light followed. He wrinkled his brow. The tightness in his chest increased. The heat in his throat and behind his eyes grew hotter by the moment. He spread the glowing shield even further. His vision grew hazy.

"Aaagh!" He let his arms fall and the magic dissipated. He sat alone on the hill outside the village.

Seri approached a moment later. "You made a shield over your entire head and shoulders," she said. "I don't think I've seen you do anything that big."

"It's not enough," Dravid grumbled.

"What are you expecting?" She knelt beside him. "You absorbed a tiny part of Forerunner's magic. You can't equal him."

"I know that. But the limitations frustrate me." He focused and drew a small bar of light in the air. He took hold of it. "I can craft small items like this, and keep them around for a good bit of time before the strain builds up. But anything beyond say, a foot in diameter... I can't keep it stable more than a few seconds."

"I think it's amazing you can do it at all."

Dravid ran his thumb and forefinger over his eyes. "I need to be better. Otherwise, I'm just a drag on you."

"What? That's not true! I would never have gotten this far without you!"

He gave her a rueful smile. "Even if that were true, you don't need me now. You've found Marshal. He has the power. He can save you when you get into trouble. You don't need me."

Seri bit her lip. "He has great power, yes. But he doesn't know how to use it. We need to teach him."

"You can do that."

"But I can do it better with you! We're a team. Our team has just grown. That's all."

"I suppose you're Bound to him now, after that rescue yesterday." Dravid knew it sounded petty, but couldn't help himself.

"I have no idea. Remember? Forerunner is suppressing our Bindings."

"Oh, right." He glanced around. "Where is Forerunner, anyway?"

"He's in the village with Marshal, actually helping people. I'm surprised. It doesn't seem like him to do physical labor for others." She hesitated. "You still talk with him, don't you?"

"Who, Forerunner? Sometimes. Why?"

Seri looked around, as if making sure no one else could hear them. "Back at the sanctuary, Forerunner said something about my 'heritage.' Yesterday, Hanirel used it too, talking about the star in my eye."

"You want me to see if I can find out what he meant."

Seri nodded.

"Well…" Dravid tossed his light bar and caught it. "That's something I can do, at least."

●●●●●

Marshal dropped an enormous pile of firewood and wiped the sweat from his forehead. His offer to help the people of Tungrorum recover from the eidola attacks had led to many chores of varying degrees of difficulty. Still, growing up in Drusa's Crossing, he worked at nearly everything imaginable. A Curse Boy couldn't be trusted with regular jobs.

How far he had come since then. His curse was gone. He could talk with anyone he wanted to. And people actually looked to him as a leader. The people of this village, in fact, regarded him as a great hero. That could lead to some problems once the word spread. They had all heard Hanirel call him the son of Varion. Trying to deny it would only make it spread faster, so he hadn't even tried.

Across the road, he saw Victor sitting at a bench with some children. Forerunner had been right about his injuries. They healed quickly. But Marshal forced him to rest today, just to be sure. To pass the time, he tried to teach the children how to play Mages & Lords.

"No, that's the Queen," he heard Victor say. "She either moves the

King to the bottom of the deck, or lets you play the next card."

One of the children asked a question.

"Yes, she goes with the King to the bottom of the deck. Very good."

Another comment, followed by laughter.

"What? No, the Queen doesn't have anything to do with the General! Why do you even ask that?"

Marshal laughed as well. Victor with children wasn't a sight he had expected to see any time soon.

"The card game reflects more truths than most people realize."

Marshal turned in surprise to see Wolf standing behind him. The former member of his squad had remained aloof throughout the last couple of days, not deigning to participate in their labors. Even Forerunner had helped.

"Have you come to finally help us out here?"

Wolf did not seem to notice the question. He continued watching Victor for a few moments. "This thing you are doing," he said at last. "It is unusual."

"You mean helping people?"

Wolf nodded. "You seem to do that wherever you go. You fought to protect us in battle. You tried to stop the entire war. And now you help these people. Yet none of them can do anything for you."

"I care about people. It's not that complicated."

"They should worship you and bring you gifts."

"Uh, no. They shouldn't."

"How else will your power grow?"

"I'm… not trying to make my power grow."

Wolf cocked his head, as if trying to comprehend this strange thought.

"Remember our friends who died in the battles?" Marshal asked. "Callus and Gallus and Albus? I don't want anyone else to die. Or suffer. Or be cursed."

"Then you should seek more power. It is the only way to stop these things."

Marshal considered that for a moment. "All right, that does make some sense. If I am to change things in this world, I will need all the power I can get." Wolf nodded in approval. "But I don't need people to worship me for that. I'd rather have friends."

Wolf narrowed his eyes.

Marshal pointed at Victor. "Victor can do things that I can't. So can Topleb. Rufus knows things about farming that I'd never think of, and that's been important for these people. And now, with Seri and her friends joining us..." He spread his arms. "I grow more powerful. Through my friends."

"You seek friendships... to gain power?"

"No, no. I seek friendships because... they're good. We help each other. And through that, I guess we gain power, but that's not the purpose."

Wolf clapped his hands. Marshal jumped. Victor and the children looked up.

"I am learning from you," Wolf declared. "This is good. When you desire it, you may ask a boon of me."

"A boon. All right. Thank you?"

Wolf nodded and turned away. The big man strode quickly away, leaving Marshal baffled.

Victor came up beside him. "What was that all about?"

"Apparently, Wolf owes me a boon."

"What's a boon?"

"I have no idea."

· · · · ·

For three days, Victor watched Marshal lead the party in assisting Tungrorum. They helped with numerous jobs, making up for those who had been taken away. Marshal tried several times to use the warpsteel blade to open a way to the Otherworld, but failed each attempt. Neither Seri nor Forerunner were able to help him. At last, they moved on, much to the disappointment of the grateful villagers.

Victor walked beside Topleb as they continued on their journey. He had little knowledge of geography or maps, and Topleb was pleased to share with him.

"We are descending out of the hill country of your land," he explained, pointing to examples of what he meant. "The mountains you and Marshal come from are now far to the northwest from here. You cannot see them. But soon... soon it will be getting warmer."

"Why is that?"

"We are descending near the coast. You notice no trees any more?"

"I haven't seen any in a while."

"They don't grow here. In fact, your trees do not grow in Ch'olan at all."

"No trees?"

"Better trees! Trees that grow wide as well as tall! Trees that grow fruit. Trees in which the animals play."

"We have some of those."

"Not like our trees." Topleb wagged his finger. "Ch'olan has the best trees."

"If you say so."

"I do say so!" Topleb exploded in laughter and Victor laughed along with him, though he wasn't entirely sure why.

A few more days passed. One morning, Topleb surveyed the terrain around them, then pointed to the west. Victor looked and saw a sparkle.

"Lake Litanu," Topleb proclaimed. He spread his arms wide and rotated in a circle. "We are in Ch'olan!"

"Are you sure?"

"I am a native son! Would I not know my own home?" He looked to the northwest. "I have come home!" he shouted, pounding his chest.

The other members of the party, in varying stages of morning preparation, looked up. "Come, all of you!" Topleb called. "Today, we walk on the soil of Ch'olan! Ixchel, daughter of the homeland, you have returned!"

Ixchel nodded. She didn't seem as excited as he did. Then again, she never looked excited about anything.

Rufus walked up, proudly wearing Marshal's old sword on his belt. "This is Ch'olan? I thought you said it was beautiful, Topleb!"

Topleb reached out and tousled Rufus's hair. "I also said you were a smart man. Maybe I don't get everything right."

"How far to our destination?" Victor asked.

"Still quite a ways," Topleb said. "We'll need to bear more to the north now, if you wish to avoid Woqan. It is a mighty city, such a great city, with pyramids marking every decade of its life."

Victor glanced back at the rest of the party. "Yeah, I'm not thrilled with the idea of another big city. Maybe after we visit this magic place."

"Uh, Victor, when we stop for the night, can you, ah, train me some more with the sword?" Rufus asked.

"Of course," Victor said. "You're probably better with a spear than I am, but the sword is a different thing. I like to think I'm getting pretty good at it."

"Again," Topleb said, miming a throw, "if you hit them from a distance, you don't have to worry about such things."

"That's why we keep you around."

Marshal joined them. "Why have we stopped?"

"Topleb wanted to let us know that we've arrived in Ch'olan," Victor said.

Marshal looked around, as if expecting to see some change. "All right. So why have we stopped?"

Topleb threw up his hands. "I am home, silly man! Is that not something to celebrate?"

Marshal grinned. "Of course it is. I was just…"

"You joked?" Victor put his hand over his heart. "Seri really is changing you."

"I can joke," Marshal protested.

"I've never heard you," Rufus said.

Marshal scowled at him.

Victor put a hand on Marshal's shoulder. "No, this… this is a good thing, Mars. We haven't had much to laugh about for a while. This is good."

"Especially since we're in Ch'olan," Topleb added.

(((69)))

"Are you certain?" Kishin asked. He leaned forward, almost letting his hood fall away. He grabbed it and leaned back, waiting.

"Yes, sir," Aapo said. "The messages were quite clear. The man you are looking for is on the road from Varioch to Ch'olan. He was last seen in the village of Tungrorum only a few days ago. They're calling him the son of Varion."

"And the facial scars?"

Aapo nodded. "He had them. And traveled with a group of people, including mages and some Ch'olanese fighters. The witnesses say he rescued the village from the Eldanim and some spirits or something."

Kishin frowned. That was a new one. But the other news interested him much more. Marshal traveled to Ch'olan. Why? The first thought that popped into his head—that Marshal sought him out—was ridiculous. It had to be something else.

He jumped to his feet, passed the startled Aapo, and paced about his room. Where would Marshal go after being freed from his curse? He had the power of a Lord. Why didn't he challenge his half-brother for the Lordship of Varioch?

Except Volraag had power too. Stolen power. Maybe Marshal sought for more. So he came to Ch'olan for...

"The high place," he whispered. That had to be it. Everyone knew it to be a place of fell magic. And Marshal traveled in the company of mages. They would help him gain new power, the power he needed to defeat his brother. It was the only possible explanation.

"Thank you, Aapo. I may be leaving soon. Pack my usual travel bag."

The servant nodded and left. Kishin took a deep breath and tossed the hood back from his face. He tired of hiding his healing from Aapo.

As he considered what Marshal might be planning, he mechanically began to gather his weapons and gear for the trip, as he had done so many times over the past twenty years.

"Will you kill again?"

Kishin whirled about, dagger in hand. The voice sounded so real. But those were the words Chimon had asked him repeatedly.

"I do not want to," he whispered, repeating his own answer.

"Yet you come to me still wearing a sword."

Kishin set the dagger down. Did he really need his weapons, if he could not—would not—kill again? He picked up the warpsteel sword. It felt so much heavier than usual. He slid it out of its sheath. The blade, so perfectly forged, gleamed even in the half-light of his room. Beautiful.

Something drew his gaze away from the sword to the back corner of his room. A staff leaned against the wall, the staff the old man left behind after the strange conversation on the road.

A staff could be a useful tool on the road. It could also be a weapon, though usually not for killing. Wasn't this semantics, though? A man could be cursed for injuring someone, not just killing. The curse might not be as bad, but it would still be a curse.

"All men are cursed."

Then what was the point? The priest said the answer came from Theon, but that didn't help. Still, he had suggested one solution. A cause to fight for.

Kishin strapped the sword to his belt, then took the staff also. He did not have a cause yet, but if he were to find one anywhere, it would be with Marshal and his companions.

If not there, then… Kishin did not like to think of where he would go if this did not work out.

(((70)))

"You have a challenge here," Victor said. "You're right-handed, but your left foot is the twisted one, right?"

Rufus nodded. The rest of the party were setting up camp, but Victor had pulled him aside.

"Normally, I would teach you how to pivot on your right foot, constantly moving your left foot. Do you think you could do that?"

Rufus demonstrated an attempt at a shifting stance. The awkwardness made Victor wince. A skilled opponent would knock him off balance in seconds, opening him up to a lethal attack.

"Let's flip that," he suggested. "You'll be more of a defensive fighter, but I think you'll live longer."

He worked with Rufus on new stances, holding his square Varioch shield forward and waiting patiently on an opening. Once it grew too dark to see, they sat in the dirt and watched the new campfire from a distance.

"Do you think we'll have much more fighting to do?" Rufus asked.

"I hope we never have to fight again." Even as he said it, Victor wondered if he truly believed that. "But after what happened in the last village, I think everyone needs to prepare for battle. We might have to fight more invaders from the Otherworld."

"Swords didn't seem much good against them."

"No," Victor admitted. "But if they cross over like the leader did, we can fight them."

They sat in silence for a few moments. Victor looked up at the stars starting to appear. Marshal talked a lot about the stars of the Otherworld. Victor wondered how different they could be. At any rate, they seemed to have power to heal, which is where starshine came from. Huh. Forerunner and Wolf could heal, and they came from there. He wondered if Marshal or Seri had made that connection.

"Thanks, by the way," Rufus said.

"What for?"

"Helping me out. I'm feeling kind of useless here, what with the mages and heroes and all."

Victor snorted. "Our curse squad is down to only four, if you don't count Wolf. Which I don't. We've got to stick together."

Victor almost couldn't hear the response. "I'm the only one now who actually has a curse."

"That doesn't matter. We're all one mistake away from being cursed, after all." He shifted so as to face Rufus. "Marshal didn't even do anything for his curse. This is the point. We're going to find a way to end all of it. No more curses."

"Do you really think that's possible?"

"I didn't think it was possible to get rid of one curse, but we did. And I've seen so many other things I never would have thought possible. Did I tell you about the floating city?"

He hadn't, so Victor spent the next few minutes telling Rufus all about Intal Eldanir. When he finished, they again shared that silence that young men often do.

"Do you think you'll ever go there again?" Rufus asked after a while.

"The Eldanim city? Nah, I don't have any reason to go back there. Marshal might, I suppose. There was this Eldani girl that seemed like she wouldn't mind seeing him again, if you know what I mean."

"He seems taken with the mage right now."

"True."

"So where will you go when this is all over?"

"All over?" Victor frowned. "I haven't thought that far ahead. I don't really know. I could go back home, to Drusa's Crossing. I had a girl there. Careen." He paused. "I haven't thought about her in a long time. I wonder if she ever thinks of me."

"Topleb will go home after we reach this other place," Rufus said. "I don't know what I'll do. I don't have much to go back to."

"You're welcome to stay with us as long as there's reason to."

With the glow from the distant firelight, Victor saw Rufus open his mouth, then close it. He looked like he wanted to say something more, but couldn't decide whether he should.

"Ho! You two!" Topleb's shout carried across the flat land. "If you're done slapping each other with sticks of metal, you might want to eat something!"

"Is he cooking again tonight?" Victor asked.

"I think he delights in tormenting us."

"If you are talking now about my cooking," Topleb called, "then you are giving me time to add a few extras to your plates!"

"We'd better move!" The two young men scrambled to their feet and hurried to join the others.

•••••

Dravid relished his role as nightly storyteller around the fire. To him, Kuktarma was home. But to this group, it was an exotic land, far away. Every story he told of his homeland sounded strange to them, especially if he exaggerated a few things. Every once in a while, however, the interruptions grew irritating.

"One day, Lord Meluhha's fourth son decided to visit a young maiden who lived—"

"What was his name?" Rufus asked.

"I don't know his name. He's the fourth son."

"You don't know the name of your Lord's son?"

Dravid scowled at him. "Of course I don't. Do you?"

"Even I know that," Topleb said. "It's Volraag. Except he is Lord now."

"That's not the same thing," Dravid argued. "He was next in line. Do you know any of his other sons?"

"Marshal," Victor said, grinning.

"Still not the same thing!"

Rufus looked confused. "Marshal?"

"I'll explain later," Victor whispered.

"As I was saying, the fourth son went to visit a young maiden who lived in the walls of the city. She was an orphan child who had grown up under the care of the chief of the Lord's guard. What the fourth son did not know, however, was that he was followed by the seventh son, the youngest—"

"You don't know his name either, do you?"

"We've established this."

"Let him tell his story," Seri put in. "They're always funny, even if he doesn't know their names."

Dravid nodded. The smile she directed his way made all of it worthwhile.

"The seventh son followed the fourth and watched as he met with the maiden. Unfortunately, the seventh son tripped over a vase, revealing his presence."

Dravid went on, describing the conflict between the two brothers. As he talked, he noticed Marshal whisper something to Seri and point to his new sword. She nodded, whispered something back, then returned her attention to Dravid.

"...but the maiden interfered, for she was tender of heart. She begged the fourth son not to be harsh with his younger brother, who was only curious about the ways of love.

"'Curiosity was the downfall of the tailless monkey of Lord Sakouna,' the fourth son pointed out."

Rufus opened his mouth to ask something, but Topleb shushed him.

"'True,' the maiden replied, 'but is it not also the defining characteristic of all seven sons of the great Lord Meluhha? Surely you do not begrudge your brother your own character traits, for was it not that very curiosity that led you to my door?'

"Her earnest words, spoken with such ardor, so moved the fourth son that he completely forgot the presence of his brother and began to kiss the maiden with all the passion of a true son of the Lord Meluhha.

"The seventh son felt uncomfortable witnessing this display and moved toward the door. The fourth son and the maiden both paid him no mind, so deep were they in their embrace. And it was at this precise moment that the chief of the guard knocked on the door."

Dravid paused for the chuckles which naturally followed. Then he went on, gesturing broadly as he described the awkward situation. As the youngest, the seventh son rarely appeared in the stories, but when he did, he always caused awkward problems for his older brothers. But often, like in this story, he managed to get them out of trouble through surprising wisdom.

As he continued to the story's ridiculous climax, Dravid kept an eye on his audience. Rufus still looked a little confused, though Topleb, Victor, and Seri all seemed to be thoroughly enjoying themselves. Marshal's scars made him much harder to read. Forerunner leaned forward, completely enthralled. He never missed a story of any kind.

And then Dravid noticed Calu. He sat apart from the others, as he often did. But his face... his eyes narrowed with suspicion. His nostrils flared ever so slightly, as if he contained anger. Did the story offend him? But no... he did not watch Dravid. His eyes were fixed on

Forerunner.

•••••

Seri looked over the warpsteel sword with her star-sight. "I don't see anything special about it," she said at last, handing it back to Marshal.

"That's surprising. I was sure you'd see something."

"Tell me again what makes these swords different."

Marshal gestured with the sword, looking frustrated. "I don't fully understand it myself. That's part of the problem. Talinir talked about the forging process, but I didn't know what he meant. And apparently, the magic they use in making it means the sword exists in both worlds."

"So when you're swinging that around right now…" Seri pointed at it. "Does that mean there's a sword swinging around in the Otherworld by itself right now?"

"I guess? Or maybe they have to do something to make that happen. I don't know. I watched Talinir fighting a monster in the Otherworld with one, while he was here with us in this world." He held it up and looked at it again. "And Hanirel used it to cross into our world. It was like he cut open the sky."

Seri nodded. "He said as much to me. But not how he did it."

"Let's try our power together," Marshal said. He held out his left hand.

Seri glanced around to make sure none of the others were too close. She took Marshal's hand. He closed his eyes, concentrating. She did her part, finding an orange beam of magic nearby and absorbing it. She let it flow through her hand to Marshal and felt his power flow back in response. Her body tensed up. His power felt so amazing, so strong.

As before, the beams of light began to encircle them, moving faster and faster. Soon, she could see nothing else. Marshal opened his eyes and grinned. She smiled back. It felt good to have someone able to share this with her.

Marshal held up the sword and focused on it. Seri watched magic flow from Marshal into the blade. Some of the beams swirling about them shifted and plunged into the sword also. A few began to writhe about the blade itself, giving it an bizarre appearance. She almost couldn't see the metal any more. But the brightness around it continued to increase. Soon, it became difficult to keep her eyes open.

"Try it now!" she shouted, then wondered why she felt the need to raise her voice. The swirling magic wasn't creating any sound... was it?

Marshal lifted the blade and drew it across the colored beams in front of them. To Seri's surprise, the beams themselves came apart and split in opposite directions. But the sword cut deeper than that. As it moved across her viewpoint, it left behind a dark gash in mid-air.

"I think it's working!" Marshal cried. He thought he needed to be loud too. Interesting.

Seri stared at the dark cut. Did it truly lead into the Otherworld? She couldn't see much of anything through the narrow gash yet.

Marshal inserted the warpsteel sword into the gash and cut down a few inches. Then he cut back across the opposite direction. Eventually, he brought the sword back up to the starting point. Both of them stared at the results.

A horizontal opening a few inches tall floated just above their eye level. Beyond it, Seri saw the stars of the Otherworld. Though she immediately felt the overwhelming awe of their immensity and beauty, she found her reaction somewhat muted this time. Memories tempered her admiration, memories of the star-like being that strode across the world coming for her after the breaking of the Bond.

"The stars," Marshal whispered. Seri pulled her eyes away and looked at him. Marshal's face showed more than awe. He looked like... like... what? Like he wanted the stars, desired them. Seri admired their beauty and power, but Marshal wanted more. He took a step toward the opening, staring up into it with total abandon.

"Marshal!"

He did not react.

Seri yanked her hand away from his. The colors faded away. The hole in the sky remained for a few more moments, then it dissolved as well. Marshal lunged for it just as it disappeared. His hand closed on nothing.

He spun back to Seri. "Why did you do that?" he demanded.

"What is wrong with you?"

"Wrong with me? The stars, Seri! Didn't you see the stars?"

"Yes, I saw them. I also saw your reaction to them."

He looked confused now. "What other reaction can there be to that beauty?"

"I don't know. Maybe some admiration combined with self-control?"

"You don't understand."

"No, I don't. You looked like you would have left all of us behind if you could get to the stars."

Marshal looked back at where the hole had been. "I would have," he said. He dropped the sword and fell to his knees.

Seri stepped closer. "What do you mean?"

"I thought... I thought I had gotten over it, after the fight with Curasir." He continued to stare up at the empty sky. "But I haven't. Ever since I first saw them, I've... wanted nothing more than to get back to them. It may be wrong, but sometimes, it's all that I can think about."

Seri tried to grasp what he meant, but the concept eluded her. This behavior from Marshal differed from all she had come to know from him.

"Are you... planning to go through the high place to the Otherworld when we reach it? Is that why you're going?"

"I don't know. I mean, it was for Talinir. I need to rescue him. And, and the curses. But if I can see the stars again..."

"You can't leave us! We need you!"

"And I need the stars. But what I need never matters, does it?"

"I don't understand at all."

"No one does."

Seri hesitated for a moment, then shook her head. Whatever this strange desire that consumed Marshal might be, she couldn't argue with it. Better to leave him alone. Her excitement in recovering her star-sight and finding Marshal: all of it seemed tempered now. Maybe things weren't what she thought them to be. Maybe Marshal wasn't who she thought he was.

(((71)))

Something had happened to Marshal. Victor didn't know what, but he saw the change. Marshal was reverting to his behavior back at the battlefront: withdrawn, moody, and quiet.

He suspected Seri had something to do with it. Marshal hadn't spoken to her in three days, at least.

Still, Victor had been busy. Training with Rufus. Learning about Ch'olan from Topleb. And his own practice. He still hadn't decided whether to switch to using the new flail. The old one felt so comfortable, so normal in his hand. The new one might be a better weapon, but he couldn't seem to get used to it.

The road ascended from the sparse lowlands and they entered a forest. Victor saw what Topleb had meant about the trees. They were enormous! They further they traveled, the higher the trees rose, forming a roof that blocked out much of the sun. Enough light made it through to show off more shades of green than Victor had ever imagined. He found it all both strange and beautiful. Unfortunately, the heat and insects diminished the appeal. He waved a large buzzing thing away from his face and found himself wishing for thrummers.

He wiped sweat from his forehead. "Is it always this hot here? The air is so... damp." Was it summer already? It seemed too early.

"Ha!" Topleb laughed. "This is not hot. This is pleasant warmth. Come back later in summer to find hot!"

"If I ever come back, I think I'll try for winter."

The good-natured banter continued as the two of them led the party up the road north. Marshal followed behind them, quiet as he had been the last few days. Wolf and Forerunner came next, speaking only to each other. Seri, Ixchel, Dravid and Rufus brought up the rear.

"Someone up there," Marshal said, breaking into the conversation. He inclined his head to point with his chin.

Victor looked ahead. A cloaked and hooded man with a staff leaned against a gigantic tree trunk at the side of the road. They had seen occasional travelers along this road, but never someone all alone.

"A pilgrim, perhaps," Topleb suggested.

"A pilgrim?"

"The high place is considered sacred by many. Some make the journey there as a spiritual adventure."

The pilgrim, or whatever he might be, noticed their approach. He straightened and pulled back his hood. He lifted a hand in greeting as Victor and Topleb neared him.

"Ho there," Topleb said.

"Blessings to you," the stranger said. "Is this the road to the high place?" His skin, dark and smooth, marked him as a native. His black hair, while full, reached only to the middle of his neck.

"It is. Are you a pilgrim?"

He nodded once. "That is my current task, the job I have chosen for myself. Are you all pilgrims as well?" Something sounded vaguely familiar about his voice, but perhaps it was the accent, so similar to Topleb and Ixchel. His eyes looked them over, then darted to Marshal and his scars.

"Something like that," Victor said. "We're on our way there."

The pilgrim hesitated for a moment. "At this time of year, there are dangerous animals in the region sometimes. Would you mind if I followed along with your group? For safety?"

Victor looked back to Marshal. He didn't react. "Well, ah, we're quite an unusual group. I don't know if we're the best company for, um…"

The pilgrim spread his arms, revealing clothes that looked about as average as you could find. "I seek nothing from you, save the safety of your companionship. I have my own food, and need nothing else."

Forerunner pushed past Marshal and approached the pilgrim, arms lifted in welcome. "Another wanderer on this life's road!" he exclaimed. "I am Forerunner. It is an honor to meet you, good sir."

The pilgrim looked a bit taken aback. "I am… Kishin."

"Oh, Kishin." Forerunner put a hand to his face. "How great is your loss! How much you have suffered! This world of curses is so unjust."

"You are… most perceptive."

"It is my job to restore that which was lost. For you, I must consider carefully. One thing you have lost can be restored almost immediately. After that… well, this should be quite interesting."

Victor stepped up next to him. "If you're feeling confused, that's how all of us feel around him."

Kishin nodded.

"I'm Victor, by the way, and this is Topleb. The quiet one there is Marshal."

"So pleased to meet you," Kishin said. He extended his hand to Marshal.

Marshal blinked, surprised to be addressed. He held out his own hand and took Kishin's. "You are welcome here," he said.

"You have no idea how happy I am to hear that."

• • • • •

Using his real name had given him a moment of panic. He hadn't meant to say it. But even so, it should be safe. None of these people had ever heard his name. Certainly, there had been no reason to offer it when he had been trying to kill them.

But who was this Forerunner person? How had he come to join Marshal's band? His words struck deep. Kishin couldn't figure out if he truly did perceive things that no one should know, or if he made wild guesses. The words could be interpreted in multiple ways, after all. Still, he found it unnerving. The tall, white-and-gray haired man that walked behind Forerunner puzzled him even more. Kishin took him for some kind of barbarian, perhaps from somewhere beyond Antises.

He chided himself for his impatience. He should have scouted the band, identifying each one before actually meeting them.

No sign of the Eldani warden, though. Out of all of them, he was the only one Kishin feared could recognize him, despite his lifted curse. His absence, though unexplained, helped greatly.

Four more in the back. He started to turn toward them when Topleb slapped him on the back. "Tell me, friend pilgrim, where have you come from? Tell me it is Woqan. I must hear of Woqan!"

Kishin smiled at him. "I have indeed come from Woqan," he said. "Are you from there as well?"

"Ah, no," Topleb said. "I live in a small village on the east side. Still, I have spent much time in the great city. But I have not visited in too long. Have they completed the latest pyramids?"

"You know the pyramid construction. It never ends." They shared a laugh, and the group resumed walking.

"I'm going to have to see these pyramids one day," Victor said.

"Indeed! I have told you many times now. And here is someone else to show that I lie not!"

"I've never said you lied! Horribly exaggerated, perhaps, but not lying."

The two men exchanged insults and boasts like old friends, or soldiers who had fought together. Kishin wondered that Marshal did not join in the conversation. He could speak; he had welcomed Kishin himself. Yet he seemed withdrawn, not interested in what happened around him.

What had changed? According to his reports, Marshal had fought to liberate Tungrorum and endeared himself to its people. Yet here he walked as if his curse had never left him.

"What has led such a unique assemblage to travel to the high place?" he asked. Such an inquiry would be expected. Anything more specific would be unusual.

"We're fulfilling promises to some friends," Victor answered. "We met some of these others along the way, and they joined up with us, just like you."

"Is all well with the Lord and Lady?" Topleb asked. "I heard there was trouble at the Passing this year."

"Yes, they are well," Kishin answered. For the next few miles, he exchanged news and pleasantries with Topleb, who was eager for news of his homeland. Victor joined into the conversation now and then. Marshal remained quiet. Forerunner did not engage him again, thankfully.

Topleb enjoyed the sound of his own voice. It did not take Kishin long to uncover bits of information he suspected the others would have kept to themselves. He learned that most of the men in the party had fought together under Lord Volraag. Intriguing. How had Marshal come to that situation?

He also learned that the two women in the back of the group made things so much more complicated, at least in Topleb's opinion. "They are always needing time and space to themselves," he complained.

"But they are nice to look at," Victor said, eliciting a laugh from his friend.

"See? You are in Ch'olan only a few days and already you become more enlightened! You see beauty in skin with a proper color, not pale like you."

"I am an admirer of the female form in all colors!" Victor protested.

Kishin glanced back but could not see the women. After the laughter subsided, he asked, "The women are from Ch'olan also, then?"

"One of them is," Victor said. "She's some kind of warrior. The other is from Arazu."

"She's a mage!" Topleb inserted.

Kishin felt a tremble. A lady mage with a warrior woman from Ch'olan. It could not be. The odds were extreme. He glanced back again and caught Forerunner looking at him with a knowing smile. Impossible. How could he know? How could this... Enough. He had to know.

"Oh, pardon me," he said, coming to a stop. "I believe my sandal has come loose. You needn't stop. I will catch up."

Topleb and Victor continued on, followed by Marshal. Forerunner actually winked at him. Maddening. The other man ignored him. He finished pretending to fix his sandal and stood as the final four approached.

"Hello," said the girl in mage robes. "Who are you?"

"I am Kishin, my lady, and I—" He broke off at the sight of her companion.

Kishin was undone.

His daughter stood before him. Dressed in the traditional Holcan warrior garb, she could not have been more beautiful. She looked strong, powerful, everything she would have wanted. Everything he would have wanted for her. And the feathers. She wore the same feathers he had left beside her the last night before he let her go.

"And you what?" The mage looked amused.

"I, I am delighted to meet you."

"I'm Seri. This is Ixchel, Dravid, and Rufus. What are you doing on this road?"

"He's a pilgrim," Ixchel said. "On his way to the high place." She looked him over with a trained eye. Kishin's sword remained hidden on his back, under the robe.

"And you are one of the Holcan. Though, I don't fully know why you're here."

"I have been assigned to guard the Lady Seri."

Kishin nodded. Just as Kuch had said. He struggled not to stare at Ixchel. Ixchel. Had he given her that name? He felt ashamed that he could not even remember. So much of his life before the curse remained a haze even now.

Dravid and Rufus each greeted him, but he paid little attention. He needed to learn more of Ixchel, but he couldn't ask too many direct questions. Perhaps he should learn more about this mage first.

"What brings a mage to this part of Ch'olan?" he asked. "One of the warriors up there said you were from Arazu?"

Seri nodded. "I'm a very long way from home. I'm... learning about all aspects of the magic of Antises, as part of my education. The high places need much more study."

Her attempt at a lie was blatantly obvious. This young woman lacked all guile.

"Of course. They have long been revered as places of both magic and faith. And Ch'olan's is the only one readily accessible."

"Oh? Have you been to the other two?"

"Oh, no. But I have heard that both are buried beneath the ground."

"I wonder how that happened." Seri seemed to be thinking hard about something. Kishin's eyes darted to Ixchel again, only to find her staring at him.

"I must speak to Forerunner," she said abruptly, and sped up to catch the others.

Kishin watched her go, his heart aching.

(((72)))

Volraag, Tezan, and Rathri waded onto shore. Tezan shook water from his boots then pointed inland. "According to the captain, that road just in sight there will take us directly to the high place."

Volraag opened his mouth to agree, then paused. Now on land, he felt something else. "My brother is near," he said.

Rathri's head shot up and he looked in every direction. "How close?"

"Not very. But not too far, either." Volraag considered for a moment. "It makes sense that he would be coming here. He was at the last site, as well. He must have a plan of some sort."

"It did not sound like it, from what our spy told us back at the war," Rathri argued.

Volraag clenched his fist and felt his power vibrate out from it. Some loose sand billowed into the air around him. "I have grown very tired of him."

"Shall I go kill him for you?"

"Not yet. I want to be sure his power is mine before he dies. I don't want any more surprises." Volraag paused again, thinking. "But... do go find out who he has with him and what they are up to, if you can. If our spy is still with them, use him. Let him come meet me at the high place, but if he has any significant help, stop them from joining him."

"It shall be done." Rathri paused and pointed at the road. "Just before you reach the high place, the path will enter a tunnel. Be careful. The tunnels were built to suppress magic. Go through it quickly."

"Wait." Volraag frowned. "How can something suppress magic?"

Rathri shrugged. "No one is quite sure. The tunnels have been in place for generations. Some natural feature of the earth itself, I suppose. Perhaps they were longer in the past, meant to trap anyone or anything that emerged from the portal." He shrugged again and set off at a light jog.

Tezan and Volraag watched him go. The wild magician turned to Volraag. "Well, the atmosphere has just improved greatly. I suspect our conversation will, also."

"Indeed." Volraag began walking toward the road. "Do you still have the hunger?"

Tezan didn't hesitate. "Yes. Why do you think I am still here?"

"As if you could escape me."

"If I wanted to, I could be gone by tomorrow morning. Without Rathri and his blades, you have no power over me."

Volraag stopped and faced him again. The ground around them both shook. "Are you sure about that?"

Tezan appeared unfazed. "I am sure. When you fall asleep tonight, I could get up and walk away." He paused for a long moment. "But I won't." Before Volraag could speak again, he rushed on: "It is not because of your supposed cause. I don't know if you even believe in that yourself any more. No. I am here because I want the power. Nothing else."

Volraag's eyes grew narrower throughout Tezan's speech. "Whatever it takes. I am not done with you yet."

Tezan took a drink from his water pouch. "I just wish I could get the salt taste out of my mouth," he grumbled.

Volraag nodded and resumed walking. No matter how much water or wine he drank, the salt taste remained, a constant reminder of the hunger for power within him. Was Tezan right? Did he even care about his cause any more? The Eldanim power that coursed through him now had changed him, perhaps more than he was willing to admit.

Regardless, the portal—and Marshal—awaited.

(((73)))

Marshal put the unusual pilgrim out of his mind, though he could hear Victor and Topleb discussing him in great detail. His thoughts, as they had for several days, followed dark paths, all of them centered on his glimpse of the stars with Seri.

Until that moment, he had put thoughts of the Otherworld's stars far from him. But now... now it all came rushing back, overwhelming him with the desire, the need to be there, to see them again. To do so, he would have to pass through the high place, leaving behind his friends, abandoning all they hoped to accomplish. If Seri's ideas were right, he would be abandoning Antises itself.

Yet he could not deny the temptation. He even had an excuse ready: he needed to go find Talinir. Wasn't that the original point of coming here, anyway? And he should do that. It was his fault. He needed to rescue Talinir. And who knew how long it could last?

Seri hadn't spoken to him since the encounter. He disgusted her. Worse, he disappointed her. She wanted him to be a king, a hero, the one to restore Antises. She knew the truth now. He was none of those things. He couldn't be.

"Is there anything I can do to help you?" He glanced to his right and found Forerunner beside him. The mysterious man seemed to always be lurking nearby, no matter where he went.

"No, thank you."

"No doubt you are pondering what awaits us at our destination."

He always seemed to know far more than he should.

"There may be more than you expect," Forerunner went on. "The high place is of great interest to certain others, you know."

In that moment, Marshal knew. "Volraag. He's near."

"He started a war over one high place," Forerunner pointed out. "If he is here, what will he do for this one?"

Marshal straightened. "We need to be ready. I'll tell the others tonight—" He stopped only because Ixchel strode up on the other side of Forerunner. She looked even less pleased than usual.

"Is this your doing?" she demanded.

Forerunner cocked his head. "To what do you refer, my dear?"

Ixchel pointed toward those at the back. "The 'pilgrim.' He just happens to be named Kishin?"

"I did not bring him here."

"But you claimed…" Her brows furrowed.

"Ah, I see. That strand of hope." He held up his fingers, pantomiming pulling on something. "You fear to let it come forth."

"It is not possible!" Ixchel's fierceness made Marshal want to step away from this conversation, but his curiosity kept him walking beside Forerunner.

"I have told you," Forerunner said. "My job is to restore that which was lost. In some cases, I act directly. In others, I sit back and wait. Things which seemed impossible… happen. As long as I am around, anyway."

Marshal couldn't help himself. "Are you saying that what we see as coincidence is actually some subtle magic on your part?"

Forerunner's smile expanded. "That is a brilliant way of stating it. Things just seem to fall into place while I'm around." He looked back to Ixchel. "Or more specifically, things are… restored."

"Some things do not need to be restored," Ixchel answered. She looked almost ready to draw her sword.

They all came to a stop and simultaneously all realized that Topleb and Victor had stopped also. Victor had drawn his sword.

"Did you see it?" Topleb asked.

"See what?"

Victor took a step toward the side of the road, sliding into a defensive stance. "Curse-stalker," he said. "A big one."

Ixchel whirled the other direction, sword already in her hand. "Another one on this side."

"There are many such creatures in this area," Topleb said. "They are drawn to the high place. This is why our pilgrim desired numbers."

"Not his only reason," Ixchel muttered.

Victor moved closer to the undergrowth. Something large just out of sight moved away. The sounds of its movement faded away. "I think we've scared it off," Victor said.

"We'll need to move with more caution," Marshal said. "Topleb, I think we can all follow the road now. I want you to move to the center of the party, where your atlatl can strike in any direction. Victor and I will stay in the front. Ixchel, you and Rufus will be in charge of making sure one of them doesn't sneak up on us."

Everyone turned to look at him while he spoke. Victor raised an eyebrow and had a funny grin. "What?"

"No, it's a good plan. Just... glad to hear from you again."

•••••

Dravid looked around. Ten people, all gathered around the same fire. All of them looked a little nervous, except Calu. All day, they had seen glimpses of curse-stalkers moving about. They couldn't tell if they kept seeing the same two or three creatures, or many more. But everyone had seen at least one.

It made sense, unfortunately. Curse-stalkers were drawn to magic, so naturally they haunted the area around a magic portal. Or high place or whatever you called it. And now they had an assemblage of magic-infused people all in one place. No wonder the beasts kept coming closer. Eventually, one or more of them would risk an attack. The inevitability worried him.

Dravid touched the burn scar on the back of his hand. It still hurt, even though his fight with the curse-stalker had been weeks ago. Did Marshal's scars still hurt? He couldn't imagine the pain the other young man had gone through. Burns all around his head. Dravid shivered.

Marshal alone would be enough to draw the curse-stalkers, with all his power. Plus Forerunner and Calu. Dravid held power, and Seri always had a little stored within her, whether intentional or not. Seri said Victor had an odd sort of power absorbed from proximity to Marshal. Even Rufus radiated some magic, because of his curse. That left only Ixchel and Topleb without any magic. And the pilgrim.

Seri, beside him, looked back out into the encroaching woods. Ixchel called it jungle, not woods, but Dravid didn't get the distinction. "They don't hunt in packs, do they?" she asked, breaking the silence.

"I have not known them to do so," Ixchel said. "But these are unusual circumstances."

Dravid noticed a gap in the group. He looked from face to face.

"Where's Rufus?" he exclaimed. Everyone else looked around in a hurry. The limping soldier was nowhere to be seen.

Victor leaped to his feet, sword already drawn. "Rufus!" he shouted.

A sudden rustle drew their attention behind Dravid. Rufus stumbled out into the light, his face white.

"What were you doing?" Dravid demanded, echoed by the others.

Rufus took a seat next to him, shaking. "I'm sorry," he repeated several times. "I had to... relieve myself. I thought it would be okay, not going far. But... one of them is out there. It came too close. So close."

Victor shook his head. "Next time, take someone with you." He looked around. "That goes for all of us. No one should be alone."

Dravid gave Rufus an awkward pat on the back. They had become, if not friends, at least close acquaintances over the past days of traveling. Their respective deficiencies made them the slowest walkers, always at the back.

"You're all right now," Dravid told him.

Rufus stared into the fire. The curse-stalker clearly terrified him. Dravid could imagine. If Varioch were like Kuktarma, Rufus had probably been warned of the creatures as a child, then tormented by the very thought of them once he became cursed. They were walking nightmares for those who bore a curse of any kind.

On the opposite side of the fire, Marshal abruptly rose to his feet. He walked around the fire and stood beside Seri. She looked up in surprise.

"Volraag is here," Marshal announced.

"What? You can sense him?"

Marshal nodded. "Since earlier today. He's very close."

"How close? Can you tell?"

Curious. She must not want to let Marshal know about her Bond to Volraag.

"No, I don't know. But I can feel him as powerfully as I could back at the war camp. He's very close." Marshal looked around. "Listen to me, everyone." He needn't have bothered. All eyes were already fixed on him. "Volraag is here. He started a war over the high place in the south. And now he's come for this one."

"Lord Volraag of Varioch?" the pilgrim asked.

Marshal nodded. "I'm sorry that you've gotten caught up in this. The curse-stalkers are not our only threat now. Volraag is here. I do not know his intentions, but they can't be good. And he may have others with him."

"The assassin," Victor said.

Rufus shivered again. Dravid glanced at him. "Maybe we should turn back?" Rufus suggested. "We can't know how many soldiers he's brought. It may be an entire legion!"

"That is not likely," Ixchel said. "To bring so many soldiers across the water to Ch'olan? It would be an invasion fleet. Ch'olan's own soldiers would be fighting him even now."

"No," Marshal said. "He wouldn't have brought an army. Only those he needed, for whatever he's doing." He paused. "We need to be ready, whatever it is. Any suggestions?"

"We stick together," Victor said. "Together, we're more than a match for him."

"I don't want to underestimate him."

"You and Seri should be enough to stop whatever he tries!" Victor said.

He was right. But Marshal and Seri hadn't been spending much time together lately. Selfishly, Dravid couldn't help being pleased, but he knew something needed to bring them back together.

"And the rest of us handle this assassin," Topleb said. "He can't be all that bad. Ixchel and Victor will show him how to fight. Victor is the Hero of Varioch. Almost as impressive as Ch'olan soldier."

Rufus opened his mouth as if to protest, but closed it again.

Dravid noticed he hadn't been included in any of the fighting discussion. He had never claimed, nor wanted to be a warrior. But it did raise the question again: why was he here? He looked across Ixchel to Seri. Did she really need him any more?

Forerunner, who sat on the other side of Seri, leaned over and whispered something to her. Dravid felt a twinge of guilt. He hadn't been able to get anything from Forerunner about Seri's "heritage" yet. Seri nodded in response to the whisper without looking at Forerunner.

"What can we expect from this high place?" she asked out loud. "Pilgrim, have you been there before?"

Kishin inclined his head in a slow nod. "I regret that I have not been as yet. Hence my pilgrimage."

"Oh, right. Topleb, Ixchel, can you tell us anything?"

"I have never been," Ixchel said. "But I have seen drawings. It is a circle, with stone platforms around it."

"This road leads straight to it," Topleb added. "We have but to follow it. We may even reach it tomorrow. If I remember right, the road curves around to the left, goes into a tunnel, then climbs to the high place's opposite side. The road coming from the other direction does likewise."

"So it is actually... high?" Victor asked. "Like a hill?"

"Of course. Why do you think they call it the high place?"

"The one in Varioch wasn't. It was underground!"

"Because you Variochs do everything upside down! It is a wonder you don't walk on your hands."

Dravid smiled. The banter between the soldiers always entertained. He envied their easy camaraderie.

"I wish we had more of a plan," Marshal said a few minutes later. "But for now, let's get some sleep. Rufus, you and I will have first watch."

Dravid took another look out into the darkness. It would not be easy to sleep knowing those creatures prowled just out of sight.

(((74)))

"This is it."

Talinir stepped forward. "I was here once before, around fifteen years ago, but I had forgotten…"

The high place, as it had been dubbed by the humans so long ago, looked like a pond on this side. Nothing distinguished it from the surrounding landscape until someone drew near enough to actually see it. The Eldanim once built a platform surrounding it, but it had been destroyed at some point in the last few decades. Talinir didn't know if the Durunim had done it, or if it had just been a casualty to the general decay of the Starlit Realm itself.

"It has been quite a journey, Talinir," Janaab observed, leaning on his spear. "I hope it has been educational for you."

"I have learned many things," Talinir said. "But the greatest mystery remains unsolved." He looked at his companion. "The mystery of Janaab."

"In the grand scheme, it matters not," Janaab answered. "If you must know, ask the girl. I told her who I am. Or who I was."

Janaab looked pensive, an unusual look for him.

"Something is bothering you."

Janaab sighed. "I would like nothing less than to go with you through the portal," he said. "I spent several years in Ch'olan. Blademaster Sakura was one of my closest friends. But… I am needed here."

"Needed for what?"

"Others are coming. I will do what I can on this side. But you will need to prepare them over there."

"Prepare them for what?"

Janaab found a rock to sit on. "You've seen the Durunim and their masters. I think they are coming. If the portals are opened… war may come to both worlds."

Talinir tossed a pebble into the portal and watched the ripples. "Isn't this portal already open?"

"It's open enough for you to pass through, or the occasional curse-stalker. But it is limited. And it is linked to the other two. I think one of the other two is now open. Everything is changing, shifting. Just like she told me."

"Who?"

Janaab glanced up at him. "I told you about the old woman in Intal Eldanir, didn't I? She also told me about this place and what would happen here."

"What will happen here?"

"She told me that the next time I saw this place… I would die."

"Then… why did you come? We could have gone somewhere else! Or you could have stopped a mile away and sent me on by myself!"

Janaab chuckled. "I should have died almost two decades ago. Instead, I ended up here. I have wandered beneath the stars all that time now—if time works the same way here. I have seen and done far more than I ever thought I would." He sighed. "I have helped through the shadows to overthrow some and manipulate others. I have had more impact on Antises here than a lifetime spent on its own soil."

"Then why must it end?"

Janaab held out his hand. It shook. "Once, I could say this was caused by the magic within me. Now… I'm simply old. Old and worn out. It is time for the next generation to safeguard Antises. To maybe do what I could not do. To save it all."

Talinir took hold of the shaking hand. "Then come meet that generation. Guide them with your wisdom."

Janaab shook his head. "I have told you all that matters. You can guide them."

"This is not necessary! You can live!"

Janaab pulled his hand away and pointed toward the portal. "If I go through that portal, very bad things will happen. I will risk undoing everything that they're fighting for."

"By your mere presence?"

"Yes!" He shook his head. "I don't know how to explain it to you. You've already noted that I'm disguising my power here. If I cross over, I will not be able to do that any longer. I will be proclaiming who and what I am to everyone in the region. And that will attract attention. I will be too weak to fight for myself by then. And if they fight for me, they may die and all will be lost. Marshal, though... he will not be weak."

He sighed.

"I am old, Talinir. I don't know how old your people live. But as human aging goes, I'm up there. I'm tired."

"What gain is there if you die?"

"Gain? There is much gain! Marshal will come into his own. And I... I will see Theon's face. And maybe get some answers to questions I've had all my life."

"I cannot persuade you, can I?"

"No."

Talinir fell silent. What else could he say? Janaab had made up his mind and could not be convinced otherwise. Yet it seemed such a waste, after all they had been through.

"How long do you have, do you think?"

Janaab gestured in a vague direction. "I'm not sure. Everything is coming to a turning point here and in Antises. I will try to restrain what happens here. I don't know how long I can last, but I think it might just be enough."

Talinir took Janaab's hand again, but this time as a farewell. "It has been my honor to know you, Janaab. I can never repay you for helping me survive."

"Help Marshal. That will repay everything." Janaab squeezed Talinir's hand with a grip surprising in its strength for his professed age.

Talinir released him and turned away. The time had come. He stepped to the edge of the "pond" and looked it over. For a moment, he considered taking it slow, stepping down and wading step by step. He took one last look back at Janaab. The old man sat on the stone, holding his spear and watching. Talinir nodded to him. And dove in.

Outwardly, the sensation felt like diving through a curtain of water. But inside, everything shifted. He left part of himself behind in the Starlit Realm, as it should be.

Talinir, warden of the Eldanim, erupted from the portal into the primary world. He grabbed the stone on the edge and pulled himself out. He closed his eyes to steady himself. After one shivering moment, he blinked and stood. All was right again. He could see both worlds at the same time.

He turned back. The overlay of the two worlds never matched up exactly, but he knew where to look. Janaab still sat, watching in his direction. The human couldn't see him now, but he could still watch over his friend. His hand strayed to his sword hilt. With the warpsteel blade, he could fight in both worlds at the same time.

And if Janaab was right, he might have to.

•••••

Victor stared at Dravid. "You want me to do what?"

Dravid glanced around at the others. Noon had arrived. Everyone spread out along the road, taking a break and trying to find some relief from the heat.

"Seri won't listen to me, and I'm guessing that Marshal won't listen to you," Dravid said. "So let's switch. I'll talk to Marshal; you talk to Seri."

"And tell her what? 'Please like my friend again'?"

Dravid wiped sweat off his forehead. Honestly, he had expected Victor to be a little dense. He was just a warrior, after all. "I've already told her that Antises needs the two of them together. But she's scared. Marshal said something to her about the stars that I don't get. She doesn't trust him now."

Victor rolled his eyes. "The stars again. Great."

"But that's where you can help! You can tell her about the Marshal you know, and how she can trust him."

"All right." Victor nodded. "I guess I can see that. But what will you tell Marshal?"

Dravid looked over at Marshal, who sat alone, staring into the jungle. "I can talk to him as one broken man to another."

Victor considered that and shook his head a little. "I... don't know what to say to that. But I'll try to talk to Seri." He adjusted his belt full of weapons and started off toward her.

Dravid turned to Marshal. He thought he knew what he might say, but hadn't come up with a specific plan yet. On reflection, that described most of his decisions.

"Marshal? Can I talk with you?"

Marshal looked up. A smile crossed his face, but didn't last very long. "Dravid. What can I do for you?" He got to his feet. Topleb and Rufus, sitting not far away, looked over at them in curiosity. Dravid ignored them.

"You and Seri need to work together," he said. The direct approach.

"I would like that," Marshal said. "But I don't think she wants to be around me any more."

"Why not?"

Marshal made a weak gesture. "She knows I can't be the hero she wants."

"Why not?"

"I just… it's not your concern."

"Wrong. I'm Seri's friend. Her best friend." Dravid emphasized the words. "Anything that concerns her concerns me. I'm here only for her. And right now, what will help her the most is for you"—he pointed at Marshal's face—"to stop moping and act like the leader you've shown us you can be."

"I can't." Marshal looked away from Dravid's pointing finger.

Dravid whacked him with his crutch.

"Ow! What was that for?"

"Look at me! You think you've got it bad because you've got scars on your face and you want to see the Otherworld's stars? I'm missing a fire-devoured leg!"

Marshal's eyes narrowed. "You don't know what you're talking about. I've lost—"

"Your mother. I know! Do you think the rest of us haven't lost anyone or anything? Hailstones! My Master, my mentor, had the magic sucked out of him so that he died a withered husk! And when he died, I lost my whole purpose in life. I'm broken. You're broken. So what? Let's get over ourselves and save the fire-devoured world!"

"You—" Marshal started, but stopped himself. He looked at Topleb and Rufus, who both tried to pretend they weren't listening.

Something big moved in the jungle a few feet away. Marshal reached for his sword.

● ● ● ● ●

Victor approached Seri. Dravid's suggestion made sense, but he had no idea how to go about it. He swallowed. "Just get started," he muttered.

Seri and Ixchel both looked up at his approach. "Hello, Victor. How close are we to the high place?"

"Topleb says it might be right around the next bend," Victor answered. "But he's not sure." He toyed with the rusty flail on his belt.

"Then we should be prepared," Ixchel said.

"About that…"

Seri raised her eyebrows. "Do we have a new plan?"

"The plan is for you and Marshal to work together." Victor took a deep breath. "And for that to happen, you have to actually talk to each other."

"We'll work together when we have to," Seri said, a sharp tone in her voice, "but that's all."

"Look, I don't fully understand why you're upset at him, but—"

"Upset?" Seri interrupted. She stood. "That doesn't even begin to describe it. He, he said he'd be willing to abandon us all! Abandon all of Antises, if he could just go look at those stars!"

"Because the Eldanim used them to save his life!"

"What does that have to do with it?"

Ixchel stood and eyed the jungle. Her eyes narrowed.

"The only one of the Eldanim you've met was Curasir, right?" At Seri's nod, Victor went on, "Well, the others—the good ones—they're kind of addicted to the whole starlight thing. Talinir, our friend, even used this kind of medicine called starshine to remind him of it. When they healed Marshal, he kind of became like them, I think. It's always pulling at him."

Seri frowned. "You're saying it's like… people who can't live without strong drink?"

"Something like that, I guess."

"I don't really want to work with those people, either."

"Ugh." Victor ran a hand through his hair. When had it gotten so long? "But it wasn't Marshal's choice. They did it to him, to save his life. Look, he's been through more tragedy than anyone I know, and yet he's still fighting. He hates himself sometimes, but… he's the best man I've ever known."

"Your loyalty to your friend does you credit," Ixchel said. "You have the spirit of the Holcan."

"Thank you?"

"Now draw your weapons. We are about to be attacked."

"What?" Even as he turned, Victor obeyed her, one hand unclipping his flail while the other pulled his sword from its sheath.

Curse-stalkers erupted from the jungle around them on every side.

(((75)))

Talinir looked over the high place. The humans here in Ch'olan had done quite a bit of extensive building around it.

The portal itself lay in a natural dip at the top of a hill, surrounded by a stone walkway made of hewn limestone. At each of the four compass points, a larger platform stretched out from the circle. At the east and west platforms, stairs descended in opposite directions, curving around the exterior of the circle and leading down to larger stone platforms at the base of the hill to the north and south. Each of those lower platforms were dominated by a large limestone pillar which reached almost as high as the hilltop portal itself. From there, the roads began to the east and west, descending into a tunnel on either side.

When Talinir took a single step into one of the tunnels, he felt an odd vibration and immediate weakness. He stepped back out and the feeling subsided. Curious.

All this Talinir had scouted out in the first few minutes after his arrival. Marshal would be coming from the west, so it made sense he should set out down that road to meet him. But he hesitated.

On the other side, Janaab still sat near the portal, as if waiting. If he went in search of Marshal, Talinir would abandon the old man to whatever fate came his way. He found himself reluctant to do that.

He could at least be waiting for Marshal when he arrived via the western road. Talinir descended the stairs from the east platform and paused at the pillar. The limestone, subject to the sometimes-harsh weather here, was pitted and crumbling. Talinir could just make out a few letters carved into the surface at eye level. No one would ever be able to tell what had been written there.

He moved on and examined the tunnel again. He did not relish experiencing that odd weakness. In an archway over the tunnel's entrance, he could discern a few letters. Only one word remained: "come." A greeting or a warning?

In that moment, he heard yells and cries of panic coming from somewhere beyond the tunnel.

•••••

Topleb's spear passed right in front of Dravid's face and struck a curse-stalker in its mouth. The creature reared back and collapsed, waving its arms futilely at the spear protruding from its mouth. Two more took its place.

At least a dozen of the monsters attacked the party from both sides. Dravid looked about, registering everything as fast as his mind could process it. He and the three soldiers here at the front of the group were being split off from the others. Forerunner and Calu looked unconcerned in the center, both of them now wielding swords of fire. Beyond them, Dravid could barely make out the others. He couldn't see Seri.

"Fall back to those trees!" Marshal yelled, pointing to the right side of the road. "We can make more of a defense with them at our backs! Dravid! One of your shields would help!"

Dravid nodded. Beside him, Rufus stabbed down into the head of a smaller curse-stalker that ran up behind them. Dravid scrambled around it in the direction Marshal had suggested, but kept his hand moving, conjuring up the largest magic shield he could handle. For the first time, he seriously regretted not taking Ixchel up on her offer to train him in self-defense.

Just in time, he lifted his new shield and blocked two of the disgusting tongues that shot out from a nearby creature's mouth. The tongues sizzled where they struck his shield. Rufus did the same with his shield.

Marshal unleashed a wave of power and blew three monsters out of their way as he, Topleb, Rufus, and Dravid reached the trees.

"Can't you just take them all out that way?" Topleb asked.

"Too much confusion! I might hit one of our friends!"

More of the curse-stalkers poured out of the jungle from both sides. The road became chaotic everywhere they looked. Marshal wielded both his sword and his power with deadly effect. Rufus and Topleb stood to either side of him, doing their best. Dravid stood behind all three, moving his shield where it was most needed. Everywhere he looked, he saw claws, teeth, tongues.

"There's too many!" Rufus yelled. "They're pushing us back into the jungle!"

• • • • •

Victor slung his flail, tripping a curse-stalker and flipping it onto its back. He stabbed down through its neck with his sword.

Beside him, Ixchel killed another of the beasts. The fluidity of her movements continued to amaze him. When the magic and rage overtook him, he knew his own movements became faster and smoother. But Ixchel seemed to possess that ability innately. Or, he reflected, she had been trained for years. He only had a few months with Talinir.

"Press the attack!" Ixchel cried. "We must drive them back!" She placed one foot on the dead curse-stalker and vaulted over it toward the next two just emerging from the jungle.

Victor followed, but took a quick look around. All of their gear lay in haphazard piles across the road. They would have to come back for it later. Seri came right beside him. She held her hands in the air, no doubt using magic to protect herself should any of the creatures get past him or Ixchel. He saw Forerunner and Wolf fighting with flaming swords. Where did they get those? Beyond them, it looked like Marshal and the others were being pushed back into the jungle the opposite direction.

He opened his mouth to tell Ixchel, but she was already at the tree line. He glanced at Seri and rushed to catch up.

• • • • •

A curse-stalker slammed against his shield and Dravid lost his balance. He fell back into a tangle of vines that covered the jungle floor here. The curse-stalker tried to bite at his glowing disc. Dravid yanked it up; the edge of the disc sliced through the monster's upper jaw, severing it cleanly. As blood ran down both sides of his shield, the creature fell back, screaming with a harsh nasal tone.

"Nicely done!" Topleb gave him a hand getting up.

Marshal put his hand on the trunk of a tree. Almost immediately, it shattered and the tree toppled. It landed on one curse-stalker, pinning it to the ground. But three more scrambled over it.

Moving into the jungle gave the warriors more options, but the curse-stalkers seemed to move just as fast through the undergrowth as they did on the road. Dravid wasn't sure Marshal had made the best call.

Slithering tongues like burning ropes shot through the air at them from two sides. Rufus cried out as one of them brushed his shoulder. Dravid tried to cut through a pair of them with his shield, but Marshal beat him to it with his warpsteel blade.

Chaos reigned over all. Dravid struggled to stay upright, keep hold of his crutch and magical shield, and help out in any way he could. The strain of keeping a magical object intact for so long soon made its effects known. The heat inside began to build up, rivaling the stifling heat outside.

Then came a moment when the curse-stalkers backed off. Everyone caught their breath, but held ready. It didn't last long.

"Is anyone else near us?" Marshal yelled.

"I don't see anyone!" Rufus answered. Topleb and Dravid added their assent.

"Everyone next to me! I'm going to blast in all directions!"

Dravid joined the other two in moving as close to Marshal as comfort allowed. The curse-stalkers lunged forward and tongues began to extend.

A wave of power erupted outward. Dravid felt the vibrations of it throughout his body. He could no longer maintain his shield and it slipped away. Around them, Marshal's power shredded the jungle, hurling curse-stalkers away, shattering bones and teeth.

In a moment, it was over. Nothing living remained in a twenty-foot circle around the four men. The devastation looked utterly complete.

Dravid swung around on his crutch to compliment Marshal. But the words died in his throat when he saw the other young man's face. Marshal put a hand to his side. It came away covered in blood.

● ● ● ● ●

Kishin moved through the jungle like a silent wraith. With one hand, he swung the staff. With the other, he wielded the warpsteel sword. Already, he had killed seven curse-stalkers.

Despite the earlier discussion about how many of the party would be attracting the creatures, Kishin could not imagine this attack had occurred naturally. Something or someone else had stirred the curse-stalkers up, doing something to make them rush out in such large numbers.

His first inclination was to follow Ixchel. But he soon saw how well she could handle herself. And the young man that fought by her side, Victor, fought with a fervor he had not possessed the last time Kishin met him. Interesting.

And so Kishin gravitated toward Marshal, in case he needed protection. He noted briefly that the two unusual ones, Forerunner and his companion, moved on down the road, having escaped from the battle.

Marshal and the three men around him had moved off the opposite side of the road and into the jungle itself. Kishin followed, passing dead curse-stalkers and broken trees. In only a few moments, he could see the others ahead of him, still fighting.

An ominous growl stopped him. Kishin turned and found himself facing the largest curse-stalker he had ever seen, at least ten feet long. Kishin smiled. At least he could keep this one away from Marshal and his friends.

The creature eyed him, as if unsure about this one. After all, Kishin radiated no magic. No curse. But still… the curse-stalker hungered for more than just magic. Fresh meat would help as well.

Kishin feinted a stab to make it flinch, but the old curse-stalker was too experienced to fall for that. Instead, it advanced step by step, keeping its eyes fixed on its prey. Unlike its smaller brethren, its legs were long enough to keep its body well above the ground. That meant if it ever pounced, it could achieve a greater height, making it difficult to avoid. And if it landed on him, Kishin had little doubt that would be the end.

He thrust the staff forward, letting his hand slide down its length to extend it as far as he could. Unable to avoid it, the curse-stalker snapped its massive jaws at the staff. Kishin pushed the staff's end down into the creature's lower jaw and vaulted into the air. He returned with sword blade down, stabbing.

His intention had been to stab straight through the curse-stalkers skull. But the wily beast thrashed to the side and Kishin's sword caught it in the shoulder instead. He lost his grip on the staff and put his weight into the sword's thrust, twisting as he did.

The curse-stalker whipped its head back. The left corner of its jaw caught Kishin in the calf and flipped him. He yanked the sword back as he fell.

Massive jaws opened and lifted, intending to come down on top of him. Kishin stared up into the maw.

At that moment, an enormous burst of power erupted from Marshal's direction. The blast caught both Kishin and the curse-stalker and sent them flying and tumbling away. Kishin struck his head against a tree, whipped around and fell face down. His consciousness fled.

(((76)))

Talinir could not bring himself to enter the tunnel. In addition to the strange effects, to do so would take him too far out of view from Janaab in the Otherworld. The cries he heard had subsided, but he knew he heard the ring of weaponry in action. He hesitated. Then he scrambled up out of the tunnel's entrance. Stone walls separated the road and platforms from the surrounding jungle. He vaulted up onto one of the walls and tried to see beyond the nearest trees and down the hill.

Nothing came into view, but then he heard footsteps coming through the tunnel itself.

Talinir dropped back onto the road and drew his sword. "Marshal?" he called.

Two very unusual travelers stepped out of the tunnel. Both appeared relieved to be leaving it behind. One towered over the other, rippling with muscles and a cascade of multi-colored hair that fell down his back. The other, dressed in the most outlandish clothes, spied Talinir immediately and lifted his hands in greeting. His face split into a huge smile as if he had just found a long-lost friend.

"An Eldani warden! How delightful to see you!" He rushed forward. Ignoring Talinir's sword, he grasped his other arm. "Why, you must be Talinir! They've spoken very highly of you, you know."

"Who?"

"Ah, you have lost much, but have already regained quite a bit!" the strange man plunged on. "Yet still you are not whole. I am Forerunner, and I am here to restore what is lost."

"Let's move on, Forerunner," the larger man growled.

"One moment, Calu. This is why I am here, after all." He looked up into Talinir's eyes. "You seek two young men. They are very close. On either side of the road, down below here. I cannot tell you which way to go, or whether they will come here to you. That is your decision." He paused and cocked his head.

"Who are you?" Talinir asked. The man's rapid-fire speaking left him little time to process the actual words. In addition, he felt sure magic vibrated through every syllable.

"I just told you that. I am Forerunner. And I see that you have lost more than you have admitted to anyone in some time. How sad. If I had the time…"

"Forerunner, he is Eldanim. Not human. He is not your task." The big man pushed past him and continued toward the high place. Talinir looked after him. Something about the stranger reminded him of the third race in the Starlit Realm. Could he be?

Forerunner sighed. "Regretfully, I must admit that he is correct. I must escort him now." He turned to go, but paused long enough to gesture back down the hill and tunnel. "Left or right. Your choice."

●●●●●

Victor's first battle had been against a curse-stalker, when it came for Marshal. In that battle, he had been almost ineffectual. As he stabbed another one through its jaw, he marveled at how far he had come since then. So many battles, so many lessons.

And swords were much more effective against these things than flails. Aelia had been quite right about that. Plus magic. Magic helped.

"We're getting pretty far from the road!" Seri said. "Shouldn't we turn back?"

Victor glanced back at her. "Look out!" she screamed, throwing her hands up. Victor spun back to see an enormous mouth full of teeth coming straight at his face. He felt vibrations passing by his ears, and the curse-stalker behaved as though its face had struck a solid wall. It flipped underneath the impact point, slamming into Victor and throwing him back.

Ixchel stabbed down into the creature's exposed underbelly. As it thrashed its last, Victor scrambled to his feet. Had they killed all of them?

Ixchel pulled her short sword free. "I do not see any more near us," she observed.

"I think you're right. That was some fantastic fighting on your part."

"You were not ineffective yourself."

Did Seri roll her eyes? "Thank you," Victor told her.

"You're welcome. It wasn't easy throwing the power past your head on either side."

"Are you saying I have a big head?"

Seri giggled. This time, Ixchel rolled her eyes. Victor smiled.

The magic that kept him moving started to subside. He could feel the vibrations in his hands slowing. But it was still enough to save him in the next moment, giving his reflexes the startling speed he needed to dodge out of the way of a sword that seemed to come out of nowhere.

Victor spun back into a defensive stance, flail hanging from his extended left arm, sword ready in the other. Ixchel stood to his left, shield and short sword at ready.

Before them stood the fear that had haunted Victor's dreams for months, though he never admitted it: the leper assassin.

•••••

Marshal stared at the blood on his hand in shock. An instant later, the pain hit him. He knew this pain. Like the time the assassin stabbed him. He almost died that time. This time… The pain grew. Maybe he would die from this one, after all.

"I guess the protection spell finally wore off." It was a stupid thing to say, but it was the first thought that came to mind.

Topleb grabbed Rufus and spun him around. "What have you done?" Topleb screamed.

Only then did Marshal notice the dagger Rufus held in his left hand. It looked very familiar.

"Where did you get that?" he asked. Again, a stupid thing to say. But his brain didn't seem able to handle more than one thing at a time. Volraag gave him that dagger so long ago. Rufus must have taken it. And hadn't he been holding a shield in that hand? When did he drop it?

"I didn't have a choice!" Rufus yelled at Topleb. "He made me do it! He—Aiiieeee!!!" Rufus broke Topleb's grip and grabbed at his own head, still holding the bloody dagger. "The pain! Ahhh! What is it?"

"It's the curse," Dravid said, his face pale. "Marshal, are you all right?" He took a hesitant step toward him.

Marshal put his hand back over the stab wound and tried to put pressure on it. Stop the bleeding. That's what mattered.

"He was your only hope!" Topleb berated Rufus. "Why? What is wrong with you?"

Rufus staggered, gritting his teeth in anguish.

Dravid tried to look at Marshal's wound. "I think... if we can get him to Forerunner or Calu... he might be all right."

That seemed right. But keep the pressure on.

"No!" Rufus screamed. "He has to die! He has to!" He lunged forward.

Topleb intervened. "Stop it! You madman! Put it down!"

The two soldiers struggled. "Don't," Marshal said. He took a step toward them and almost lost his balance. Dravid caught him by the arm.

"Put... it... d—" Topleb gasped suddenly. He let go of Rufus and staggered back.

"Topleb?" Marshal asked. Then he saw the dagger in his friend's chest.

"No," Rufus said. "I didn't mean to." He took a step back himself. His eyes widened and his mouth fell open in a silent scream. He clapped both bloody hands to his head. Marshal couldn't be sure, but it looked like blood also poured from his nose and ears. The scream became audible at last, a horrible, wet, gut-wrenching sound that gurgled to an abrupt halt. Rufus collapsed and rolled on the ground, whimpering and holding his head.

Dravid helped Marshal lean against the remains of a tree and then tried to catch Topleb. But the Ch'olan warrior was too big and only dragged Dravid down with him. He fell to his knees and Dravid rolled onto the ground next to him.

"Topleb," Marshal whispered. "Not you."

Topleb looked up and met Marshal's eyes as Dravid scrambled back up next to him. "You b-brought me home, Marshal," he said, his words interspersed with gasps. "Thank y-you."

"No, no, no," Dravid said, trying to find a way to stop Topleb's bleeding. But it was too late.

Topleb fell face-forward. Dravid's hands came away, holding the dagger. He looked helplessly up at Marshal.

Two more of his men dead or dying. Marshal's brain finally caught up. He sank to his knees beside Topleb, still trying to hold on to his own wound.

Whatever quest he had wanted to achieve, whatever purpose Aelia had hoped for him... None of it mattered. None of it would ever come to pass. They were dead. They were all dead. And he would join them soon.

• • • • •

Volraag stepped up and looked out over the Ch'olan high place. So different from the one in Varioch. He wondered what had happened in his homeland to bury that one so deeply. Someone must know. He made a mental note to ask Curasir. Considering the vast differences, he wondered what the condition of the third high place would be like.

Tezan stepped up beside him. "This is different. I thought it would be sealed, like the other one." He looked at the stone columns. "What do these stones mean?"

"Maybe it's sealed in a different way," Volraag said. He turned to the right and walked to the southern platform. "Look here." Tezan joined him and they both examined a spot in the platform wall. Unlike most of the limestone, this particular spot showed no signs of decay. Two hand-shaped indentations showed clearly without damage.

"Try it," Tezan urged.

Volraag shook his head. "Not yet. We wait for my brother." He turned back to the portal.

"Why?"

"With his death, I will have more power. Whatever Curasir has in mind this time, I want to face it with all the power I can." He looked out over the jungle. "By now, the spy will have struck, if Rathri motivated him correctly. And Rathri himself may be involved."

"You'll know when he's dead, right?"

"Yes." Volraag pondered for a moment. He stepped to the edge of the platform and called out as loud as he could. "Marshal!" His voice echoed back from the portal. A curious effect. "Marshal! I'm waiting!"

"Is that wise?"

"Why not? I already have more power than he does. What can he do?"

Nothing happened. In the distance, Volraag thought he heard a rumble. Marshal using his power?

"Someone's coming." Tezan pointed to the eastern platform, with its stairs winding down toward the west. Volraag turned to look.

A tall figure ascended the stairs, coming into view slowly. He stopped at the top and looked them over. Volraag considered his muscles and strangely-colored hair. Who was this?

•••••

The assassin lunged past Victor's flail, sword outstretched. Seri shrieked and jumped back. Ixchel appeared in the way, her shield catching the sword in mid-air, even as she tried to counter with her own sword thrust.

Victor attempted a strike of his own, only to have it parried by another sword. The assassin wielded two at a time and seemed totally unconcerned to be facing two opponents. In fact, his eyes kept darting toward Seri. Was she his primary target?

The assassin looked the same as he had back in Volraag's command tent. He wore a Remavian Guard uniform, red cape and all. Rathri! Volraag had called him Rathri.

"We meet again, hero." Rathri's voice mocked and unnerved. The raspiness of it sounded painful; did it hurt him to speak?

Ixchel had been impressive against the curse-stalkers, but now she fought with a skill that seemed beyond human. She moved back and forth, stepping in and then back, thrusting and slashing with her short sword. Her shield seemed to know where to go all by itself, blocking every counterstrike from the assassin. She never took her eyes off Rathri's face.

At the assassin's first attack, Victor felt the magic surge again within him. Beside Ixchel, he felt like a stumbling brute, but he knew his movements were much faster than what he would normally be capable of. He stabbed with his sword, then spun in the opposite direction, narrowly dodging a counterstrike from Rathri. He brought up his old flail in an upward arc, but Rathri leaned back far enough to dodge it, simultaneously making another slash in Ixchel's direction.

Even with all this, they seemed barely able to hold their own against this opponent. Rathri dodged, parried, and struck back so often that Victor felt like he spent most of his time on the defensive. How was that even possible? A thought struck him.

"Seri! Is he using magic?"

"Oh!" He couldn't see her, but Victor knew Seri would be activating her star-sight and watching their battle.

Victor ducked. How had Rathri gotten a slash that high? And his swords... they looked Eldani-made. Not warpsteel, but just like the one Victor used, that Talinir had given him.

"He's... he's magic—I mean, he has magic, but... it's something new. I can't tell what he is!" Seri sounded frustrated.

Rathri slammed a blow down at Ixchel, who raised her shield to block it. He used the momentum to launch himself into the air, flipping over her and slashing at her back in the process. Victor thought the blade nicked her shoulder. Rathri landed out of Victor's reach. Even as Ixchel spun around, he tossed one of his swords up into the air, grabbed a dagger from somewhere within his clothes, and threw it at Seri.

Halfway toward her, the dagger abruptly shifted and flew off into the jungle in a different direction. Seri had been ready, using her own magic to deflect it.

Rathri parried Ixchel's attack and caught his falling sword without looking at it. If he hadn't been in imminent danger, Victor would have stood in awe. The assassin's skill defied understanding.

"My Lady!" Ixchel shouted. "You should go!"

Victor charged back into the fray. "Yes! Find Marshal!" he called back. "Stop Volraag!"

"But—"

"Go!" Ixchel screamed.

Victor didn't turn to look, but he heard Seri moving away through the underbrush. She needed to go, but he hoped she didn't run into any more curse-stalkers on the way.

• • • • •

Dravid shoved the dagger into his belt, wiped blood off his hands, and grabbed his crutch. He pulled himself up and then moved back to Marshal's side. A sense of urgency filled him. "Come on," he urged. "We need to get you to Forerunner or Calu!"

"It's too late." Marshal's voice was almost too low to hear.

"No, it's not. We can do it."

At that moment, a voice echoed down to them. "Marshal!"

Marshal's head came up.

"Marshal! I'm waiting!"

Dravid glanced up the hill. "Was that him? Volraag?"

Marshal nodded. "I guess... I should face him one more time." He gritted his teeth, took hold of Dravid's outstretched hand, and pulled himself up. A fresh flow of blood erupted from his wound and around his other hand.

"I'm not the best person to lean on," Dravid said weakly.

"We'll make do," Marshal answered. He took a halting step up the hill. "We only have to make it up there. For the end of all this."

(((77)))

"Who are you?" Volraag challenged.

The tall man ignored him and looked down into the portal with a smile. He took a step toward the edge.

Volraag released a short burst of power that shook the stone around them. "Answer me!"

The mystery man finally looked in Volraag's direction. His eyes began to glow. "I am Calu, little human. Oppose me at your peril."

Volraag took a step back. Calu's voice vibrated with magic. What was this?

"Despite whatever power you may have accumulated here, you cannot stand against me. I am—"

"There you are!" cried a second voice, also vibrating. A second man joined Calu on the platform. Far smaller, he boasted the strangest clothing Volraag had ever seen.

He looked toward Volraag and Tezan, an enormous smile on his face. "Ah, more guests! You must be Lord Volraag. Am I right?"

"And who are you?" Tezan asked.

The smaller man made an elaborate bow. "I am Forerunner, and I am here to restore that which was lost." He lifted a hand, palm up, in some kind of supplication. "Each of you have lost something, something dear to you. I tell that it is not the end. What was lost—"

"Why are you here? Where is Marshal?" Volraag interrupted.

Forerunner took a step closer, spreading his arms out. "Marshal? I'm not here with a Marshal. I am merely escorting my friend here back to where he belongs. And, as I said, to restore that which was lost. But you…" He tilted his head, examining Volraag. "You do not admit to losing anything, do you?"

"Volraag! I'm here!" called a weak voice behind him.

Volraag turned and looked down over the wall. Two figures climbed into view on the lower platform. One held a crutch, but the other, who seemed to be bleeding, stared up at him with a horribly-scarred face.

"Marshal!"

·····

Kishin winced as he came back to consciousness. His head ached.

But he had no time. He still held his warpsteel sword, but had dropped the staff in the blast that tore apart everything around him. Marshal's doing, no doubt. He considered hurrying on, but somehow couldn't abandon the staff. He searched quickly and found it beneath a pile of shredded palm leaves.

Voices came from above. One sounded like Forerunner, but he couldn't make out the others.

Something moved off to his right. A curse-stalker might still be alive out there. Maybe more.

He could try to find Marshal's path and follow him, or head directly up toward the high place. He decided on the latter course of action. Marshal would be going there, anyway, as would the others. And Volraag might be there.

Kishin sheathed his sword and hurried up the hill as fast as he could.

·····

Seri pushed aside a branch, then recoiled. Ants covered it! Why was this place so strange? If the heat wasn't bad enough, there were bugs everywhere! And Ixchel had grown up here. Maybe that explained some things about her.

She glanced back over her shoulder. She could hear the clang of weapons colliding and an occasional grunt or inarticulate yell from the combatants she had left behind. Victor and Ixchel would be all right. Both of them were amazing in their own ways.

But that assassin... something very strange there. He glowed with magic, but not like anyone else. The closest comparison she could think of would be Curasir, but he had been stealing magic from the Masters. The assassin's magic looked... confused. As if one type of magic were buried beneath another, or entwined together somehow.

She kept moving, then realized a pull on her heart led the same way. Volraag.

At the top of her ascent of the hill, she saw a stone wall about three feet high. When she reached it, she found herself looking down into the continuation of the road, now narrowed to a seven-foot-wide path paved with the same stone as the walls on either side of it. It had apparently just emerged from some kind of tunnel. Above the path, the hillside grew abruptly steeper, leading to some other stone structures she couldn't make out from here. Seri pulled herself up onto the wall.

"You must be the girl."

"Oh!" Seri almost fell off the wall. How had she not noticed the Eldani standing there, just a few feet away?

He looked different from Curasir or Hanirel. While he still possessed the same angular features and the unnerving perception of being taller than he looked, his features were somehow... kinder. She would have said softer, but that didn't make any sense. His hair, darker than her own, somehow encouraged her.

"I am Talinir. I believe we possess some mutual friends." His voice, warm and friendly, immediately put her at ease. She slid down onto the path.

"Talinir! Of course! You're one of the reasons we're here. Marshal wanted to rescue you from the Otherworld. But you're already out, so I guess that's good."

"Indeed. Where is Marshal?"

"I'm not really sure. We got attacked by curse-stalkers and split up. He didn't come this way?"

"No." Talinir gestured vaguely up the path. "Two others did. Someone called Forerunner?"

"But not Marshal? I wonder what happened... oh! Victor! And Ixchel!" Seri pointed back the way she had come. "They're fighting!"

Talinir drew his sword. "Victor is fighting someone called Ixchel?"

"No, no, no! Ixchel is my friend. They—they're both fighting an assassin. He looks like a leper, and he's—"

Before Seri could finish, Talinir vaulted over the wall and vanished.

• • • • •

Marshal looked up at his half-brother. He had not seen Volraag's face since that day in Drusa's Crossing. The day everything changed. The day he found out they shared a father. The day Volraag gave him a dagger that had just been used to stab him and kill Topleb.

Volraag hadn't changed in that time. His blond hair and beard somehow still looked impeccably trimmed, even in the sweltering heat. His triumphant smile did what nothing else had done: it made Marshal want to survive long enough to wipe it off his face.

"Go find Seri and the others," he told Dravid.

"Are you sure? You can't—"

"Go!"

Pain made Marshal almost double over. Despite his best efforts, blood still oozed from his side. He could not go on much longer this way. He leaned against the limestone column. Why was it here, anyway?

Dravid gave him a concerned look, but turned and began ascending the stairs that led around and up toward the high place.

With a rumble of power, Volraag landed in front of Marshal. Chips of limestone rained down around them both. He straightened up and looked Marshal over.

"You're barely on your feet. Did you really walk all this way from the battlefield, only to die before you could do anything at all?"

"Maybe... not."

With a scream of pure anguish, Marshal unleashed a blast of power at his half-brother. The limestone column shattered into a million shards that slammed into the wall.

But Volraag stood unmoved and unharmed.

• • • • •

Kishin watched over the wall's edge at the high place. When Volraag jumped off the opposite side, he almost went after him. But something inside him urged caution. Bide his time.

Volraag's flunky waited on the platform. He looked nervous, like he wasn't sure what he should be doing.

Calu and Forerunner were arguing about something. Calu pushed Forerunner aside and began to descend to the glistening portal.

"Will you kill again?"

Again, the voice came out of nowhere. Kishin's neck twisted as he tried to look in every direction. Why did he keep hearing that question?

From the opposite side, where Volraag had gone down, came a ferocious rumbling.

• • • • •

Dravid leaned against the wall. Marshal's blast tore up everything behind him, but he was far enough around the corner that it didn't reach him. Barely. Idiot.

Marshal had ordered him to leave, but it felt wrong somehow.

Also, whoever designed these stairs should be executed. Even an acolyte stonecutter knew every step shouldn't be a different length and height. And some of them had crumbled with age. It would be a difficult ascent for anyone, let alone a one-legged man with a crutch.

Jamana could have handled these steps with ease. Better than he handled the tunnels back on Zes Sivas, anyway.

Dravid scowled and pulled himself up to the next step. Somewhere up there he would find Seri and maybe the help Marshal needed.

• • • • •

Seri ascended the stairs as fast as she could. Not an easy thing to do when they were all different widths and heights. How annoying.

"That is not what they said when they sent me!" Was that Forerunner's voice? It came from up above, followed by another voice she couldn't quite make out. Calu?

"But that is not what I've seen here! They're not all like that! You know this!"

"Enough!" Definitely Calu.

Seri picked up her pace.

• • • • •

Victor dodged again. He envied Ixchel's shield. In close-quarters fighting like this, it certainly came in handy. Especially against an opponent like Rathri. The assassin kept up the attacks, never letting up for even a moment. How he could do that against two opponents at the same time baffled Victor.

He and Ixchel kept shifting positions, trying to keep themselves on opposite sides of Rathri to make it more difficult on him. Yet somehow, he shifted with them, keeping them closer together than they intended. The terrain always seemed in his favor as well. No matter how they shifted, he kept the high ground. Twice he used a nearby tree to his advantage.

Rathri dodged underneath a swing of Victor's flail. He lunged in, his blade scoring a light scratch across the left side of Victor's stomach. With his other hand, he deflected a thrust from Ixchel.

Victor could think of several maneuvers that might work, but all of them would leave him open for a devastating counterstrike if he failed. If only he could communicate with Ixchel. Yeah, that would work. Perhaps Rathri would be willing to take a break for a few minutes if he asked nicely.

Ixchel grunted as one of Rathri's swords cut her arm near the elbow. That was it. If they didn't do something soon, he would wear them down. He showed no signs of slowing himself.

Victor waited for the right moment. He caught Ixchel's eye, but had no way to let her known his intentions. If this worked, she would have the perfect opening, at least. He had no doubt she would take it.

When the moment came, he took it. Dodging a large swing from Rathri, Victor dove forward, swinging his flail at the assassin's legs. As he went down, he lifted his own sword up to deflect any counterstrikes.

To his shock, Rathri leaped into the air, planting a solid kick on Ixchel's shield. She stumbled back a couple of steps from the impact, leaving Rathri free to turn his full attention to Victor on the ground.

One sword knocked Victor's own out of the way. The second came down in what would be a killing stroke.

And then a warpsteel sword inserted itself in the way, saving Victor and knocking Rathri off balance for the first time in the entire fight.

"You shouldn't have left yourself that open."

Victor looked up at a strange but familiar face.

"Talinir!"

The Eldani warden smiled and faced the assassin. "You're not the one I expected, but if you stand against this friend of mine, that's all I need to know."

"Then you will fall with them," Rathri said. He launched forward again.

•••••

"Pathetic."

Volraag took one step and punched Marshal in the face. His half-brother went down, rolled once, and clutched at the bloody wound in his side. His sword clattered away.

"All this time, I've been imagining an epic confrontation between the two of us," he said, stepping closer. "I would win, of course, but it would be a struggle of might and magic." He looked down at Marshal. "Instead I find you almost dead already and..." He kicked Marshal in the side, eliciting a loud cry. "...my own powers make me almost invulnerable to yours."

In truth, the invulnerability surprised Volraag. Only recently, practicing with Tezan, had he discovered how to use his Lord's power as a kind of shield, radiating outward from his body. But even so, he should not have been able to completely ignore Marshal's attack. The new power absorbed from the Eldani must have made the difference.

He looked up. Tezan waited for him. And others were arriving. Stealing Marshal's power would have to wait. And yet, if he left him here, one of the curse-stalkers might find him. Volraag felt fairly certain if that happened, their father's power would come to him. But after everything else that had happened, he didn't want to take the chance.

Something Rathri said came back to him. He bent and grabbed Marshal's tunic, prompting a groan. With little effort, Volraag dragged him back up the path, then down the steps into the tunnel.

The tunnels were supposed to suppress magic or something like that. Maybe it would be enough to keep Marshal in place and keep anything else from finishing him off.

"Farewell, brother. Once I've dealt with your friends, I'll come back for you."

(((78)))

Seri stepped up onto the platform next to Forerunner. Calu stood just below, about to step out into the glistening portal. On another platform to her left, Tezan, the false king, stood watching. What was he doing here?

Calu stepped into the portal and sank in. He took another step. It looked like he waded into nothing more than a pool of water.

"Why isn't he going right through?" Seri wondered aloud.

"The portal isn't fully open," Forerunner said. He leaned in close to Seri and said in a much lower voice, "He will cross over in just a few seconds, unless you stop him."

"Why would I stop him?" She answered in the same quiet tones.

"Once he enters the Starlit Realm, your world will be in grave danger."

"Why are you telling me this? I thought he was your friend."

"Let's just say I have grown rather fond of this world in the time I have spent here." Forerunner's face suddenly brightened. "Oh! One of the decisive moments approaches. I have someone I must speak to!" He took off on a run around the right side of the portal.

Seri watched him go, then turned back to watch Calu, now waist-deep. How could she stop him? She glanced over at Tezan, still wondering about his place in all this. She blinked, activating her star-sight, and gasped in wonder.

Before, the portal had appeared as a glistening, water-like substance. With her star-sight, it became a whirlpool of endless colors swirling all in one direction. It reminded her of the effect she saw when she and Marshal combined their powers, but on a much greater scale.

She studied the colors. At first glance, they appeared to fill the entire area, but on closer examination, she could see some gaps. Maybe that's what Forerunner meant about it being partly open. Then to keep it closed, she needed to tighten things up.

She knelt and grasped two of the largest swirling beams of light and pulled. Usually, when she grabbed a beam of magic, it rushed into her. These beams fought back, pulling against her and the swirling portal simultaneously. She held tight, wondering if she were making any kind of difference.

"What are you doing, child?" Calu asked, turning to look back at her. His eyes narrowed.

• • • • •

Victor whooped as he scrambled to his feet. Rathri could not possibly take on all three of them. In fact, he seemed focused entirely on Talinir. Victor took a moment to catch his breath.

He glanced at Ixchel. She nodded at him, then swung around to the left. Victor duplicated her movements in the other direction.

Seeing their motion, Rathri sheathed one of his swords while using the other to deflect Talinir's swing. He grabbed something from his belt and threw it to the ground. Smoke erupted in a blossoming cloud.

Victor coughed and stepped back.

"Trickery," murmured Talinir. He held a defensive stance, warpsteel blade aimed at the cloud.

Ixchel hesitated, then dropped back as well.

As the smoke dissipated, Victor saw no sign of Rathri. For a moment, he breathed a sigh of relief, but it caught in his throat as he remembered the assassin's efforts earlier. His true target. Seri.

"Come on!" Victor charged up the hill.

• • • • •

Dravid gritted his teeth and pulled himself up another step. Only three more to go. He paused to look over the edge.

Seri stood on a platform opposite him. She did something with her hands, but he couldn't make it out. Calu seemed to have descended somewhere, as Dravid could only see his top half. On another platform to the right, Tezan stood alone. Dravid scowled at the sight of the man who had tried to become king.

Another rumble came from below and Volraag launched into the air.

Had he killed Marshal, then? Before Volraag landed, a hand grabbed Dravid's shoulder and he whirled to find himself looking up at Forerunner.

"This is the moment, Dravid!"

"What are you talking about?" Dravid put the point of his crutch onto the next step.

"I told you you would have a choice to make. That you could choose what would be restored to you. This is it. You must choose, and choose now!"

Dravid pulled himself up to the step. Two more. "Why now?"

Forerunner released his shoulder and pointed first toward Calu. "It all comes down to right now. While Calu struggles against Seri to move through the portal, his magic spreads throughout it. All you have to do is cross this platform and slide down into it yourself." He paused for dramatic effect. "And your leg will be healed."

As easy as that? Dravid put his crutch onto the next step.

Forerunner pointed back down the steps. "Or the other choice. What do you want: your leg or your purpose?"

"How is my purpose down there?" He pulled up again. Only one more step to the platform.

"Volraag has left Marshal to die. And he will die." Forerunner tilted his head. "Unless you go back to him."

"What can I do?" Dravid put his crutch onto the platform.

"You can save him. You have the power. And you're the only one who can."

"Why don't you go save him?"

Forerunner glanced back. "My purpose is here. Yours is there. Or here also. It's your choice, as I said."

"That's—"

"That's the decision you must make. I never said it would be easy. Choose, but choose swiftly. Your healing or your purpose. What will be restored to you?"

Dravid stared at him. He looked down at Calu, then to the right where Volraag landed next to Tezan. Everything was happening too fast. How could he possibly make this kind of decision now?

Forerunner began to run back around the platform. "Choose now!" he called back.

The portal was so close. Only a few steps and Dravid could have his leg back. Then maybe he could turn and run back down to Marshal... No. If he had learned anything from Forerunner over the past few weeks, he knew he spoke the truth now. He had to choose. Healing for himself or life for Marshal. And if he saved Marshal, then helping him, a man he didn't even like, would become his purpose in life?

His crutch shifted.

• • • • •

From his hidden vantage point, Kishin saw what none of the others could, so focused were they on their individual tasks and desires. He had to act now.

He leaped out onto the walkway directly in front of Forerunner, who skidded to a stop. The flamboyant man, shocked to see him, nearly lost his balance. Kishin ignored him and raced in the opposite direction, toward the eastern platform. "Theon grant me speed," he whispered.

Seri concentrated on something, holding her hands out apart. Calu, in the center of the portal, began to manifest some kind of beam of golden light in his hands. Volraag grabbed Tezan's shoulder and pointed at Calu.

All of these things Kishin noticed, mostly through his peripheral vision. His focus lay just beyond.

He grasped the staff with both hands near one end and planted the other on the stone walkway. He vaulted over Seri, who stared at him open-mouthed. In the air, he shifted his grip and brought the staff swinging forward.

He landed on the platform with a shout.

Rathri's descending sword slammed into his outstretched staff only inches above Seri's head.

• • • • •

Marshal moaned. His face felt wet. Why? It took a few moments to realize he lay on the stone path in the tunnel. The wetness came from his own blood, pooling around him.

In all of his journeys, with all the wonders he had seen, he never thought it would end like this. Volraag was right. Pathetic.

He failed everyone. Mama. Nian. All of his squad. Dead now. And what hope did the others have against Volraag without him? Victor. Seri. If not dead already, they would be.

Aelia told him he had a purpose in this life. This was it?

A tear rolled off his cheek and hit the pool of blood. A tremor radiated out from it.

He still had his power. But not much else. He wouldn't last much longer. Any attempt to move now would only make him bleed out even faster.

He tried directing a burst of power upward, hoping to signal the others somehow. But the magic went nowhere. Something about the cave blocked it? That seemed to fit with his luck. Nothing worked. No hope.

But he released power a moment ago. Down. Into the ground. Another idea came to him. An idea born of madness. It could destroy him and maybe everyone else. But it might just destroy Volraag.

Marshal let his eyes slip closed, but did not let himself slip any further. He knew if he did, he would be gone. Power flowed out from his body into the ground. Tremors radiated outward. Further and further he let his power spread in an ever-increasing radius.

In his mind, Marshal put words to the power. "Magic. Magic is here. Come."

"Come," he whispered.

• • • • •

Varion had been a horrible father. But Volraag had learned one important thing from him: when an unexpected possibility appears, seize it.

The strange man—Calu—had threatened him, but now appeared trapped within the portal. And now he manifested some kind of magical spear? He glared at Seri, whom Volraag had not seen arrive. "Release me!" the stranger shouted at her.

So many others. A hooded man with a staff ran in front of the other stranger who called himself Forerunner. Rathri appeared out of the jungle to the right. The cripple stood on the western platform. But only one mattered at the moment.

Volraag pointed to Calu. "Tezan. He bursts with power. I want it."

Tezan nodded and reached out.

(((79)))

Dravid surprised himself. The choice wasn't that difficult after all.

He turned and began to descend the stairs as fast as he could.

• • • • •

Kishin drew his sword just in time to deflect Rathri's second attack. His brain struggled to comprehend. Looking at the assassin felt like looking into a twisted mirror of what he had been not long ago. All he had heard about a second leper assassin was true somehow.

"A staff, Kishin? Really?" The leper's voice rasped as if every syllable were painful. Kishin's own curse had never been that bad. At least he had kept his voice.

"How do you know me? Who are you?" Kishin yanked back on his staff at the same time his opponent pulled back on his sword. The two came apart and both assailants stumbled.

"I am what you could never be. I am the god of death."

Kishin spun the staff, being careful not to hit Seri. As the leper ducked, Kishin slashed low. Somehow, his opponent dodged between the weapons, stabbing forward with both of his own swords. Kishin brought the staff down in time to deflect them both, but the blades came within an inch of his face.

"You are no god," he growled.

"When you bow to me as your life's blood drains, you will know the truth."

• • • • •

Chaos surrounded Seri.

Out of nowhere, the pilgrim leaped over her and saved her life from the assassin. Volraag joined Tezan and now they...

Seri's star-sight showed her an unexpected horror. Just as Calu had been about to throw a magic-formed spear at her, Tezan reached out. As she had seen him do back on Zes Sivas, he pulled at Calu, siphoning his power. A thick beam of golden light erupted from Calu's chest and rushed into Tezan. The spear dissolved.

Tezan's other hand shot out. The power flowed from it and into Volraag, who lifted both fists out to his sides in exultant pleasure.

Should she let Calu go? Forerunner said their world would be in danger if he went through. But if Volraag gained all of Calu's amazing power, wouldn't that be just as bad? The strain of holding the portal began to tell. Her arms vibrated. But so did everything else. A low tremor shook the ground.

She looked up to see Forerunner rejoin her. "What should I do?" she cried.

For the first time since she had known him, Forerunner's face showed real fear. "I don't know," he whispered.

•••••

Victor stumbled on the first step. Was it his imagination, or was everything shaking? Ixchel took advantage of his mistake and rushed past him. Talinir came right behind.

"Marshal!" Victor shouted.

•••••

Kishin parried another attack, then used the momentum to strike back. Even though he had not fought with a staff in years, he wielded it well enough as a secondary weapon to keep his opponent on his toes. And he needed every advantage here. It did not take long to realize this assassin equaled him in martial prowess. He might even be better.

Out of the corner of his eye, Kishin saw Volraag's flunky with arms outstretched. And Volraag seemed to be glowing brighter with each moment. That could not be good.

"Somebody stop him!" Seri screamed behind him.

Stop who?

"He is giving Volraag more power," Forerunner said. "I don't know if he can be stopped."

Anyone could be stopped.

Kishin spun around the assassin, intending to swing the staff at Volraag's companion.

The leper dropped one sword and grabbed the staff. He sneered at Kishin.

"Not like that."

• • • • •

Dravid sat and slid down the final steps into the tunnel. Marshal lay unmoving in a large pool of blood. Already dead? No. The ground still shook beneath them. It had to be Marshal doing that.

Now what? Forerunner said only he could save Marshal. But how? Dravid ran his hands through his hair. What could he do?

Forerunner and Calu healed people. Dravid had absorbed some of Forerunner's power. Could he do the same? He pulled himself next to Marshal and considered. He knew how to create semi-solid items of magic. That didn't seem to be of much use here.

A movement caught his eye. He turned and stared in horror as a curse-stalker approached the stairs leading to the tunnel entrance. It looked down at the two of them. A hiss escaped its lips.

A second curse-stalker appeared beside the first. Its twin tongues flipped out a few feet, as if testing the air, then returned to its mouth. It took a step down toward them.

• • • • •

Kishin pulled on the staff. Rathri pulled back.

He shot a glance at Tezan and Volraag. Volraag's tunic tore apart. His muscles were growing!

Seri whimpered.

Footsteps approached on the stairs, but they would not be soon enough.

The choice belonged to Kishin alone.

• • • • •

Dravid felt for his power. He might be able to hold his own against one curse-stalker, but not two.

The ground rumbled again. Marshal kept releasing steady pulses of magic. Why? His power summoned these creatures right to them!

The curse-stalker put its foot on the top step, hesitated, then pulled it back up. The other one looked all around at the tunnel entrance. Then both of them turned and disappeared in the other direction.

Dravid realized he was holding his breath and let it go. He turned back to Marshal. By now, his hand glowed with the familiar warmth of the golden power.

When Forerunner healed Dravid, he held his hand over the wound. Dravid reached out and held his hand over Marshal's wound. Blood continued to ooze out of it, but very slowly. Was that good or bad?

Dravid closed his eyes and focused. What did he know? When using the magic of Antises, a mage needed to focus on the vibrations emitted by all things. Trying to channel magic into a living thing involved sensing the life within that thing and focusing the magic in between it. Yet now he wielded a different magic, one he didn't fully understand. He didn't want to channel between life; he wanted to preserve life.

Still, focusing on life might help. Except Dravid had never mastered that ability. Seri could do it; her skills far exceeded his. Why wasn't she here?

Dravid shifted and nearly slipped. So much blood. This would never work. He was a failure. Again. Always. Every time he tried something, every time he truly desired something, he failed.

Restore his purpose? "What purpose?" he groaned.

Marshal's head moved. His eyelids flickered, but he didn't look up. "You... have a... purpose." The words came out of his mouth through great effort, but Dravid couldn't be sure Marshal even knew he was there. With the last word, a rush of breath escaped Marshal's mouth.

The ground stopped trembling.

No. He couldn't fail without at least trying again. "Don't go yet," he snapped.

Dravid focused. Life. Where was it? He stared at his own glowing hand. At first, he sensed nothing. It couldn't be. No vibration. No life. No. No... There. He felt something. Deep down inside Marshal somewhere. Life! It had to be.

Dravid's mouth went dry. Heat began to build behind his eyes. His chest grew tight. He focused, increasing the power that flowed out of his hand. He formed no shapes, did not take hold of it. Instead, he let it flow down into Marshal's still body. The glow increased, growing brighter and brighter the more power he released. He had no idea what was happening, but that had to be a good sign.

The light grew too bright to watch. Dravid closed his eyes, gritting his teeth against the heat that grew behind them. His hand shook.

"Ahhhhh!" He let his emotions erupt in an inarticulate cry behind his gritted teeth.

Finally, he could take no more. He released the power and slumped forward over Marshal, gasping for breath as the heat and tightness subsided.

And then Marshal's chest lifted in a deep breath.

• • • • •

Kishin released the staff and spun back to his left. As he turned, both hands grasped the hilt of his warpsteel sword.

"Will you kill again?"

"Yes," Kishin breathed.

The sword pierced through Tezan's chest.

(((80)))

Seri released the portal just as multiple things happened all at once. As she turned, she saw all of them.

Something moved on the opposite platform.

The pilgrim turned and stabbed Tezan.

Calu disappeared through the portal.

The pilgrim's staff clattered off the walkway into the portal as well.

Ixchel and Victor emerged from the stairway.

The leper assassin, no longer fighting the pilgrim, turned and launched himself at Seri. Exhausted from holding the portal shut, she could only stare at the sword's point coming toward her face.

And that's when Forerunner stepped in the way. And took the sword meant for her.

•••••

Kishin felt the curse take hold the moment his sword slid out of Tezan's chest. Tezan's eyes froze, and he toppled back next to Volraag. "I was... almost king..."

As it had many years before, the sensation started in Kishin's hands. A numbness began in his fingers and spread rapidly throughout his body. His brown skin faded into a pasty white. Small white objects, the remains of his hair, began to rain to the ground.

The numbness seemed to steal into his soul. Where was the staff? It fell, but where? He turned and saw Forerunner stabbed. Another curse. But no. Like himself, that killer already possessed the worst curse a man could have.

Like himself.

And he chose it.

●●●●●

Volraag stared at his hands. Such power! How was it possible? Who had that strange man been? The power felt similar to what he obtained from the Eldani, but so much... more. It even transformed him physically! His body had grown, ripping his clothes in multiple spots.

Inwardly, he felt better than he had his entire life. A warmth suffused his body, which, in light of the unbearable heat in this atrocious country, would seem to be a bad thing. Except he felt the warmth and nothing else. The heat no longer bothered him.

Tezan's body fell beside him. For a moment, he didn't even react. It seemed so inconsequential compared to his new power.

But Tezan had been his. Killing him demanded consequences. He turned to see who had done it and found another surprise.

"Kishin? You?" There could be no mistaking that corrupted face, so similar to Rathri's. "You work for my brother now?"

Kishin lifted his sword. "I serve—"

Volraag didn't wait for the answer. He unleashed his power. Kishin flew backward over the edge of the hill and tumbled down out of sight.

A growl came from behind him. Volraag turned, ignoring Rathri and the others, and saw two curse-stalkers emerging from the stairs on the western platform. Curious. He had been told they avoided the portal. His new power must have drawn them.

A smile broadened his face. Whatever drew them, it made no difference. Even these creatures were far beneath him now.

●●●●●

Marshal came fully awake with a start. He blinked and sat up. Dravid rolled off him and lifted himself up on his hands.

"Marshal?"

Before answering, Marshal felt for the wound in his side. Blood still covered it, as well as everything else. But he could find no sign of the wound itself. It was gone.

He looked to Dravid. "Did you do this? Did you heal me?"

Dravid gave a half-smile. "I guess I did."

"Amazing." Marshal got to his feet. A few moments ago, he had slipped away, convinced he would soon be with his mother. He even heard her words about purpose.

Yet now... he felt completely normal. No. He felt invigorated. As if he had just awoken from a nap and taken a quick swim in a cool pond.

"Are you all right?" Dravid sounded weary. Of course he would, if he used magic on this kind of scale.

"I feel great," Marshal said. He picked up Dravid's crutch, then reached down and pulled Dravid up as well.

Dravid took the crutch, keeping his eyes on Marshal. "I can't believe it."

"You doubt your own work?"

"I've never done anything like that before. I, I don't know what to think."

"I think we should go find the others," Marshal said. He turned, but Dravid caught his arm.

"Careful. I saw two curse-stalkers out there."

"Oh. It worked, then."

"What worked?"

Marshal chuckled. "If I couldn't go after Volraag myself, I figured I could summon something else to bother him. So I've been letting my power flow all over the place. I figured any curse-stalkers left in the area would come this way."

"You're lucky they didn't come eat us!"

Marshal looked around. "I think they're scared of this cave for some reason. Volraag seemed to think I would be safe here, anyway."

Dravid awkwardly adjusted his stance and looked out. "I don't see them now."

"Then let's go."

•••••

Forerunner fell back onto Seri. She caught his body, trying to keep him from rolling away.

As Volraag blasted the pilgrim off the high place entirely, Ixchel screamed and launched herself at the assassin. She engaged him with a flurry of quick thrusts and slices, forcing him back from Forerunner and Seri.

Victor came after Ixchel, followed by Talinir. Both of them started toward the fight.

"Victor!" Seri screamed. He stopped abruptly as if something had grabbed him and yanked him back. Seri felt an odd vibration in her throat. Maybe something had.

Talinir pushed past Victor and joined Ixchel.

Seri spared a glance for Volraag. To her surprise, curse-stalkers appeared on the walkway and ran toward him. Good enough for now.

Victor knelt beside her and looked at Forerunner. "That looks bad. Can't he heal himself?"

Forerunner shook his head slowly. "Calu took most of my power with him," he wheezed. Blood trickled from his mouth. "He deemed me unworthy of it, because I grew too fond of you humans."

"Then he only has one chance," Seri said firmly. She wrapped her arms around Forerunner, ignoring the blood. "Help me, Victor."

"Help you what?"

"Help me take him into the portal."

Victor glanced back at the fight happening just behind them. "But I should—"

"Victor! This man saved my life! I have to help him. You know what that's like, don't you?"

Victor nodded and sheathed his sword. "Whatever you say."

•••••

Volraag spread his arms and laughed at the curse-stalkers. He was dimly aware of a fierce battle happening on the eastern platform. Rathri versus some of Marshal's companions. But it didn't concern him. Nothing really did, any more. He moved beyond it all.

The nearest curse-stalker opened its mouth and two tongues shot out. Volraag caught them as they wrapped around his arm. He yanked on the tongues and pulled the creature to him. Its eyes bulged as Volraag caught it by the jaw. He twisted the huge head around until he heard the satisfying sound of the neck snapping.

He dropped it and the second curse-stalker scrambled over its body and leaped at him. Volraag flicked his fingers and power blasted the creature off the platform and down the hill.

So easy.

•••••

Seri shifted and took hold of Forerunner's feet as Victor lifted his upper body. Together, they moved to the edge of the walkway.

"Should we throw him in?" Victor asked hesitantly.

"No! You don't throw a dying man!" She glared at him.

"Sorry. I've never crossed into another world before!"

Seri took a step off the walkway. She found just enough of a gap to stand before stepping into the portal itself. She nodded and Victor joined her.

"This... won't work," Forerunner whispered.

"Be quiet and let me save you!" Seri snapped.

She took a deep breath and stepped into the portal.

•••••

Talinir tried to take it all in. Too much was happening all at once. Where was Marshal in all this chaos, anyway?

Fighting the assassin took most of his focus, but he kept checking on Janaab. After Calu fell through the portal, he remained lying on the ground in the Otherworld. Janaab checked on him, appeared to recognize him, and moved away. What could that mean?

Talinir appreciated the help from the girl, Ixchel. He instantly recognized the traditional Holcan garb, of course, as well as the fighting style. Against any normal human opponent, she would be formidable.

But the assassin was not normal. His moves, his fighting style, seemed an amalgam of so many others. Talinir recognized elements of the Holcan, traces of Mandi sentinels, the Remavian Guard... and something else beneath it all. Ixchel's involvement made it difficult to discern. It might be easier to fight this opponent one-on-one. Having another involved made everything slightly more unpredictable.

The close quarters made it more difficult. The assassin stepped back to the corner of the platform, allowing Ixchel to swing out to his left, onto the walkway leading to the southern platform and Volraag. Talinir stayed to the assassin's right. Because of the angle, he couldn't move entirely opposite Ixchel.

The assassin wielded two swords of medium length which Talinir immediately recognized as Eldani-make. Though rare, he could have obtained them from his targets over the years. He couldn't have visited the Starlit Realm, could he?

Ixchel slammed one sword away with her shield, then used her momentum to spin in the opposite direction to attack. The assassin struck Talinir's sword downward with his own so that he could use the same weapon to parry Ixchel. It left him open for only a fraction of a moment. Talinir brought his sword back up and managed to score a short slash on the assassin's right side.

In response, the assassin feinted at Talinir, then delivered a devastating double-sword strike at Ixchel. She caught both blades on her shield, but it staggered her back several steps. Talinir knew that move.

In that moment, he realized the truth. But his mind fought against it. It could not be true.

"Who are you?" he demanded.

"I am Rathri. It is all you need know."

• • • • •

Kishin lay almost senseless. The warpsteel sword had somehow absorbed much of Volraag's blast, though it still sent him flying. If not for the sword, every bone in his body would be broken. Even so, he felt battered and bruised all over his now curse-ravaged body.

For the second time in his life, he had taken on a living death. What remained for one such as him, save real death?

He staggered to his feet and picked the sword back up. At first, he thought his hand shook. But the sword itself was shaking. Perhaps it still held the magic from Volraag within it?

Kishin looked up the hill. Maybe he could still do something here, after all.

(((81)))

Victor stared. This was the Otherworld that so consumed Marshal? It looked... like the aftermath of a forest fire. And an earthquake. And maybe a war.

But then his eyes looked up, as he knew he must, and saw the stars. He had to admit, they were majestic. So many colors and sizes! The light of this place, though dim, came only from the stars. Did that make it always night here? None of the others ever mentioned daylight.

"Where's Calu?" Seri asked. Victor blinked and looked down. Forerunner lay there, barely breathing. Seri knelt by him. The portal lay a few feet away. He didn't remember moving away from it, yet here he stood.

"What are you doing here?"

Victor spun to see an older man staring at them. He wore tattered clothing and had dark splotches on his skin... wait... hadn't Seri described meeting a man like this?

"You!" Seri cried. "How...?"

The older man glanced over his shoulder, then hurried toward them. "You should not be here at this time," he said. "This is all wrong." He barely glanced at Victor, then looked down at Forerunner. "And what are you doing with him, of all people?"

"You have power!" Seri pointed at him. "I know it. I don't know whether you're really the King or not, but I can see your power. Can you heal him?"

The supposed King shook his head. "I don't possess that kind of power, my dear. You should know that."

"It's... all right," Forerunner said. "I... did what I thought was

390

right."

"You saved me!" Seri said. "I can't let you die!"

"There is no Bond... I am not human and bound by your Law."

"I don't care! How can I save you? Where's Calu?"

"You mean that one?" The older man pointed with his spear. "He's not in any condition to help you right now."

Victor looked and found Calu lying on his back not far away. His eyes were closed, but his chest rose and fell.

"...said I would die like a man." Forerunner's voice had grown faint.

"You don't have to," Seri said. "Hang on. We'll find someone and..."

"They mean you harm, Seri. Do not trust them." Victor and Seri both had to lean in to hear Forerunner.

"Who does he mean?" Victor asked.

The old man sighed and leaned on his spear. "He means the gods."

• • • • •

Marshal raced up the steps, feeling better than he had in days. Behind him, he heard Dravid cursing the stairs. He would catch up when he could. For now, Marshal had a purpose, and a job to do.

He burst out on the platform and looked around. Talinir! Here! Alive! And he fought against Volraag's assassin with the help of Ixchel. But where was Seri? And Victor? Volraag stood alone on the southern platform, but he looked different. Larger. Wilder.

"Volraag!" he cried. "Face me!"

His half-brother turned, a smile of ecstasy on his face. Marshal hesitated. Volraag's eyes glowed, like Wolf's. What had happened to him?

"Marshal! Not quite dead after all, eh?" Volraag spread his arms, and his hands curled into fists. "Come, brother! Let us end this face to face!"

Marshal felt his power building up inside him. He locked eyes with his brother's glowing ones. "Let us," he responded. And the power erupted.

• • • • •

Talinir dodged another strike from Rathri. He could not ignore the evidence any longer.

"Ixchel! Go help Marshal!"

The warrior woman nodded and disengaged, leaving Talinir alone versus the assassin. Time to learn the truth. The fundamental basis of all Rathri's fighting came from the Eldanim. More specifically, it came from the same warden training Talinir himself had experienced.

"How can you be a warden?" he cried. "You're human!"

"I have never been human."

Talinir's mind raced. He could see Seri and Victor in the Otherworld, speaking with Janaab. But Rathri was not there. He had no presence, no essence at all in the Otherworld. That meant...

"You unfolded yourself into this world," he realized. "And then did something horrific enough that a curse came for you." Which meant Rathri's true curse went far beyond his leprous appearance. He had been trapped in a human body, cut off from the Starlit Realm.

Talinir deflected Rathri's swords with his own and leaned in. "How long?" he asked. How long had he been like this?

Rathri leaned back. "Lifetimes!" he snarled. In a moment, he reversed the attack, slashing at Talinir. "Humans did this to me. And I will see them all suffer for it!"

•••••

"The gods?" Seri looked up. "What do you mean?"

The old man pointed toward Calu again. He stirred and began to lift himself off the ground. "Like that one," he said. "The other race that lives here. They came to humanity long ago and proclaimed themselves to be gods."

"You mean... the ones our people worshipped before learning of Theon and his Law," Seri said. "They're here? Oh, the golden people!"

The man nodded. "You've seen them then. I should have expected that."

"Seri..."

She looked back down at Forerunner. His face had gone very pale. Nothing could help him now.

"Ask your... mother," he whispered. "Your... heritage..."

"What?"

"They sent me, to prepare for their return. They... will come. And they will..."

"Yes?"

The four stars in Forerunner's eyes faded and disappeared. His body went limp. A hint of gold colored light washed out from him into the ground. The soil around his body softened.

"No..." Seri moaned. She closed her eyes. At times, Forerunner had deceived her, inspired her, tempted her, encouraged her, and manipulated her. Yet here at the end, he seemed sincere. He had given his life for her. What more could anyone do?

"Wolf?" Victor's voice made Seri open her eyes. He approached the now-standing Calu. "Wolf? It's Victor. Are you all right?"

"I am home," Calu said, his voice shaking with more magic than ever before. "Be thankful that I do not strike all of you down for her actions." He pointed at Seri.

The old man stepped in the way. "I might have something to say about that."

Calu looked him over with a quizzical expression. "Who are you, human?"

Victor turned to look at him as well, but his eyes widened as he looked beyond. "Theon's wings!" He drew his sword and took a step.

Seri rose to her feet and turned as well. She gasped.

● ● ● ● ●

Kishin reached the stone walkway in time to see Ixchel charge toward Volraag. The Eldani warden fought the assassin. As for Volraag... he and Marshal looked to be locked in some kind of magical duel. Both held their hands out toward the other. The air between them seemed to warp and twist, distorting vision through it. The walkway between them crumbled.

But Ixchel... She was trying to attack Volraag from this side! Even as he moved in behind her, Kishin could see her mistake. Volraag had grown in power. He couldn't miss her, could he?

Ixchel shouted as her sword came down toward Volraag. It ricocheted off an invisible barrier, knocking her off balance. She staggered back several steps.

Volraag laughed. One of his hands swung around toward her.

Kishin leaped into the way, holding the warpsteel sword up. A force struck it, almost tearing it from his grasp. But he held firm and stepped in closer. The sword continued to absorb magic. But how much could it take?

● ● ● ● ●

For the second time since arriving in the Otherworld, Victor found himself staring. This time, he felt no awe. Only horror.

An army approached. An army of extremely tall and dark beings. Some of them rode on fearsome creatures that made the curse-stalkers look small. Durunim. An entire army of them.

"Edin Na Zu," he whispered.

"What?" Seri asked. "Where did you learn that? I don't think it's appropriate here, and…" She trailed off. "Or maybe it is."

Victor looked to Wolf. "Friends of yours?"

Wolf smiled. "Our army approaches. Once the portal is fully opened, they will sweep into your world."

"I thought… I thought you wanted to help people," Seri said. "Forerunner talked that way. Why an army?"

"You have forgotten us," Wolf answered. "Forerunner was one of those sent to begin restoration. And so we shall. We shall restore things the way they were before the Laws of Cursings and Bindings. Before Theon. Haven't you and Marshal discussed this very thing?"

"You were listening to us?" Seri sputtered. "But, but this isn't what we meant! It definitely doesn't take an army!"

Victor tried to count the oncoming horde. He couldn't tell much in the odd light here, but… thousands. Easily thousands of enemy soldiers. Far more than Varioch's or Rasna's forces at the other high place.

"No," Wolf said. "It takes many armies. This is only one of them. A new age is about to begin."

Only one? Victor's heart sank. If that were true, it would take all of Antises united to stop them. And even then, it might not be enough.

"Not if I have anything to say about it." The man in the tattered clothing started toward the army, holding his spear in both hands. "This is why I am here."

•••••

Dravid pulled his crutch up onto the final step. He really was quite sick of these things. But his annoyance vanished at the sight of Marshal and Volraag engaged in some kind of magical combat.

It took only a moment to size things up and they did not look good for Marshal. His face looked tight, teeth gritted as he concentrated. Dravid could see his arms shaking. The stress must be immense.

Volraag, on the other hand, did not look the least bit stressed. In fact, he looked pleased with himself. He waved one hand at two other figures Dravid couldn't make out through the warped air. Then he returned his full focus to Marshal. He pulled both hands back a bit, then thrust them forward.

The stone walkway between the two combatants had already crumbled apart in many places. But as Volraag focused, the stone at his feet not only crumbled; it turned to powder that spread into the air around him. Inch by inch, Volraag's power pushed forward, pulverizing the stone. Inexorable, it moved toward Marshal.

Marshal began to yell, something Dravid couldn't make out, but it didn't seem to make any difference. Volraag's power continued on its way, drawing closer and closer to its target.

Marshal wouldn't give up and couldn't stop Volraag. Dravid had only moments to make yet another fatal decision.

He shoved himself forward in a dive, dropping his crutch.

He crashed into Marshal and both of them tumbled off the walkway.

As they struck the portal, the stone behind them erupted.

The world vanished, and Dravid saw… stars.

(((82)))

Volraag lowered his hands. Once again, Marshal eluded him. He watched the gravel rain down on the portal. Interesting. Most of it no longer fell through into the Otherworld. The portal had reached its limits, perhaps. It might not let anything else through again for a day, a week… or until he opened it like he had the other one.

He turned to see who remained. "Kishin. Still alive, I see." His last burst of power had knocked his former assassin back a few steps, but he resumed his pose, defiant as ever. Behind him stood… "Ah, Holcan. I regret that your lady seems to have left us. I wished to speak with her."

"Then why did you send your assassin after her?" Ixchel demanded, gesturing toward Rathri.

Volraag watched Rathri duel an Eldani. Where had he come from? They seemed quite equally matched.

"I gave no such command. Rathri exceeded his orders. I will speak to him about that. Rathri! To me!"

Rathri dodged and flipped backwards away from the Eldani. He ran around the other side of the walkway, but paused when he came to the destroyed platform.

"Enough of this," Ixchel growled. She jumped down to the portal.

Her bare feet landed on its surface and went no further. As Volraag anticipated.

"What is this?" Ixchel looked about in confusion. She stomped a few times.

The Eldani stepped to the edge and looked down. "The portal is closed," he said. "This one does that."

"When will it open again?" Ixchel asked.

"I don't know." The Eldani shook his head. "Hours. Days. It is unpredictable."

Volraag kept part of his attention focused on Kishin, the most dangerous opponent left. He seemed to be struggling with his sword. Odd.

"There is another possibility," he announced, and moved to the spot in the platform wall he had discovered.

"What do you mean?" the Eldani asked.

Volraag placed one of his hands into position. "I can open the portal for good."

•••••

Marshal rolled to a stop. What just happened? He shook his head and blinked. His eyes first focused on Dravid, pulling himself up onto his elbows a few feet away.

"Why did you do that?" he called.

Dravid looked at him with confusion on his face. "I saved your life," he said. "He was about to destroy you!"

"You don't—" Only then did Marshal realize his environment. He immediately looked up and lost himself in the stars.

Days ago, when he saw them with Seri, it had awakened his desire to be here far more than he anticipated. Now, at last, the light of the stars shone on his face once more. The beauty overwhelmed him, as it had done the first time. He could only stare. He lay still in the dirt, eyes fixed on the blazing heavens.

Seri's face intruded in his vision. "I suppose this is where you leave us?" she asked. "You could at least acknowledge what's going on around you for a moment."

Marshal scrambled up. "Seri! I—" He broke off, looking around at the others. Victor helped Dravid up, handing him a staff to replace his missing crutch.

"What about the others?" Victor asked. "Are they all right?"

"Ixchel and the Eldani were fighting," Dravid said.

"Topleb and Rufus?"

Marshal looked at Victor helplessly. He didn't know what to say. Somehow, Victor understood. He bowed his head in grief. Marshal groaned, then noticed Forerunner's still body on the ground. Dead? Marshal looked closer. He saw tiny springs of green growing all around Forerunner's body. Living plants? Here?

A snort from Wolf drew his attention. The big man stood nearby, a smile of triumph on his face. Marshal followed his gaze.

"Who's that?" He watched the lone figure moving out toward the approaching army.

"We don't know his name," Victor said. "But he's the one who claimed to be the King of Antises."

Marshal felt a sudden pull within him toward the stranger. He took a step. The stranger paused and looked back over his shoulder at Marshal. Something about him seemed familiar, somehow.

"This is for you." Marshal read the stranger's lips more than heard him, as a mighty roar came from the army.

"Grandfather?" he whispered.

•••••

Seri gasped. Of course the old man, the King, must be Marshal's grandfather! It made perfect sense! Varion must have blasted him into the Otherworld instead of killing him, and he'd been here ever since. But why had he never returned? Why stay here all these years? He could have returned to his daughter and grandson, helping them through their hard life, using his power if needed, and...

Oh. Of course. Every Lord and every mage and countless other people were constantly searching Antises for the lost King. If he had returned, he would have been found eventually. Here in the Otherworld, no one could find him. Why had Varion not recognized him all those years ago? Had his arrogance blinded him?

All of this rushed through Seri's mind in seconds, the time it took for the King to turn back to the army, take a deep breath, and lift his spear into the air.

With her star-sight active, Seri watched enormous power, hundreds of beams of colored light, flow out of the King's upraised spear, shattering it in the process. The power rushed up into the air, something she had never seen a magic-user of any kind do before. The sheer spectacle of the beams of light exploding upward into the vast star-filled sky blinded Seri for a moment. She rubbed her eyes.

And then the power came back down, swirling in multiple tornadoes of light, each of them composed of dozens and dozens of beams spinning in a cacophony of colors. Where each tornado struck the ground within the Durunim army, massive eruptions exploded, scattering dozens of soldiers in every direction. In just a few seconds, the King took down hundreds of Durunim.

The rest of the army halted, some of them even backing away.

The King lowered his arms and collapsed like a rag doll.

• • • • •

Dravid could not stop staring. From the moment they fell through the portal, he experienced wonder after wonder.

First, the stars. Seri had undersold them. They were magnificent. Dravid joined Marshal in admiring them for a moment before Seri's interruption. Victor helped him get up, handing him a smooth staff to use in place of his crutch. Curious. The staff looked identical to the one the strange pilgrim carried.

And then… then the King—he had to be the King with that kind of power!—tore apart the front lines of an entire army! Dravid barely had time to recognize that an army approached before it happened.

As Seri and Marshal ran toward the fallen King, Dravid and Victor both turned to Calu to see what he would do now. They glanced at each other, then back at the supposed god.

To their surprise, Calu stood still, as if unconcerned. He continued smiling.

Calu noticed them watching him. "Your time has almost come," he said, looking at Dravid.

"What does that mean, Wolf?" Victor asked.

Calu rolled his eyes. "My patience with you is nearing its end, Victor. I forgave much due to your kindness while I was… not myself. But that has a limit. My name is Calu. Should you need to address me, you will use it. And soon, you will use it in worship."

While Calu spoke, Dravid's eye caught a movement in the air, silhouetted against the stars. Another wonder: a tall figure soared through the air. In a burst of dirt and gravel, he came to a landing near Calu. Though his form looked much different here in the Otherworld, Dravid recognized him immediately. Curasir.

Dravid shifted awkwardly. The staff was a poor substitute for his crutch. And he was so tired.

Curasir bowed to Calu, then turned toward the humans. "Oh, good. You're all here." He glanced toward the portal. "And my other pawn moves into position. Everything… is as it should be."

• • • • •

Talinir reached down a hand and helped Ixchel back onto the walkway. Still reeling from the revelation of Rathri's nature, he tried to reason through Volraag's arguments.

"I don't trust you, son of Varion," he declared. "Why should we let you do this?"

In truth, Talinir alone could see what took place in the Starlit Realm. He saw the death of Forerunner, Janaab's decimation of the Durunim army, and Curasir's arrival. And on this side, he couldn't understand the appearance of a second leper assassin: the one who had tried to kill Marshal. Yet this time he seemed to be on their side.

"You will not 'let' me do anything, Eldani," Volraag said. "You have no way to stop me. However, I speak the truth. If I open the portal, your friends can return. If I do not..." He shrugged. "They stay there."

"And if he does, it opens the way for an invading army," Talinir said in a low voice for Ixchel to hear.

But the leper assassin heard him too. "I cannot allow that," he said.

Volraag placed his second hand against the stone. A vibration rose from the portal itself.

"Why are you here, assassin?" Talinir demanded. "Who are you?"

He turned those life-filled eyes surrounded by death toward Talinir. "I am Kishin the Cursed," he said. "I was the greatest assassin Antises has known." He turned his eyes to Ixchel. "But once, long ago, I was merely Kishin... a father."

Ixchel's intake of breath seemed louder than the portal's shaking.

Kishin turned and launched himself at Volraag.

• • • • •

Marshal knelt beside the old man. The King. His grandfather. It had to be. But he looked like every last bit of energy had flowed out of him. Knowing how tired he felt after using magic, Marshal wasn't surprised.

"Are you... are you Evander?" he whispered. "Aelia's father?"

The old man lifted a shaking hand. Strange black patches dotted his skin. He touched Marshal's face, tracing one of the rope-like scars.

"I haven't heard either of those names in so long," he answered in a quiet voice. "Evander was once my name. I've gone by others since then."

"Then you're my grandfather!"

Evander nodded.

Marshal had another realization. "You're the one who helped me after my battle with Curasir!"

"Yes. I took care of you, though I don't think you ever saw me."

"Don't look now," Seri's voice intruded. "But Curasir is here now."

"Help me up," Evander said.

Marshal lifted his grandfather to his feet, surprised by how little he weighed. They both turned to face the others. Evander's eyes first went to Dravid and Victor.

"All four of you? Together already? That... but no. Three of the four."

"What—?" Seri began.

"Oh, how delightful!" Curasir called. "You've found each other. I must say, that was quite a demonstration there, old man. But I still have over half of my army left. And I don't think you have another one of those in you."

"I slowed you down," Evander said, then coughed violently. "That's... all that matters."

Curasir spread his hands. "For what purpose? Volraag is about to open the portal permanently. Then I can bring this army through, and as many more as I want." He nodded to Calu. "In service to our masters, of course."

"Masters?" Victor asked.

Curasir rolled his eye. "You are the most obtuse of all these humans. It's not even amusing. How do the others even stand you?"

Marshal let Evander sit down against a large rock, then turned to Curasir. "I beat you once already. Shall we go again?"

Curasir snorted. "You had help." He gestured at Seri. "But I am not here alone this time. If we were to fight, it would not go well for you. But that is not my purpose here now."

"Then what is?"

Curasir looked toward the portal. "I am here to watch this open and reward my faithful pawn."

"Your pawn stole some of my power," Wolf growled.

"Did he? Then nothing can stand in his way now."

$$\bullet \bullet \bullet \bullet \bullet$$

Kishin crashed into Volraag, knocking him off balance. He whipped his sword up and across, cutting a gash across Volraag's chest and right arm.

The young Lord staggered against the stone wall. But even as he regained his balance, the wounds began to close. Impossible!

Volraag looked down and chuckled. "I guess it pays to absorb the right kind of power." He lifted his hand and a wave of vibratory magic blasted at Kishin.

Once again, the warpsteel sword absorbed the attack. Rathri ran across the portal toward them, but Talinir jumped down and faced him. Ixchel hesitated, but stood firm behind Kishin.

Volraag paused. "I have got to get one of those."

"Your power won't reattach your head if I cleave it from your body!"

Kishin feinted a blow toward the neck, and Volraag dodged instinctively.

Kishin whirled and threw the sword at the stone wall, embedding it next to where Volraag had been placing his hands.

"Eldani! The sword! I don't know how, but I know you do!"

Continuing the motion, Kishin spun and dove over Talinir and into Rathri.

● ● ● ● ●

"Marshal... hear me." Evander's weak voice barely caught his attention. He knelt once more next to his grandfather.

"I am dying," Evander said. "Don't argue. I knew it would... be today."

"But I just met you!" Marshal's anguish could not be contained. Not another death. Not again.

"I... am sorry that I wasn't there for you. Or Aelia. By the time I even learned... that I could go back"—Evander's frail body was wracked by coughing again—"I... thought I could do more for Antises here. I may... have been wrong."

Of course he was wrong. How would Marshal's life have been different had this man returned to it? Aelia might still be alive! Marshal didn't know whether to be angry, sad, or frightened. All three warred within him.

Evander pointed toward the regrouping army with a shaking finger. "If the... portal is opened, they will invade our world. These gods... will try to take control... of everyone."

"But Volraag is on the other side. And I can't get through now."

"Yes. You can." Evander placed his hand on Marshal's and guided it to the hilt of his sword.

"I don't have enough power to stop him," Marshal whispered.

"You will."

"Grandfather, I—"

"I have... always loved you, Marshal. I have fought... here... for you. And now you must fight... there... for me. For all of us."

Marshal bowed his head, and held Evander's hand. He swallowed hard. To do as Evander asked meant leaving his grandfather to die here. And it meant leaving the stars, perhaps forever. It would be the hardest thing he had ever done. He didn't have the strength. He couldn't.

A hand rested on his shoulder.

"We're here for you, Marshal. Whatever you need." Victor.

Another hand gently touched his other shoulder.

"You can do it," Seri whispered. "I believe in you."

"We all do," Dravid added.

"This sentimental drivel is making me sick," Curasir said loudly. "I do hope Volraag speeds things up."

Marshal stood and drew his sword. He smiled at his friends, then turned to the portal.

"It's time I put an end to all this."

(((83)))

What had that idiot Kishin done now? Volraag turned and looked at the sword stuck into the wall. What difference did that make?

He turned back. The warrior girl stood a few feet away, shield up, sword at ready. Kishin and Rathri rolled across the portal. And the Eldani turned to look back at him.

So feeble, all of them. He could destroy them all with a single burst of power, now that Kishin had released that annoying sword. He lifted his hands.

The Eldani was faster. His hand whipped up, and he cried out, "*i hatel indalanim!*"

The warpsteel sword exploded.

• • • • •

Marshal did not look up. He knew that if he did, his determination would waver. Another look at the stars and he might never leave. But they pulled at him, even so. How they pulled. He gritted his teeth. A tear escaped his left eye.

"If you leave now, you might never return," Curasir called.

Marshal stifled a whimper. He had a purpose. "In this world," Aelia had said. Not the Otherworld. His purpose lay in Antises.

"I made you an offer before," Curasir continued. "It's not too late, Marshal. We can remake this world."

"Will you shut up?" Victor snapped. Marshal smiled. Whatever he did now, he had friends backing him up.

He looked at the portal. How to do this, exactly? He stumbled on the uneven ground and stepped out onto the surface of the portal itself. As anticipated, it felt like solid ground. He walked into the middle and looked around.

"You can do it!" Seri called.

Marshal lifted the blade and stabbed down, holding his breath. The warpsteel sword penetrated through the portal's surface without any resistance. He paused for a moment and looked at the others one more time.

Dravid moved beside the others. He, Seri and Victor all watched. Evander sat where Marshal left him. Curasir argued something with Calu.

Marshal turned the sword in a circle around himself, slicing cleanly through the portal's surface.

And plunged through.

●●●●●

Seri lowered her gaze as Marshal disappeared through the portal.

"Seri..." Evander's whisper drew her attention. Had she ever told him her name?

She bent close to hear him. "I'm here."

"You and Marshal, together," he managed. "Heal the worlds. End the curses."

"We dream of that," she said. "But we don't know where to even begin."

"You need... help." He lifted a single finger and pointed. Seri followed it and saw Dravid, still watching the portal.

"He is... channel. But... one... more..."

Seri lowered her ear close to Evander's lips.

●●●●●

Volraag pulled himself up from the pile of gravel. What had just happened? He blinked dust out of his eyes and shook his head.

Rathri's hand grasped his shoulder and pulled. He got to his feet without difficulty. His clothes were torn in many places, even bloodstained, but he could find no wounds. His new power protected him again.

He looked back. The entire southern platform had been obliterated by the exploding sword. Nothing remained but a hole in the hill. He could no longer open the portal.

The Eldani and the Holcan stood on the opposite side of the portal, pulling Kishin up onto the walkway. He appeared to have been stabbed in the gut. Rathri's doing, no doubt.

This had gone on long enough. He should have blown them all away when they first arrived. Time, at least, to correct that error. He lifted his hand.

Marshal exploded out of the center of the portal, warpsteel sword in hand. He landed in a crouch, and pointed the sword at Volraag. "Let's try this again."

Volraag laughed, a deep laugh that shook his upper body, throwing his head back. He looked down at Marshal and unleashed his power.

• • • • •

Victor paced back and forth. "There has to be a way we can help him," he muttered. "We should have all gone through the portal with him."

"We can't leave Evander," Seri said, pointing at the old man. She seemed shaken, and not by Marshal's departure.

"We don't even know what's going on!"

"I can see," Curasir said.

"I didn't ask you!"

"But he can," Seri said. "He has one eye on our world all the time!"

"Fine." Victor whirled on Curasir. "What do you see?"

"Marshal started out well," Curasir answered. "He confronted Volraag, probably with some suitably dramatic statement about destiny or something. And then they started blasting at each other. So crude. Marshal used the warpsteel sword a little, but he doesn't know well enough how to use it. I'm afraid it won't go well for him now. He's already being driven back."

"How do we even know you're telling the truth?" Dravid demanded.

Curasir put a hand to his heart. "Why would I lie? I'm winning."

"I can feel it in my Bond! He's in great danger." Victor growled. "We have to help him!"

"How?" Dravid asked. "Even if we could get through the portal, we don't have any way to harm Volraag. He's too powerful now!"

"There must be a way! You're both mages! Can't you think of anything?"

"Seri might be able to open a way to our world, but... no. Volraag has a Lord's power and... part of a god's power. I don't know if anything can hurt him."

"A god." Victor turned and strode to Wolf. "W- Calu! I need your help."

"Why would I help you?"

"Because, when you were lost and everyone called you Wolf, we helped you! We took care of you. We kept you alive!"

Calu nodded. "I acknowledge this. And I have granted Marshal a boon in return."

"What's a boon?"

"Seriously?" Dravid said. "It's a favor."

"That's what I need!" Victor said. "A favor. How can I stop Volraag?"

"The boon was granted to Marshal."

"I'm doing this for Marshal! I claim it on his behalf!"

Calu frowned and considered for a moment. He glanced at Curasir. "Get the army moving. It won't be long." Curasir smiled and dashed away.

"Devouring fire!" Victor shouted. "God or no god, you will help me save Marshal, or I'll—" How did one threaten a god?

"Give me your weapon."

"My—?"

"Your weapon."

Victor reached for his sword hilt.

"No. The other one."

The flail? Victor removed it from his back. Only as he handed it over to Calu did he realize he could have used the new flail. He had taken the old one out by instinct.

Calu looked at the flail for a moment, his expression unreadable. "You have something else that will help. A stone, I believe."

A stone? Oh! Victor dug in the pouch at his belt and pulled out the Ranir Stone. It had been there so long, he had gotten used to its weight and forgotten it. He held the stone for a moment. Aelia had given it to him, calling it valuable beyond his understanding. Yet when he tried to use it to call for help, nothing happened.

"You can't trust him," Dravid said, limping up beside him.

"I have to," Victor said. He held the Ranir Stone out to Calu. "For friendship."

Calu studied him, then took the stone. "For friendship."

•••••

Marshal gasped in pain. Volraag's power exceeded his. Dravid had been right. He had no chance.

He pushed through the pain. The last time he used his power this extensively had been against Curasir months ago. He had no desire to break the bones in his hands again, so he let the power flow out through his whole body. It hurt everywhere.

Yet for all his efforts, Volraag seemed unfazed. He held one hand up toward Marshal, pushed back, power against power. He lifted the other hand and sent another stream of power toward Talinir and Ixchel.

"No!" Marshal cried.

Talinir held his own warpsteel sword up, absorbing or blocking Volraag's attack and shielding Ixchel. They would be all right, as long as Volraag couldn't turn his full power against them.

Marshal tried again to use his own sword in the same way. He felt it absorb some of the power, but it seemed to be pulling at his own power at the same time. That wouldn't work. He tossed it away and focused.

He could do this. He had to. Everyone depended on him. This was his purpose. Wasn't it?

Volraag laughed. "Why did you think this time would be different?" He leaned back and then thrust his hand forward once more.

Power unimaginable pushed back at Marshal's own. He felt it pouring around the edges of his own blast, forcing it back and back toward him.

In the end, he had no chance. Volraag's power struck him.

Marshal flew across the portal's surface and slammed against the walkway on the north side. His head wavered and fell. For a moment, he could see through the portal to the other side. Evander's tired eyes looked back at him. "Grandfather," he whispered. "I failed you."

Volraag seized Marshal by the hair and lifted him. He threw one last burst at Talinir to drive him back, then drew a dagger from his belt.

"Goodbye, Marshal."

• • • • •

Calu held the weighted end of the flail in one hand and the Ranir Stone in the other. He brought the two together and murmured something Victor couldn't hear. A soft, golden glow burst from his hands and surrounded the two items. The brightness grew until Victor couldn't see any more.

Beside him, he heard Dravid make a sharp intake of breath.

The glow faded. Victor stared at his flail. The Ranir Stone had become a part of it. In fact, it looked as if the iron ball on the flail's end had simply been fused into the stone itself.

Calu offered him the flail's handle. Victor took it, still staring. He touched the stone tentatively and found it cool.

"Amazing," Dravid whispered.

"The boon is fulfilled," Calu said. "And all debts, all connection that I have to you, or Marshal, or any other human is now repaid. We are friends no longer."

Victor shook his head. "You have strange ideas about friendship. It's not an obligation."

"Regardless. I have spoken."

Victor spun on his heel and ran back to the portal. "Seri! I need you!"

She stood. "What do you mean?"

"Get me through!"

"I can't do that!"

"You've done it before," Dravid pointed out.

"And I've never been able to do it again!" she argued. "Except with Marshal's help, with the sword."

Victor grabbed her upper arm and looked into her eyes. "Please, Seri. I'm begging you. Try!"

"All right, all right. I'll try." She cast one last look at Evander, then moved to the edge of the portal.

"You can do it," Dravid said. "This is a portal already. You just need to open it."

"Easy for you to say," Seri muttered. She reached a hand out and seemed to be trying to grab things only she could see.

The pull of Victor's Bond to Marshal hadn't been this strong since the ravine. Victor felt as if his own heart would burst out of his chest. "Hurry, hurry!"

"I'm trying!" Seri snapped. "I feel it too, you know!" In the moment, Victor had forgotten that Seri was now bonded to Marshal also.

She seemed to grab something else and then pushed. "I think… yes… Victor, when I say, you need to jump right in front of me."

Victor began to swing the Ranir flail, as he thought of it now.

"Almost…"

He braced himself.
"Now!"
Victor leaped through the worlds.

(((84)))

Dravid watched Victor's head disappear through the portal. Now only he and Seri remained. Would Seri be able to open it again for them to escape?

"The time has come," Calu announced.

Dravid turned, holding on to the staff. "The time for what?"

Calu pointed at Seri. "I told you there would be a price to pay. It is due now."

"What does he mean?" Seri asked.

"When he saved your life," Dravid said, "he said there would be a cost. I said I would pay it."

"Dravid! Why would you do that?"

He shot a look at her. "To save your life, of course! I would do anything for you, Seri."

"...oh..."

He took a deep breath, then turned back to Calu. "I'm ready. Will you let Seri go?"

"She is free to leave whenever she is able," Calu said. "You, however, are not. You will serve me, crippled one."

Dravid nodded. "For how long?"

"Until I grow tired of you, or your mortal life expires."

•••••

Victor burst into the regular world like diving through the surface of water. Volraag stood almost right in front of him, bringing a dagger toward Marshal's neck.

The Ranir flail rotated once more.

411

The dagger pierced Marshal's skin.

Victor screamed, bringing the flail up and forward. The chain hooked under Volraag's right arm. The stone swung up under it and smashed into his face.

The dagger fell. Marshal collapsed. Once again, the Bond was fulfilled.

Volraag skidded across the portal's surface from the impact, rolling and clutching at his face.

•••••

Talinir gasped. Not because of Victor's sudden appearance.

In the Starlit Realm, a hero breathed his last.

A tear formed in Talinir's right eye.

And Marshal's hand began to shake.

•••••

"You can't have him!" Seri shouted. She stepped in front of Dravid and glared up at Calu.

"He agreed to this," Calu said calmly.

"Well, I didn't! You can't have my friend!"

Calu cocked his head. "And again, we come back to this concept of friendship. Fascinating."

Dravid touched Seri's back. "Seri."

She turned, tears filling her eyes. "You can't go with him! Not for me!"

Dravid's hand shook as he reached out and brushed away one of her tears just as it spilled out. "For you."

"No! I can't lose you!"

Dravid took a deep, shuddering breath. "Do you remember back on Zes Sivas when I lost my leg, and you stayed with me?"

Seri nodded.

"I complained that you were going to be the death of me, and you… you said you were going to be the life of me."

Dravid had tears in his own eyes now. That made Seri's spill out all the more.

"And you were!" Dravid went on. "You saved me. And now… now I've saved you. And I get to be your life. Literally. Going with him is the price for your life!"

"It... you don't have to... we can fight him!"

Dravid shook his head. "There's an army coming. We can't fight. You need to go, as soon as you can."

"But... but he said we would need you, and..." She looked toward Evander. "Oh!" Seri put both hands to her mouth. Evander slumped over, unmoving. "He's gone."

Dravid took hold of her shoulder and pulled her closer. She shot her eyes back and forth from his face to Evander's still form. "Listen to me," Dravid pleaded.

Seri lost control. She grabbed Dravid and embraced him fully, wrapping her arms around his back. He held her with one arm, hesitated for a moment, then dropped the staff and wrapped the other arm around her. They adjusted for the imbalance and held each other tightly.

"I will come back," Dravid whispered. "We need to know more about these so-called gods. I'll learn all I can, and then come find you!"

"How? You know their power. How will you escape?"

Dravid pulled back enough to look into her face. "I'm a mage," he said. "I'll think of something."

"Are you finished?" Calu asked.

"No!" Seri snapped. She had to do one more thing, at least.

She looked at Dravid, studying his face. That beautiful skin. Those eyes. She would never forget him. Especially not if she...

Before she could analyze it any further, Seri pulled Dravid's face toward hers and put her lips against his.

Dravid's eyelids went up, but he responded, holding her even tighter and returning her kiss with a fervor that surprised her. In fact, the passion in the embrace and the kiss pulled on Seri in ways she had never imagined. The thought of continuing down that path terrified her, but she didn't want it to end. She let herself go, feeling like something overwhelming and powerful swept her away.

Dravid broke the kiss at last, pulling away. He stared at her, the longing in his eyes unmistakable. "You had to wait until now..." he whispered.

"It is time," Calu said. "No more delays. Come, servant."

Seri helped Dravid balance while she reached down and fetched the staff for him. How would he get by without a crutch? This wouldn't be enough. She handed it to him wordlessly.

Dravid took a faltering step toward Calu, then stopped. He looked back at Seri. "If I don't say it now, I'll regret it forever," he said. He searched her face, then nodded. "I love you."

Seri swallowed hard. He loved her? She loved him too, but... was it really that way? Did she even understand what love meant? She hadn't thought...

Dravid smiled and turned back. He stumbled after Calu as the big man strode away to meet Curasir and the army. They would be here soon.

"I love you," Seri mouthed the words, unable to give them any volume.

Dravid looked back, as if he heard her. He nodded.

Seri stood alone beside the portal as the army drew near. She took a last look at Evander. As much as she wanted to chase after Dravid, or stay to bury this old man, she had no choice. Her Bond to Ixchel had been pulling at her since Forerunner died. Her Bond to Marshal had subsided when Victor left. But now another Bond, not as powerful but still insistent, pulled at her. Volraag.

(((85)))

Marshal felt it coming before his mind could grasp it. A gust of wind came out of nowhere, providing welcome relief from the humidity. His hair waved in its flow.

Victor, who stood in his defensive stance beside Marshal, felt the breeze too. He glanced around.

A pressure enveloped Marshal, covering every inch of his body. He knew this feeling. He knew. The pressure forced its way into him, swirling and growing, filling his chest. The pressure came from inside now, growing with each moment. This had happened to him before, in the temple, when Varion died and Marshal received his power.

But this was greater. So much power. Growing and growing and growing. No one could contain power like this.

Victor said something to him, but he couldn't hear it. Across the portal, he saw Talinir and Ixchel, both staring at him. Talinir's mouth hung open. Ixchel's sword and shield hung loosely from her hands.

And still the power grew.

On the other side, Rathri stared at him with undiluted hatred. He yelled something and hurled his sword at Marshal.

Marshal watched it approach in slow motion. He put out his hand and touched the oncoming sword with his finger. The blade did not so much shatter as it crumbled. Dust rained down on Marshal's arm.

And still the power grew. A King's power.

Volraag, still holding his face, looked up. His eyes, full of pain and anger, stared at Marshal around his fingers.

Evander. He was dead.

Marshal threw his arms skyward and let the power erupt. This time, no temple ceiling and walls accepted the blast. Instead, it poured into the sky. So much power flowed out of him that it became visible, distorting the very air. Far above, the clouds swirled, conforming to the vibrations that reached to their very height.

Marshal lowered his hands, staring up in wonder. Had he done that? As if in answer, a gentle rain began to fall.

The drops splattered against the portal's surface... except in the middle, where the drops disappeared as they struck. In fact, the area where they disappeared was growing...

"The portal's opening!" Victor cried.

•••••

Seri emerged from the portal near the edge where she had first entered. Ixchel dropped her sword and grabbed at her arm.

"My Lady!"

"Ixchel! I'm all right. I just..." She wavered and Ixchel caught her. Together with Talinir, they lifted her out of the portal. Rain spattered against her face and robes.

"Where's Marshal?" She turned.

The high place had changed dramatically since she left. The southern platform was completely gone, and the western one wasn't much better. Rathri and Volraag stood on the walkway nearest to it. Victor and Marshal stood on the northern platform.

"Did you open the portal?" Talinir asked.

"No, I was surprised that I walked right through it!"

"Then it must have been Marshal's power."

"Marshal?" She looked back at him, blinking to activate her starsight. Oh. "Theon's pillars!"

Marshal glowed with incredible power, far more than he had possessed a few minutes ago. The King's power... united with a Lord's power. How did he contain it all? How did he even survive? "The Heart of Fire," she whispered. Marshal's body contained the Heart of Fire. Tezan's false version now seemed so petty.

She glanced at Volraag, seeing his massive power as well, but it seemed somehow diminished in the greater glow of Marshal's strength.

As she watched, she saw Marshal gather up power in his hand, preparing to throw it. "No!"

Seri launched herself free of the other two and ran around the portal.

"Seri? Where's Dravid?" Victor asked.

She grabbed Marshal's arm just in time. "Stop!"

Marshal looked at her with furrowed brow. "Seri? What is it?"

Seri took a few steps and stood between Marshal and Volraag. "Don't hurt him any more. We need him."

Marshal lowered his hand. In that moment, Seri knew her Bond to Volraag had been fulfilled. The slight feeling of knowing where he stood evaporated.

A head emerged from the portal, tall and dark and rippling with strange energy.

"Durunim!" Talinir shouted.

"Everyone run!" Marshal commanded. "I'll deal with this!"

"Where?" Victor asked. "I think both sets of stairs are destroyed or blocked…"

Marshal pointed down the side of the hill and a shockwave rushed down it, throwing dirt, stone, trees, vines and brush aside, forming a path to the ground below.

Rathri yanked on Volraag's arm and they hurried down together. Victor hesitated, then followed them with Seri. Ixchel and Talinir, carrying the pilgrim, soon caught up to them.

Marshal came at the end. Seri watched him descend, wondering about his new power. Did he close the portal himself?

In answer, a tall figure of the Durunim appeared silhouetted at the top.

• • • • •

Marshal stopped at the base of the hill and looked back up. If the army came through, then Ch'olan would be devastated. He could not allow that.

"You are not welcome here!" he called to the Durunim. "Leave now, or face the consequences."

The figure did not move.

Marshal closed his eyes. He knew he now had the power to do what he wanted, but he wasn't sure he knew enough to control it well.

"For Topleb!"

He pointed at the hill in front of him. Dirt and rock began to erupt beneath the portal.

"What are you doing?" Talinir asked.

Marshal ignored him and pushed his hands to either side. The hill came apart under the portal, throwing tons of debris in either direction. The rain's intensity picked up at the same time.

"Marshal?" Seri asked.

"Stay back!" he warned.

He swept his arms further apart. The rest of the dirt and rock came apart. The portal plunged down to the same level as Marshal himself. The Durunim warrior fell back inside it. Just as well, with what he was about to do.

Marshal brought his hands back together and clapped. This wasn't much different from what he had done at the battlefield, but on a grander scale.

The portal fell deeper, below his feet. Dirt, rock, trees, everything poured down on top of the portal. Much of it fell through, but enough trees and rocks began to form a barrier.

"Marshal, no!" Seri screamed at his side.

He ignored her and focused his power. More debris poured in, beginning to pile up.

"Stop it!" Seri grabbed his arm and pulled.

Marshal clapped again. Fragments of the old platforms and walkway, tons of dirt, tree trunks, and more covered the portal, burying it. Marshal kept pouring it on until he built a new hill, piled on the ruins of the old one. Seri pulled at his arm for another minute, then let him go and sank to her knees, weeping.

He let the power diminish gradually until nothing remained but a cloud of dust. He pushed gently with his power, blowing it away along with the rain for a moment. He hadn't known he could do that until he tried. The rain reasserted itself right away, resuming a steady fall that began to muddy the torn-apart ground around him.

He looked down. What was wrong with Seri?

"Dravid..." she sobbed.

Dravid? "He didn't come back?" Marshal suddenly felt a pull. His Bond to Dravid.

"Calu kept him. And now he can't escape!"

Marshal glanced at his new hill. He felt a sick feeling settle in his stomach.

"There are other ways," Talinir said.

Seri shook her head. Ixchel knelt beside her and put an arm around her shoulders. "We will find him," she said. Her voice shook as well.

Seri stood. "No. I have another task first."

Marshal looked around. Victor stood closest. His flail looked...

different. Talinir stood beside him. At his feet lay Kishin, but...

"The assassin?"

Talinir nodded. "He stopped Volraag from opening the portal sooner. I do not understand his actions."

Ixchel knelt beside Kishin. Marshal thought she whispered something, but he couldn't tell. When she stood and moved back to Seri's side, she left behind one of her green feathers, carefully tucked into Kishin's hand.

Victor pointed. "What about those two?"

Rathri held his remaining sword at ready, eyeing all of them. So strange to see two leper assassins. How did they both end up like that? Volraag stood beside him, hunched slightly. His face looked horrible. His cheek, jaw, and nose all appeared broken. And they weren't healing instantly, like his earlier wounds. What *had* Victor done to that flail?

Marshal pointed at Volraag. "This ends here, brother. Will you surrender?"

Volraag shook his head.

"Don't be ridiculous," Rathri snarled. "Of course he doesn't surrender."

"Don't make me—" Marshal began, then stopped. Make him what? What could he do to them? They weren't trying to kill him now, so he couldn't kill them. Or could he? He was both a Lord and King now. The curses did not apply to him. But they would apply to any future children, should he ever have any. He could not do that.

"No." Seri stood in front of him, hair and robes dripping wet. "Let them go."

(((86)))

Everything within Seri told her to turn and leave. Take Ixchel and abandon all of them. Find a way to go after Dravid instead. Yet she knew what she had to do.

She took a deep breath and turned to Volraag. "The third portal is in Kuktarma, just south of the border with Arazu. You will need help to get there. I should go with you."

"What?"

"Are you crazy?"

"My Lady?"

Seri ignored the cries from her friends. She focused on Volraag. "Well?"

Volraag looked to Rathri. The assassin nodded. "Lord Volraag seems unable to speak at present," he said in his abrasive voice. "But I believe he accepts your offer." Volraag nodded, then winced. "We should leave as soon as you are prepared."

Seri turned back to face the others, who stared at her in disbelief.

"Did you leave your mind behind in the Otherworld?" Victor demanded.

Seri tried to smile, but couldn't keep it on her face. The emotions were still too raw. If she weren't careful, she'd start sobbing again, and that would derail everything.

"I have to do this," she said softly.

Marshal's face almost broke her. Through his scars, he looked... he looked like a little boy whose best friend has just joined those who mock him for being different. Such a specific simile. It... had happened before. When she was a child. She was the best friend. And like then, she was abandoning someone who needed her.

420

Except this time, she acted for the greater good. She didn't understand everything, but she knew… she knew she had to go with Volraag now. The future of Antises depended on it.

"There's no way I can make you all understand," she said, cognizant of Rathri and Volraag within hearing distance. "I have to go. It's what needs to happen now."

"I will go with you," Ixchel said.

Seri felt a weight slide off her tense shoulders. She had hoped, but hadn't been sure. "Thank you, Ixchel."

"I do not agree with your actions in the slightest," Ixchel went on. "But you are my Lady. I will protect you even in this."

Seri nodded. Later, she could try to explain to Ixchel alone. Maybe.

"Don't," Marshal said.

Seri choked up. That one word was too much. How to make him understand? How?

"We will meet again," she said in very measured words. "I can't tell you more than that yet."

She made a slight curtsy. "After all, you're my King now," she added.

Marshal only shook his head slowly, rain dripping from his hair and across his scars.

"I thought you understood," Victor accused. "I thought you… I don't understand you at all. Who are you?"

"Victor." She bit her lip and squeezed her hands together for a moment. "Thank you for saving my life. I will always be grateful."

"What?"

She turned and walked toward Volraag, Ixchel falling in beside her. Those first few steps may have been the hardest ones she ever took.

• • • • •

Marshal watched her go. Why? How? What did it mean?

"Is it because of Dravid?" he asked aloud. "I can go after him. Right now, if you want."

Seri stopped, but she did not turn around. "No, Marshal." Her voice broke.

He took a step after her. "I will bring him back. I swear."

She lifted a hand. A slight tremor ran across Marshal's chest. Had she done that? He had never been more confused in his life. He understood attacks. He understood mockery. But this? Betrayal. After all they had just been through. After losing Topleb and Rufus. After meeting his grandfather, then losing him. After stopping the invasion. He didn't understand at all.

Marshal sank to his knees in the mud. The rain, at least, began to subside.

Seri seemed to gather herself and resumed walking, Ixchel at her side. Volraag and Rathri turned, and the four of them continued on to the end of Marshal's carved path. There, they turned to the south and disappeared behind the trees.

Marshal felt himself sinking down inside. What now? He had been counting on Seri to give him guidance once they found Talinir. She wanted him to go to Zes Sivas. But he couldn't go without her. What would be the point? He didn't want to be a King. He wanted to get rid of the curses.

And he had no idea where to go from here.

"But I didn't save her life," Victor said.

Marshal looked up at him. Exhaustion dragged him down. What was Victor saying?

"I never saved her." Victor cocked his head. "But she saved me!" His eyes widened. "She saved me!"

Victor dashed a few feet down the muddy path, then turned back. "Do you get it? The Bond!"

What?

Victor pointed in the direction Seri had gone. "I'm Bonded to her now! That's what she was trying to tell me, without letting Volraag know! I'm Bonded to her!"

Marshal shook his head. A lot of Bonds had been formed and fulfilled in the past few hours. Everyone had been fighting and saving each other. He could still feel Dravid on the other side.

Victor whooped and swung his flail in a circle, slinging water in all directions. "Don't you get it?"

"Explain it to us, Victor," Talinir said. "I don't know what you're raving about, and Marshal clearly doesn't, either."

"Watch!" Victor said. He covered his eyes with his free hand, then turned in a slow circle. He pointed southwest with his flail. "There! She's that direction!" He opened his eyes and looked back at them, grinning.

"She wants us to follow her! Don't you get it? That's why she reminded me of the Bond!"

Marshal got to his feet. "We can follow her?" he repeated, feeling stupid as he did.

"Yes! I could always tell how to find you were when we were Bonded, but even more so when you were in danger." He pointed after Seri again. "She's in constant danger now. I know exactly where she is!"

"But... why?"

Victor lifted his hands and shoulders. "I have no idea!" But he kept grinning.

Talinir stepped up. "I do not understand the girl's movements, either," he said. "But it seems she is acting with some purpose in mind. Do you trust her?"

Marshal thought for a moment. Despite their quarrels, in the Otherworld Seri told him she believed in him. Could he do any less?

"I do trust her."

Talinir nodded. "Then it appears our course is clear." He smiled. "And... it is good to see you again, Marshal."

Marshal swallowed past a lump in his throat. In all the chaos and battle, he had almost forgotten. "Talinir—" he began.

The warden swept him into a hug while Victor laughed. Marshal found himself lifted up and spun around. He couldn't help laughing as well.

Talinir set him down and chuckled. Then his face sobered. "I do have one question, though."

"What is it?"

Talinir pointed to the unconscious form of Kishin. "What do we do with him?"

(((87)))

"Come, Jamana." Master Korda's booming voice echoed through the palace's wide spaces. Jamana picked up his pace. He still didn't know why they had been summoned back to Tenjkidi. Master Korda did not seem to know, either, or at least was not being very candid about it.

Jamana had been to the Lord's Palace only once before, when he had been chosen to become an acolyte for Mandiata. That trip had been at night, and he had seen little of the palace's interior. Of course, its looming minarets dominated the view of Tenjkidi throughout his life. But inside was a different story. He wanted to stop and stare at each new room, each new work of art he spied on walls and in corners.

Unfortunately, Master Korda seemed to know exactly where to go, and led the way without pause. Jamana adjusted his grip on Aharu's book and hastened to keep up.

At last, they exited another large room through a wide open doorway and entered an enormous terrace. Two structures dominated the terrace, both of them containing elaborately carved stone coffins surrounded by rows of flowering plants. Jamana came to a halt.

"Is this…" He trailed off.

Master Korda turned back to him. "The Tombs of the First and Last Lord," he announced. He reached out toward the nearest of the two. "Lord Sundinka lies here, of course."

The other tomb then held the body of Sakouna, the first Lord of Mandiata, from the days of Akhenadom.

"Each time a Lord dies, the previous Lord's body is removed and taken to the Tombs of the Lords," Master Korda continued in a softer tone. "Thus, someday, these two will definitively be the first and last Lords."

Since Volraag had stolen Lord Sundinka's power, he might truly be the last Lord of Mandiata. Jamana hoped not. There had to be a way to undo that travesty.

"My Lord!" Master Korda exclaimed, bowing. Jamana turned in the same direction, bowing as well. He looked up and saw Lord Bakari, Sundinka's son. At his side walked Komadi, the current ranking mage of Tenjkidi's court. Bakari wore the traditional garb of Mandiatan royalty, though without, Jamana noticed, the tiger pelt his father had worn. Also without his power. Jamana's senses detected only faint traces of magic within Komadi, and nothing from the young Lord.

"Rise, Master Korda," Lord Bakari said, his youthful voice sounding odd in this solemn locale. "I am pleased you could come so quickly."

Master Korda nodded, and gestured to Jamana. "My acolyte Jamana, my Lord. He carries the book we found, and—"

Lord Bakari raised a hand and Korda stopped. "I did not summon you back home to hear of books," he said.

"But this alters what we knew of the beginnings of Antises," Master Korda responded. "It is monumental."

Lord Bakari shook his head. "I am not concerned with the past, Master Korda, but the glorious future." A smile lit up his face. "Monumental, you say? Something has occurred that will shake the foundations of Antises forever. And Mandiata will lead the way into a new order, a majesty unknown to our ancestors... save those in the far distant past, perhaps."

Master Korda seemed at a loss for words for the first time since Jamana had known him. "Then I... beg your Lordship to share this discovery with us. What have you found?"

"It is not *what* I have found."

"They found us!" Komadi said in excitement. Bakari glared at him. "I apologize, your Lordship." Komadi shrank back.

A third man approached behind Lord Bakari. "Here is the one who will explain," Bakari said. He stepped aside.

The newcomer was shorter than the young Lord, but dressed more elaborately. His outfit appeared to consist of several lengths of cloth, each a bright color, wrapped around his body in an intricate fashion and hanging from his arms. His hair, white as snow, belied his age, which Jamana could not discern. Twin gold chains hung around his neck and draped across his chest.

But his magic power radiated in a fashion unlike the Masters or Lords. Jamana glanced at Master Korda and saw that he looked confused as well.

"Greetings, noble mages!" The white-haired stranger cried. "I am Harbinger. I am the omen, the forerunner. I have come to pave the way, to restore that which was lost."

"I… do not understand," Master Korda said. He looked to Lord Bakari, but Harbinger stepped closer.

"I have been among your people for some weeks," he said, looking into Master Korda's face. "My task has been difficult, but highly rewarding. And now it draws to a close."

"Why is that?" Korda asked.

"Because I need prepare the way no longer." He smiled, folded his arms, and stepped back.

Lord Bakari gestured to the other side of the terrace. "Behold!" he cried.

Jamana and Master Korda turned. A tall figure appeared from behind the First Lord's tomb. Physically, he appeared Mandiatan, though taller and more strongly-built than even Master Korda. He moved with the easy stride of a man with no concerns or worries of any kind. His clothes resembled Harbinger's, but seemed finer, the colors brighter. On his shoulders, he wore a pelt Jamana could not identify. Yellow-orange fur appeared toppled with spots like a leopard, but interspersed with jagged stripes, as well.

But the most impressive thing about the newcomer had nothing to do with his appearance. Jamana noticed Master Korda stiffen a few seconds before he felt it as well. Power radiated from him, power greater than that of any Lord or Master. Yet something about it felt… different. It did not seem like any of the power of Antises he had felt in anyone else. Harbinger radiated a similar power, he realized, though nowhere near this intensity.

"Welcome, mages." He spoke, and his voice resonated with authority and power. Magic vibrated through every word he uttered. "I am delighted to meet you. We have much to discuss."

"We are pleased to meet you also," Master Korda answered, bowing again. Jamana echoed his movements. "I am Master Korda and this is my acolyte Jamana. I'm afraid I don't know you."

"Fear in my presence is a good thing," the stranger said. "For your ancestors feared me. But they loved me as well."

"Ancestors?"

"Harbinger, proclaim my name to them."

Harbinger stepped forward and bowed deeply to the stranger. Then he turned back to the mages.

"Master Korda, you are in the presence of the inimitable, the immortal, the mighty Nummotem."

Master Korda drew in a sharp breath. Jamana did not recognize the name, though it sounded familiar. "Master?"

"Do you not know me, little acolyte?" Nummotem held out a hand and golden light blossomed from it. He shaped it into a circlet and placed it on his own head. He looked down at Jamana.

"I am one of your gods, the gods you abandoned when you came to this place." The terrace shook as if another earthquake were beginning. Jamana fell to his knees, as did the other four. Nummotem remained standing.

"I have returned. We are all returning. And Antises will never be the same again!"

For more information on Antises,
upcoming books, and more,
visit timfrankovich.com

(Join the mailing list and receive a free short story,
featuring the origin of Kishin!)

If you enjoyed this book, please post a review!
There's no better way to spread the word.

Glossary

Caution: These listings may contain minor spoilers.

Aapo - Kishin's household servant

Adhi - A mage acolyte from Kuktarma, studying on Zes Sivas.

Aelia - Marshal's mother who willingly sacrificed herself to lift his curse. Daughter of Evander.

Aharu - Sibling of Akhenadom. Founder of the priesthood. First High Master Mage of Antises.

Ajaw - Lady of Ch'olan. Wife of Lord Rajwir. Commander of the Holcan.

Akhenadom - Called "the Great." At the time of the Great Cataclysm, he led six people groups from their original homes to the land of Antises. He introduced them to the worship of the one god Theon, and presented to them Theon's Book of the Law. In return, the six people groups proclaimed him the first King of all Antises.

Albus - A soldier in the army of Varioch. Cursed for murder and assigned to the curse squad.

Alpin - Former Master Mage of Varioch. Murdered by Curasir.

Amnis River - A branch of the Trebia River that flows along the western side of Varioch and its southern border with Rasna.

Antises - The union of the six lands of Rasna, Varioch, Ch'olan, Mandiata, Arazu, and Kuktarma. Ruled from the island of Zes Sivas in the middle of Lake Litanu, which borders all six lands.

Arazu - One of the six lands of Antises. Arazu is located on the eastern side of Lake Litanu, between Mandiata and Kuktarma. Arazu is the smallest of the lands, but claims the oldest culture and strictest traditions.

Bakari - The young Lord of Mandiata. Son of Sundinka. The first Lord of a land without possessing any magic power (due to Volraag's theft).

Balaes - A blacksmith in the village of Drusa's Crossing. Father of Careen.

Book of the Law - A compilation of the moral and ceremonial laws of Theon, written by Akhenadom.

Calu - The name of an ancient god of Rasna.

Callus - A conscript in the Varioch army, twin brother to Gallus. Assigned to the curse squad.

Careen - A young woman of Drusa's Crossing. Daughter of Balaes. Was in a relationship with Victor prior to his departure.

Cassian - General of Varioch's army. Placed in charge of the war with Rasna by Volraag.

Cataclysm, Great - The event which motivated the six people groups to follow Akhenadom. Details about it are apocryphal at best. Descriptions range from earthquakes to volcanic eruptions to extreme weather events to floods, perhaps a combination of all of these.

Cato - A young man of Varioch who seeks out Forerunner.

Chimon - An elderly priest at the temple in Woqan.

Ch'olan - The northernmost of the six lands of Antises, bordered by Varioch and Mandiata. Ch'olan is known for its fierce warrior traditions and its stone monuments, especially pyramids.

Conclave of Mages - The organization of magic-using professionals based in the Citadel of Mages on Zes Sivas. The Conclave is led by six Master Mages - one from each land - and includes numerous lesser mages of varying degrees of proficiency.

Curasir - A scheming member of the Durunim, who can make himself appear as one of the Eldanim.

Curse-stalker - A large reptilian creature that is drawn to magic. Since the primary sources of magic encountered by most common people are those who are cursed, this gave rise to the idea that these creatures only hunted cursed individuals. Curse-stalkers possess two long tongues that excrete some form of acid while absorbing magic energy.

Cyra - Volraag's concubine.

Diabol - The devil. Rarely mentioned in the religion surrounding the worship of Theon. Mostly used in epithets.

Djatan Desert - A large desert marking the eastern extent of Antises, primarily connected with Mandiata, but also bordering Arazu.

Dravid - A former mage acolyte. Lost his leg during one of the earthquakes on Zes Sivas.

Drusa's Crossing - A village in the mountains near the border between Varioch and Ch'olan.

Durunim - Former members of the Eldanim whose physical form has been changed through an unknown process. They now wage war against the Eldanim on behalf of mysterious masters.

Efesun - A large town in Varioch, located on the shore of the Trebia River, near the Great Plains.

Eldanim - A magical race of non-human beings. Eldanim exist both within the primary world and the Otherworld (or Starlit Realm). This creates a strange dichotomy for human eyes, as their physical shape within each world is different. For their part, Eldanim can see both worlds at the same time. Their physical appearance within the primary world is similar to humans, though generally taller with much sharper, angular features. One eye appears all black, with tiny pinpricks of light. Their physical appearance in the Otherworld is several feet taller.

Eidolon - An apparition, often seen as a misty human-like form. In reality, the eidola are Eldanim or Durunim who have shifted their primary essence into the Otherworld. "Eidolon" is the name used by residents of Varioch and Rasna. In Arazu, they are called **Gidim**. In Ch'olan, they are called **Tzitzimitl**.

Eniri - A young woman of the Eldanim who resides in Intal Eldanir. She works in the healing profession.

Enuru - Current Lord of Arazu, husband of Lilitu.

Edin Na Zu - A phrase of uncertain origin in Arazu. Used as an epithet. Has some connection to the Djatan Desert.

Evander - Father of Aelia, grandfather of Marshal. King of Antises (in self-imposed exile).

Forerunner - A mysterious man who possesses a strange magic unlike the usual magic of Antises. Sent to the land of Varioch.

Gallus - A conscript in the Varioch army, twin brother to Callus. Assigned to the curse squad.

Ganak - Current Master Mage of Kuktarma. Part of the Conclave of Mages on Zes Sivas.

Gidim - *see* **Eidolon**

Gnaeus - A conscript in the Varioch army, cursed with a twisted hand. Assigned to the curse squad.

Great Plains - A wide, open area of land on the western side of Antises, bordering Varioch. Generally considered to be the location of Intal Eldanir.

Hain - Master Mage of Arazu. Part of the Conclave of Mages on Zes Sivas. Mentor to Seri.

Hanirel - A member of the Durunim, who can make himself

appear as one of the Eldanim.

Harbinger - A mysterious man who possesses a strange magic unlike the usual magic of Antises. Sent to the land of Mandiata. It is probable that others like him or Forerunner were sent to each of the six lands.

Hauk - A boatman who works for the mages on Zes Sivas.

Harunir - A member of the Eldanim, resident of Intal Eldanir. Husband of Indala, father of Eniri.

Holcan - An order of female warriors in Ch'olan, trained from an early age in multiple fighting techniques. Usually assigned to guard and escort the Lady of Ch'olan (wife of the Lord).

Indala - A member of the Eldanim, resident of Intal Eldanir. Wife of Harunir, mother of Eniri.

Inkil - A news broker in Woqan. Often employed by Kishin.

Intal Eldanir - The primary city of the Eldanim. While floating above the ground, it can be shifted from the primary world to the Otherworld (and back).

Ixchel - A young member of the Holcan. Assigned by Lady Rajwir to serve Seri.

Jamana - A mage acolyte of Mandiata. Serves on Zes Sivas under Master Korda.

Janaab - A name used by Evander during his wanderings in the Otherworld.

Junia - A young woman of Varioch who seeks out Forerunner.

Kanna - A small town in Varioch, near the border with Rasna.

Kawal - A man of Woqan. Kishin's second murder.

Korda - Current Master Mage of Mandiata. Part of the Conclave of Mages on Zes Sivas. Mentor to Jamana.

Kishin - An assassin of Ch'olan. Cursed with a form of leprosy.

Komadi - A mage assigned to the Lord's court in Tenjkidi,

Mandiata.

K'uh - A word for magic in Ch'olan. An ancient belief (pre-Antises) connected magic with each individual's life force. This led to human sacrifice in some communities.

Kuch - Blademaster of Ch'olan. Responsible for training warriors, including the Holcan.

Kuktarma - One of the six lands of Antises, bordered by Arazu on the north, and the sea on the south. Known for its walled cities and the antics of the current Lord's sons.

Laws of Cursings and Bindings - A set of magical laws put in place by the first Conclave of Mages. Anyone who willingly violates one of the moral laws of Theon, as described in the Book of the Law, receives a magical curse appropriate for his action. Magical Bindings are formed between family members and other close relationships. In addition, special Bindings are created when someone rescues another person from serious danger or potential death.

Lilitu - Lady of Arazu. Wife of Lord Enuru. Sponsored Seri's membership in the Conclave of Mages.

Lake Litanu - A huge freshwater lake in the center of the six lands of Antises, bordered by all. The island of Zes Sivas is in its center.

Lords' Betrayal - An event that followed the creation of the Laws of Cursings and Bindings by the Conclave of Mages. The first six Lords of Antises twisted the Laws to attempt to exempt themselves from the curses. Instead, curses for their actions fell on their children.

Lucia - A young woman of Varioch who seeks out Forerunner.

Mages & Lords - A card game popular throughout Antises (with some variants) dating back to the Lords' Betrayal. Small deck with limited cards. On a player's turn, he flips over the top card of the deck, then decides whether to play it or put it back on the bottom of the deck. Object of the game is to collect either six Lords & King or six Mages & High Master Mage.

Makaan - Former Blademaster of Ch'olan. Mentor to Kuch and Kishin.

Malena - A woman from Rasna who serves Forerunner.

Mandiata - One of the six lands of Antises, bordered by Ch'olan and Arazu. Known for exotic wildlife, elaborate architecture, and high respect for the dead.

Marshal - Son of Aelia and Varion (rape). Grandson of Evander. Half-brother of Volraag. Inheritor of the powers of both a Lord (Varion) and King.

Meluhha - Current Lord of Kuktarma. Father of seven sons, whose escapades have been documented (and exaggerated) in dozens of stories that his people delight in repeating.

Merish - A conscript of Varioch. Stole a sword and received some form of mental damage as a curse. Rarely if ever speaks. Assigned to the curse squad.

Mukuy - A man of Woqan. Kishin's first murder.

Nehesy - Son of Aharu. Second High Master Mage of Antises.

Nian - A priest of Mandiata. Decided to go on pilgrimage to all six lands of Antises. Never made it to Rasna.

Nummotem - The name of an ancient god of Mandiata.

Otioch - Leader of Varioch's Remavian Guard. Confidant of Volraag.

Otherworld - A parallel world separated from the primary world. Similar in shape/geography, but lacking most water and vegetation. No sun or moon, but lit constantly by enormous stars of varying colors, leading to its other name, the **Starlit Realm**.

Passing - An annual event on Zes Sivas, where the King and Lords of all six lands are instructed to surrender their magic power for one hour. The power returns to the land temporarily and seems to keep it from breaking apart.

Plecu - Current Master Mage of Rasna. Part of the Conclave of Mages on Zes Sivas.

Raeton - Capital city of Rasna. Known for spectacular pillars.

Rajwir - Current Lord of Ch'olan. Husband to Ajaw.

Ranir Stone - A stone given by Aelia to Victor. Aelia used it for sending a message to the Eldanim. The magic involved is unknown. Appears as an ordinary rock.

Rasna - One of the six lands of Antises, bordered by Varioch on the north, and the sea on the south. Known for the pillars of Raeton and little else.

Rathri - An assassin employed by Volraag. Appears to possess a leprosy-style curse similar to Kishin.

Regulus - One of the three Consuls who control the economic power of Varioch.

Reman - Capital city of Varioch.

Remavian Guard - Elite warriors of Varioch, recognized by their red capes. In service to the Lord and his household.

Rufus - A conscript of Varioch. Once stole food from his neighbor and received the curse of a twisted foot, causing him to limp. Assigned to the curse squad.

Sakouna - The first Lord of Mandiata, from the time of the founding of Antises. Apparently, he had a monkey.

Sandu-Emuq - Capital city of Arazu.

Sekou - A Master Mage who wrote extensively about wild magic.

Seri-Belit - Mage of Arazu. Prefers just Seri. Possesses the unusual ability to "see" magic due to a "star" in her eye.

Simmar - Former Master Mage of Kuktarma. Murdered by Curasir.

Sipak - A legendary beast of the sea, described in stories of Ch'olan.

Siratel - An elderly woman of the Eldanim. Appears to have the ability to foresee a person's future to some extent.

Starlit Realm - *see* **Otherworld**

Sundinka - Former Lord of Mandiata. After his power was stolen by Volraag, he was murdered by Rathri.

Talinir - A warden of the Eldanim.

Tenjkidi - Capital city of Mandiata.

Tezan - A wild mage who, under the control of Lord Tyrr, attempted to convince everyone he was the lost King of Antises. Fell under the control of Volraag, who used him to steal power from Lord Sundinka.

Theon - The god worshipped (or at least acknowledged) by the majority of Antises.

Thrummers - Insects about one centimeter in length. Bites like a mosquito, but less painful. Mostly harmless. Especially attracted to those with magic, as it absorbs tiny amounts of magic when it bites. The insect's abdomen glows in response with an intensity and color based on the magic's potency.

Titus - A young man of Drusa's Crossing.

Topleb - A conscript in the army of Varioch, originally from Ch'olan. Assigned to the curse squad.

Trebia River - A river that flows on south along the western edge of Varioch, next to the Great Plains.

Tunaldi - A ferocious beast of the Otherworld, comparable in size from a hippopotamus to an elephant. Carnivorous. Attracted to magic.

Tungrorum - A small village near the border between Varioch and Ch'olan.

Tyrr - Current Lord of Rasna.

Tzitzimitl - *see* **Eidolon**

Tzoyet - Current Master Mage of Ch'olan. Part of the Conclave of

Mages on Zes Sivas.

Varioch - One of the six lands of Antises. Bordered on the north by Ch'olan and the south by Rasna. Known for aggressive leadership.

Varion - Former Lord of Varioch. Father of Marshal (by rape) and Volraag. Murdered by Rathri.

Victor - A young man from Drusa's Crossing. Bound to Marshal since they were boys.

Volraag - Current Lord of Varioch. Son of Varion. Half-brother of Marshal. Stole power from Lord Sundinka of Mandiata.

Wolf - A conscript in the Varioch army. Speaks very little. Seems confused and withdrawn most of the time. Assigned to the curse squad.

Woqan - Capital city of Ch'olan.

Zes Sivas - An island in the center of Lake Litanu. Center of magic and authority for Antises. Most of the island is covered by the Citadel of Kings and the Citadel of Mages, two interwoven fortresses.

Acknowledgments

Publishing a second book is much different than publishing a first book. You have expectations! I hope I've been able to meet them.

My thanks to David Farland and the Apex Writers Group for education, enlightenment and encouragement. Continued thanks to my beta readers Stephen Tallman, Allen Perkins, and NJ Kharme.

And a special thank you to everyone who read the first book and demanded to know what happened next! (And now you'll be bugging me with the same question again.)

This series, *Heart of Fire*, will have four books. That's the current plan, anyway. The next two are on their way. At the same time, I have other books I'm working on that may come out between these titles.

If you want to keep track of my progress, you can connect on timfrankovich.com, my Facebook author page, Twitter, etc. But the best way, which keeps you informed and gives you exclusive previews, is to join the mailing list. Sign up on the website. (You'll get a free story too!)

About the Author

Tim Frankovich has been exploring fantastic worlds since third grade, when he cut up a grocery sack and drew a Godzilla-meets-superheroes story. Since then, he's gotten a little bit better at the writing part (not so much with the drawing).

His goal as a writer is to transport readers to another world, make them care deeply about characters in dire situations, and guide them deeply into life itself.

At the moment, he is probably suitably conscious somewhere in Texas with his beloved wife, awesome four kids, and a fool of a pup named Pippin.

Made in the USA
Monee, IL
06 January 2021